Advance Praise for I Love You Today:

"Love, sex, lies, and advertising in the era of *Mad Men*. Compelling and provocative."
— James Wiatt, former Chairman   Morris Agency

"I enjoyed *I Love You*   romp through the *Mad Men* era told   r me, it was a trip down Memory La   in the late 1960s). I not only liked it, I lived
— Pamela Fiori, author a   ner editor-in-chief, *Town & Country*

"Marcia Gloster paints an intimate portrait of life in 1960s Manhattan, as one young woman strives to make her way professionally and personally in the challenging art design world. An accomplished artist herself, the author brings her own insight and in-depth experiences to the story and delivers a narrative that highlights both career struggles and characters searching for true connection in the midst of a social and sexual revolution. Readers looking for a peek into the magazine publishing and advertising world of that era will be intrigued!"
— Marilyn Brant, *New York Times* bestselling author

"A good view of the glamorous magazine business in New York by someone who has obviously been there. A solid novel, a good read, sexually intriguing."
— Jay Ingram, author of *Living Zen*

"A well-researched glimpse into a woman's turbulent struggle in a male-dominated career during the late 1960s. It pulled me right in, from the wrenching love story that could never have a happy ending, to the ultimate strength shown by the main character. An overall compelling journey."
— Andrea Hurst, author of *Always with You*

"Marcia Gloster fearlessly takes us through the days of unlimited sexuality and power in the world of advertising. And here's the twist: we see it through the eyes of a woman who must compete with men in suits while wearing a mini-skirt, the uniform of the day. Gloster knows the terrain like a trusted river guide."
— Jacqueline Sheehan, *New York Times* bestselling author of The Tiger in the House

I LOVE YOU TODAY

I LOVE YOU TODAY

A novel by

MARCIA GLOSTER

To my parents, who wouldn't approve but would still be proud. For every woman who has been driven to pursue her passions, be they work or love.

The Story Plant
Studio Digital CT, LLC
P.O. Box 4331
Stamford, CT 06907

Copyright © 2016 by Marcia Gloster
Author photo by Maureen Baker

Story Plant Paperback ISBN-13: 978-1-61188-243-8
Fiction Studio Books E-book ISBN: 978-1-943486-99-1

Visit our website at www.TheStoryPlant.com

First Story Plant paperback printing: April 2017

Printed in the United States of America

Life is like an onion;
you peel it off one layer at a time,
and sometimes you weep.

Carl Sandburg

March 1971

New York City

She barely registered the long black limo slowing at the curb. They were standing on the corner of Sixty-Sixth and Park, no place for an argument in late March. The night had turned bitterly cold, slush freezing into black ice making sidewalks treacherous. The wind lashed their faces but did little to restrain Rob's anger.

Out of the corner of her eye she saw the back door open. A young woman, maybe thirty-one or thirty-two, a couple of years older than she, stepped carefully out. Jet-black hair was piled on top of her head and her dark eyes were outlined in black. Despite the cold, she was wearing a short, form-fitting black dress, black stilettos and black gloves that came to her elbows. Long jeweled earrings swayed as she walked in what appeared to be slow motion toward them, all the while staring at Rob. He caught Maddie's look and turned, his harangue ending abruptly in mid-sentence.

She stopped a few feet away, her eyes never leaving his face. "Why are you standing there arguing with her," she said in a strong yet seductive voice. "Come with me."

Maddie stared in amused disbelief; the girl was the image of Holly Golightly, that is if Holly Golightly had been a hooker. As outrage replaced amusement, she took a step toward her. "Get out of here and leave us alone."

Ignoring her, the woman repeated her offer. Without a word Rob walked to the car and slid in. The woman followed. Neither looked back.

Maddie watched the car for several blocks, sure it would stop and Rob would get out. But it continued on slowly becoming a distant shadow.

Part 1

Perhaps our only sickness is to desire a truth which we cannot bear, rather than to rest content with the fictions we manufacture out of each other.

Lawrence Durrell

Chapter 1

September 1966

New York City

The phone was ringing as Maddie unlocked the door. She ran to pick it up, hoping it was one of the employment agencies or even Danny. Either would have been acceptable, but at that moment the employment agencies took precedence. The week before she had quit a job she loathed—one she had only taken because she thought it would advance her career. It hadn't.

As for Danny Gladstone, she had met him at a party a few months before. He was tall with dark blond hair and blue eyes—in other words, attractive. Yet what had drawn her to him was his apparent shyness, unusual for such a good-looking guy. She imagined, in these sexually liberated days, that he could have any girl he wanted. But somehow, to her surprise, he lacked the expected attitude of self-congratulatory arrogance. He was a marketing manager for AW&M, a large and prestigious advertising agency and had expressed amazement that she was already an art editor at what he described as "the tender age of twenty-four."

Maddie liked him; he was fun for movie and dinner dates on Saturday nights, which over several weeks had evolved into the inevitable sleep over. Midweek dates, however, always ended with a kiss at her front door. He explained that he liked to get to the office early and didn't want to bother her on workday mornings. She opted not to tell him it wouldn't have been a bother. What she did appreciate about him, although he was almost thirty, was that he was in no rush to "nest," even though many of his friends were already married and pushing him in that direction. She wasn't ready to take it further and neither, apparently, was he. She had made it clear that her career came first.

=

The call was from Mr. Collins, an employment agent she'd met with several times. Although it had only been a few days since she had quit her job, she was very much in need of a new one, hopefully as soon as possible. It wasn't so much that the working conditions had been deplorable—it had more to do with the attitude of the company in general and her boss in particular. The publishing company occupied several floors in an old, rundown building on West Forty-Sixth Street, in a part of the city known as Hell's Kitchen. It took Maddie two subways plus cautious weaving through streets populated with aggressive drug dealers and preening, cat-calling prostitutes just to get to the locked entrance.

She had been hired to design a magazine called *HandiWoman*, sort of a how-to for the "modern, take-charge woman" who didn't want to wait for her husband to tackle small chores around the house. Articles dealt with a variety of subjects from how to fix a leaky pipe under the sink while keeping your housedress tightly wrapped around you, to articles on efficient floor cleaning and even simple carpentry—as if simple was the only way a woman could manage it. Although she found the writing occasionally condescending and the photography uninspiring, she tried to make the layouts as visually appealing as she possibly could.

Herb, the short, balding, cigar-smoking production director who headed up her division had made it abundantly clear that hiring her—a female—was a joke. It amused him to march through the art department smoking his stinking cigar, smoothing his greasy hair and muttering under his breath that it wasn't a woman's place to unplug a sink; it was a man's job, as was her position as art editor. He liked to sneer, "I guess if that's what women want these days, who am I to deny them? As long as they look nice and have dinner on the table by six." After that he'd give her what he considered a meaningful look, remove the cigar from his mouth and mutter, "Maybe that's what you should be doing." Some variation of that monologue was repeated at least once a week. She did her best to ignore him.

Her editor was another grouchy man in his fifties. He wore tweed suits that smelled of mothballs but was at least polite if not particularly friendly. Her days were spent laying out pages, meeting deadlines and hiding in her small, cluttered and worst of all, windowless cubicle. It was one of many in the large dingy room that comprised the art department, all occupied by men in their forties and fifties and all art editors of insignificant magazines dealing with do-it-yourself carpentry, auto-repair and plumbing.

Another of her problems stemmed from a photographic machine called a "Lucy." Basically a black vertical coffin, it had lights and knobs that allowed one to enlarge or decrease the size of a photograph in order to fit it into a layout. It was a useful piece of equipment but, in order to access it, she had to step up on a small platform, bend over to see the image and then trace it into her layout. It had been designed sometime in the dark decades before the sixties, long before miniskirts were ever a thought, much less a reality. After the first couple of times, she realized the office had become unusually quiet. Looking behind her, she saw all the men had stopped working and were grinning as they stared at her ass.

Exasperated, she went to Herb, asking sweetly if he might consider turning the "Lucy" so it faced the wall. "I don't think I can do that," he said with a nasty leer. "Why not give the guys a little thrill? After all, you should be grateful you even have this job. You could have been hired as a secretary." Feeling a quick stab of anger, Maddie turned her back and walked out of his office. *Better than calling him an asshole to his face.* She later found out that he had indeed objected to hiring her, the first female in the art department, but had been overruled by the somewhat more enlightened owner of the publishing company.

=

It wasn't the first time she had experienced discrimination. After graduating from college and in search of her first job, she had what she considered a successful interview at a prestigious Madison Avenue ad agency. Stan Marks, the creative director, was anxious to hire her, but it had to be blessed by one of the senior partners, a Mr. Harper.

A few days later, at her second interview, Mr. Harper strode in, the perfect image of the Madison Avenue ad man: flannel trousers perfectly pressed, blue and white striped shirt perfectly starched, the perfect red and blue rep tie with coordinating suspenders. She expected him to crunch when he sat down. He didn't; he remained standing.

After looking through her portfolio, he was complimentary. "You're quite talented. You'll make a good art director one day," he said, nodding at no one in particular. Although she should have been optimistic at that moment, she had a feeling that less than positive news was coming. "But, I can't hire you. You would have to work in the bullpen. All our art assistants start there. They follow up the art directors on layouts, but they also spend a good deal of time cutting mats for presentations."

She stared back at him, undaunted. "All the layouts in my portfolio are matted. Most, in fact, are double matted. I cut every one of those myself. I can handle a mat knife as well as any man." She hoped she hadn't sounded too indignant.

He indulged in a smile. "But, my dear, the boys in the bullpen swear like longshoremen; it's part of the tradition. I'm afraid that having a girl in there would inhibit them and their work might suffer. We wouldn't want that, would we?"

"I can swear, Mr. Harper. Would you like to hear a few words?" she asked without thinking. Inside she cringed a little. *But why not? We all swore like crazy in art school; especially after accidently cutting ourselves with our mat knives.*

She glanced at Stan but he didn't meet her eyes. With a forced smile, Mr. Harper summed it up, "I understand, but I'm afraid it just won't work. You see, we've never hired a girl before in the art department." After shaking her hand, he wished her well. With a quick glance at Stan, he left. She was speechless; *I can't be hired because boys won't want to swear in front of me?*

Stan shook his head. "I had hoped to make you the exception, Maddie. I'm sorry. I thought we had a shot at this. This agency will have to face reality someday, but unfortunately today isn't it."

Taking a breath, she said she understood. She was disappointed but not all that surprised; throughout college and even into her first months in New York she had been repeatedly warned that as a female in the testosterone-controlled land of advertising meant she could be trapped forever as someone's secretary.

The only nice part was that she and Stan became friends. He took her to glamorous restaurants such as Romeo Salta and The

Twenty-One Club where, over several glasses of wine he explained how difficult it was for women, particularly creative women, to break through the long established male dominance in advertising.

"Maddie, even if this new feminist movement lasts, I think it will still take several years, maybe even a decade for women to become accepted at agencies. Although Mary Wells is making a name for herself at Jack Tinker, most women are still destined to remain as secretaries or at best, low-level assistants. I'd hate to see that happen to you."

"I can't even type. The problem is that at almost every interview I'm asked if I've had any experience working in an art department. But don't I need that first job in order to get experience?"

"It's a vicious cycle Maddie and we've all been there. I think you should try the big magazine publishers like Condé Nast, Hearst or McCalls. Shelter, family and fashion magazines are where women are making the most inroads." He took out a business card and wrote down several names. "These are my contacts. Use my name and don't take no for an answer. Just keep calling. Something will open up. It always does."

She looked at the card trying not to be intimidated by well-known names at *Vogue, Mademoiselle* and *Holiday*. "Thank you, Stan. I'll start making calls tomorrow."

That was the last time she saw him. He called a few weeks later to tell her he was fed up with the restrictive policies of his own agency and was moving back home to Minnesota where he planned to start his own graphics company. She wished him well and asked him to stay in touch, but she never heard from him again.

By the time he left New York, she had finally landed her first job at *Today's Bride*. When the stone-faced personnel director questioned her on her skills, Maddie did her best to maintain a cool exterior. In answer to, "Can you do mechanicals as well as paste-ups?" she said, "Yes," at the same time wondering if there was a difference. To the question, "Do you have experience in specifying type?" she responded, "Of course," thinking, *as long as it's Bodoni or Caslon* and wishing she had majored in graphic design instead of illustration. When the woman questioned her about her typing ability, she answered simply, "I typed my papers in college, but it's not my strong suit."

When the woman finally cracked a smile, saying, "Well, in an art department it may not be so important," Maddie relaxed, knowing she was home free.

She was fortunate that her art director, Joan Kendall, had the patience of a saint. Whenever a very nervous Maddie asked her a tentative question, she went out of her way to explain in detail. Over the next two years Maddie worked her way from apprentice to assistant art director without ever having to type more than a simple photography schedule.

The magazine was run entirely by women and while she found it a welcoming and nurturing environment, there was an underlying current of sniping and bitchiness. The only male was the publisher, an older man with white hair who wisely hid in his office most of the day. The editor in chief and the managing editor ruled and everyone who worked there, especially the assistants, herself included, marched to their beat. Meetings in the musty pine-paneled conference room were frequent and not to be missed, and all layouts and artwork had to be presented and approved by deadline. Lunch could be taken, but not for one minute over an hour.

Never a morning person, she barely made it to the office at nine. More often than not, she stashed her coat with the receptionist (whom she had made it a priority to befriend), grabbed some papers and walked in as though she had indeed arrived on time. Occasionally the managing editor, a dour woman who wore calf-length dresses buttoned to the neck and had a handkerchief eternally pushed up under her sleeve, would catch her, giving her a stern look along with a small shake of the head. And yet Joan didn't appear to mind; especially since Maddie was always willing to work late and they never missed a deadline. She was sure the presence of a man or two in the office might have tempered it all.

Today's Bride was considered a glamour job and while she was fortunate to have gotten it, she was aware that the more prestigious the magazine, the less it paid. Although the first stirrings of feminism were beginning to be felt and more opportunities for women were opening up, the concept of pay-equality was barely a whisper in the wind.

She accepted the job at *HandiWoman* because it paid more and gave her the title of Art Editor. It was only her second job and she wasn't an assistant; she had her own, albeit small and somewhat obscure, publication. Despite her unpleasant boss and the grumpy men who worked there, the final straw was the time card that had to be stamped in a machine as she entered and left every day, just like in a factory. (Hours were strict: nine to five or pay was docked.)

After only a few months, finding it intolerable, she quit and decided to freelance while looking for another job.

=

The call from Mr. Collins was good news: there was an opening at a magazine called *Status*.

Chapter 2

By the time Rob arrived at the Cattleman it was 12:45. As he made his way around the unfortunates huddled impatiently at the entrance while vainly attempting to catch the maître d's eye, he inhaled the aroma of charred meat blending enticingly with whiskey and tobacco smoke. Across the room Ken and Evan were already seated at a corner table working on their first martinis. Ted, one of the waiters, caught Rob's eye and nodded: his Johnnie Walker Red was on the way. Wednesdays had become a welcome routine with the three of them meeting for a moderately wet lunch and catching up on industry gossip.

Ken Henderson was a senior art director at *Time-Life*. His division included a new group of so-called "coffee table" books. Some of them, hugely oversized and mostly on art or photography, fit the bill; all they needed were legs. Ken and Rob had been friends for seven years, since the day Ken had hired Rob for his first job. After working as Ken's assistant at *Time-Life* for four years he moved on to become an associate art director at *The Saturday Evening Post* and *McCalls* and then to *Cavalier*, where he finally achieved the title of art director.

Cavalier was considered a cooler version of *Playboy* and, while it attracted some of the best writers of the day, in Rob's opinion you couldn't beat several photo shoots a month with barely clad, voluptuous and, more often than not, friendly girls. He had left over a year before after being recruited to redesign the format for *Status*. Although he considered the magazine to be somewhat frivolous — the very name reeked of exclusivity — he viewed it as a significant career move, one that would be his stepping-stone to the glamorous and more lucrative realm of advertising. He had been gratified by the mention in the New York Times, a write-up with a photo in Advertising Age and, perhaps most importantly, an invitation to join the elite Art Director's Club.

Evan Breen, their more recent acquaintance, was a printer's representative. He continually wined and dined Ken and Rob, making sure they used his services as frequently as possible.

After ordering the London broil, they BS'ed about who had just gotten or left a job, if they had resigned or been fired and why, and most important, who was sleeping with whom. Publishing in New York was a small, inbred community and news travelled fast. By the time they finished it was almost two thirty and Evan asked if they wanted a Drambuie or Anisette before returning to work.

Rob shook his head. "Thanks, Evan, but I have to get back. I'm interviewing someone for the assistant's job at three."

Ken folded his napkin neatly on the table. "What happened to Nancy or whatever her name was?"

Rob drained the last of his scotch. "I had to fire her. She was an okay assistant, but she was beginning to make demands. To be fair, I did find her another job."

"Wow," Evan said. "When you're tired of a girl, you get her a job? You're a nice guy."

Ken grimaced. "No, Evan, he's not," he said, signaling the waiter for the check.

Rob laughed. "I somehow doubt she saw it quite that way. What she really wanted was for me to leave my wife and move in with her. That's a definite no-no. Never going to happen. She had to go, no ands-ifs or, unfortunately any more of her pretty little butt. I got her an interview at another magazine and told her I'd call."

"And have you?" Ken asked, leaning back his chair and lighting a Camel.

"Have I what?"

"Called her," Ken said, sounding impatient. "You know what I meant."

Shaking his head, Rob started to get up at the same time noticing several young women at a nearby table glance his way. At a slim 6'3" with dark hair and green eyes, he was accustomed to it. Ladies had always been in plentiful supply. He smiled back and they giggled. One actually blushed. *Sweet*, he thought.

As they left the restaurant, Ken turned west toward the *Time-Life* building and Evan joined Rob heading downtown to the *Status* offices at Thirty-Third and Park where he currently presided as art director.

Evan asked if he knew anything about the person he was interviewing.

Rob snapped open his lighter and lit a Marlboro. "A girl."

"Maybe you should hire a guy," he suggested, trying to keep pace.

"Why?" he said, exhaling smoke. "I like having girls around, especially if they're pretty and have good figures."

"And what if she's not? Pretty that is."

"Then maybe I won't hire her."

"Why am I not surprised? I'm coming with you. I want to see this one."

Rob stopped and put his hand on Evan's shoulder. "No Evan. Go home to your wife tonight and be a good boy."

"And you? Are you going home tonight?"

"Yeah. I stayed in the city last night."

"With who?"

"You mean with 'whom?' Gotta go, man. Talk to you later."

As he entered the office, a man was just leaving but stepped aside to let him pass. Thinking about the interview with his potential assistant, Rob barely glanced at him, only noticing that he was carrying a portfolio from AW&M, a big ad agency.

Chapter 3

Maddie exited the subway and walked a block to the *Status* offices, arriving just at three. The stark simplicity of the reception area surprised her: a white leather sofa and a glass coffee table stood on a small beige area rug with two matching Barcelona chairs on either side. The only color came from large fashion photos that covered the walls behind the couch and reception desk. She had expected a bit more glitz.

The receptionist was tapping rapidly on her typewriter while talking equally as rapidly on the phone. Seeing Maddie, she looked up with an impatient expression on her heavily made-up face and whispered that she'd call back. Maddie told her she was there to see Mr. MacLeod. After an appraising glance, the receptionist unwrapped a piece of Juicy Fruit, popped it in her mouth and dialed an extension. Maddie straightened her skirt, suddenly wondering if she should have worn something other than a suit.

Have a seat," the girl said in a bored voice, indicating the couch. "His secretary will be right out."

Maddie sat, feeling nervousness creep in and her earlier, all-too-fragile confidence beginning to fade. A few minutes later, a short dark-haired young woman in a miniskirt came in and introduced herself as Tara, Mr. MacLeod's secretary. Maddie followed her along a corridor lined with several windowed offices on the left and a bright open bullpen area on the right where it looked like some assistants worked in different sized cubicles. On the far side she saw two more large, sun filled offices. In one of the doorways two men stopped talking and glanced at her.

Tara stopped at the second to last office, looked in and grinned. "Rob, this is Miss Samuels, your three o'clock appointment." There seemed to be an inside joke somewhere in there, but Maddie didn't get it. Not then.

As she walked in he stood up, buttoned his suit jacket and stepped forward to shake her hand. She caught her breath; not only was he attractive, he had bright emerald green eyes and perhaps the longest eyelashes she had ever seen. *Wasted on a man*, she thought, trying not to stare. *Or, perhaps not.* His dark brown hair was cut short with long sideburns that framed his handsome face.

She sat down on one of the metal and leather chairs that faced his desk. A large drawing board, covered in layout sheets, rolls of galleys and photo stats was to his right. On the left, flat files were piled high with books of typefaces and stock photos. The office wasn't designed for so much furniture; there was little room to move around.

He sat back and asked her to tell him about herself. Interviews generally didn't faze her, but this time she was unusually flustered. She began by mentioning *Today's Bride*, saying that she had liked working there.

"Why did you leave? You weren't fired were you?"

"No. Not at all. It was just becoming uncomfortable. I'm not sure it's something I should talk about."

Her answer seemed to intrigue him. A smile lit up his eyes and he leaned forward, elbows on his desk. "Now you have to tell me, Miss Samuels. I promise I won't tell anyone. Was it some sort of conspiracy?"

"No," she stammered, wishing she had never brought it up. "Nothing like that. I was very close to Joan, the art director who hired me. She was a great teacher, actually a mentor for me. I was a kid just out of art school. But after two years her husband was offered a job at Publicis, the big ad agency in Paris and they decided to move there. Before she left she tried to have me named as art director. By then I was doing half the work on the magazine anyway. But the publisher told her he had already decided to bring in a well-known art director from a rival publication." She stopped, unsure how to proceed.

"So what was the problem?"

"Well," she took a breath, "not only was he hiring her, but his weekly meetings with his so-called 'investors' were really long afternoons at the Biltmore, a few blocks away."

He leaned back in his chair and laughed. "You had to leave because the publisher was screwing…pardon me, sleeping with the new art director?"

She bit her lip, sorry she had mentioned it and realizing she had backed herself into a corner.

"It wasn't quite so simple. Over the first couple of months she did everything she could to make my life miserable. Suddenly I wasn't allowed to cover photo shoots and then she didn't even want me doing layouts. She began quietly bringing in her own team. By the time everyone realized what was going on, there wasn't anything anyone could do about it. I spoke to the publisher who I knew liked me, but he said it was now up to her. It was out of his hands. So I resigned." Taking another big breath, she looked at him, hoping she hadn't said too much.

He shook his head. "Too bad. It sounds like you were happy there."

"Yes. I was."

He asked her to tell him more: what her goals were and did she really want a career or just a job until she found the right man to marry.

His questions didn't surprise her; she had been asked the same things at every interview.

"Mr. MacLeod. I have no desire to be married. I'm focused on my career. I hope to be an art director one day."

"And how do you plan to become one?"

She looked back at him wide eyed. It was a question she had never been asked. "I guess I'll just have to keep on working and learning. I'm very motivated, Mr. MacLeod. If something needs to get done, I'll make sure it happens."

He nodded, green eyes flashing. "I'll bet you will. Let me have a look at your portfolio."

As she stood up, she noticed him glance at her legs. She wondered if her skirt was too short but not wanting to appear self-conscious she stopped herself from smoothing it down. Standing next to him, she answered his questions as he leafed through the pages.

"Miss Samuels, can you leave the portfolio with me? Unless, of course, you have other interviews today."

"Yes. I mean, no." She wanted to kick herself. *What is wrong with me?* "Yes, I can leave it, and no, I don't have any more interviews today."

He smiled, amused at her obvious discomfort. "Good. I'd like to show it to the managing editor. I've already seen several potential candidates and I expect to make a decision later today."

She thanked him and he shook her hand, holding it she thought, a bit longer than necessary.

=

She left the building optimistic, yet wondering why she had become so rattled; that never happened to her. True, she hadn't anticipated that he would be quite so attractive, not to mention attentive. Usually her interviews were a lot more straightforward than that. But then, maybe it was just her. While she wanted the job, she was also afraid she might like the art director thrown into the deal.

Pushing that thought out of her mind, she noticed a phone booth on the opposite corner and reminded herself she had promised to call Suzanne after the interview. She answered on the first ring and suggested they meet at the Third Avenue El, a coffee shop directly across the street from Bloomingdale's. Named for the elevated subway that had been torn down in the early fifties, it was poorly lit and filled with artifacts and memorabilia that went back to the turn of the century. Maddie was sure it survived more on nostalgia than the quality of its food.

She had met Suzanne Weisman her first summer in New York. They were the same age, but Suzanne had married at nineteen and now at twenty-four she was trying to get pregnant. And yet she had confided to Maddie that she really wasn't very happy with her husband, a lawyer, who tended to be arrogant and dismissive.

"Why do you stay married to him?" Maddie had finally asked one day.

Suzanne sighed. "No one in my family has ever, and I mean ever, been divorced. I can't imagine it. Besides, what would I do?"

"You could get a job and then you'd have a chance to meet other, nicer men. If you can't stand him now, kids probably won't make it any better."

Looking painfully resigned, she had shaken her perfect dark brown pageboy. "No. I just don't see that happening. Maybe having a baby will help." She stopped suddenly, glanced around and whispered, "Although I have to tell you that we hardly ever have sex anymore. Andrew was insatiable before we got married when we had to sneak around, but now he hardly seems interested in sex at all."

Maddie resolved to remember that conversation should she ever, even remotely, consider getting married.

=

Suzanne was already at the coffee shop when Maddie arrived. She slid into the narrow booth, taking care not to snag her pantyhose on the cracked red plastic seats. After they ordered Cokes, Suzanne asked about the interview. Maddie said she thought it had gone well and, by the way, the art director happened to be quite attractive. She was surprised when Suzanne suddenly looked serious. "Attractive is one thing," she said firmly, actually shaking her finger at Maddie. "The first and most important question is, is he married?"

"Good question. I don't know."

"Well, was he wearing a ring? Don't tell me you didn't look." She sounded exasperated.

"No. I didn't. You know I never think of those things. I'm not interested."

"You will be, Maddie, if he is."

"I have no intention — I repeat — no intention of ever dating my boss. Besides I don't even know if I have the job. I have to call..." she glanced at her watch, "actually in a few minutes." Looking around she saw a pay phone on the wall near the restrooms.

Suzanne looked at her. "You really want this don't you?"

"Yes, I do," she said, knowing there may have been more to that answer than just the job. Suzanne knew it too. "Be careful what you wish for," she said softly.

Chapter 4

Rob watched Miss Samuels leave; she looked almost as good from the back as she did from the front.

He had been somewhat surprised when she walked in. She was tall and slender but appeared to have curves in all the right places, at least from what he could tell from the suit she was wearing. Not beautiful, but certainly pretty with short dark brown hair, big brown eyes and an irresistible sprinkling of freckles over a cute nose. Her skirt was quite short and her legs were what he considered spectacular. All that and an excellent portfolio.

After a brief conversation with a photographer about an upcoming photo shoot, he picked up her portfolio and wove his way through the maze of cubicles to the two executive offices across the floor, one belonging to the publisher, the other to the managing editor. Most of the editors and assistants were at their desks either writing or making phone calls. The place was still buzzing at five thirty.

The only unoccupied cubicle was the one directly across the hallway from his office. That was for the art assistant, the position he was hoping to fill today. Jules Warner, the publisher was out at a conference and had left all decisions to Fred Buckingham, the managing editor. They had met at *Cavalier* where Fred had been editor in chief. It was he who brought Rob in to become the art director for *Status*.

Fred had just returned from a meeting and now had a glass of a rare scotch resting on the corner of his desk. "Want some?" he asked.

"Sure, a short one, thanks," Rob said, sitting down opposite him. "I have to get out of here soon. Maybe try for the 6:24." He put the portfolio on Fred's desk. "I think this is the one I want to hire."

Fred looked at Rob over his glasses. "I noticed her earlier, on the way to your office. Are you sure this is a good idea? You really have to learn some self-control. If you can't, then hire a guy." But he looked through the portfolio and nodded. "This looks good. If you think she can do the job, go ahead. Just no dating this one. Promise?" He looked at Rob with a sardonic smile. "You know it creates a dreadful tension in the office."

Rob laughed and took a sip of the twenty-year old single malt. They touched glasses. "I promise," he said.

He finished the drink, feeling a pleasant warmth settling in and all too aware that he wasn't going to feel that at home. Allison was guaranteed to be in one of her bitchy moods, harping about him not making it home last night. He had told her a business meeting had run late and he had stayed with Fred.

As he entered his office the phone rang. Thinking it might be Allison he almost didn't pick it up. "Ah shit," he muttered and reached for it. It was Jackie, the girl from last night. In a seductive voice she said she knew he had to get back to the 'burbs but suggested they meet somewhere near Grand Central for a quick drink. It was tempting, but he already knew there would be nothing quick about it.

"Jackie, I'd love to, but I have to get home. I'm about to miss my train as it is. I'll call you tomorrow, I promise."

"I've heard that one before," she said, her tone not quite so seductive, and hung up.

He shook his head. She was pretty and willing, if a bit empty headed. Suddenly Tony, one of the editorial assistants barged into his office. "There's a phone call for you, Rob. Tara left so I picked it up. I'll switch it to you."

Rob thanked him and waited until it rang. It was Miss Samuels, the girl he had interviewed earlier. He had almost forgotten he had asked her to call.

Chapter 5

Maddie's first morning at *Status* consisted primarily of Tara showing her around and introducing her to everyone in the office. Most of the senior editors were older, but several writers and assistant editors were about her age. She knew it would take a while before she got all the names straight and could figure out exactly who was an editor and who was an assistant.

After the introductions Tara brought her back to Rob's office. As she sat down across from him, she said, "Mr. MacLeod, I just want to thank you again for offering me this job."

He looked at her with a wicked grin. "I think if I'm going to call you Maddie, you should call me Rob. How's that?" Maddie blinked, feeling a slight electric current run through her. Tara smiled knowingly and went to get coffee from the cart that came to the floor every morning and afternoon. Maddie asked for black, as did Rob.

Rob settled back in his chair and looked at her. Feeling unusually self-conscious, she glanced around the office and then back at him. Meeting his intense stare, she suddenly experienced that rare but unmistakable recognition that sparks between two people before they truly understand what it means — especially in a situation where it shouldn't mean anything at all.

Breaking the brief but palpable silence, he asked how much she knew about the magazine.

"Just what I've seen and read in a few issues."

He nodded and lit a Marlboro. "*Status*, as the name implies, is a bit on the snobbish side. As you know we are owned by the Cassini brothers. One is a fashion designer and the other a rather acerbic gossip columnist who contributes at least a couple of pages every month. We cover quite a lot of fashion, travel and culture, not to mention celebrity gossip, as well as the kinky nightlife that's lighting up the city right now. By the way have you been to Max's Kansas City?"

"Yes, but not to the back room. Although I did see Andy Warhol and his entourage walk through a couple of times."

"Then you know what I'm talking about. But that's only part of it. What makes us special is our publishers like to proselytize to our readers about what's in and what's out, particularly in so-called New York Café Society. What's 'in' right now is the snooty sorority known as the 'ladies who lunch.' Last month debutants were 'out.' Next month who knows? Although some of the articles are newsworthy, others are just plain ridiculous. Is there more than one person in the entire world who has any interest in reading an article on how to care for their Rolls Royces? With the accent on the s?"

She laughed. She was finding him very charming.

Suddenly serious, he began to describe her job. "Maddie. I know you can design pages, but I think it would be best if you work closely with me, at least at the beginning. I'll give you a couple of sections such as travel and 'Nights Out' which includes the restaurant columns and we'll go from there. I'll be working with you on concepts and illustrating articles as well as incorporating different design elements and fonts into your layouts. It's important to keep the magazine contemporary but consistent and at the same time liven it up with different graphic treatments."

"That sounds fine Mr., um, Rob. I look forward to it." She hoped she wasn't blushing, and yet spending time with him did sound fine, that is until she reminded herself to stop thinking it. "What about photo shoots? If you have one coming up, I know all the model agencies and stylists. I'm sure I can help with that."

"I expect you to. In fact, I'm looking forward to you coming on location with me." She wondered if there was more to that statement than just photo shoots. She had been there less than two hours and they were already flirting. She told herself to take it down a notch.

"Come on. I'll show you your work area. It's kind of small, but assistants here don't get a lot of space."

She stopped suddenly, "Thanks, Rob. You've just given me a clue how to tell the assistants from the editors."

"I have?"

"Yes. By the size of their cubicles." Suddenly realizing what she said, she grimaced and looked away, her face scarlet.

Laughing, he said. "That sounds like a dirty joke. The editors will love it."

Biting her lip, she followed him to her cramped workspace. It was, as she expected, in the bullpen, but directly across the hallway from his office and to the left of the entrance.

The wall behind her was solid only to a height of about four and a half feet; the rest was glass to the ceiling. If she turned she could see directly into Rob's office which was partially glass as well.

The large drawing board had the usual metal T-square and triangles as well as a partially completed layout taped down on it. Next to it was a white wooden taboret with a large jar of rubber cement, a well-used circular tray with pencils, kneaded erasers, razor blades, ruling pens and all the other supplies that it took to complete a mechanical. He handed her several typed pages of an article and about a dozen black and white photos. "I want you to begin with this layout. It's two spreads on a couple of galleries in an area below Houston Street called Soho."

"I've heard about galleries opening there," she said, taking the photos.

"Maybe next time you can come with me."

She wanted to say she'd like that but stopped herself. What he said felt seductive, although she wasn't sure he meant it to be.

The photos showed the exteriors of two recently renovated galleries. Through a plate glass window in one of them, the edge of what looked like a Lichtenstein was visible. Another shot, taken from an angle across the street, showed small piles of garbage and odd pieces of metal littering the ancient cobblestones in front of the other. The reconstructed classical façades, juxtaposed with the detritus of an area all but abandoned for decades, were stark and dramatic. She wondered if many people would actually choose to venture down there.

"These are great photos."

"Thank you."

She looked at him in surprise. "They're yours?"

"Yes, Maddie. I do quite a bit of photography. I covered this article."

She breathed a sigh of relief, glad she had said she liked them.

Suddenly he was all business. "When you've finished laying out the spreads and spec'ing the type, bring it back to me and we'll go over it. Also, remind me to get you together with Jaime, the fashion editor so you can find out what he's planning."

After Rob returned to his office, Tara came over and asked if she'd like to have lunch with her and a couple of the assistants. She happily accepted.

=

At the local coffee shop Cynthia Alter, one of the writers, began probing her for details. Was she married? No. Living with someone? No. A boyfriend? Sort of. Why did she leave her last job? She explained briefly and they all laughed. Finally, what did she think of her boss? She said she'd have to let them know. She saw Tara glance at Cynthia and Sarah, a copyeditor, with that same knowing smile she had last seen in Rob's office the day of her interview.

"What? Is there something I should know about?"

Sarah put down her BLT. "We just think you should be aware that Rob, Mr. Handsome we call him, can be very moody. Since he got his name in the papers, he thinks he's a big time art director and we're all his serfs."

Cynthia cut in. "We're pretty sure he was going out with his last assistant. Every time she went to his office she'd fix her hair and put on lipstick. At first he was nice to her but after a few months he turned nasty. Then one day she was gone. Just like that. Fired."

"You're kidding."

"No, Maddie," Cynthia said. "Watch out for him."

Maddie picked up her Coke, thinking it was good that she had heard this. Better to know sooner than later what she might be dealing with.

=

In the next weeks, she worked closely with Rob. She never felt he was particularly moody; although he could be abrupt at times with the editors and assistants. When he reviewed layouts with her he was more often than not complimentary. If he did have a comment on the design of a page or the choice of a typeface it was posed as a suggestion, not a command. He asked her to sit in on meetings with fashion photographers and she accompanied him to a few shoots. It wasn't long before those same photographers began sending her invitations to what always turned out to be raucous parties at their huge, unfinished lofts way over in the West Twenties. She went with Cynthia and Tara to a few and each time saw Rob come in with several friends and a tall blonde hanging on his arm. Once, noticing her, he smiled briefly, then turned away. Cynthia saw his look and sniffed. "Be careful of him. He's treacherous."

"What do you mean?"

"He has a different girlfriend every week. Although from the looks of this one, I'd say she's lasted longer than most."

Maddie shook her head. She didn't need any more warnings; she had already resolved to keep her distance.

=

By that time, she obviously knew he was married. She was also aware there were nights he didn't go home to Darien. When Suzanne had asked her weeks before if she had noticed a wedding ring and she had told her no, it was because he didn't wear one.

One morning, about a month after she started, Tara arrived a bit late. Sitting down at her desk in her cubicle opposite Maddie, she immediately began typing. Maddie glanced at her, curious to know what was going on. Tara usually came around, coffee in hand, to say good morning and chat for a few minutes about upcoming meetings or office gossip. That day she stayed put and Maddie wondered if something was wrong. Before she could think much about it, she saw Rob walk in, a small blue bag tucked under his arm. His shirt and tie looked new, but she was sure his suit was the same one as yesterday. For some reason she glanced at Tara who was watching him as he went into his office and closed the door. As Tara looked back, Maddie frowned and shook her head. Tara shrugged and smiled.

Maddie was glad not to be in her high heels. Since she had begun working with Rob he had been occasionally flirtatious and, though they had caught one another's eye from time to time, she wasn't about to let anything come of it. A little flirting, all things considered wasn't such a bad thing. And while she occasionally wondered what he'd be like to go out with, that thought was usually banished as quickly as it occurred.

A few days later, after he had gone to lunch, Tara came over to her.

"Come into Rob's office for a minute," she said softly, looking around to see if anyone was watching.

"Why?"

"Just come with me. I want to show you something."

Curious, Maddie followed her. Tara flipped on the light and went around his desk where she searched under a few papers, pulling out a rectangular envelope.

"I picked up these from the photo store this morning on my way in," she said. "Have a look."

Maddie took one of the glossy photos from her. It was a picture of two small children; a towheaded boy, about two and a girl with blond curls who looked about four. Rob's kids, she could easily see the resemblance. Tara handed her anther photo. This one was of an attractive but somewhat chunky woman with short, curly medium brown hair. "Look at her," Tara commented with a grimace. "Look at those fat legs. No wonder he cheats on her."

Maddie backed away, having no desire to see or hear any more. "Tara, that's his business and yours if you want it to be. But if I were you, I wouldn't choose to be part of his harem."

Tara sighed, taking care to replace the photos where she had found them. Maddie returned to her drawing board wondering briefly about Rob's wife and how she coped with his obvious infidelities. She shook off the thought. What he did with Tara or anyone else was none of her business.

Chapter 6

Suddenly it was the day before Thanksgiving. Maddie was seeing Danny on a regular basis and had plans to go out with him that night. He called late in the afternoon apologizing that he had to entertain a liquor client who was in town for the holiday and wanted, as he said, to "hit the bars." He asked if he could come over after but admitted it might be late.

She tried to hide her disappointment. "It's all right, Danny. I know you have an early flight tomorrow."

"Thanks, Maddie. You know I'd rather spend the evening with you." He paused as though he was about to say something else. She waited, half-hoping it would be something affectionate.

"I'll call you over the weekend," was all he said quickly. She hung up, reasoning that words of affection might take them to another level, one that perhaps neither of them was quite ready for. As much as she liked him, something was missing. Maybe it was that he was too serious, too much of a grown up.

Cynthia had a date with her new flame, Michael, and asked her to join them. She thanked her, but declined, saying she might as well go home, have a glass of wine and chill out. She was expected at her mother's house in Westchester the next day and she wasn't particularly looking forward to it.

=

By six she was getting ready to leave the office but first went to drop off some layouts on Fred's desk. He grunted his acknowledgement, shrugged on his leather coat and said he'd look at them Monday. Maddie liked him; he was in his mid-fifties, a big man who dressed with a decidedly English flair and was known to enjoy fine dining as well as the drinks that went along with it.

Rob had mentioned that he was working on a cookbook specifically for men that, not surprisingly, included an extensive section on the finer points of mixing cocktails. That triggered a thought and she stopped in the doorway. "Rob said you were writing an article for the special section we're doing on food in April. I didn't see it on the schedule."

Carefully arranging a plaid cashmere scarf around his neck, he nodded. "Not to worry. I'll have it ready when I return. Have a lovely weekend."

After wishing him the same, Maddie went to get her coat and leave. As she crossed the room, she noticed a sheet of paper pinned to her chair. She looked around, but everyone had already left. *Have a drink with me?* was all it said. Perplexed, she glanced around again, seeing Rob standing in the doorway.

"Are you coming?" he asked with a grin.

"You want me to have a drink with you? Tonight?" She wondered if she sounded as surprised as she felt.

"Yes, Maddie. That's what the note says. I have to catch a train to Connecticut but I was hoping we could have a quick Thanksgiving drink before I leave."

"Um, I guess so," she said as warning bells began to chime in her head. "Let me stop in the ladies' room and I'll be right back." He nodded.

She was grateful the bathroom was empty. Taking out her hairbrush, she looked in the mirror. *Maybe I should just say no or tell him I have plans. One drink, then say I have a date and have to leave. Anyway, he has to catch a train. Why am I so nervous?*

Taking a breath, she lined her eyes, put on lipstick and dotted on some Cabochard, her current favorite fragrance.

He was waiting in the reception area with her coat. Helping her on with it, he told her they were going to The Four Seasons. *Nice, but not exactly around the corner from Grand Central.*

Leaving their coats at the coat-check, they climbed the stairs to the bar, which not surprisingly was a mob scene. Rob was ordering scotch for himself and bourbon and ginger ale for Maddie when three of his friends showed up. Looking surprised, he introduced them as Ken and John and someone else—a tall guy with black hair and blue eyes. She didn't catch his name. Ken and John were both art directors at *Time-Life* and the other guy did something with printing. That was all she could hear; the noise was deafening. When they finally snagged a table, Ken and John had insisted on telling her stories about "the old days" at *Time-Life*. Apparently Rob and John liked to play pranks such as gluing down pencils, mat knives, kneaded erasers and the like on Ken's drawing board. Rob had laughed and whispered denials in her ear.

=

She didn't know what time it was when Rob suggested they go to a rugby bar uptown on Third Avenue. *A rugby bar?* She said she should probably go home. But all three of them protested, insisting she had to come along. The next thing she knew they were on the street and the tall, black-haired guy, whose name was Evan, was hailing a Checker cab.

The rugby bar was smaller than the Four Seasons and even more packed. The bar was on the left and although there were a few tables and booths, most were unoccupied; everyone was standing and milling around. It was as though they had crashed a party where everyone knew each other.

The walls were covered with flags from different teams and long pennants swayed in a thick haze of cigarette smoke under a patched tin ceiling. The noise level was earsplitting and the place reeked of old beer. When they walked in, everyone turned to look at them — then shouted their welcome. Rob was in his element, shaking hands and saying hello to guys Maddie was sure he had never met before. His friends weren't quite as outgoing. She wished she had been more firm with him and gone home.

Rob ordered drinks and within minutes was caught up in an arm wrestling contest with one of the rugby players. Maddie was squashed between Evan, who was egging him on, and Ken who was glancing around at some tough looking girls in miniskirts. John was slouched in the corner chatting up one of the waitresses. Maddie looked at her watch; it was after eleven and she was getting hungry. After Rob lost more arm wrestling matches to a few more of the players — all the while doing shots in between — she shouted in his ear that she was starving and wanted to leave, with or without him.

That got his attention and he finally got up saying it was time to go. Everyone began bellowing, insisting that they had to stay but he waved them off, promising he'd return soon.

They managed to squeeze through the drunken crowd and made it outside. Ken quickly flagged down a cab to go to the West Side. With pointed looks at Rob, John and Evan said goodnight and climbed in with him.

Maddie gratefully breathed in the cold air, expecting Rob to say goodnight and take the next taxi that came along to Grand Central. But he grabbed her hand, saying he wanted to get a hamburger at Willie's, another bar a couple of blocks away.

Willie's, however, had closed early for the holiday and they walked down Third Avenue finding only a Chinese restaurant still open. The waiter said they were about to close but he would let them take out whatever they wanted. All Maddie wanted was to go home; she no longer cared if she ate or not. She'd had too much to drink and was trying her best to remain lucid. Rob, who had drunk far more than she, appeared to be just fine and ordered a few things from the menu. She had a Coke while they waited and asked him about the next train to Darien. He assured her there was still time. Taking the bag of Chinese food, he steered her down Third to Seventy-Second Street, turning left toward her apartment building halfway down the block.

They sat at her small dining table drinking, eating and laughing about the rugby bar. "Did you actually know anyone there?" Maddie asked.

He shook his head. "No. I just thought it would be a trip."

"It was certainly that," she said, watching Rob navigate with his chopsticks "You're good with those."

"Okay, Maddie. Put down your fork. It's easy. I'll show you."

"Um, I'd rather not."

Despite her resistance and state of sobriety, he insisted. Giggling, she repeatedly dropped whatever it was she was trying to pick up.

"This isn't working. Everything is too slippery."

"Come on, Maddie. You can do it," he said, taking her hand and showing her how manipulate them. He was leaning in close to her, his hand warm around hers. She looked at him, liking his easy smile and becoming comfortable with him. She warned herself not to get too comfortable.

After she managed to pick up a couple of lo mein noodles, he applauded. "A few more and you'll be a pro."

"Why do I doubt that?" she said, dropping a water chestnut.

He laughed and looked around. "I like your apartment. It's sort of an eclectic mix of old and modern."

"My mother had a few things, like this old table, in the attic," she said, successfully picking up a few more noodles. "I add to it whenever I can afford something new, like the leather couch."

"It's nice Maddie. Cozy."

Glancing at her watch, she said, "Rob, it's almost one. Are you sure the trains are still running?"

"I just missed the last one."

She sat back, incredulous. "What? Well, you can't stay here."

"Why not?"

She couldn't believe he was smiling. "Because I'm not going to sleep with you, that's why. You're married and you're my boss. Isn't that enough?" She crossed her arms and stared at him.

"Are you serious?" he asked, looking at her as though he couldn't believe what she was saying.

"Yes, Rob. I have no intention of getting involved with you."

"We don't have to get involved," he said with a grin.

She shook her head. "Come on. You know what I mean."

She saw a flash of impatience in his eyes. "All right, Maddie. If you're really sure about this, I'll try and rent a car. Do you have the Yellow Pages?"

"Yes. It's on the top shelf in the closet, but I don't think I can reach it."

He got up reluctantly, his good mood having vanished. She stood next to him as he reached for the phone book. When he looked down at her, she caught her breath and almost gave in; he was too attractive, too seductive. And she was about to pass this up? It would have been so easy. But sleeping with her married boss was a Pandora's Box not to be opened.

Rob sat on the couch and irritably dialed several rental car agencies. They all told him the same thing: there was not a rental car to be had in Manhattan until Friday at the earliest. He shrugged and said he'd call a couple of his photographer friends; perhaps he could stay with one of them. Neither was home but he left Maddie's number with their answering services to call back.

Maddie shook her head in frustration; she couldn't exactly throw him out. She pointed to the couch.

"No. I don't sleep on couches," he said, getting up. They faced one another and then he laughed. She did as well; it was a ludicrous situation.

"Okay, Rob. You can sleep in bed with me but no sex. Agreed?"

"Fine, Maddie. Whatever you say." She wondered if she'd still have a job next week. She was sure no woman had ever turned him down.

She dug out her least sexy nightgown; a long, flannel high-necked ruffled number that she only wore when she was sick. "Go ahead, get undressed," she said, "I'm going to the bathroom to change." After brushing her hair and teeth, she emerged resplendent in the least sexy nightwear anyone over twelve had ever worn.

He was standing by the far side of the bed in the shortest, tightest boxer shorts she had ever seen. He looked at her and laughed. "You even look cute in that."

She dragged her eyes away and turned the covers down. "Look Rob, I don't want you to think I'm a prude, but I just can't get involved with you." She cringed as she said it; she was far from a prude. But as much as she had had to drink and as sorely tempted as she was, her instincts were screaming, *stay away; this can only lead to trouble.*

"I understand, Maddie," he said with a small smile. He slid under the covers and a few seconds later moved toward her. "No, Rob. Just no." She turned her back to him.

"Not even a kiss goodnight? A small one?"

She kissed him quickly on the lips. Far too quickly to feel anything and again turned away from him. He sighed and moved over. She was so tired that she fell asleep immediately, only to be awakened a couple of hours later by the phone ringing.

Half-asleep, she picked it up hearing a man's voice ask if Rob was there. *Rob, huh?* Vaguely, she remembered him leaving her number with some photographer's answering service. "You don't have to leave," she mumbled, handing him the phone. "It's too late. Just go back to sleep."

He thanked the guy for calling and said he'd call tomorrow.

It's already tomorrow, she thought, beginning to doze. She felt him move toward her and as she started to say no he began to kiss her.

She put her hands against his chest, intending to push him away but then his mouth was on hers and there was no more resistance. Without thinking, her arms were around him and she was returning breathtaking kisses. He pushed up her nightgown and began kissing her neck and breasts. She helped him unbutton it and pull it off. By the time it landed on the floor he was kissing his way down, all the way to her toes which, while watching her through the faint light, he kissed slowly, one by one. Her head thrown back, she caught her breath, wondering if he felt the electric current running between them. Slowly he started back up, spending some quality time between her thighs. She was gasping by the time he rose above her and took her slowly. She heard herself moan, and then her hands were running down his back, his skin satiny and smooth, trying to pull him closer. He resisted, suddenly patient and deliberate; he was used to getting what he wanted and he had waited her out.

Later, lying close with his arm around her she had no idea what to say. It soon became obvious that talking wasn't what he had in mind. In the thrall of quickly gratified lust, his attentions didn't cease, not that she wanted them to. Lightly dozing between intense bouts of lovemaking, it was as if she had no choice but to surrender to his sensuality. She had almost forgotten how pleasurable it felt to be with a man who not only knew what he was doing, but did it so superbly. Wherever he led that night, she willingly followed.

=

It was just becoming light when she felt him move away from her. "It's after six. I have to be on the next train," he said, already reaching for his clothes. Still half asleep, she got up, smoothed her hair and made her way to the closet to get a robe.

"No," he said in a soft voice. "Come here. I want to see you naked." In a daze, she turned to him, realizing she had the hangover from hell. He didn't appear to notice. He looked at her and taking her in his arms, he held her for a few seconds. "I have to go," he whispered into her hair. She nodded, trying to get her eyes to focus. At the door he said he'd try to call over the weekend.

She returned to bed still feeling his touch and inhaling his scent on the pillow. It was a night that left her wanting more, even though, for all the obvious reasons she knew she shouldn't. It wasn't only that he was married; the greater problem was that she'd be spending every weekday with him in the office.

Despite their occasional glances, she hadn't expected to connect with him quite so easily, not to mention quickly. Now she wondered what to make of it. Was she just another one of his conquests—a few drinks and a one-night stand? Maybe that would be best; they could smile at one other and leave it at that. And yet, while the sex had been extraordinary, there was something more, some indefinable chemistry that had existed since the moment they met. Pulling up the covers, she told herself to stop over-thinking it and go back to sleep.

Chapter 7

Rob made the 7:15 train with minutes to spare. He considered that pretty good since he was often late and it wasn't only for trains. He knew he was going to catch hell when he got home and, though he usually winged it, he needed to think about how he was going to explain last night.

He had picked up a *Post* with the intention of trying to clear his head by reading the sports page, but he couldn't get Maddie out of his mind. He had asked her to have a drink more because she intrigued him than wanting to get her into bed, at least at that moment; and anyway he had to get home. Besides, he had promised Fred.

He had made the right decision in hiring her; she was quick, smart and organized, and if she had a question, it was intelligent. He was tired of telling his assistants exactly what they had to do every minute of the day and he'd always been amazed how few people actually thought for themselves. He'd had some productive conversations with her about concepts and design, but whenever he mentioned taking it out of the office, even for lunch, she always smiled and backed off. And yet he'd catch her staring at him when she didn't think he noticed — a hard girl to read. On the surface she was professional and proper, but underneath she was just plain sexy. It wasn't only him; he had seen the looks the other guys in the office gave her as well.

He had forgotten that he had spoken to Ken earlier that day. He'd mentioned that he might stop at the Four Seasons after work with his new assistant; that is, if he could convince her to go out with him. He never expected Ken to show up, especially with John and Evan, no doubt to check her out.

Maddie had been talking with Evan when Ken moved beside him. "What exactly do you have in mind for her?" he asked.

"Come on, Ken. This is just for a drink. I'm going to catch the next train. Well, maybe the one after," he said, glancing at his watch.

Ken touched his glass to Rob's. "Sure you are," he said with a grin.

After a few more drinks, he remembered the rugby bar. He had ended up there one drunken night with an acquaintance from England and suddenly it seemed like a cool idea. He had been right; the place was a blast. Maybe if he hadn't been drinking so much he wouldn't have lost all those arm wrestling matches.

He shouldn't have let his dick overtake his brain, but by the time they got out of there he pretty much knew he wasn't going home. He wasn't sorry that Willie's was closed, although they had great bacon cheeseburgers. But he lucked out with the Chinese place; it gave him the perfect excuse to go home with her. He had thought everything was going great until she blindsided him by saying she wouldn't go to bed with him. At first he thought she was kidding; once he made it to a girl's apartment, sex was a no-brainer. He understood her apprehension about sleeping with a married man and especially, as she said, her boss. *Hard to argue with that; a sure recipe for trouble.* By then he was beyond caring; she had become a challenge.

When they finally got to the bedroom and she came out in that silly nightgown he was pretty much resigned to his first-ever failure. *I have to remember to thank Hal for calling back at three in the morning, otherwise I would have left hung over and horny—a night truly wasted.*

But it hadn't been wasted—far from it. After the phone call he had gone for it one more time. He had thought that under that proper exterior she might be timid, even inhibited, but after he surprised her with that kiss, he knew he had her. Once he got her nightgown off, a feat in itself, he couldn't believe how great her body was. He wanted to fuck her right then, no foreplay, nothing. But he forced himself to slow down, to take time fondling and playing with her. He wanted her to ask for it.

The train stopped with a lurch and he glanced out the window. Stamford; Darien was only a couple of stops away. It was time to concentrate on what would be waiting at home. He lit a cigarette, his mind drifting back to Maddie. He'd expected her to be just another minor conquest; give another girl a thrill. Now he wasn't so sure; there was something about her that intrigued him. Sure, the last two girls he had been with were more beautiful. They looked great on his arm, but once in bed the blonde was definitely faking it and the brunette was so passive he had wondered if she was even awake. If you couldn't have a decent conversation and they were dead in bed, why bother? And yet he did and seldom asked himself, outside of today, why?

He told himself to cool it. He had to focus on how to handle Allison. He had called her from the rugby bar saying he was out with clients and would be late. In retrospect it was probably a mistake; she had to have heard the racket in the background. But he was pretty plastered by then and having too much fun to give a shit. Now, unfortunately, he'd have to suffer the consequences. *What the hell.* He'd been down that road before.

Fortunately, his old Ford woody was parked at the station, otherwise it would have been a long walk home. He decided to chill out for a few minutes. He lit a cigarette and turned on the radio. Dylan was singing "Blowin' in the Wind." It fit his mood. He had met him a couple of times at *Cavalier* and thought he was a cool guy.

He mashed out the cigarette and put the car in gear. *So now I'm going to have to face Allison's hostility when all I want is to spend some time with the kids and maybe watch a football game.*

He had been correct about the hostility. It began with the silent treatment; Allison didn't even bother to ask why he hadn't come home last night. Most likely she would wait until the kids were in bed that night before she started screaming at him. Meanwhile he was going to have to sit through an endless Thanksgiving dinner with her family and his and try to pay attention while avoiding the image of Maddie with her long legs wrapped around him. *What a fuck up! Time for a drink.*

Chapter 8

Before leaving for Harrison, Maddie called her mother to let her know she'd be taking a train an hour later than she originally planned. Sounding exasperated, her mother snapped that some of her guests had already arrived and why was Maddie always so late not to mention that her stepfather, who was about to leave to pick her up, would now have to wait another hour. Maddie was impressed that she got it all out in one breath. She shrugged it off, accustomed to her mother's sharp responses. Besides she was too preoccupied thinking about the night before to let it upset her.

=

Her mother hadn't always been so on edge. Her parents had met and married in New York, driving across country a couple of years later when her father had gotten a job as an engineer at Douglas Aircraft in Santa Monica—a job that had kept him out of the war.

It was only a few years later, after Maddie was born, that her strong-willed mother became disenchanted with marriage, Maddie's father, or more likely both. To supplement their income, she went to work for the May Company where she had risen rapidly through the ranks. Within a couple of years, she was promoted to head buyer for ladies' sportswear.

Maddie was seven when her parents separated and her father moved to Seattle to work at Boeing. After the divorce her mother dated a series of wealthy men, most of whom Maddie didn't particularly care for. One of them, a lawyer, owned a palatial home in the Hollywood Hills and promised her a pony. While Maddie understood it was a bribe, she imagined she could live with it. But it was never to be; her mother met and married Harry Colton, a businessman from New York, only a few months after their first date. Before Maddie knew it, they had packed up the furniture, her grandmother and Skippy, her dog, and moved to a big white two-story house in Scarsdale. Within a couple of years Maddie watched her mother evolve from a dark-haired working woman to a blonde Scarsdale socialite who pursued golf, bridge and scotch with equal fervor.

=

Her mother was waiting impatiently at the front door, her face already set in a frown.

"You said you'd take the earlier train. What happened?"

"Nothing Mom. I was out a bit later than I planned last night and overslept."

Her mother seemed to lighten up. "You were out with Danny?"

"Um. No. He had to leave for Chicago. I was with a couple of friends from the office." She kissed her mother's cheek. "Look, I'm sorry. But I'm here now." She walked quickly in the direction of the living room, almost making it before her mother remarked that her skirt was too short and she was wearing too much eye makeup. Before she could respond, Harry asked if she wanted a drink. Grateful for his intervention, she said she'd have a Tab. He looked at her curiously. "You usually have Old Grand Dad and ginger ale. Why suddenly a Tab?"

She wasn't about to tell him she was still a bit fragile after all the drinking and love making the night before. She felt a twinge just thinking about lying entwined with Rob, not to mention the rest of it. "I'll just start with that, Dad. Maybe I'll have one later." He nodded, still looking a bit perplexed.

=

It was after four and already getting dark but the expansive living room was lit with tall lamps and overhead spots bathing wall-sized abstract paintings in bright light. Barely visible through the floor-to-ceiling windows was a swimming pool, now covered for the winter, and tired gardens where a few withered roses still clung to bare stalks. The living room had several seating areas, including one that faced a massive stone fireplace that could easily have handled a good-size pig. That's where everyone had gathered, deeply engulfed in feather-cushioned couches and working their way through cocktails and hors d'oeuvres.

Maddie was still recovering from her mother's barbed remarks when her grandmother glided out of the kitchen carrying a bowl of her famous chopped liver. She stopped and looked up at Maddie. "You look tired, Maddie. Aren't you getting enough sleep?"

=

All through her childhood Maddie had measured herself by her grandmother's five-foot height. When she passed her at about age nine, it had been strangely satisfying. As a child she had been close to her grandmother, spending happy summers at her narrow, sky-blue painted house on Venice Beach. But all that changed when her parents divorced. After her father moved out, her mother and grandmother continually bad-mouthed him in front of her as though trying to turn her against him. Instead, it had backfired, causing anger and resentment against them and resulting in a protective attitude toward her father. Even as she got older, she still had to contend with her mother's and grandmother's ire. Ever fearful of confrontation, she eventually learned to keep her distance.

As for her father, he remained in California, eventually marrying an attractive widow in San Jose and adopting her two small children. Although Maddie spoke to him several times a month and occasionally visited on school vacations, she was never comfortable in his home. His new wife was possessive and sharp tongued. The best times were when he took her out to museums or to wander the intriguing streets of San Francisco.

=

Maddie rolled her eyes, sorely tempted to explain in detail why she looked so tired. She went with the white lie. "I've been working late, Nana. We have deadlines coming up and I've been out with Danny a couple of times this week." *Well, once anyway.*

"You should have invited him. You've been dating him long enough. Maybe we should meet him."

"He left this morning for Chicago to visit his parents for the holiday. Perhaps another time."

She sniffed and placed her chopped liver on the table where it was immediately attacked by her mother's best friend Kitty, her husband Norman, and Will and Maureen, a couple of her parents' golf club cronies. Their two zit-faced, nerdy adolescent daughters were slapping at one another while making grotesque faces. Maddie decided she never wanted children. Glancing at her mother, she wondered if she had ever felt the same.

Kitty patted the couch next to her and Maddie sat down, lit a cigarette and waited for the next comment that was sure to follow. While the men argued the pros and cons of Ronald Regan having just been elected as governor of California, Kitty looked her up and down as if trying to find some flaw that hadn't been identified as yet. "Your hair is too short," she said flatly.

Maddie tried not to grit her teeth. Kitty had been best friends with her mother since before she was born and they were a perfect match — both equally critical of just about everything and everyone on the planet.

"Kitty, it's the style today. Besides, I have to be at work early and I don't have the time to fool with it."

"Then get married and let it grow. You're twenty-four, what are you waiting for? Find yourself a nice Jewish doctor."

Maddie rolled her eyes at the cliché. "I actually went out with a Jewish doctor. He was boring. And why does he have to be a *Jewish* doctor?"

Kitty shrugged. "He doesn't. He can be a lawyer. Whatever you like. We're all very open-minded here."

"I'm not sure I want to get married."

"Don't be silly. Every girl wants to get married. What would you do otherwise?"

"Live life on my own terms and maybe one day become an art director. Hopefully at a big magazine."

Kitty glanced at Maddie's mother who shook her head and took an extra long swallow of her scotch. She'd heard it all before.

"Nonsense. When you meet the right man you'll change your mind. And don't forget, it's just as easy to fall in love with a rich man as a poor one."

Maddie wondered what she might have to say about one who was married.

=

Other than her mother asking what was she day-dreaming about, she made it through dinner basically unscathed. She was tempted to say that she was thinking about making passionate love with her married boss and wondering, not when, but *if* he would call.

After dinner everyone returned to the living room and her step-father brought out his vast collection of brandies. Maddie excused herself and retrieving the overnight bag she had left in the entry, went to her bedroom. It felt impersonal, like a hotel. But then she had never lived here; her mother and Harry had built this sprawling modern house after she had graduated from college. The old white clapboard house in Scarsdale was the one that possessed her memories from high school; many that she treasured and some she'd just as soon forget. The day she graduated from college she had moved directly—as in do not pass go—to the city. Harry had generously offered to pay for an apartment until she could manage it herself, which, he had added, hoped would be soon.

By the time she returned to the living room everyone had left. The room was dark, but embers still burned in the fireplace. She lay down on one of the massive couches, letting her thoughts drift to the night before. She reviewed it minute by minute: when Rob had first taken her hand, his smiling glances, how they had ended up at her apartment and how inevitable, despite her protests, it had all been. She sighed and closed her eyes, picturing herself in his arms and wishing, despite all the difficulties, for it to happen again.

The next thing she knew it was dawn and the fire had burned to ashes.

Chapter 9

Danny arrived back Saturday and, as promised, called her. That night they went to see *Georgy Girl* at Cinema 1 and to their usual Chinese place around the corner on East Sixtieth Street. Afterwards she told him she wasn't feeling well and escaped back to her apartment. As much as she had wanted to see him the night before Thanksgiving, too much had happened and there was no way she could be with him that night. He looked disappointed but kissed her and said he'd call tomorrow. She knew he would.

By Sunday afternoon she was becoming anxious. She made coffee in the barely walk-in kitchen and drank it while absently perusing the holiday ads in the Sunday Times. Unable to concentrate, she got up and went to the window and pulled up the blinds, the pallid sunlight doing little to brighten the apartment or her mood.

She called Suzanne and was relieved when she asked her to come over. She and Andrew had been away for the holiday and Suzanne didn't yet know about her night with Rob. After a quick shower, Maddie threw on jeans and a sweater, picked up a couple of coffees and French crullers at a nearby coffee shop and rang her doorbell twenty minutes later. Andrew didn't bother to move, just glanced over the sports pages of the *Times* and grunted what she assumed was hello. Apparently a football game was about to begin on TV. Maddie wondered what it was with guys and football.

Suzanne ushered her into her eat-in kitchen and closed the door. "What happened?" she asked.

Maddie sipped her coffee and described her night with Rob. Suzanne frowned. "What the hell are you going to do now? Did you ever think about that before jumping into bed with him?"

"Yes. That's why I put on that ridiculous granny gown. I also considered putting a few rollers in my hair but it's too short." They looked at each other and laughed. "That probably would have done it," Maddie admitted.

Suzanne gave her a knowing look. "But you really didn't want that did you? Come on, it's me you're talking to."

Maddie closed her eyes and took a breath. "I honestly don't know. But after that three o'clock phone call when he kissed me, I couldn't resist him anymore." She looked at Suzanne. "What do I do now?"

"You have a choice: say no to him or have an affair. But don't expect him to leave his wife. And, by the way, what about Danny?"

"Danny?" she shook her head. "I guess I should be glad he's there."

"Be careful with him. Don't screw it up."

"No, I don't think that's a problem. Anyway, who knows where this is going? Probably nowhere."

Suzanne looked doubtful, but with a sudden smile, she said, "Now I have some news. I'm pregnant."

Maddie jumped up and hugged her. "That's great, Suzanne. I'm happy for you."

"I'm happy too. Except for my grumpy husband, everything is perfect." She paused and gave Maddie a serious look. "But you better make sure you stay on the Pill."

Chapter 10

For Rob, the best moment of the Thanksgiving weekend was Saturday afternoon when Allison took Val to a friend's house and left Tommy alone with him. They built a fort with blocks and afterwards Rob read him a couple of stories. Later, he stretched out on the couch in the den with Tommy on his chest and they both fell asleep. The den was his hangout. When he wanted to work, have a quiet drink or watch TV alone, that's where he went. There was a large leather couch, a small wet-bar set into a wood paneled wall, a vintage drawing board with a scrolled metal base and a TV. It was where the kids watched Bugs Bunny and Casper cartoons on Saturday mornings. Occasionally Val would venture in and ask him to draw something. They'd get comfortable on the couch and she'd tell him what she wanted him to sketch: a cat, a puppy or their house. Then Tommy would wander in, climb on his lap and demand he draw something special for him. It always caused a small uprising that was easily circumvented by giving them each crayons and craft paper that Rob kept nearby for just those moments. He always tried to make time for the kids; it was their mother who was becoming increasingly demanding and shrill.

The worst moment, as he expected, was returning home from Thanksgiving dinner. While they were at her parents' house, Allison either continued to ignore him or made small, snide remarks. Despite the fact that Rob's parents and sisters were sitting across from her, Allison's mother kept casting venomous glances his way. He ignored her.

After arriving home Allison put the kids to bed. Already anticipating what was coming, Rob kissed them goodnight and went downstairs to the den.

By the time he reached the bottom step Allison was already screaming. "I can't fucking believe that you didn't come home last night. What the hell is wrong with you? And don't tell me you were out with clients…"

He cut her off. "Cool it, Allison. The kids can hear you."

She stamped into the den after him and slammed the door. "You're suddenly worried about the kids? If you cared about them, you would have come home last night instead of going out with floozies."

Rob poured a drink and sat down on the couch. There was no point arguing; they'd been through this before and he had to let her vent. When she finally stopped to catch her breath, he said, "If you're through yelling at me, perhaps you'll give me a minute to explain."

She glared at him, her face red with fury. "I want the truth," she said through clenched teeth.

"Look Allison, I'm sorry. Of course I planned on getting home to you and the kids. But since Fred was away, Ed, one of our ad salesman, asked me to have a few drinks with a new advertiser. You know, tell him more about the magazine. I planned to have one drink and, well," he shrugged and shook his head, "you know how it goes. One drink became two and then they wanted to go to another bar. By the time I looked at my watch I had already missed the last train."

"So tell me, Mr. big art director, where did you stay?" He didn't miss the sarcasm in her voice.

"Ed and I barely made it to his apartment. I slept on his couch." *Yeah, sure.* But inwardly he cringed. "When I called you I couldn't hear a thing and later I didn't want to wake you up." When blatantly lying, he'd always found it best to sound as sincere as possible.

She sneered at him, "You didn't have to worry. I didn't sleep."

He sighed. "Alli, forgive me. Come sit next to me. I'm truly sorry." When she shook her head, he patted the cushion next to him. "Please?"

"No," she snapped.

He stood up, took her hands and kissed them. When she didn't move, he drew her to him and kissed her gently. "I'm sorry," he said. "I truly am. I won't do it again."

"You've said that before. You're lying to me."

He was beginning to feel anger creep in but forced himself to remain calm. He tried again, convinced a bit more cajoling would help. "You know when I'm out with advertisers or at meetings time gets away from me. But you also know that I love you." She stopped and stared at him, looking like she wanted to believe him but not quite ready to.

"Come upstairs with me. I want to make love to you."

"No," she said and began to pull away.

He held her tight. "Alli," he whispered. "I love you. Please."

He could feel her giving in. She stepped back, her voice softer. "We'll see. Let me turn off the lights.

"Leave them, Alli. I'll turn them off later. Come with me. You have no idea how much I want you."

She sighed and nodded. Following her upstairs, he congratulated himself on another masterful performance.

=

Saturday night they were invited to a cocktail party given by one of Allison's country club pals. The hostess was one of her tennis partners and had just married — for the second time — a guy who lived a few blocks away. Most men Rob knew in Darien liked to play in the city but preferred to marry, and remarry, closer to home.

He was getting a beer when he saw Tom Bartlett, an acquaintance from high school. He didn't look like he wanted to be there any more than Rob did.

"I hear through the grape vine that you're now a big art director at a trendy magazine," he said.

Rob shrugged, not wanting to appear immodest. "I've been there about a year and a half and I'm thinking it may be time to move on. I don't want to stay in publishing forever."

After looking around, Tom took a card out of his wallet. "My wife hates it when I discuss business at parties. But what the hell am I supposed to do, talk about gardening?" He handed the card to Rob who glanced at it before slipping it into his pocket. "Call me. I just moved over to LRG, and we're always looking for fresh young talent. From what I hear, you just may be it. Are you interested in getting into advertising?"

Rob felt a jolt of excitement; that was precisely what he wanted. Staying cool, he said, "Sure, Tom, I'm always interested in something new."

As they talked, a couple of the wives sidled up to chat. Rob controlled his irritation; he couldn't continue the discussion with Tom with these silly twits standing around and doing their best to flirt. Forcing a smile, he gallantly lit their cigarettes as they fluttered their eyelashes at him through the smoke. *Nothing unusual,* he thought, convinced that if he ever made a pass at either of them, they'd tuck their tails between their skinny legs and run home screaming. Or maybe not; he wasn't in any rush to find out. After they walked away with a few backward glances, Tom gestured across the room. "Look at that." Rob turned, seeing their tall, dark-haired newly remarried hostess. She was wearing a low-cut blouse that accentuated her ample cleavage. As she glanced back at them, Rob smiled in appreciation. Even if he was tempted, which he had to admit he was, he wouldn't go near her. Too close to home.

Those thoughts brought him back to Jackie—and Maddie—neither of whom, fortunately, were too close to home. Jackie was pretty and energetic in bed but that was about it. Maddie was something else, and he didn't know what to make of her. Most girls were easy to read and just as easy to get into bed. But not her; there was something about her he couldn't quite grasp.

He turned to get another beer and saw Allison staring at him. *Oh shit. Now what?* He went to her and put his arm around her waist. "Having a good time?" he asked, not caring if she was or wasn't.

"We should leave soon," she said. "We promised to stop at my parents' house on the way home."

Stopping at her parents, who were also having a cocktail party, was about the last thing in the world he wanted to do.

=

Rob had met them not long after meeting Allison at a party given by a mutual friend. She was short and slender with dark blond curls. When he picked her up for their first date he had shaken hands with her father, making sure to look him in the eye. He had greeted her mother with a smile but could already tell she wasn't particularly pleased. He didn't know why and it didn't matter; they were only dating. No big deal. They had gone out for a few months on and off, then suddenly it was more on than off and in retrospect he should have been more careful.

At twenty-two he was living at home while trying to save enough to move into the city. One day she had called him at his parents' house. She was frantic and said they had to talk; she was pregnant. He was far from ready to get married, but what could he do? He had to marry her; there was no choice. He already knew her parents would be furious; their idea of a husband for their only daughter was one of the vacant-minded boys from the country club. She had dated a bunch of them, but they hadn't held her interest, he guessed, as he had. They had only had sex a few times before she got pregnant. His mistake, one of the rare times they were alone in her house, was convincing her to take her panties off. It was spontaneous and rushed. Now, too late, he realized spontaneity might not always be a good thing. His parents were shocked, of course. Especially his mother, a dedicated Catholic to her very core. His father just shook his head and wished him luck. It wasn't that they didn't like her, they did; it was her snobbish family that worried them.

Her parents were, to put it mildly, enraged. They didn't approve of him and the last thing they wanted was for her to marry him; but again, there wasn't much choice. Unwed mothers were anathema and besides, she really did want to get married. She was in love and adamant. So he told her he loved her. Hell, maybe he did, then. It wasn't such a bad deal; she was cute and her parents were loaded. He just went along with it. What else could he do?

After everyone calmed down, her mother announced that they would have a big, white (the emphasis on *white*) wedding at the country club. Rob said he would prefer a small ceremony with just a few friends and family. His parents agreed, but she ignored their suggestion and by then Allison was on board with the whole thing. But it had to be accomplished quickly; no one could know that she was pregnant. "It would be a scandal," her mother said archly.

So there he was, along with his parents, (who were shocked and disappointed that he had gotten a girl pregnant, yet were delighted with the girl) his sisters (both less than delighted), a few relatives and friends mixed in with about a hundred and fifty of Allison's parent's "closest" family and friends. The country club was filled with early autumn flowers and candles. Tables were set inside and out on the large stone terrace where a band was playing. It was a lavish affair and yet all he could think about was how in hell had he managed to get himself into this predicament and if he could run away. But there was no running, and after a few drinks he steadied himself and it all went, as her mother pronounced, "swimmingly."

Thanks to his parents' generosity they went to Acapulco for a short honeymoon, returning to a large white-shingled house that Allison's father had bought them as a wedding present. It had three bedrooms, no doubt in anticipation of more grandchildren, a good-sized living and dining room, a remodeled kitchen—so Allison could learn to cook—and of course his small den. It was larger and in a better section of Darien than where he had grown up and it felt ostentatious to him. But then, no one had bothered to ask him. Allison's father wanted only the very best for his little girl and all Rob could say was "thank you." Whatever misgivings he might have had were simply ignored. His friends commented, with a slap on the back and a few sniggers, that he was "set for life.'" He wasn't so sure.

=

The Thanksgiving weekend ended in relative peace. He was about to leave Monday morning to catch the 7:43 to New York when Allison asked what time he'd be home. Thanksgiving might be over but it hadn't been forgotten, not by a long shot and he didn't miss the edge to her voice. Despite his little flings, which were fun but basically meaningless, he wasn't unhappy at home. Allison was a good wife, but the girls in the city were sexy and seductive. He had been single for too brief a time and only too late realized he had never given himself a chance. Yet why leave a good thing when he could go out, have his fun and return to his nice house? The only difficult part was coming up with creative excuses.

He told her he'd take the 7:04. "Don't be late," she whispered in a less than loving tone.

=

On the train he took out Tom's card. He'd call him that afternoon and set up an appointment. Moving from publishing directly to advertising was a big step, but one he was determined to make. That chance meeting could be the break he needed.

He had spoken with a couple of headhunters only a couple of weeks before and both had told him the same thing; ad agencies never hired art directors from magazines, even one who had received art director's awards and recognition for his creative covers. For one issue he had gently spoofed a well-known society lady, known as a "social butterfly" by finding a model who resembled her and having butterfly wings airbrushed on to her partially nude torso. In the photo she was looking over her shoulder with an insouciant wink. That his bosses had allowed him to publish it amazed him.

The response at first had been outrage that, fortunately for Rob, had turned to delight when everyone who was anyone, at every dinner party on Park Avenue told the socialite what a simply smashing idea it was and that they wanted to be the next to make such a splash. A couple of weeks later the society lady's husband reciprocated by taking out a couple of ads for his bank.

Despite his successes, the headhunters had insisted that he consider taking a job in the promotion department of a corporation such as Seagram's or Revlon in order to make the transition. Those art departments dealt with catalogs, store signage, brochures and advertising to the trade. To Rob it was design purgatory and he was determined to cross the bridge to advertising in one step. He was almost twenty-nine and after his first taste of celebrity he was convinced he was ready for the big leagues.

Glancing out the window at the stark landscape, he reminded himself that there was a lot to do in the office that day, although Maddie would be there to take some of it off him. *Maddie.* What the hell was he going to do about her? Had he told her he would call over the weekend? He couldn't remember. Probably it would be better to leave it alone; maybe just say it had been a special night, but she was right, it wasn't a good idea to get involved. After all, he had promised Fred, hadn't he? And now he had a major career move to consider. But underneath, what he really wanted was to make love to her again and soon. Just thinking about it was making him hard. He shook his head and lit a cigarette.

Chapter 11

By Monday morning Maddie had worked herself into an unshakable state of anxiety. She would have to face Rob having no idea what to expect. There were too many questions, too many what's and what-if's. She asked herself repeatedly, *What is it that I want?* and, *Should I see him again?* She wasn't getting answers primarily because she couldn't stop imagining what it was that *he* might want. And what if he said it had just been an impulsive, not-so-quick drink that turned into a one-night stand? In fact, shouldn't she be the one to say it? Either way they'd simply return to being co-workers, certainly not friends. They had never been friends to begin with.

While she was fretting over questions with no answers, she was trying to get dressed. By the time she left for work her bed was awash in discarded skirts and sweaters, all of which had looked perfectly fine last week, yet this morning for some unfathomable reason, nothing fit the way she would have liked. Finally giving up, she chose a black skirt and grey sweater, grabbed her coat and slammed the front door on the way out.

=

The phone rang the second Rob entered his office. He answered it, surprised to hear Jackie's voice. She got right to it, asking if they could meet that night. "After all," she purred, "we haven't been to-gether, if you know what I mean, for a couple of weeks. You didn't even call me before Thanksgiving."

Rob shook his head. The girl was relentless and he was very well aware of what she meant. Not that he minded, but he wasn't in the mood to deal with her at 8:45 in the morning. He promised to call her later in the week. "Sure you will," she said, the purr turning to a hiss. He stared at the phone. Maybe he'd call her, maybe not. He had other things on his mind.

While he was talking with her, he saw Maddie come in. He didn't look up. He wasn't sure how she would react after their night together and knew he had to be careful; all he needed was another assistant casually dropping by his office twelve times a day and leaning over his shoulder to point out something non-existent on a layout while whispering in his ear. Still, there was something about this one that was different.

Reminding himself to play it cool, he picked up an envelope. "Good morning, Maddie. I hope you had a nice weekend. Can you come into my office for a minute? I want to go over these contact sheets before the meeting."

He had come up behind her and registered her surprise as she turned to look at him. With a barely whispered "Good morning," she followed him to his office. He dropped the envelope on his desk and looked at her, his voice low. "I thought about you all weekend."

"You did?"

"Yes, Maddie. I would have called but things got too hectic. How about I make it up to you. Have a drink with me tomorrow after work."

After hesitating, she nodded. "All right."

He had considered, if only for a split-second, that she might say no, that they shouldn't let it go any further than it already had. And yet he wasn't really surprised she accepted. Rejection wasn't in his vocabulary.

He slipped several contact sheets out of the envelope. It had been left by a photographer who had covered a "Happening" at Andy Warhol's Factory over the weekend. He glanced at them and, all business again, handed them to her. "Take these, we'll discuss them at the meeting."

At the door she glanced back with a small smile. He felt that smile as though it were a kiss. He shook his head. It was time to focus on work; the Monday morning editorial meeting was about to begin.

=

Rob was the last to crowd into Fred's office. At one time there had been a conference room but it had been sacrificed to make more space for the bullpen. Since several of the assistants were women, Fred no longer considered it a "bullpen." He now referred to it affectionately as the "chicken coop."

The editors sat in chairs they had dragged in, but due to lack of space, the assistants, including girls in short skirts, were relegated to the floor.

By the time Rob squeezed in, preferring to stand, the production director was already haranguing one of the writers. "Your article was due last Friday," he snarled. "If you miss one more deadline, we'll replace it with something else."

The writer glared back at him. "Fuck you. Excuse me ladies, but if you cut my article there will be hell to pay." Holding back grins, the editors looked up as if examining the ceiling tiles while the assistants sniggered. Every week it was the same, the editors continually complaining about pages allocated for their stories and the production director bitching about deadlines.

Rob shook his head and glanced at Fred, who, looking exasperated, shouted for everyone to shut up so they could get on with the meeting. They began with the social editor who announced he would be attending Truman Capote's "Black and White Ball" that night at the Plaza. "It may be the party of the decade if not the century," he sniffed.

Fred was nonplussed. Society snobbery bored him. "When will you have the story ready?"

"I should have it by the end of the week."

Fred nodded. "Get it done quickly. You know we'll be scooped by *Life* and the other weeklies."

"I'm writing it from the social angle. They'll be concentrating on the Hollywood crowd."

The production director cut in. "Finish it by next Monday and I'll hold six pages for you."

From there the meeting moved on to other editors and writers, variously reporting on the Broadway scene, new clubs, a famous golfer and even a cooking school. The pompous travel editor went last, complaining that he "simply loathed" the photos provided by the public relations agency for the Bahamas. Maddie looked up and in a quiet voice suggested they chuck the photos and instead use illustrations to liven up the piece. He frowned, but nodded, "Not a bad idea." He seemed to be searching for her name.

She glanced quickly at Rob, who nodded with a small smile.

After the meeting ended Fred and Rob went out for lunch, both of them requiring at least a cocktail or two. Maddie's name never came up.

Chapter 12

Trying to calm the butterflies in her stomach, Maddie dressed in a long ivory turtleneck sweater over a black-and-white checked miniskirt and knee-high boots. In an attempt to avoid the agitation of the previous day, she had laid everything out the night before. Despite that a few of her anxieties had been put, at least temporarily, to rest—most significantly that she wasn't merely a one-night stand—she was still uptight, anticipating what the night might bring and the next round of uncertainties that would be sure to follow.

It had gotten cold enough to wear her lynx coat and she dug it out of the closet where it had been stored all summer. Joan had bought one when they were at *Today's Bride* and Maddie had loved the soft warmth of it. She had splurged and bought one, paying for it over several months.

When she arrived at the office, Tara sidled up to her. "Got a date tonight?" she asked in a snippy voice. Maddie forced a smile, wondering if she could possibly know.

Rob had asked her to meet him at Laughlin's, a pub a few blocks away on Third Avenue. When he left the office at six, Tara walked out with him. Maddie watched them nervously before going to fix her makeup.

=

Quinn, the bartender saw her first. Glancing at Rob, he nodded his approval and pointed to a booth near the back. The room was already crowded with single guys and girls who worked in the area. The world was changing, Rob thought, and girls were no longer apprehensive about going to bars by themselves. (His mother had told his sisters never to go into a bar alone; the men would think they were prostitutes). But it was 1966 and the recently coined "happy hour" was beginning to take hold. Occasionally a quick drink turned into "a quickie" back at someone's apartment. Rob considered himself a great supporter of another new term, "free love."

Quinn asked Maddie what she wanted and she told him an Old Grand Dad sour. He nodded and said he'd bring it back to the booth. As he placed her drink on the table, along with another scotch for Rob, he squinted at her, "Do you really like these? They're so sweet."

"Yes. Actually I do. But I can't drink too many of them."

"Nobody can," he muttered, returning to the bar. As if on cue, Rob reached across the table and took her hand. "Then I think we should finish our drinks and go to your apartment."

She stared at him; he certainly wasn't wasting any time. For a second she considered saying no, if only to be coy. Then she asked herself why; the man was married—there was no place for this relationship to go. It would no doubt be at best a short-term affair, so why not just go for it and enjoy the moment? Although she liked Danny, he was a bit on the conservative side. While he was a sweet and caring lover, he didn't have the fire that Rob had in, or for that matter, out of bed. After one night of Rob, she wanted more.

"Sure," she said. "Why not?"

=

In the taxi she tried to think of something, anything, to say. What, she asked herself, does one talk about when on the way to make love for the second time with your married boss? The weather? Maybe a photo shoot coming up? Before she could become even more nervous, Rob put his arm around her shoulders and began kissing her, not stopping until the taxi driver impatiently announced that they had arrived. Maddie stepped out blushing, aware she was a bit disheveled.

After paying the driver, he rushed her past the startled doorman and up to her apartment where, unleashing an insatiable desire, they practically tore one another's clothes off. Without warning, he picked her up and carried her to the bedroom. By the time she landed on the bed he was already kneeling between her legs. Breathless with desire, she pulled him forward, sighing softly as he entered her. He didn't rush, allowing sensation to build between them until he stopped abruptly, put his arms under her and turned over, pulling her on top of him. She gasped in surprise but stayed with him as they moved together. Letting go of her hips, he began caressing her breasts. At exactly the same moment she leaned over to kiss him and suddenly unbalanced, they rolled off the bed, unfortunately at a somewhat crucial moment. It didn't matter; they lay on the floor laughing and with barely a pause, continued.

Finally climbing back in bed, they released each other. Maddie got up, somewhat unsteadily, to get a glass of water. Rob lit a Marlboro and asked if there was a beer. She said she thought there might be a can or two in the fridge. As she reached for one, he came up behind her, picked her up and sat her on the counter top.

"What are you doing? It's cold," she yelped, trying to get down. But he held on and started caressing her. "Maddie," he said solemnly, "I'm going to make love to you in every room in this apartment." Balancing her carefully, he began to do just that.

But he wasn't quite through with her. Whispering, "There's still another room to go," he carried her, giggling and with her legs wrapped around him to the living room couch. They later agreed it may not have been the most comfortable place to make love, but it was certainly fun. Laughing, she finally pushed him off. "Rob, there are only three rooms in this apartment and now that you've accomplished your goal, maybe we should go get something to eat. I'm starving."

"So am I," he agreed, reaching for her.

"No, Rob. Not again. Not until you feed me. Do you want to take a shower?" She thought they'd eat something and he'd catch the next train. It was only nine thirty.

"No, Maddie," he said with a smile in his eyes. "I'm afraid we're going to have to come back here and do this all over again."

She grinned at him. "Are you always this insatiable?"

He laughed easily. "When it comes to you, obviously I am."

While she loved his answer, she wondered if returning to her apartment was such a good idea and if he shouldn't be going home. And yet she felt it wasn't her place to question his decisions.

=

Maddie had lived on the Upper East Side for almost three years but couldn't think of anywhere to go. On Third Avenue they turned uptown and Rob pointed to Allen's, a dimly lit bar on the far corner of Seventy-Third Street.

"Have you ever been there?" he asked. She shook her head and wrinkled her nose, "No. I've always thought it looked sort of grubby."

"Come on," he said taking her hand. As he expected, Allen's was essentially a neighborhood saloon with scuffed wooden floors and a long bar that gleamed with years of careful polishing. Old iron lanterns hung from a stamped tin ceiling painted a dull grey. Well-worn wooden chairs and tables were scattered around the large room that retained the scent of old whiskey and cigarettes.

It was about ten and not many tables were occupied. There was an empty booth in the window alcove opposite the bar and they took it. Rob ordered Johnny Walker Red, a bourbon and ginger ale for her and asked for menus. They both decided on cheeseburgers, rare with fries.

Before the food came, Rob went back toward a corridor with a sign for the restrooms where he made a phone call. Maddie watched him, uncomfortably aware that he was calling his wife. When he returned to the table, he said nothing about the call and she didn't ask.

Instead, they drank, ate and talked about their jobs, their dreams for the future and his childhood growing up in Darien as the only son of a doting and deeply religious Catholic mother. Maddie asked if he had rebelled when he was a kid.

"I did some really dumb things." He said with a grin. "But my friends and I were in high school and they were just pranks, like painting and feathering the statue of one of the town's founders. There was never any real harm done, but all the cops in town knew us by the time we graduated. Anyway, my mother always dragged me and my sisters to church on Sundays so our sins could be forgiven. By the time I was twelve I had it figured out. I could do whatever I wanted during the week and on Sunday confess a few misdeeds. I'd never tell all of them; it would have taken too long. After the priest told me how many Hail Marys and all that, I'd make sure to look contrite, do a run around the beads and everyone was happy. I wouldn't be going to hell after all. A least not that week."

He laughed as he described the first time he had sex. "When I was fourteen, one of my mother's friends from out of town came to visit for a weekend. After dinner that Saturday she asked me to bring her overnight bag upstairs to her bedroom. When I did, she took my face in her hands and kissed me. While everyone else was talking and drinking downstairs, she invited me into her bed."

Maddie looked at him wide eyed. "And?"

He laughed. "And what? I wasn't about to refuse her. She was a really nice lady."

"Did she go to church with your mother the next day?"

He grinned. "Of course, Maddie. We all did."

Lighting a cigarette, he said now that he had told his story, it was her turn. She shook her head. "Maybe another time," she said, thinking he was still that same mischievous kid, except that his "pranks" were more grown up and he now answered to no one. Those Sundays at church had been abandoned long ago.

After ordering Irish coffees, they moved on to less scandalous subjects. She hadn't known that he was a fine artist; not only did he draw, but while still at Parson's he'd had illustrations accepted and published in magazines. "But now," he said, suddenly serious, "I think it's time for me to leave publishing."

"What do you mean?"

"Maddie. No one knows this but I'm starting to look for a job in advertising."

She felt a stab of fear; if he left *Status* what would happen to her? And not only as his assistant. She wanted to ask him more, but he was already signaling the waiter for the check.

Chapter 13

Rob opened his eyes to weak light seeping through the blinds. Still half asleep, he wasn't sure where he was. He turned over and saw Maddie. Her back was to him and the covers were crumpled down to her waist. He was immediately aroused, which no doubt would have happened crumpled covers or not. Simply put, girls just turned him on.

He began caressing her and she backed up closer to him. He told her to stay still and began making love to her. She arched her back and caught her breath. It was a warm, sweet moment and he knew it didn't get much better than this—at least at seven on a weekday morning. Usually he couldn't get out of a girl's apartment fast enough, but for once he was in no hurry.

He guessed they slept because when he looked at the clock it was almost eight. He kissed her neck, told her it was getting late and he'd go first. He asked if there was an extra toothbrush and a razor and she pointed to the bathroom. Still half asleep she told him to take a towel from the linen closet. In the shower, he found an old metal razor that was as dull as he expected it to be. *That's what we guys have to contend with the morning after. They shave their legs with the damn things.* He found extra blades, but no shaving cream. At least she didn't appear to have her dates staying over like some other girls he knew. *But then, who am I to talk?*

When he came out of the bathroom she hadn't moved. "Time to get going, Maddie. We don't want to be late," he said with a touch of irony. She forced her eyes open and glanced up at his well-toned body wrapped in a pink towel. "Pink isn't exactly your color, Rob."

He laughed. "If I take it off we may never get to the office."

She groaned and sat up. "I hope I have some Bufferin left."

The bathroom was still foggy from Rob's long shower and she rummaged through the messy medicine cabinet muttering to herself that she should probably straighten things up a bit.

She reached for the Bufferin, hearing the satisfying click of a few pills.

"There was no shaving cream," Rob said standing in the doorway still wrapped in pink.

"I don't use it. I use soap."

"Well, I didn't get a great shave," he complained, rubbing his chin.

She was sorely tempted to reach for the pink towel. Instead she gave him a light kiss. "You look fine, Rob."

=

As they exited the subway he said he was going to buy a new shirt and tie; he couldn't show up in the office with the ones from yesterday. He didn't mention that he would bet that Tara would catch it, but hopefully not connect the dots.

Tara. She had been an unforeseen, one-night fling. After flirting with him for months, she began waiting until he left so she could walk out with him. One rainy night she asked if they could have a drink. He wasn't really interested; she wasn't exactly his type, and besides she was his secretary. It may have been the scotch more than anything else, but opportunity knocked and who was he to turn it down? They ended up at her apartment in Queens. He didn't consider himself a snob but he definitely preferred his women in Manhattan. If he couldn't get a taxi, at least he knew where the subways were.

The next day, feeling a little awkward, he had taken her to lunch, explaining it could only be that one night. Surprisingly she agreed, saying it had been fun and she understood. He was relieved; he needed her on his side. She was the one who fielded the frequent and probing calls from Allison and made up appropriate excuses for where he might or might not be.

=

Rob slipped quietly into his office without Tara noticing. He stashed the bag with yesterday's shirt and tie under his desk and drank some much needed black coffee, at the same time still cursing himself for that slip up with her.

Looking at his watch, he was surprised it was almost nine thirty and he better get on the horn to his wife. He was steeling himself for a less than pleasant conversation when Fred barged into his office, trailed closely by Maddie who was looking everywhere but at him. Considering they had just gotten out of bed, he understood her reticence. It was going to require a lot more coffee if this was going to be some sort of confrontation. But the office gossip was evidently silent, at least as far as he and Maddie were concerned.

Fred wanted to know about the next day's photo shoot. "Where's Jamie? We have to pick the dresses."

"They were just delivered. He'll be here in a minute," Maddie answered.

Two minutes later Jamie rushed in, dropping his armload of gaudily colored dresses on Rob's desk. Rob grimaced.

"I'll move them in a minute, Rob. Chill out. They're from different designers so just tell me which ones we're going to shoot." One of the worst kept secrets in publishing was that the number of pages an advertiser bought directly affected the amount of editorial coverage he received. Editors eternally swore it wasn't true, but in Fred's words, that was pure bullshit and precisely why he had called the meeting.

Ed, one of the ad salesmen, bolted into the office. He and two other space salesmen as they were called, occupied the offices next to Rob. The editors, as well as Maddie and Rob tended to ignore them despite the fact that they were the ones who brought in the advertising, essentially the revenue that supported the magazine and paid their salaries.

"Make sure you use a couple of dresses from Ferndesigns," Ed said catching his breath. "They're running spreads in the next two issues."

Rob nodded impatiently and Jamie held up two color blocked mini dresses. "We'll definitely be using at least one of these."

Ed thanked him and ran back to his office.

Fred asked Maddie about the models and scheduling for the shoot. After checking her notes, she answered him. Risking a quick glance at Rob, who looked at back at her with a grin, she blushed and shifted her gaze to the window, staring out at the less than fascinating view of the brick building next door.

Rob reached for a cigarette thinking he wanted to fuck her right there.

"I assume then that we're all set," Fred said looking pointedly at the three of them. He stood up and lit one his endless cheroots. "Looking forward to seeing the shots next week."

Jamie nervously gathered all the dresses together, told Maddie he'd have them ready to go to the location in an hour, nodded at Rob and scurried out the door.

"He's such a wimp," Rob said, looking at Maddie. She smiled, the first he'd seen that morning and it lit up her face. "I better go and get everything ready for the shoot," she said.

He was about to pick up the phone to call the photographer when he noticed a pile of messages on his desk. Seeing Tara staring at him from the doorway, he didn't have to guess who they were from. "She must have called eight times this morning, Rob. I'm running out of excuses." She glanced at Maddie and back at him. "I think you better call your wife." She turned on her heel and walked out.

There was no way out of it. Picking up the phone, he dialed and swiveled around to the non-existent view outside the window, hoping Allison would be out. No such luck. She started with her usual accusations and he let her yell; there was no point interrupting. He had told her yesterday that he'd be in a late meeting and planned to stay at Fred's. This time she asked for Fred's number. She didn't exactly ask, she demanded it. She said she had called information but had been told Fred's number was unlisted.

"How convenient," she snapped.

Rob breathed a palpable sigh of relief. "Fred's here," he said, trying to mask his sarcasm. "Do you want me to get him so you can ask if I was there last night? Really Allison, are you going to start checking up on me?"

"You should have called me from his apartment. I don't care if it was late," she said in a softer tone.

"You're right," he admitted. "But I hate to wake you." *Bullshit. I just don't want to have to listen to you bitch at me.*

"I've told you before, it's all right. I'm usually not asleep anyway. I'm awake worrying that something might have happened to you. And I insist that you give me Fred's number." Her tone had reverted to shrill.

Ignoring her, he said he'd be on an early train and in a seductive voice told her to get the kids to bed early; he really missed her. That calmed her down. He lit another cigarette and looked across at Maddie. There was no time to think about her; he had other things on his mind. Most important, he planned to work on his portfolio that night. He had already called Tom and made an appointment to meet with him at the agency in two weeks. He needed to be ready.

Later that evening he barely said goodnight to Maddie, adding that he'd see her the next morning at the shoot.

Chapter 14

Maddie arrived at the Fifth Avenue apartment just before nine. Although a short distance from her small one bedroom, it was miles away in prestige, size and elegance. It consisted of nine spacious rooms with wood paneling, fireplaces and high ceilings. Heavily curtained windows obscured dramatic views of Central Park, most likely to block sunlight from fading the silk brocade sofas and eighteenth-century Baroque paintings that graced the lacquered, gilt edged walls. Despite its opulence, Maddie doubted she would ever have any desire to live in such a place; it was about as personal as a museum.

Rob strode in just as Neil, the photographer, began setting up the first shot. After shaking hands and giving a perfunctory nod to Jamie and Maddie, he proceeded directly to a huge pink marble bathroom that had been designated as a changing room. Inside, two models were having their hair and makeup done. Rob entered to squeals of glee as they both jumped up and began kissing him. Maddie glanced in seeing one of them in a very small black bra and even tinier bikini panties hanging on to him and whispering. They laughed as he patted one on the bottom and gently extricated himself telling them to continue getting ready.

Maddie wasn't crazy about photography shoots. She had done too many of them at *Today's Bride* and the novelty had worn off. They required intensive planning, layouts to follow, clothes to be pressed and pinned in time to be ready for the next shot, not to mention making sure the outfits looked all right as the models moved on the set. That day they were lucky; the models were cooperative and happy to do whatever Rob asked of them.

Neil had brought a transistor radio and music blared, as usual at a photo shoot, even in a Fifth Avenue apartment. Beginning with the mellow sounds of Simon and Garfunkel's "Sound of Silence," it progressed to the Beatles and Stones and even the Byrds, with a bit of Sonny and Cher's "Babe Don't Go" thrown in.

By the end of the day Maddie's ears were ringing, but the loud music kept everyone upbeat and moving. She was relieved that the owners hadn't returned home. With clothes strewn all over the expensive furniture, wires for the strobes snaking over the Persian carpets and half-naked models running back and forth in between shots, she was afraid they'd have heart attacks.

They finished by five thirty and after a discussion with Neil, Rob announced he was going to call the office and then leave to catch an early train. Feeling a stab of disappointment, Maddie watched as he picked up a phone in a hallway and began jotting down notes as he spoke with Tara. At one point he gave a small laugh. After hanging up, he dialed another number, this time speaking softly. She noticed him glance at her and turn away quickly. She had little doubt he was talking with some girl. She wasn't jealous, but she experienced a sinking feeling and reminded herself that she had no hold on him; he was free to do what he wanted. Although, she mused, his wife might not exactly agree with that.

On his way out the door, he stopped briefly to speak to Jamie and cheek-kissed the still scantily clad models. Maddie reminded herself to be glad she had a date with Danny that night.

=

Rob left the apartment satisfied that the photo shoot had gone well. When he had phoned Tara, she told him he'd had quite a number of calls; not much of a surprise since he had been out of the office all day. There were, naturally, several from Allison and he told her to call and tell her he'd take the 6:23 train. After rattling off the rest of his messages she cleared her throat and in a phony sweet voice said, "Your friend, Miss Simmons called. Shall I call her back for you?"

He laughed. "It's okay Tara. I'll deal with that one myself."

"I'm sure you will," she answered in a sardonic tone.

Miss Simmons answered on the first ring.

"Hi Jackie, I got a message that you called." He shook a Marlboro out of the box and lit it with his lighter.

"Well, hello Mr. MacLeod. I haven't heard from you in a couple of weeks. I thought you might like to come to an early Christmas party with me tonight."

"Sounds like fun Jackie. Unfortunately, I have to go home."

"Who said anything about you not going home?" She was whispering seductively and it was turning him on. For some unknown reason, he glanced at Maddie and experiencing an unusual pang, he made a decision.

"No can do, Jackie. I'll call you soon." He winced as she slammed down the phone.

On his way to the elevator, he stopped suddenly and returned to the apartment. Maddie was packing up the dresses and looked surprised to see him. "How about having dinner with me next Tuesday?"

She smiled, her eyes shining. "I'd like that, Rob."

Chapter 15

The following week, on the night of their date, Rob told Maddie he'd made a reservation at Saito for seven-thirty. Fortunately, they were in his office because she looked at him in wide-eyed shock.

"That's the Japanese restaurant that specializes in raw fish. I don't think I want to eat sashimi or whatever it's called."

His smile was indulgent. "You won't have to eat anything you don't want. Trust me. I'm sure you'll like it."

At four she was surprised to see him preparing to leave. With his coat in hand, he said quietly, "I just got a call for a meeting at an ad agency. It shouldn't run late, but I think you should go home and wait until I call. Just in case."

"What agency?" she whispered.

"Not now, Maddie. I'll tell you about it later."

=

When she got home she took a shower, dabbed on Cabochard and turned on the boob tube. *The Girl from Uncle* was on NBC and she watched it until *The Red Skelton Show* came on. She was glad Rob had warned her he might run late.

Two hours later, she wasn't so sure. How was it that he had been so attentive earlier and now he wasn't calling? By eleven she was angry. She switched to the news; maybe there had been a disaster in midtown and that's why he hadn't called. According to Walter Cronkite, however, all was quiet in the city of New York.

The phone rang, startling her.

Rob sounded excited. "Sorry I didn't call earlier Maddie. I was with a couple of guys from the advertising agency. After my interview they insisted I join them for a drink."

A drink? That was one hell of a long drink.

"Are you there?" he asked when she didn't answer.

"Yes, Rob. What do you want me to say? That I like being stood up?"

"No, no. I didn't stand you up. I would never do that to you." He paused and she could hear someone speaking to him. "All right," he mumbled. "I'll just be a minute."

"I'm going to hang up now."

"Maddie, stop. I have to go. The guys are leaving. I'll be right there.

"No, Rob. I'll see you in the office. Goodnight." She hung up feeling her heart beat wildly as all those lovely anticipatory butterflies congealed into a lump in her stomach. She hoped she'd still have a job the next day.

She got out of her clothes and into one of the T-shirts she slept in, wishing she had a Seconal or whatever those feel-good pills in *Valley of the Dolls* were called.

The doorbell rang, surprising her. She grabbed her robe. *Now what?*

Rob was standing there with an apologetic look on his face.

"What are you doing here?"

"I already told you Maddie, I wanted to see you," he said, moving around her and throwing his coat on the couch.

"No, Rob. Go home and see your wife."

"I don't like my wife," he said in a quiet voice. He stopped, as though stunned at his own admission.

They stared at one another in silence.

Wrapping her robe around her, Maddie sighed and asked if he wanted coffee.

"No. But I'll have a beer." He followed her to the kitchen. "Please forgive me. I had an incredible evening and it just got away from me. But you're the one I wanted to share it with. Sorry about Saito."

"It's okay."

He looked at his watch. "Come on. I know you haven't eaten. Neither have I. Let's go to Allen's."

She relented; she couldn't have eaten anything before, but now that he mentioned it she was ravenous.

=

After they ordered, her curiosity having overruled her irritation, Maddie asked about his meeting.

He attacked his hamburger with vigor, saying all they had done was drink. And talk. And drink some more. No one had even mentioned having dinner. He said he had been with Tom, an acquaintance from Darien, and John Langer, a senior partner of the agency.

Maddie could actually feel the energy emanating from him.

He drained his beer and signaled the waiter for another. "John told me they were usually wary of hiring someone straight out of publishing, but he had heard about my reputation and said if I thought I could cut it, they might be willing to give me a shot. I'm sure you can understand that there was no way I could leave or refuse to go with them for drinks. I was even afraid to get up to make a call. I didn't want to break the good vibes."

"So now what?" Maddie asked.

He reached for her hand. "Maddie, the art director on Cosette, their big cosmetic account, is leaving. He's already given notice. I think it will be a couple of months, probably early February before it opens up. There's no guarantee I'd get the account even if I do get a job there, but it's worth a shot."

His excitement was contagious and she leaned over to kiss him.

"Don't congratulate me yet. There are still more interviews and I'll have to present some ideas. As many magazine layouts as I've done, coming up with ads is something else entirely. I have a lot of work to do in the next couple of weeks. Now do you forgive me?"

"I guess I'll have to. But do me a favor, call me next time. You were going to get that offer, phone call or not."

Chapter 16

That Friday, as she was about to leave a meeting in Fred's office, Maddie heard him ask Rob what he was doing for the weekend. Rob stopped in the doorway. "Going skiing in Vermont with a couple of my buddies. Want to come?"

Fred laughed, "Don't break a leg."

Maddie was taken aback. Their long nights of making love — interspersed with affectionate murmurs and occasional industry gossip — seldom touched on the reality of his day-to-day existence outside the office. Still, she thought that after Tuesday he might have mentioned it. After they returned from Allen's he had gone on at length about how much he loved to ski, describing his excitement and the ecstatic rush of speeding down winding mountains trails. He said it was almost, but not quite, as great as sex and how perfect it would be if he could take her away with him for a weekend. She had hugged him, thrilled with the thought while omitting the fact that she had never even thought about skiing.

And yet here it was, three days later and not a word about it. She guessed the reality was that guys tended not to communicate what they didn't think was relevant at the moment. In truth, all too often they didn't even bother to communicate what actually was relevant.

=

Danny had invited her to a birthday party on Saturday for his friend, Luke Berman, an account exec at AW&M.

Luke's wife, Sue, opened the door and with a squeal of delight threw her arms around Danny. He rolled his eyes but hugged her back. With her arm still around him, she looked at Maddie and in a true Brooklyn accent said, "Is this man the best? We just love him. Not only is he successful, but so gorgeous. You better not let go of him."

Maddie blushed. "That's quite an endorsement."

Danny laughed. "It's okay Maddie. I pay her to say those things."

After meeting Luke—he was the one with the funny birthday hat—Sue introduced her to their friends. Danny had mentioned that the guys worked at AW&M, either as account executives or media buyers, all of them on the business side. When she asked if any of the wives worked, he shrugged, "I doubt it. Why would they?"

It took only minutes before those same wives cornered Maddie. They all proclaimed to adore Danny, one confiding that she wished he was her husband instead of Ron, the balding guy with the paunch sitting on the recliner. A tall brunette—Maddie had already forgotten their names—whispered they were glad to see him with a new date; he had been devastated after his last girlfriend had broken their engagement. It was something he rarely mentioned; to him it was the past and he preferred not to dwell on it.

They all expressed surprise that she was an assistant art director at a well-known magazine. After one of the nosier women sarcastically suggested that she was probably only working until she found the right man to marry, she forced a smile and excused herself, saying she wanted to get another glass of wine. Instead she went to Danny, who despite her interrupting a boisterous discussion on football, made room on the sofa and put his arm protectively around her.

After a dinner that was long on wine and advertising gossip, Sue brought out the birthday cake: a pair of large pink breasts with candles stuck strategically around rosy nipples. As everyone laughed and clapped, Sue turned to Maddie with a grin. "I ordered it from the Erotic Bakery. One of Luke's accounts is Bali, but they wouldn't make a cake of a bra."

=

They were the last to leave and after ringing for the elevator, Danny kissed Maddie and put his hand under her sweater, stroking her breasts. She tried to relax, thinking that Rob certainly slept with his wife and there was no reason she shouldn't go to bed with Danny.

After all, this is the decade of free love and since everyone else is doing it, why not me? But deep down she was beginning to desire only one man and he was married.

When they arrived at her apartment, he kissed her and led her into the bedroom. He unzipped her dress but stopped abruptly and began taking off his own clothes. After putting his sport jacket and slacks carefully over a chair he turned back to her.

In bed he caressed her breasts and kissed her neck. As she reached down to stroke him he groaned and moved over her. He made love silently but energetically and all too quickly he whispered, "Are you ready Maddie? I want you to come with me."

"Yes," she sighed, wishing it were so.

He rolled off and hugged her close. "Maddie, I love making love to you."

"You too," she murmured, wondering if he, like Rob, would ever say, "I love fucking you?" She didn't think it was in his vocabulary. Actually he never swore, at least not in front of her.

=

The next morning, he left around ten to meet a bunch of his friends at the Carnegie Deli on Sixth Avenue. He had asked Maddie to come with him, but she declined.

"Danny," she said slipping on her robe. "I truly have no desire to watch your friends gorging themselves on pastrami sandwiches while telling outrageous stories about playing high school football, not to mention squeezing into a packed subway to Yankee Stadium for a Giant's game where you'll end up end up drinking beer and shouting invectives at the players for the next three hours."

He laughed and kissed her, "It's okay Maddie. I understand. I'll call you when I get home."

After he left she made coffee and collapsed on the couch with New York Times. By one o'clock she was becoming restless. She made herself a grilled cheese sandwich and picked up the *Valley of the Dolls* — something, anything, to take her mind off Rob. An hour later she put the book aside and called Suzanne who asked if she wanted to come over.

"Probably not. I haven't even bothered to take a shower and I'm too lazy to even think about getting dressed."

Suzanne yawned. "I know how you feel. I'm still in my night-gown. What's going on with Rob?"

"He's fine, he's sexy, and oh yeah, he's married. What more is there to say?"

"You're becoming involved, aren't you? I'll bet he's on your mind all the time and right about now you're wondering if he's going to call." That was something Maddie hadn't even admitted to herself.

"Did Danny stay over last night?"

"Yes. There was no way I could get out of it. Sometimes I think he actually helps balance what's going on with Rob. I know he's every-thing a girl could want but I'm beginning to feel like I'm using him."

"Concentrate on Danny, he's good for you. Rob's never going to leave his wife. He's got all the girls he wants and now he has you. You don't want to become known as his girlfriend. Who'll ask you out then? Wouldn't you rather be with someone who wants to spend Saturday nights with you?"

"Of course I would. But it's only been a few weeks and Christ-mas is coming. I think I should wait and see what happens. Maybe by then it will be over anyway." She shivered, hoping she wasn't being prescient.

Hearing a shout, she asked, "What was that?"

"Andrew's glued to the football game on TV and now he wants lunch. No way can he make his own sandwich. Gee, I don't remem-ber signing up for lunch."

Maddie laughed and said she'd call her tomorrow.

=

After hanging up, Maddie glanced outside. Through the window of the apartment across the street she could see two people argu-ing. *Why is every relationship so difficult?* Why wasn't anyone happy with what they had or whom they were with? Look at Rob, married only five years. When had he begun to cheat? And Danny's fiancée? What had she needed that he didn't have? Maybe she had met some version of Rob. And in her own life, her parents had divorced after ten years. Everyone was searching for love but no one seemed hap-py when they found it.

She recalled a quote from D.H. Lawrence: "Love is the flow-er of life, and blossoms unexpectedly and without law and must be plucked where it is found, and enjoyed for the brief hour of its duration."

Maybe that was the answer; *the brief hour of its duration*. Her generation had grown up watching sugary-sweet Hollywood movies that gushed sentiment: Doris Day and Rock Hudson exchanging chaste kisses in Technicolor leading them to believe that love and romance, not to mention happiness, would last forever. And if love did equate with happy, was happy even the right term? Probably not. Perhaps that all too "brief hour" was all there truly was before the inevitability of dissatisfaction set in. In that case, why not indulge herself with Rob. Better to enjoy the moment, forget the questions and not worry about the outcome.

The phone rang, breaking her reverie. She was sure it was Danny letting her know the Giant's had lost again. She didn't particularly care, but it had been a bad season and he and his friends had become very emotional about it.

She was surprised to hear Rob's voice saying he wanted to see her and would be there in half an hour. Even more surprising was that she should "be naked."

"What?" she shouted, not believing she had heard him correctly. But he had already hung up.

Be naked? What the hell is that about? Whatever it was, there was no time to think about it and she ran for the shower. After dotting on some Cabochard, she straightened up the apartment, washed the dishes and changed the sheets, not believing she'd ever end up making love with two men in two days. She shook the thought away; it wasn't the moment to ponder that existential predicament.

She put on a long red-velvet robe that had only a thin tie to keep it closed. It had been a gift from her mother last Christmas, and she wondered what her mother would think of her wearing it to greet her...her what? She stopped, suddenly asking herself what Rob was to her. Certainly not a boyfriend. She supposed he'd have to be called her lover. That sounded very serious, like something out of a French or English novel. She was still trying to process the thought when the doorbell rang.

Taking a breath, she went to answer it, loosening the tie so the robe fell seductively open.

Without a word, Rob picked her up and threw her over his shoulder. Ignoring her shouts to put her down, he dropped her on the bed.

"Rob," she laughed. "Didn't you go skiing?

"Yes, Maddie. There was a snowstorm so we left early." Without hesitation he began kissing her while trying to get his own clothes off—not an easy feat with layers of ski clothes. She was giggling and attempting to squirm out from under him, but he held her down. "Stop moving. I want you. Now."

"Rob…"

"Don't say a word."

It was as though he hadn't had sex in a long time. He had her on top, on her knees, in every configuration he could devise. He was strong, moving her as though she were a doll, caressing her one second and roughly thrusting into her the next, backing off and telling her she couldn't come, not until he allowed her. She was screaming with desire while he continued to whisper and tease, holding off until they reached the moment when desire becomes too intense for conscious thought and only sensation remains.

"How is it I can't get enough of you?" he whispered.

Warm and drowsy, she stretched out against him. She knew no answer was required; she had learned that sometimes silence was best.

He turned to glance at the clock. It was close to six-thirty. "I have to go. I should have been home by now."

Maddie kissed him lightly, wishing desperately that he didn't have to leave. As she was about to get up, he grabbed her hand and she turned back to him. He was staring at her with a look that might have said volumes, or perhaps it was just that—a look.

=

Danny called about eight-thirty. Maddie had fallen asleep while watching the Ed Sullivan Show.

"You sound tired," he said.

"A little. How was the game? Did the Giants win?" *Do I really care?*

He laughed. "No. Another rout. By the way I meant to tell you I may be in your office this week."

She sat up, suddenly alert. "How come?"

"It seems my bourbon client wants to run a couple of ads in *Status*. In exchange he's asking for some sort of event or promotion."

He paused and she heard papers shuffling. "Yes. I'm meeting with Fred and Jim, the sales guy. Wednesday I think. I met Fred a few months ago, before you were there. Funny, I never thought about it till now."

Yes, funny. "Well, let me know when you'll be coming over." She had to force it out. That was all she needed; both of them in the office at the same time.

Chapter 17

Luckily Allison hadn't found out that Rob had gotten home three hours after his skiing buddies. To maintain the peace, he made up his mind that he would attend a few Christmas parties, but he wouldn't stay overnight in the city.

Nevertheless, the following Wednesday he called Maddie into this office and asked her to come with him to a party that night. She told him she couldn't; she already had plans. She didn't mention she was going to AW&M's annual Christmas bash with Danny.

The rest of the day Rob acted cool to her and she was beginning to wonder if she had made a mistake. But she wasn't about to tell Danny she couldn't go with him. She assumed Rob took it for granted that she'd be available whenever he wanted. It was her own fault; she hadn't said no to him since their first night together. She imagined him going through his little black book (didn't they all have little black books?) and calling another girl. *No,* she thought sardonically, *he probably has their numbers memorized.*

She had been relieved that he hadn't asked who she was going out with. He didn't know about Danny, not yet anyway. But she was afraid that that was about to change — any minute in fact.

It was about three when she saw Danny following Ed, the ad salesman, along the far side of the bullpen to Fred's office. She watched as he stopped and appeared to ask a question. Ed pointed to Maddie and Danny waved. Forcing a smile, she waved back.

Just over an hour later she held her breath as he left Fred's office and made his way over to her.

"So this is it," he said with a wide grin. "The center of *Status's* creativity."

"Not quite, Danny." She hoped he was in a rush to leave.

He wasn't. "I have good news. It looks like we'll be placing some ads in your magazine and also having a promotional party for my bourbon client."

Out of the corner of her eye, she saw Rob approaching. "That's great Danny. Come on, I'll walk you out."

She was too late. Wishing she could become invisible, she introduced them: Rob as the art director and Danny, as just Danny. Biting her lip, she watched as they sized one another up. They even stood up straighter as they shook hands. Danny started explaining why he had been to see Fred, and Rob, feigning interest, wasted no time asking about his agency, adding quietly that he was considering making a change. Danny suggested that Rob come over to talk to AW&M and handed him a business card. Maddie could see Rob preening, convinced if he had feathers he'd be ruffling them about now. Anticipating what was about to happen, she stood frozen as Danny turned to her and with a smile said, "Maddie. I'll see you later."

Rob glanced quickly at her and then at Danny, his surprise obvious. With a look of irritation, he returned to his office. That night he left without a word to her.

=

The Christmas party at AW&M was a booze, beer and grass fueled mob scene. Christmas decorations papered the walls, the Beatles and Stones blasted from immense speakers and mistletoe had been hung everywhere. It didn't take long before an art assistant and a media buyer, two people who at any other time would have ignored each other, were locked in a passionate embrace. Another couple glanced around furtively, then headed with great stealth toward a copywriter's empty office, the copywriter chasing them and yelling, "No. Get out. No fucking on my desk." Two prim and proper secretaries got bombed, unbuttoned their bowed blouses and did the Watusi on a desk as one of the art directors ran for a Polaroid camera. To cap it off, someone threw up behind the Christmas tree.

Despite the raucous revelry, Maddie couldn't stop thinking about Rob. How could he be angry at her? Did he think she stayed home the nights he wasn't with her? She tried to drown those thoughts with too many glasses of champagne and knew she'd pay for it the next morning.

At midnight Danny, never a weekday lover, said he had an early meeting and, to her relief, left her at her apartment after only a few kisses.

Chapter 18

It was the last day in the office before the Christmas holiday and Maddie could barely concentrate on her work. She had several pages to release before five o'clock and had to stop herself from turning to look at Rob. Whether or not he was aware of her glances she didn't know. He hadn't looked up and, except for a few clipped comments about work, he'd hardly spoken to her in the last two days. She was cropping a photo stat with a razor blade when she inadvertently nicked herself. Grabbing her finger, she jumped up quickly; bleeding on a mechanical was practically a sin. As she ran to the ladies' room, Rob looked up.

"What happened Maddie?" he said, following her down the hallway.

She looked at him with tears in her eyes. It wasn't so much that her finger hurt; she was relieved that he was finally speaking to her.

Seeing her bloody hand he said, "Go put it under cold water. I'll get a couple of Band-Aids."

When she returned he was waiting at her drawing board. "I see you managed not to bleed on your layout."

"No, Rob. I wasn't about to redo the whole thing."

With a smile, as though there had been no tension between them for two days, he took her hand and gently wrapped a Band-Aid around her finger. He asked if she might possibly be available for lunch.

Feeling her anxiety dissolving into relief, she simply answered, "Yes."

He said to meet him at Laughlin's for lunch at two, he would go directly to the train from there.

=

Rob watched Maddie make her way through the cheerfully inebriated crowd, noting a few guys turn to glance at her. He'd been pissed at her for turning him down but after a couple of days realized he missed her, a rare feeling for him. He'd likely miss her next week as well; he had promised Allison he'd take time off. For whatever reason, he hadn't mentioned it to Maddie. He'd explain that he needed the time to work on the agency presentation.

In truth, he'd been putting it off and was only beginning to admit to himself that he was more than a bit stymied on ideas. His justification was too much work at the office, not to mention all the partying before the holidays. He'd already called John Langer to reschedule his interview for the week after New Year's. He'd have to be ready; he couldn't postpone it again.

He helped Maddie off with her coat and she sat down opposite him. After they ordered, she said, "It seems all the editors have left for the holidays. Except for you it looks like the inmates will be running the asylum next week."

He smiled. "I don't think I'll be coming in either, Maddie. I need to spend time with the kids and work on the presentation for the agency. I'm sure you and Tara can handle anything that comes up. I'll try to call you if I can."

=

If I can? "All right, Rob." What else could she say? Since they never discussed his life at home, it was as if it didn't exist. Alone and immersed in one another, they talked and laughed and made love. She greatly doubted that after he left he experienced the same wrenching emptiness. Perhaps it was time to think less about the romance and more about the reality.

She was glad she hadn't left herself without options. Danny was going home to Chicago for a few days, but he'd be back Tuesday. He had gotten tickets for *Auntie Mame* on Thursday and there were parties over New Year's weekend. She reminded herself to be grateful that he was in her life.

"What are you thinking about, Maddie?"

"Nothing, Rob," she said looking at her watch. "We should order. You have a train to catch and I should get back to the office."

He reached in his pocket and took out a square box, placing it on the table in front of her. She looked at it and then at him.

"Go ahead, Maddie. Open it. I promise it won't bite."

She untied the red ribbon and took out a heavy silver bangle bracelet. She caught her breath, trying to quell a surge of emotion.

"I have a friend in the Village who makes unusual jewelry. I hope you like it."

"Rob. It's beautiful. Thank you. But I didn't get anything for you. I wasn't sure what to do. I mean, because…"

"It's okay Maddie. Having you is enough."

She leaned across the table and kissed him. As she moved back he got up and took her in his arms, his kiss deep and lingering. Hearing hoots and shouts of "get a room" behind them, they moved apart, laughing. Every time she had doubts he somehow managed to make her feel that he really did care.

Chapter 19

Christmas eve turned out to be better than Rob expected. After Val and Tommy baked cookies with Allison, they ran into his den asking him to draw a picture of Rudolf the Red Nosed Reindeer to leave out for Santa. Later, after helping decorate the tree, they were so wound up it was impossible to get them into bed. It was almost ten thirty by the time they finally collapsed on the floor. After carrying them upstairs, Allison, to Rob's surprise, hugged him, saying what a wonderful day it had been. He kissed her, thinking that despite the tension between them, it truly had been.

Allison brought out wrapping paper and ribbon as Rob, contemplating putting together a dollhouse for Val and a train set for Tommy, poured a couple of large scotches. They had a few drinks, talked and laughed and by the time they finally put all the presents under the tree, he was looking forward to going upstairs with her. He was also looking forward to the rest of the weekend, which would be taken up with visiting family and friends and many, many parties. Whatever thoughts he had about preparing for his interview were once again put aside.

It appeared to be going well except for an unexpected moment at his father-in-law's house on Christmas day. Allison's brother's family was there, along with Rob's parents and sisters.

After opening their gifts, his kids and their cousins began shouting and rampaging around the house. Allison's father made himself another martini and pulled Rob aside. He had the distinct feeling it wasn't to wish him Merry Christmas.

"Rob," he said, his voice dropping to a deep confidential baritone, "I want to speak with you man to man. Alli has mentioned that you've been staying rather frequently in the city these last weeks. I hope that, ah…nothing is going on with you. I wouldn't want you to make my daughter unhappy."

Maintaining his composure, Rob looked back at him—all decked out in his English tweed jacket and silk ascot—thinking he was a pompous prick. And yet he had to be respectful; his father-in-law might be an asshole, but he was a rich and powerful one. "You know, Don, I would never do anything to hurt Allison. I love her and she's the mother of my children. But things have been unusually hectic at the office lately and there were some nights when I had to go out with advertisers or attend meetings that unexpectedly ran late. Fortunately, the managing editor is a close friend and I'm always able to camp in with him."

"I understand. But you must also understand that I want my only daughter to be happy." He took a generous gulp of his martini. "Just so you know, I expect the best from you." Rob was grateful he didn't clap him on the back.

He returned to the living room to find Tommy fighting with one of his cousins and Allison's mother glaring at him.

=

Monday morning, he closeted himself in his den. After thinking about advertising concepts on and off for days, he hadn't come up with anything remotely original. He finally admitted to himself that he was in unfamiliar territory and he was going to need someone to brainstorm with.

He was well aware that until the early sixties art directors weren't expected to be creative or even think; they were simply handed whatever ideas, good or bad, that account executives and copywriters came up with. Having no input, they did little but draw and lay out whatever they were told. Now, through the collaboration of copywriter and art director, advertising was being produced with far more inspiration and creativity. That's where he wanted to be; coming up with concepts and visuals that would, he hoped, resonate with the consumer and, to be honest, maybe even win an award or two.

Tuesday afternoon, after Allison took the kids to Stamford to return a few gifts, the house was blissfully silent. Nevertheless, nothing seemed to be working. Giving in to his frustration, he decided to call Maddie. Even without advertising experience, she was someone to bounce ideas off.

Eleanor, the receptionist, put him through and Maddie picked up sounding surprised.

"Maddie. I can't talk right now, so just listen. I'm coming to the office tomorrow. Do you think you can work with me on some ideas for the ad agency? I'm just not tracking and I thought you might be able to help."

"Sure, Rob. Let me think about it. What direction are you taking?"

"That's the problem. I'm having trouble narrowing it down. I have to go. See you around ten."

Chapter 20

Not wanting to destroy the mostly good feelings of the last few days, Rob told Allison he had to go to the city for a few hours the next day. He promised to take the 4:23 to be in time for yet another cocktail party.

On the train he asked himself what the hell he was doing. While he may not have been totally in love with his wife, he adored his kids and they had a good life in Darien. Despite the probing discussion with his father-in-law, he felt that Allison's parents had become more accepting of him.

He also admitted to himself that he was becoming too involved with Maddie. The week before he had come dangerously close to saying things he might later regret. He considered it might be time to back off—not necessarily break up, just slow it down. He wasn't about to commit to her or any woman. Besides, he was confident he'd be moving to a new job soon and who knew what lovely creatures might be awaiting him there.

Anyway, he reasoned, Maddie wouldn't be totally alone; she was obviously dating that guy he had met in the office, Danny something. He wondered what their relationship was and without warning felt an unfamiliar twinge. Ignoring it, he lit a cigarette and decided he'd talk with her after they worked on the advertising project. Even better, so as not to be too crass about it, he'd wait until after New Year's. He'd take her to lunch, definitely not to her apartment. He knew from experience that public places were better for that sort of thing.

=

The office was practically deserted when he arrived, most of the assistants taking advantage of the editors' absence to show up late.

Tara was nowhere to be seen but as he expected, Maddie was at her drawing board working on a layout.

He wasn't quite ready to face her. As he entered his office he was surprised to see a pile of magazines stacked neatly in the middle of his desk. He looked up seeing Maddie standing in his doorway.

"Did you bring in all these magazines?"

"Yes. I thought we could go through the ads together and come up with some ideas. Oh, and by the way, hi Rob. It's nice to see you." He picked up on the faint sarcasm in her tone.

"Sorry Maddie. I'm preoccupied with this interview. How was your Christmas?"

"Fine, Rob. How was yours?"

Trying to break the strained formality, he gave her a quick kiss. "It was good. Let's talk about this stuff."

"Have you decided what products you want to focus on?"

She was standing close to him and he felt her warmth. He wanted to touch her, but recalling his thoughts on the train he restrained himself.

"That's one of the problems. I haven't decided."

"Well, since the job you're going for has to do with cosmetics, why don't you start there?"

He shook his head, asking himself why hadn't he thought of that; it was so obvious. *Maybe too much booze over the weekend.*

=

Maddie wanted to ask what was wrong; why was he so cool to her. Had something happened over the holidays? Had he suddenly decided to become a loving, faithful husband? She doubted it. But a thread of unease was scratching and her instincts were beginning to scream trouble.

Putting her fears aside, she pulled over a chair and started leafing through an issue of *Vogue*, tearing out ads she thought might be relevant. Rob picked up *The Saturday Evening Post*, *Look* and *Life*.

"I've been looking at a lot of beauty and cosmetic ads since you called yesterday," she said. "Whether they're photographed or illustrated, they're all basically interchangeable, just a pretty face, a shot of the product and a boring logo."

"I agree. But it's still the basic idea that's eluding me."

She sat back and looked at him. "Think about your *Status* covers. Where did those ideas come from?"

He nodded. "You have a point. Maybe I've been approaching this wrong. It's my concepts for the covers that got me this far."

"I think you're trying to go too broad; you need to narrow it down. Maybe begin with a single product like lipstick or nail polish." She looked past him, obviously in a groove, "Or maybe both. You don't see too many combination ads," she said, sounding surprised at her own thoughts.

She went to get her purse, rummaging around until she found a couple of lipsticks. "Look at these; what can you do with them? If you want more, I'll ask Tara. She just came in. I'm sure she has some in her bag."

Rob shook his head. "Thanks, Maddie. That was just what I needed. Let me think about it. We'll talk in a little while."

"Great," she said, looking at him with a question.

"Let's have a late lunch. You know I can't stay tonight," he said, turning to his drawing board.

=

Aware that she had just been summarily dismissed, Maddie returned to her cubicle. Yesterday she had been excited and flattered when he called asking for her help. She wasn't really surprised; over the last months she had realized that coming up with ideas for illustrating articles was becoming her strong suit. Rob had even begun turning over more stories to her in recent weeks.

After his call she had anticipated a morning with a lively exchange of ideas. She'd spent time trying to come up with a few rough concepts, not to mention going out of her way to bring in all those magazines. In truth, she seemed to have offered more ideas than he had come up with. And yet that suddenly didn't matter; what mattered was that she felt let down and anxious to know why he seemed so distant.

Looking across the sparsely occupied bullpen, she wondered again what would happen if he left. No doubt they'd bring in a new art director; she was sure they'd never consider her. Then what? Would he want his own assistant as had happened at *Today's Bride*? She glanced back, watching Rob through the glass. He was holding one of the lipsticks and sketching on tracing paper.

=

An hour later he called for her. He asked her to flatten out her hand and put the lipsticks on an angle between her fingers. "Maybe this will work," he said, taking a few shots with a Polaroid camera. "Do you think anyone has nail polish here?"

"Maybe. Why?"

"I have an idea for a visual that combines lipsticks and nail polishes. A design that matches or relates the colors. Maybe something about shine."

"Or gloss? That's a big word today."

He jotted it down. "Good idea."

Maddie smiled; he was finally getting into it. "I can go out and buy some for you."

He looked at his watch, "It's okay. I can take it from here. Meet me at Laughlin's in ten minutes? And by the way, thank you."

=

At three o'clock the Wednesday between Christmas and New Year's, Laughlin's was deserted. In contrast to the pre-Christmas gaiety, only a couple of old men were hunched over the bar smoking and nursing drinks. Anemic December light filtered through the dirty windows doing little to dispel the pervasive gloom despite the red and green candles flickering on the tables. Maddie wished Rob had chosen someplace cheerier.

He was already in a booth with a tumbler of scotch in front of him. "Let's order," he said in a terse voice. "I have to catch a train."

She stared at him. "What's going on, Rob? I have the feeling there's something you're not telling me."

"Don't be ridiculous. Everything is fine." He softened his tone. "I told Allison I'd be on a four something train. Otherwise I'd have stayed in the city."

"Really?"

"Of course, Maddie."

After the waiter brought their food he sat back, drained his scotch and ordered another. "Thanks again for this morning. You really seem to get it. Why don't you think about going into advertising?"

He sounded distant, like an interviewer. What happened to the man who only days ago had been so affectionate?

"I like publishing. Maybe someday I'll be tired of it and want to try something new. But not yet. I'm glad I could help." She paused and took a breath. "What is it, Rob? You seem unusually tense."

"I told you I have a lot on my mind."

She stared at him, unconvinced.

"What are you doing for New Year's?"

The change of subject was abrupt, coming out of nowhere. He had asked the one question she never expected, especially with the tension that was hanging between them like a sinister cloud.

"I'm going to a party. I assume you are as well?" she said, trying to steer the conversation back to him.

He ignored the question. "Are you going with *Danny*?" he asked in an unusually sarcastic tone.

"Actually, yes. Can you ask the waiter for another Coke?"

"Let's not change the subject. Tell me about Danny. Do you date a lot? Is he planning on staying the night?"

"I usually go out with him on weekends, Rob. My relationship with him has nothing to do with you and me. Why are you suddenly questioning me?"

He leaned on the table, his voice harsh. "Because, Maddie, I want to know."

She could hardly breathe. What was happening with him? His questions were not only aggressive; they were disturbing.

"So, Maddie, will you be having a sleepover date?"

She faced him, feeling tension tighten her entire body. "Do we really have to discuss this? I don't ask if you sleep with your wife, do I?" Her words startled her; she had blurted it out without thinking.

A flash of irritation crossed his face. "Maddie, it's very simple. Yes, I sleep with my wife. Whether I want to or not, it's expected and that's the way it is."

Refusing to escalate the discussion, she put her hands up in a placating gesture. "Okay Rob. What do you want me to say?"

"That you won't sleep with him."

She stared back at him in shock. *So there it is; the old double standard.* He could, she couldn't. She thought that mindset had gone out with the Eisenhower era—just another hypocrisy left over from her parents' generation. *Obviously not.* Was it possible he was still mired in the fifties?

She reached for his hand and was relieved he didn't pull away. She didn't want to fight, especially knowing she wouldn't be seeing him for almost a week. "All right Rob. I understand."

"So you won't let him stay over." It wasn't a question.

She shook her head. "I only want you to be happy. Whatever you say." It was easier to tell him what he wanted to hear than fight about it.

As they got up to leave, he took her in his arms and kissed her deeply. "This should keep you until next week," he said, gruffly pulling her against him so she felt his erection.

She wished she could stop the small shocks that invariably coursed through her body whenever he touched her. Even though she was angry, his hold on her was visceral and the power of it was beginning to frighten her. Breathless, she kissed him back. "I hope so."

"You hope so? No, Maddie. I need to believe you."

"Yes, Rob."

"I have to go." He slid his knee between her legs. "Keep this warm for me. Only me. I promise I'll call you this weekend." She nodded again, choosing not to mention that until anything changed in Rob's marriage, and she was well aware that might never happen, she'd continue to do what she wanted.

=

Rob walked to Grand Central asking himself why, out of nowhere, he had questioned Maddie about her plans for New Year's. He had purposely never asked her anything about her weekends before; he simply hadn't wanted to know. But since that twinge earlier that morning something was bugging him

What triggered his curiosity was her answer that she was going to a party; something about the way she said it sounded forced. That's when he realized she was sleeping with the guy. It had to be Danny; he had seen phone messages from him on her drawing board. What capped it was her out-of-the-blue comment about having sex with Allison. He had to admit she had balls. *Hell, Allison is my wife. I can fuck her anytime I want.* He knew it was irrational, but he suddenly didn't want any man touching this girl.

He stopped abruptly in the middle of the sidewalk all but deaf to the invectives muttered by pedestrians forced to swerve around him. Regaining his bearings, he glanced around. He had walked ten blocks from Laughlin's and was now on East Forty-First Street standing conveniently in front of O'Casey's, another old Irish bar. He lit a cigarette and glanced inside. *Screw the train. So I'll be late. Allison will just have to live with it.*

Chapter 21

Riding bareback along a deep turquoise sea, thighs gripping a sleek black horse cantering in slow motion. Ahead, dark craggy cliffs pierce a cadmium yellow sky. In the distance a man waits, his face obscured by grey mist. Urging the horse forward.... a harsh ringing intruded.

The surreal dream dissolved as Maddie reached for the phone, cursing whomever would dare to call so late. Fumbling with the receiver, she grunted a not-so-friendly "What?"

"Maddie, I'm on Fifty-Fifth and Third. I want to see you."

Of course, who else? "Rob? What time is it?"

"Twelve thirty."

She lay back on the pillow, eyes closed. "I thought you were going home."

"After the interview the guys asked me to go to PJ's for a quick drink. You know how it goes. It wasn't so quick. See you in about twenty minutes. Go back to sleep."

"I seem to remember you telling me that you weren't going to stay in the city anymore."

"I changed my mind. Let me go. We'll talk when I get there."

=

Maddie yawned and reluctantly got out of her warm bed. Hadn't it been only yesterday, the first day back at the office after New Year's, that he had told her he'd have to go back to Darien every night? No more sleepovers until "things" at home calmed down. Although he had made sure to add that they could still have late nights. It sounded like his home life was deteriorating, or maybe Allison was finally giving him ultimatums. She was surprised it had taken so long.

Yesterday, she had been afraid he would ask again about Danny, but he actually apologized, saying he'd had a lot on his mind before New Year's and he hated to think of her with another man. Before she could thank him he abruptly changed the subject. "If I decide to leave Allison, it will have nothing to do with you. It's my decision, my choice. This has been coming for a long time, long before I met you."

She had stared back at him, afraid to ask where that totally out-of-context remark had come from.

=

Rob had fully intended to go back to Darien after the six o'clock interview at LRG. Since it had been billed as another informal get together with John Langer and Tom, he'd been surprised when Mark Reinhold, another senior partner—and the R in LRG—joined them. Although it turned out to be more of an intense interview than an informal meeting, it had gone well and afterwards they had asked him to join them for drinks at PJ's. If this was the scene after work, most, or even some nights he could get used to it very quickly.

It was after eleven by the time they left with encouraging comments and handshakes all around. Feeling confident, he decided he'd have one more drink; there was still time for a late train.

Returning to the bar, he noticed a few girls clustered at the far end. He felt a rush of anticipation as one of them, a tall redhead, extricated herself and with a quick glance back at her friends, wedged herself in next to him. They began to talk and he bought her a martini. After asking where he worked, she tossed her hair and said she was trying to become a model. Holding back a sardonic smirk, he thought about Jackie—not to mention several other girls he'd gone out with—whose one and only ambition in life was to become the next Jean Shrimpton or Twiggy. Thinking he'd already made far too many calls to Eileen Ford, he put down his drink and said he had to make a phone call. That's when he called Maddie, picturing her in bed and realizing that was where he wanted to be. Returning to the bar, he paid the tab and told the smiling girl he was sorry, he had to leave. Her smile faded to a frown of disappointment. Grabbing a napkin, she wrote down her number and in a seductive voice told him she'd look forward to his call.

As he hailed a cab, he glanced at the napkin and started to put it in his pocket. Instead he dropped it in the street. He had enough problems; tomorrow night, once again, there would be hell to pay at home. By the time he arrived at Maddie's apartment he didn't care.

=

Maddie awoke to the sound of the door opening. She glanced at the clock; it was almost two. *Some twenty minutes.* She was learning that guys tended to operate on a different clock than girls and, all too often, time was merely a relative term. Especially after a cocktail or two.

Rob came in sounding breathless. "Sorry, I know it's later than I told you but the guys kept on talking and drinking."

"It's okay Rob. I just want to go back to sleep."

That thought lasted until she felt his hands sliding over her body and then his kisses. He had brushed his teeth—he now had his own toothbrush—yet she could smell the booze and cigarettes still lingering on his breath. It didn't matter; there was no way, once he began touching her, that she could resist him. She wondered if she had some sort of addiction to him, or, more accurately, to sex with him.

He stopped abruptly and she looked up at him. "What is it Rob?" she whispered.

He ran a finger over her lips and leaned down to kiss her gently. "I should have gone home tonight, Maddie, but I couldn't stop thinking about you. I had to see you."

She put her arms around his neck. "I don't know what to say, Rob."

"I don't think we should say anything. It will only make our lives more difficult."

Difficult or not, she longed to hear his words. "I know," she whispered.

Chapter 22

Saturday morning Rob was in the backyard with Val and Tommy trying to build a snowman out of about three inches of wet snow that had fallen the night before. The kids were giggling and throwing snowballs at him when the back door opened and Allison stomped out, her face contorted with barely concealed anger. She announced it was time for lunch and then a nap. The kids looked up in surprise and began whining that it was too early; they wanted to play with Daddy some more. She was having none of it. With a venomous glance at Rob, she called them back inside.

He hadn't expected her to be friendly after the night he had stayed in the city, but that had been three days ago. He had explained with great sincerity that he couldn't very well refuse to go out with the agency guys, that it had gone later than expected and one of them had generously invited him to stay at his apartment. As always, he was sorry, sorry, sorry that he had neglected to call. She had merely shrugged, shaken her head and turned her back. The silent treatment was, as always, worse than her screaming at him.

Following the kids into the kitchen, he noticed several bags from the market and figured she had likely made a stop at her parents, no doubt to bitch some more about him. After all, despite Daddy's man-to-man talk at Christmas, he had dared to stay one night in the city. *One night?* Was it really that big a deal? In truth, he knew it was.

After fixing the kids lunch, she herded them upstairs. They had been perfectly happy before with him; now they were both cranky. He swore under his breath and looked in the fridge; lunch hadn't included him. He found a couple of chicken legs, grabbed two cans of beer and went down to the basement to work on a small wood sculpture he was carving for Maddie. Earlier he had roughed out a few more concepts for his next interview at the agency but hadn't accomplished much. It was easier working with Maddie; at least they could trade ideas.

He had just begun carving when the peace was shattered by Allison charging down the stairs. Three days of ignoring him were about to end. He was tempted to tell her it was time to lose some weight, but he was already in for enough trouble. Better to keep his mouth shut and wait for the explosion.

Without taking a breath she started screaming. "I want to know what's going on with you. I can't believe you stayed in the city again. You never even bothered to call. I thought you were going to stop this, but you just do what you want and continue to lie to me." She paused, either to catch her breath or expecting him to say something. Receiving no response, she started in again. "I can't take this anymore, Rob. Does your secretary even tell you when I call? Is she one of your girl friends? And how about the other sluts I'm sure you're hanging out with, not to mention fucking? I'm not stupid. I know you're not having that many meetings. We used to have a good marriage. Now I'm not sure we have one at all."

"I assume you went to see Daddy again?"

"What if I did? My father never stays out all night. Not unless he's on a business trip and then he always calls. None of my friends' husbands stay out all night. Only you." She sat down on the wooden stairs and glared dry eyed at him. "So what are you doing, Rob? Tell me. I really want to know."

"You really don't get it do you?" he asked through gritted teeth. "Right now I'm working for a magazine and they're paying me to work there. Sometimes I have to take people out and sometimes those are late nights and I forget to call. Now I'm interviewing for a new job. If they ask me to go out, I go. It's part of the dance. If I get it, I'll be making more money. Lot's more. This is work. There are no other girls." She shook her head. "I don't believe you. You're lying." She got up and started up the stairs.

"No, Allison. I'm doing this for us," he said trying to sound appropriately contrite.

She looked down at him. "My father thinks I should divorce you. My parents never trusted you, but I told them they were wrong, that you really loved me. You only love yourself. You don't even think about the kids."

"I'm taking the kids to my folk's house later."

She started to object and he finally lost it. He got up and walked threateningly toward the stairs. "Don't you say a fucking word. They're going to see their grandmother and grandfather and you have nothing to say about it!"

"Screw you," she yelled and ran upstairs, slamming the door at the top. He hoped she didn't lock it.

He cooled off with a beer and calmed down by working on the sculpture. When he went back upstairs the kids were having milk and cookies in the kitchen. They ran over and hugged his legs. He looked down at them, unaccustomed sorrow softening his anger. Things were going downhill fast, but he wasn't about to give in to Allison or, for that matter, her father. Come what may he would do what he wanted.

He told the kids to get their coats; they were going to Grandma's house. They yelped happily. As he was getting them ready, Allison, her arms crossed, glared. "Don't be too long, Rob. And don't let them eat anything. It'll spoil their dinner."

He returned her look. "I think we'll stay for dinner. Why don't you call Daddy and tell him that?" He had a few other adjectives to add but held his tongue. The kids were watching intently and they'd be learning those words soon enough.

=

Monday morning, he practically bolted out the door with no thought other than getting out of the house. On the train he had time to think. Unless he seriously began coming home every night he knew his life with Allison would only deteriorate further. But he didn't want to; he wanted Maddie. When he thought about her he was happy and every time he thought of Allison he got pissed off.

Chapter 23

Rob had made sure to arrive at LRG on time, give or take a few minutes. The receptionist was pretty but vacuous, no doubt the plaything of one of the senior partners. After she pointed one blood red fingernail at the grey sofa, he continued to stand and talk with her, if only to alleviate a rare attack of nerves.

In his portfolio were several new concept boards for lipstick and nail polish. He had even added one more for a mascara that promised to lengthen eyelashes — something that Maddie had joked about with him. Jokes or not, this interview, the fourth within the last month, was live or die.

Mamie, John Langer's secretary, came in briskly and whisked him to John's office. Looking up from a phone call, John pointed for him to sit. Rob sat down on a sleek Eames chair in the even sleeker white and dove-grey office.

Hanging up, John looked at Rob, his face set in a grin. "So, Rob are you ready for the real interview? Your way into this agency is now through Charlie, and let me warn you he's not exactly a pussy. Either he likes you or he doesn't. If he offers you a drink after he's wrung you out, you're home free. Otherwise, it's been nice knowing you. I'll walk you up to the creative floor, better known as the madhouse. After that you're on your own."

Rob followed him to a curved staircase where, somewhere above, he heard Miles Davis playing "Green Dolphin Street."

They walked through an open bullpen cluttered with drawing boards, work areas and flat files. Layouts with roughed-in copy and loosely drawn sketches were pinned to large, moveable corkboards. It was well after six, but the place was buzzing with artists who appeared to be working frantically with assistants and copywriters.

Rob stopped abruptly as a guy in overalls flew by on roller skates. John laughed. "Don't mind him. That's Bradley, one of our best copywriters. We let him do what he wants as long as he doesn't run anyone over."

Before proceeding, Rob looked around, wondering what other traffic might be going by. Across the floor he saw several brightly lit offices and one slightly darkened, where the jazz seemed to be emanating from. It turned out to be the office of Charlie Gianelli, the senior creative director and the G in LRG.

He was on the phone with his back to them. Hearing John's voice, he swiveled back and quickly terminated the call. He glanced first at John and then at Rob, his look far from friendly. After turning on his desk light, he lowered the stereo and asked them to sit down.

Looking at his seating, Rob smiled. Charlie's chairs were a couple of pairs of airline seats; one with a Pan Am label still attached. Glancing at John, he asked, "Would you prefer the aisle or the window?"

John laughed. "Take them both, Rob. I have to make a call. I'll leave you guys to get acquainted."

Charlie leaned back in his seat; his was larger, obviously first class. He was a big man in his early forties with a shock of black hair that contrasted with cobalt blue eyes. He was wearing a Jefferson Airplane T-shirt and jeans. Rob suddenly felt uptight in his Pierre Cardin suit and rep tie.

"I hear you're the wonder boy from the magazine. You know there's a big, no, huge difference, between publishing and advertising. Two beasts, I would say with very different feeding patterns."

Rob nodded, maintaining his confidence wasn't easy; the guy was obviously out to challenge him.

"Understood, Charlie. But after meeting with John and a couple of the other partners, they felt I should get to know you. After all you're the head creative honcho here."

Charlie lit a cigarette. "Indeed I am. Want one?"

"Thanks," Rob said taking a Marlboro. Charlie tossed him his lighter and Rob lit up.

"So tell me what makes you think you can work here? This isn't about pretty magazine photo shoots. You actually have to think at an ad agency. Come up with concepts, campaigns, ways to sell your product to the consumer — the right consumer. Mrs. Smith might read your nicely illustrated article in *Status*, but when she turns the page it better be your ad, Mr. Art Director, who's going to sell her pantyhose or face cream. We succeed when she not only knows the name and benefits of the product but wants, actually feels the need, to buy it. Do you think you can do that? Whether you like it or not, you have to live this shit — eat, breathe and sleep with it — even when you're fucking some chick other than your wife." He smirked. "Maybe we should put you on the Modess account."

Rob knew he was being played, but he wasn't about to be intimidated. That was usually his position.

"You know Charlie, I've had a fair amount of experience with women and I will tell you they eternally fascinate me. So, man, whatever works. Go for it. I'm hot to do this and I'll work with you on whatever you think I'll fit in to."

Charlie nodded, rubbing the space between his dark bushy eyebrows while exhaling smoke rings. "Let's see your boards. And talk to me about why you chose the product, your goal and how you got to the solution. And by that I mean the actual ad. I want to understand your head, where you're coming from. Are we cool?"

Rob nodded and opened his portfolio. "I think we are."

After glancing at a few boards, his face unreadable, he picked one up, gazing at it for a minute. "Okay. Not bad. How'd you get here?"

Rob mentioned going through magazines, looking at beauty product and cosmetic ads and realizing how similar and boring they were. "I asked myself how could I make the visuals jump off the page."

In the ad Charlie was holding, a girl in a sequined mini dress was twirling in a circle of hot brightly colored spotlights, the colors refracting off her dress. She had just turned so that she was looking directly into the camera, blond hair flying out behind her. Her lips gleamed with hot pink lipstick — Rob had added Vaseline to bring up the gloss — and her hands were raised to show the matching, and flashing, pink of her nails.

"Where'd you get the photo?" Charlie asked, his look deadpan.

"I shot it. One of the photographers I know let me use his studio."

Charlie sat up a bit straighter. "Seriously? You shot this?"

Rob nodded.

"Who's the chick?"

"A friend." *Thank you Jackie.* He'd paid dearly for that photo—an entire night of her, not to mention lying not only to Allison but to Maddie as well. He felt guilty about Maddie, but not enough to avoid using Jackie as his model or for that matter, agreeing to her price.

"Nice friend. Your copy's not bad. Needs work but I see where you're going with it."

Along with Maddie he had come up with the line: "Make Your Nights Shine with Cosette's Hot New Glosses." He also outlined his—or was it Maddie's—idea of making small lipsticks and nail polish that a girl could tuck in her purse—subliminally insinuating overnight dates. "It's the swinging sixties, Charlie. I think the idea of portability could be popular."

Charlie looked back at him with a frown. But then he nodded and Rob knew he had him. "Could be, MacLeod. With some work and research, it just could be."

After that it went smoothly. Charlie liked some of the boards more than others, but Rob had anticipated that. He hadn't expected a home run; all he needed was to get on base.

After talking for few minutes, Charlie pulled a couple of glasses and bottle of Chivas out of a cabinet. "Care to join me?"

=

Leaving the building on Forty-Sixth and Madison, Rob was ecstatic. He had accomplished the impossible; he was now an art director at LRG. He was also pretty confident he'd get the Cosette cosmetics account.

He headed straight for PJ's. Not finding anyone he knew at the bar, he ordered a scotch, double and went to the pay phone to call Maddie. Who better to celebrate with?

He let the phone ring a dozen times before hanging up. On the edge of anger, he looked at his watch. It was almost 8:30 and he was sure she was out with Danny. He blamed himself for not mentioning that tonight was his final interview. Whether it was superstition or not wanting to create expectation, he now realized he should have hedged and told her he'd call later. Curbing his annoyance, he returned to the bar as the redhead from the week before walked in with her gaggle of friends. Without hesitating she made a beeline for him, purring, "I hoped you would have called Rob, but here we are again."

"Martini?" he asked, not remembering her name.

As she chattered on, he considered his options. The one he chose didn't include her. If he took the next train home and announced his news to his ever-loving wife, he might make some valuable points.

After telling the girl, for the second time, that he had to leave she picked up her martini, muttered, "Screw this," and flounced away. He shrugged and went out to find a taxi.

=

The next morning Rob asked Maddie to come into his office. She smiled, her eyes bright. He felt a flash of irrational irritation, not sure if it was at her for not being home the night before, or at himself for not making sure she was there when he wanted her.

After she sat down, he closed the door. She looked up at him expectantly.

"Maddie. I got the job."

"I knew it," she shouted, jumping up and hugging him.

He laughed. "Sure. Why not? If anyone sees us, it doesn't matter anymore," he said putting his arms around her.

"I'm so happy for you Rob. I know you'll be a huge success."

"Have dinner with me tonight. I'll take a late train."

"Yes, of course."

"Now you better sit down."

"Okay. So what is it?" He stared at her, dragging out the moment.

"What?"

"How would you like to be the art director here?"

She sat up, her eyes wide. She had been afraid to even wish for such a thing. There weren't many female art directors in publishing and the few who held that title were, for the most part, at women's magazines.

"Are you serious?"

"Yes, Maddie. I've already spoken to Fred and he's agreed. If I stay on as a consultant, which means coming down here and working with you a couple of evenings a week, he'll give you the job." This time she got up and, putting her arms around him, gave him a long, deep kiss.

It wasn't until she stepped back from Rob's embrace that she noticed a couple of editors standing in the hallway, their mouths open, staring at them.

=

Rob made a reservation at Surabaya, a small restaurant tucked away on East Seventy-Third Street. They had found it one night while walking home from a party. He had wanted to celebrate their new jobs at Twenty-One, but Maddie had demurred, saying she preferred someplace more intimate.

They were given a corner table in the back and he ordered a bottle of Dom Perignon to celebrate. Maddie shook her head.

"It's okay Maddie. I can afford it."

Touching her glass to his, she wished him well. As she put hers down, he took her hand and kissed it. "I owe a lot to you."

"I'm glad I could help, Rob."

"I can't quite get it through my head that I'm an art director at LRG."

She wanted to say the same about herself, that it was a night for both of them to celebrate. But he was already going on excitedly about the agency, the accounts and the people he had met there. She sipped her champagne, smiled and listened.

As they left, he took her hand and began walking uptown toward her apartment. When they arrived at her building she turned to him for a kiss.

"No Maddie. I'm coming up with you. This is a night for us to be together."

"But you'll catch hell, won't you?"

"What else is new?" he laughed.

=

That night, lying warm in his arms she thought she had it all: the beautiful and charming man, the incredible lover, the artist with a splendid future who loved her. That he hadn't quite said it didn't even matter. It was the moment that counted, one that would invariably last until the next afternoon when he'd leave to take the train to Darien. She had no doubt that tomorrow night she'd bury her head in her pillow and ask herself for the hundredth time what she was doing. And yet she wasn't about to ask him to leave his wife. She was afraid of what might happen if he did. Would he, newly liberated from marriage, still desire her or might she become insignificant? It was a disturbing possibility that the status quo might be preferable to a questionable future.

Part 2

You know what charm is: a way of getting the answer yes without having asked any clear question."

Albert Camus, The Fall

Chapter 1

Late January 1967

Maddie followed the editors and assistants to Fred's office. It was the usual Monday meeting, although for her there was nothing usual about it. She felt she was treading on glass, anxiously aware of Rob's absence and yet anticipating her new position. Glancing around, she wondered who was on her side. Jaime, Cynthia and Tara had gone out of their way to wish her well, but she noticed a couple of the older editors in a corner speaking in low tones while casting less than warm glances her way.

Fred stood up. "First of all, even though we had a party last Friday for Rob, who has gone on to bigger and hopefully better places, we really never gave Maddie a proper welcome as our new art director."

There was a brief round of applause. Maddie forced a smile and tried not to fidget. She reminded herself that she hadn't asked for this job; she'd been given it. Nevertheless, she questioned if she was quite ready for it.

When it came time for her part of the meeting she went through her notes, gently letting a few of the editors know they were late with their articles. The travel editor glared at her with belligerence, but Chad, the somewhat younger Nightlife writer, nodded, promising he'd have it later that day. She glanced at Jaime who he said he'd meet with her later about the cover for an upcoming issue which would feature a socialite in a designer dress; although they yet to choose the socialite or the dress. She made a note to call Neil, Rob's favorite photographer. She would have liked to try someone new but this wasn't the time; she needed to establish herself first.

After the meeting, Fred asked her to stay behind. After lighting a cigarette, he said, "That went well, Maddie. You handled yourself very professionally. I know we should have talked last week, but with Rob leaving things got away from me. I want you to know that we all have great faith in you. You're a good designer and with Rob's assistance I'm sure things will continue to run smoothly.

"I know you must have questions, so let me address the ones I believe you're most concerned with. I have to tell you that in recent months the magazine has both gained and lost advertising. Unfortunately, we seem to have lost more than we've gained. I hate to cut pages, but I'm afraid April will be a quite a bit thinner than March, our fashion issue. That said, I've hired a new space salesman who I feel will recapture the ad revenue we require to keep going. I'm giving him Rob's office, although you will, of course have free access to Rob's files and books."

After a morning of cautious optimism, Maddie suddenly felt like she had turned to stone. If it were Rob or another man, would Fred have said "*he* handled himself very professionally?" Wasn't that just a tad patronizing? And would he have given away Rob's office to a salesman? *No way.*

"Also, I hate to tell you this but I can't promise you more than a ten dollar a week raise. Our erstwhile owners insist that you are on trial for a couple of months. If all goes well and our advertising improves, you'll get an increase. Also, since there will be fewer editorial pages, at least for the short term, they feel you should be able to handle it yourself. I'm sure Rob will help out when he comes in during the week."

Maddie stared at him in disbelief. Was she on some sort of probation? And wasn't it insulting to get practically nothing for this promotion? Not to mention she was now expected to turn out an entire issue by herself, something that had previously taken two people to accomplish. Maybe she should speak up and ask for more. Yet she was reluctant, afraid her position might be more tenuous than she had previously thought. She was sure Fred expected her to be grateful for the opportunity and indeed she was. But what began as a special day had quickly turned sour. Gathering up her notes, she stood up. "I fully intend to do my best Fred, and I appreciate your confidence in me. I'm sure you understand that I had hoped for more."

"Be patient, Maddie," he said, already picking up the phone and beginning to dial.

On the way back to her cubicle, which seemed somehow smaller than before, several writers and assistants congratulated her again. She hardly heard them. Fred had said those directives were coming from the owners. Although outwardly admiring of women, she was sure that underneath their thin façades they were just as sexist as all the other men who had the position and opportunity to wield any sort of power.

She wanted to cry, but what good would that do? There was no time to feel sorry for herself. That day alone she had appointments with a couple of illustrators, several articles to read and assign for visuals, models to cast for a shoot and that was before even touching a layout. She looked at her watch wishing for Rob to call.

Chapter 2

Rob accompanied John to a large conference room where a couple of account executives, art directors and copywriters were waiting to introduce him to the agency's accounts. One was Modess (Charlie hadn't been kidding). Another was Trim Tobacco. Trim, a thin filtered cigarette rolled with pastel colored paper, was targeted to young women and just about to hit the market with an extensive campaign. Next was Cosette. Although their hair-care products were well entrenched at Doyle, Dane, and Bernbach, LRG had captured the newly formed cosmetic division the year before, launching a line of nail polishes and lipsticks with an extensive campaign in women's magazines. To the dismay of both LRG and Cosette, however, the products were currently lagging in the market and the word on the street was that Cosette had invited other agencies to pitch for the account. Not about to let it go, John asked Rob to bring in his layouts with the photographs of Jackie.

By the end of the day Rob's head was spinning. But he had gotten the team he wanted — the one working on the new Cosette presentation. He was confident he could save the account.

Due to space constraints he was sharing an office with Larry Woodson, a tall, dark-haired art director about his age currently working on the Trim account as well as Kunchie Krisps, a breakfast cereal. He was settling into his workspace when Larry arrived closely trailed by two secretaries holding large cups of coffee. He, like Charlie, had traded his suits for jeans and T-shirts, this one with a picture of Jim Morrison. A sport jacket was thrown over a hook behind his drawing board.

Larry glanced at the girls and winked. "I guess you've come to meet my good-looking new roommate. Sure beats the last guy who was here."

They came closer, looking like two deer caught in headlights.

"It's okay, he doesn't bite." He looked at Rob. "Or do you?"

"Only sometimes," he replied, as one of the girls, a pretty blonde, put a cup on his desk.

"I'm Nancy and she's Kimmy. If you need anything let me know. I work for Charlie."

"Thank you," Rob said.

Larry put his arm around Kimmy. "I think I need something now. How about it?"

Kimmy poked him with her elbow and he laughed. "You better take me, he's married. But then, maybe not too married. What do you think?" he winked at Rob again. Rob smiled and held his tongue; it was possible that Larry was going to be a pain in the ass.

As the girls left, Larry patted Kimmy's bottom. She giggled and looked back with a grin.

"This is a happy place Rob. Great accounts, great girls. What else could you want?"

Rob laughed. He was liking the agency more every minute.

=

The next time he looked at his watch it was almost seven-thirty. He'd been so engrossed in his work that he'd forgotten to call Maddie. He called her office but no one picked up. He tried her at home, once again getting no answer. He imagined her celebrating her first day as art director with Danny and felt a tight knot of jealousy.

At the station in Darien he called again. Not getting an answer, he hung up and went home.

=

Hoping she would hear from Rob, Maddie held off making plans for that night. Disappointed that he hadn't called by five, she returned a call from Danny.

The receptionist put her through and he picked up on the first ring. "Maddie, I'm glad you got back to me. I made reservations at La Fonda del Sol."

She was in no mood to celebrate, still asking herself if a man would have been handed all those caveats: no office, no real raise, no assistant. She wasn't sure she could explain her frustration to Danny. He would likely utter the predictable male spiel to "just be patient," knowing, in truth, that patience had nothing to do with it. Rob for sure would understand the inequity. But then, Rob hadn't called.

"That sounds nice, Danny but I'm not really dressed for La Fonda. Maybe we should go somewhere else."

"No, Maddie. Meet me there at eight. That will give you plenty of time to go home and make yourself even more beautiful than you already are."

She sighed. How was it that she couldn't manage to fall in love with this terrific man who only wanted the best for her? What was he missing? And what was it about Rob that made her light up at just a glance.

"All right. See you at eight."

"That's my girl. I want to hear about your first great day as an art director."

Oh yes. A great day. She was an art director in name only; nothing else had changed except that she was now on her own. And Rob hadn't even bothered to pick up the phone to call.

=

At the next Monday meeting, Fred asked if she had heard from Rob. Tight lipped, Maddie turned away and shook her head.

By Thursday afternoon, Suzanne, with whom she had spoken, or more likely complained to at least twice a day for the last week, insisted she call him. "Why stand on ceremony?"

"If he wants me he knows where I am. He has to be the one to call. He hasn't even been in touch with Fred."

"Don't be so rigid, Maddie. The fifties are over. These days girls call guys all the time. Stop torturing yourself."

"I can't Suzanne. If it's over, it's over. I already feel it. I don't need to hear it. Fred's tried to reach him but he hasn't even returned his calls. How could I have been so stupid?"

"You're not stupid, you're in love. Maybe this is for the best. Be thankful you have Danny and that he does love you."

At the end of the day, Maddie was in Rob's old office looking for one of the typography books he'd left her. He had been her guide on typefaces and she missed his help. With tears in her eyes she grabbed the book, angry for allowing herself to fall in love with him.

She heard someone walk in. Thinking it was Al, the new ad salesman, she said she'd be out of his way in a minute. Hearing no reply, she looked back seeing Rob standing in the doorway.

All she wanted was to run into his arms, but instead she stepped back. When he didn't say anything, she moved toward the door.

"Where are you going Maddie?" he asked, blocking her exit.

"I'm going home. Can you please get out of my way?"

He shook his head. "Not without a kiss."

"Have you lost your fucking mind?" she said, trying to keep her voice down. "I haven't heard from you in over a week and now you expect me to kiss you?"

"Not only kiss me, Maddie. Make love to me as well. But that can wait until after we talk."

"What could you possibly have to say to me? Or maybe you'd like to look at some layouts. You can tell me if you approve of the typefaces I'm using."

"Actually I spoke to Fred before I came over. He was annoyed I hadn't called before, but he understood that it's taken me some time to get organized at the agency. By the way, he thinks you're doing great. You actually got some editors off their asses."

"He said that?"

He reached for her hand. "Yes, Maddie."

She pulled away.

"Please don't be angry with me. This last week was crazy. I had the agency to deal with plus all the tension at home. And yet I couldn't stop thinking about you. To be honest I did think it might be better to end it. Every time I picked up the phone to call you, I put it down. I didn't know what to say."

Holding back tears, she backed away. "I don't want to hear this."

He suddenly looked tired. "Maddie, listen to me. I didn't come here to break up with you. I came to tell you that I want you in my life."

"I've been in your life since October, Rob. What more do you want of me?"

She saw him hesitate and take a breath. "I also wanted to tell you that I'm in love with you."

Seeing her eyes fill with tears, he took one step and enfolded her in his arms. She clung to him.

He smiled down at her. "I'm telling you I love you and you're crying? Aren't you happy?"

Burying her face in his chest, she nodded.

He kissed her tears. "Come on. Let's get out of here."

=

After settling in at their window table at Allen's, Rob took her hands in his. "I thought about you constantly last week. I tried not to, but I realized I missed you. I can talk to you and you get where I'm coming from. You understand what I'm saying and more importantly what I'm not saying. Hell, I'm not sure I would have gotten the job at the agency without you." He paused. "I'm a better man with you."

Maddie felt herself blush; those were words she never expected to hear.

Rob didn't miss it. "To be honest I never expected to fall in love with you. I thought you'd just be a fling." He looked wistful. "And yet I think I've loved you since that night at your apartment when we fell off the bed. You were laughing and looked so happy."

"I'm not sure that was love, Rob. Maybe more like lust."

"Whatever it was, here were are. But not without big problems. I'm afraid things in Darien have gone from bad to worse. Allison has spoken to a lawyer, no doubt about divorcing me. This is serious."

Maddie hesitated, almost afraid to ask. "What happens now?"

"I don't know. Please be patient with me, Maddie. Just know that I love you and I want us to be together. That is, if you want me."

"I think you know the answer to that."

He signaled for the check. "Let's finish our drinks and go back to your apartment. Unfortunately, I can't stay. I've spoken with a friend who's a lawyer. He told me in no uncertain terms that I shouldn't even be seeing you, much less stay all night."

=

After Rob left, Maddie curled up in bed. He had been gentle, making love so the heat and intensity built slowly between them. There was no rushing, just deep kisses, soft caresses and loving words that made an already sensual moment even deeper.

She was still awake and replaying his words when the phone rang. Hoping he was calling from Grand Central to tell her once again how much he loved her, she picked it up with a breathy "Hello?"

The voice that responded was a woman's. "Is this Maddie?" she growled.

Maddie caught her breath as her heart began to pound.

"Well, is it or not?" she snapped again.

Maddie managed a "Yes," in a much weaker voice than she would have liked.

"Good. Is my husband there? You know, Rob?"

"No."

"Oh come off it. I know he's with you. In fact, I know quite a bit about you."

"What is that supposed to mean?"

Her tone was dismissive. "Just what I said. Figure it out for yourself."

When Maddie didn't respond, she continued. "You might as well talk to me. Just remember, it's me he comes home to."

"Allison. I have nothing to say. I don't want to talk to you." She was about to hang up when Allison shouted, "Don't you dare hang up that phone!"

Maddie held the receiver away from her face. It looked like a snake about to bite, but it gave her a few seconds to become more alert. "What do you want from me?"

"Are you stupid? What do you think I want? I want you to stop seeing Rob. You must realize you're breaking up my family."

Slightly more in control: "I don't think so, Allison. I think this is something between the two of you that's been going on long before I met him. I can't tell him what to do."

"Does he tell you he loves you? He says it to me all the time. I'll bet you didn't know when he's finished with you he comes home and makes passionate love to me."

Maddie steadied herself against the table. "Good bye, Allison. Don't call me again." She hung up trembling and wishing there was some way to warn Rob before he arrived home. But there was no way to reach him and nothing she could do.

=

It was sleeting when Rob got off the train. Still preoccupied with Maddie, he barely felt it. While he loved her and wanted her in his life, leaving Allison and the kids weighed heavily on his mind. After a few drinks it was a decision that seemed simple, but in the cold light of day the reality became overwhelming.

Allison wasn't making it easy. She had become even more distant since he had started working at the agency. It was as if she had no interest other than bitching at him about coming home late every night. One evening after calling three times, Larry joked that she obviously couldn't wait to have him home. He didn't bother to explain that it was more out of suspicion than desire.

As he drove into the garage he realized the house was dark. Angry though Allison may have been, she always left a couple of lights on. Perhaps she hadn't felt well and had gone upstairs without thinking about it. He didn't mind; it would give him some time to wind down. He took a beer out of the fridge, picked up the newspaper and headed for the den. On the train he had started reading an article about the generation now becoming labeled as "Baby Boomers," and he wanted to finish it before going to bed.

He switched on the light and stopped cold. On the couch was a pile of neatly folded sheets topped by a blanket and a pillow. On the pillow there was a note and a couple of grainy black and white photos. He dropped the newspaper and picked up the photos. Both were of him and Maddie. In one they were holding hands and laughing, in the other they were kissing. Taking a breath, he picked up the note: "Get rid of your whore or get a lawyer."

He took a sip of beer and read it again. It said the same thing the second time. He grabbed a bottle of scotch and poured a generous shot. After downing it, he did it again. He sat down on the couch, his head in his hands. He had to think.

Chapter 3

Maddie had hardly slept. If Allison knew about her she must have had Rob followed. The feeling of being spied on was in itself a violation. She couldn't stop picturing mysterious men with hidden cameras following Rob and her around Manhattan. At the same time, she felt a strange empathy for Allison; she had been driven to find answers to a question that no woman would ever choose to acknowledge.

=

Rob didn't arrive at the agency until almost eleven. He had called, saying there was an emergency at home. Indeed, there was—Allison had it all planned; the night before she had even parked the kids at her mother's house. In the morning, when he went upstairs to get his clothes, she had told him almost gleefully that she had dozens of photographs of him and Maddie at various places around the city, including entering and leaving her apartment building. What had resulted was a screaming, name calling and invective filled fight. He had slammed out of the house.

By the time he got to LRG he still hadn't calmed down. Larry looked at him from across the office. "You look like shit, Rob. What happened?"

"Not now Larry."

Larry sniffed. "Women, no doubt." Rob looked back at him, his eyes glaring and Larry shut up.

It wasn't until after five that he had time to call Maddie. By then there were two messages from her on his drawing board.

As soon as she picked up, he asked, "Did she really call you last night?"

"Yes," she whispered, as if anyone nearby could have heard his question.

He lit a cigarette. "Crazy fucking bitch. She told me she did but I wasn't sure I believed her. I'm sorry I've gotten you in the middle of this. I slept on the couch last night and it looks like I'll be there for a while." He stopped and took a drink; he wasn't alone, all the guys had tumblers of scotch or bourbon sitting on their desks or drawing boards well before five. "She's given me an ultimatum—you or her."

Maddie reached for a cigarette. She didn't smoke much—only in social situations. This definitely didn't qualify as a social situation.

Rob broke the silence. "I'm not giving you up."

In that second she knew he had made a decision. And yet it wasn't all that simple. "Rob please think about this. I'd hate to lose you but I don't want to be the reason you're breaking up your marriage."

"I told you before Maddie, this began long before I met you. Everything that's happened since has made it worse and I take responsibility for that. You have to understand that it's not your fault and I don't want you to feel guilty about it. I have to go to Connecticut tonight but I told Fred I'll come down to your office Monday. We'll talk more then."

=

To add to the tension, that night her mother called. They usually spoke once or twice a week; her mother generally asking questions which, unless they were about work, Maddie refrained from answering. She mentioned that she, Harry and her grandmother were invited to a birthday party at the Waldorf the following Thursday and, planning on staying overnight, they had taken a suite. Maddie waited, already knowing what was coming.

"Why don't you stop by for a drink," her mother said in a saccharine sweet voice. "And bring your new art director friend. About six. The party is at seven."

Once, just once, when her mother had asked about Danny, rather than telling her everything was fine, Maddie had mentioned that she was going out with an art director. She knew she had made a mistake but it was too late to take it back.

"Sure Mom. I'll ask him, but we're both pretty busy.

"We?" she asked, sounding surprised.

"Um, yes. He's my boss. Well, not anymore. He's working at an ad agency now." She knew she sounded flustered but didn't seem to be able to stop herself. "And you should also know he's in the middle of a divorce." *Not quite the middle, but hell, might as well get it all out in one shot.* She held her breath.

"Oh." That was it, just "Oh." Maddie could hear her mother's wheels turning. "And how old is he? Does he live in the city?"

She groaned. "Mom, he's twenty-nine and he lives in Darien."

"Darien?" she said, rolling it around on her tongue. "I take it he's not Jewish?" She paused. "Well, I'll look forward to meeting him anyway. We'll expect you at six." Her curiosity had overruled her obvious annoyance that Maddie was dating her married boss, or ex-boss who, by the way, wasn't Jewish. She was surprised she hadn't asked if he was circumcised.

=

The following Monday night, after a couple of rushed hours at Maddie's apartment, Rob told her he had an appointment to meet with a divorce lawyer after work on Friday. He said that Allison was basically not speaking to him and she had explained to the kids that Mommy wasn't feeling well and that's why Daddy was sleeping downstairs.

As he was leaving she mentioned that she had to meet her mother and stepfather for a drink at the Waldorf Thursday evening.

"Great. I'll go with you."

"What about what your lawyer said?"

"Screw that. I've been going home every night. Unless she has more guys following me with cameras that should satisfy her."

"You don't think it's a bit soon? I can tell them you're too busy to leave the office."

"I'd like to come with you. I'll have to meet them eventually, so why not now?"

"Rob, I can think of several reasons for why not now. I think we both know they won't approve of me dating, and that's the word, *dating* as opposed to *sleeping with*," she pointed at him for emphasis, "a married man."

He pulled her close. "I love you and you love me. I will get divorced. That is if I manage to live through this separation agreement. It'll be fine. I'll just use my natural charm."

She shook her head, doubting any amount of "charm" on his part was going to make any difference. What mattered was only that she was dating a married man. A separation agreement, as they were all aware, was not a divorce.

=

Harry opened the door to an expansive, lavishly decorated suite. Maddie gave him a kiss on the cheek and glanced around, aware that the living room alone was larger than her entire apartment. Rob stepped forward, looked him in the eye and shook his hand, saying, "Mr. Colton, I'm Robert MacLeod. I'm very pleased to meet you."

Her mother, golden haired and resplendent in an emerald green chiffon gown emerged regally from the bedroom. Rob, like a big puppy, practically bounded over to her, shook her hand and introduced himself. Maddie could see that on first impression she was impressed.

"Your eyes match my dress," she said with a small smile. Maddie was glad to see that smile; it was likely to be the last one of the evening.

Her mother asked for Dewars on the rocks and glanced at Rob, who said he'd have the same. She turned a cool gaze on Maddie. "Just don't stand there, Maddie, have a drink."

Maddie had never liked scotch and anticipating what was coming, she needed to be alert. She said she'd have a Tab.

At that moment her grandmother waltzed in from the other bedroom; five feet of tightly corseted righteous indignation sausaged into a black beaded dress. Her blue rinsed hair was coiffed to perfection in short, tightly wound curls.

As they all sat down on plush velvet couches, Maddie noticed her mother had stopped smiling.

Here it comes.

"So, Rob," she said pleasantly, "Tell us about yourself. I understand you're an art director? You and Maddie met at *Status*?"

"Yes," he answered easily. "I left a few weeks ago. I've just started working at LRG."

She nodded, taking slightly more than a sip of her scotch. "And you, Maddie? Will you remain at *Status*?

"Yes, Mom. I already told you they gave me the job as art director."

Her stepfather nodded. "I assume that means you'll be getting a raise?"

"I hope so. It hasn't been discussed yet." She hoped she sounded convincing.

Her grandmother, taking birdlike sips of sherry and regarding Rob with reptilian eyes, suddenly sprang into action. She leaned forward and said, "I understand, Rob, that you're a married man."

Maddie stopped breathing. Rob nodded. "Yes, Nana. I know that's what Maddie calls you and I hope you'll allow me to do the same?"

Maddie was surprised to see a small smile crease her stern demeanor.

"At the moment I am still married. I'm in the middle of a difficult separation and within the next month I expect to be living in the city. I've already started looking at apartments."

Maddie glanced at him, hoping surprise didn't show on her face. As far as she knew, the only apartment he had looked at was hers. She lit a cigarette.

"But don't you have children?" she asked.

"Yes, and it makes me very unhappy to have to leave them. But I'll have full visitation rights and see them frequently. I wish this wasn't happening, and please understand that this began quite a while before I met Maddie. She's had no part in my decision. It would have happened even if we hadn't met and it's entirely my problem to deal with. It was just that after working together for a few months we began to realize there was something special between us." He paused and smiled. "I guess we never know what the future will bring."

Maddie wanted to applaud.

Her mother cast a meaningful glance at her stepfather. "We understand," she said, picking up a cigarette out of a silver box on the coffee table. Rob jumped up to light it for her. She blew out smoke and looked up at him. "Thank you," she said politely. "I agree with you Rob. No one knows what the future holds. But yours, no matter what, will be complicated, not to mention costly. I worry about Maddie, that she's not being drawn into an untenable situation. What, for example, happens if by some chance this separation doesn't go through? Not to mention the divorce?"

He leaned forward, his hands clasped, almost, but not quite as if in prayer. "I understand your concern, Mrs. Colton. But I can only tell you it will. Maddie has become very important to me. I wouldn't have come to meet you if she weren't. I'm aware this is a difficult situation. But I will get through it."

Both her mother and Harry looked doubtful, but nodded. Maddie glanced at the door, desperate to escape.

Harry looked at his watch. "We should go downstairs. We can't be late, it's a surprise party."

After shaking her parents' hands, Rob took her grandmother's hand and actually kissed it. Maddie rolled her eyes and, on the way out the door, gave each of them a peck on the cheek. Her mother, Harry and grandmother got off at the floor with the ballrooms and Maddie and Rob continued to the lobby.

"I think that went well, all things considered," Rob said sounding confident. Maddie couldn't even speak. He didn't yet know her overly critical and sharp-tongued family.

She grabbed his arm. "I need a drink."

He laughed. "I don't think I've ever heard you say that before."

=

When her phone rang the next morning at work, Maddie already knew who it was. Her mother barely said hello. "Maddie, you have to get out of this relationship. He's a very charming young man. Very slick, I'd say."

"I don't think I'd describe him as slick, Mom."

"It doesn't matter and don't interrupt. This is not a relationship for you. I don't trust him. I know you never listen to me but I'm not sure he'll ever get divorced. And yes, I've heard your nonsense about not wanting to getting married. It doesn't matter. You simply must not go out with someone else's husband. Do me a favor and think hard about that."

"Okay, Mom, I will. How was the party? Was Mr. Ender surprised?"

"Very," she replied crisply, aware that Maddie was changing the subject.

"What are you doing today?"

"I think I'll stop at Saks and Bergdorfs and do some shopping. Do you want to meet me at the Palm Court at the Plaza for lunch?"

Ob yes. Right after I cut off my right leg with a dull mat knife. "Can't Mom, we're on a deadline. Next time you're in the city though."

A few minutes later the phone rang again. *Please, not my mother again.* She answered with trepidation. "So, how did it go last night?" Thankfully, it was Suzanne.

"I guess as well as could be expected. Except my mother says she doesn't trust him and he's slick."

Suzanne laughed. "She's not far from wrong."

"Come on. He loves me and I love him."

"Yes I know, but there's still something..."

"It's okay, Suzanne."

Chapter 4

The executive floor was humming. Secretaries moved briskly, carrying carafes of coffee and platters of bagels and Danish pastries, making sure the conference room looked perfect. They had all been given free manicures the day before with the new prototype nail polish and had been told to keep "flashing those nails." Their glossy lipstick matched and they had been instructed to wear their trendiest and shortest mini dresses.

Rob was standing at his drawing board staring blindly out the window while trying to calm his racing pulse. After several intense weeks of work, the Cosette presentation was finally about to happen. Whether it was nervousness or anticipation, he needed a drink to steady himself. He couldn't get to the cabinet in the conference room, but there were a couple of bottles in the office of one of the writers on a liquor account. They had, from time to time, sampled them in the evenings. The writer wasn't there but Rob went in anyway, picked up a paper cup and poured a shot of a new imported vodka. He would have preferred scotch, but vodka had no smell. He tossed back a couple and threw the cup away, already feeling the warmth pacify his nerves. Returning to his office he chewed a breath mint, just in case. Picking up some hastily written notes that he and Maddie had put together the night before, he went downstairs to the executive floor. His performance was about to begin.

The conference room was set up with his boards on the far end of the large rosewood table. It might be the agency's presentation, but this campaign was his baby. Hearing a commotion behind him, he turned as John came in with the president of Cosette's cosmetics division. Following them, a couple of LRG's senior partners were chatting like old buddies with three marketing people from Cosette.

Bringing up the rear were the LRG account executives. They were the ones who would be interfacing with the marketing group, that is if they kept the account.

John introduced Rob and everyone shook hands. Coffee was offered by a pretty secretary. One of the marketing people, a stunning brunette and the only woman in the group, asked if she was wearing the new nail polish. She nodded and smiled brightly, perfect pink lips shimmering over bright white teeth. Rob thought they might want to consider pitching the Gleam account.

John took the lead, saying that what they were about to present was a new and far more daring advertising campaign for cosmetic products than had ever been envisioned, much less undertaken.

He nodded at Rob. "We think our concepts are so strong that I'm going to leave it to my art director, Rob MacLeod, to introduce them to you."

Rob stood, wishing he could wipe off his sweaty palms. It was rare for an art director to take on a presentation, especially his first time out. But confident of success, he had assured John that it was he, and he alone, who could present the campaign best. Now facing the client, he began to feel that confidence wavering.

Steadying himself, he turned his focus to the boards stacked on the table. Picking them up one by one, he placed each on a separate easel and began describing what they represented. All faces, determinedly unsmiling, were turned in his direction. Aware the room had become deathly quiet he concentrated on explaining his concepts and his direction for the brand. After all the boards were in place, he heard a collective gasp from the Cosette contingent. He froze and glanced at John who appeared to be holding his breath.

He had reached the point where no further explanation was necessary; the images would either speak for themselves or not. It had taken him days of working with models and a photographer on the city streets and in Central Park to get the essential mood, action and colors he envisioned. He had poured every bit of his creativity into it, working late into the nights to make the presentation perfect. Now it was basically live or die. Taking a breath, he looked back at his work; the semi-circle of layouts glowed with beautiful, laughing models dancing, running, even riding a scooter. They weren't static, no longer just a head with a logo and pictures of the product. The ads projected glamour combined with activity and movement. At the bottom he had added small swatches of colors along with a re-worked cursive logo.

With no change of expression, the president nodded at Rob. "The boards are strong, Rob, but what happens when they go into a magazine like *Vogue* or *Harper's Bazaar*? The paper the magazines use won't give you those colors."

Rob had anticipated the question. "Then this is what we'll do," he said, picking up a copy of *Vogue* and letting it fall open to an insert of heavy gloss paper. Everyone leaned in. Even on the smaller scale the images jumped off the page. "I'm proposing that we print our own inserts for the magazines. If we use a heavy gloss stock we'll not only be able to control the color but the magazine will fall open, as it just did, to these spreads. I've also found a printer who may be able to provide a glittering ink that will be ours alone. We're calling them 'Metallics.'"

He watched as the president sat back in his chair and surveyed his marketing group. They stared back at him without expression. No one said a word.

After what seemed like torturous minutes, but was more likely just seconds, the president pounded his fist on the table. "Genius," he said. "You guys did it."

He got up and shook Rob's still clammy hand. "MacLeod, this campaign will put us on the map. But now you've actually given us work to do. We'll have to review not only our budget but our media buy as well. We might want to consider expanding both. Congratulations."

Rob heard a collective sigh as the Cosette people all started talking at once. After more discussion, the meeting broke up with vigorous handshakes all around. The brunette, Rachel something, Rob didn't catch her last name, handed him her card and said she'd look forward to discussing the campaign further with him. He barely acknowledged her, too stunned by the moment for his usual quick response.

He returned to his office amidst shouted out congratulations and handshakes. He called Maddie. "I can't talk now. Meet me at Twenty-One tonight at nine."

"You got the account?"

"More like I saved the account. Prepare to celebrate. I love you." Before she could tell him the same, he hung up.

=

It was actually closer to nine thirty when he arrived. Maddie had chosen to wait in the vestibule, glancing frequently at her watch. As she stood, he wrapped his arms around her and kissed her deeply. She could feel waves of excitement radiating from him; she had never seen him so happy. On the way to their table, a couple of well-dressed men in dark suits stood up and congratulated him. He thanked them and shook their hands. When they were seated she asked who they were. Rob laughed and shook his head. "I don't know. Apparently word has gotten around."

There had been no mention of going back to Darien. After dinner, with too much wine and champagne, they returned to the apartment where she surprised Rob with yet another bottle of Dom. She poured two glasses, congratulating him again.

=

It was in bed that he surprised her by becoming unusually aggressive, no doubt a combination of newly gained confidence and power mingling with excessive amounts of champagne. His kisses were deep and passionate, and breathless with desire she tried to pull him on top. He resisted, whispering, "No, Maddie. You have to wait. We're doing this my way."

He reached for the bottle of Dom and began pouring it slowly over her body. She arched back from the cold and cried out, trying to push him away. Holding her down he sensuously licked the champagne from her breasts down to her parted thighs while teasing with his fingers until she begged him to take her. Moving over her he watched her face as he thrust into her. When she moaned with desire, he pulled back, "I told you, not yet. You can only come when I tell you." It was only after more caresses, when the heat between them became palpable and they could sustain the intensity no longer that he pulled her on top, her screams mixing with his groans as they came together in a shattering orgasm. Breathless and sweating, she collapsed on his chest.

"Maddie," he breathed softly, holding her close. "There's no one like you. No one like us." He reached for the glasses with the last of the champagne and handed her one. Touching his glass to hers, he said, "Tell me you love me." Although sore and thinking she might have a few love bites the next day, she whispered, "You know I do." He kissed her and whispered that she belonged to him and him alone.

The next morning, he woke up alert and randy, making love to her quickly before rushing off to receive more accolades at his office.

Chapter 5

Maddie wasn't having a good morning. Coffee had helped clear her hangover, but she'd had to wear a turtleneck sweater to hide the marks on her neck.

Rob had surprised her with his intense passion, if that's what it could be called. Success and confidence obviously acted as an aphrodisiac for him. At the same time, she was almost ashamed to admit how aroused she had been.

Jaime intruded on her thoughts, announcing that Fred wanted to see them in his office. She picked up her coffee, already knowing there would be a confrontation.

Fred got right to the point. "Maddie, I know you don't like this dress, but it's going to be the cover of the June issue whether you or I like it or not."

Jaime held it up but she ignored him, she didn't need to see it again. It was an unusual dark coral with an empire waist and small flap pockets on the hips. What designer, she wondered, would ever put pockets with flaps on hips and why? Weren't most women wide enough? It was also too long, hitting at the knees when everyone, including Park Avenue matrons, were wearing miniskirts, fat legs or not.

"Give me something to work with Fred. If I put this on a model, she'll look ridiculous, even if I have it shortened. And where do you shoot something like this? It's a dress only a middle-aged, conservative woman would wear to lunch and we just shot a socialite for the April issue. I don't think you want to overdose on socialites."

"No, Maddie. But that wasn't a fashion story. This is."

She stopped, suddenly in thought. "La Grenouille or Quo Vadis. That's where they go. Tavern on the Green. Maybe we can shoot there."

"See?" Fred said, "You came up with a solution."

"Not quite. La Grenouille would be perfect for this dress, but I doubt they'll let us photograph there. I'll make a couple of calls. I have another idea. Do you think you can find an actress? Someone other than a skinny model who can carry off this boring dress."

Fred frowned. "We've never used actresses. Only the big news magazines put celebrities on their covers. Remember Liz Taylor and Richard Burton on the cover of *Life* magazine in 1963? They were filming Cleopatra. It turned out to be the perfect confluence of bad movie and delicious scandal. I wish we could grab something like that. But I digress. Didn't we originally discuss using a socialite?"

Maddie shook her head. "Please, Fred. Not again. Anyway, this dress is horrible. Any society lady will either expect an interview or a butterfly cover like the one Rob won an award for."

He grimaced. "You may be right. I'll call someone I know at William Morris. See what I can do."

"Fred, why are we using this dress?"

He looked sheepish. "The designer signed a contract for three pages in the next three issues."

"In other words, they're buying editorial."

"Think of it as supporting our advertisers, Maddie."

Shaking her head, she went to Rob's old office. Al, the new salesman, was out attempting to sell pages. She wondered if there was any way he could manage to sell them without promising editorial in exchange. Sitting down at his desk, now covered with rate cards and scrawled notes instead of Rob's layouts and sketches, she dialed the operator, asking for the numbers of Tavern on the Green and La Grenouille.

An hour later, after having been politely admonished by the manager at La Grenouille that they didn't allow anything so crass as photography on their premises, she received permission to use Tavern provided that she would agree to a hefty location fee and guarantee the shoot would be finished by ten a.m. That meant they'd have to start by six at the latest. She was on the phone explaining the situation to Neil when she heard the phone ring at her drawing board. She ignored it. A few minutes later Tara came in saying there had been several calls for her.

"I can't take them now, Tara. I have to get this shoot organized. Why can't Eleanor screen my calls or take messages rather than letting my phone ring? She always told Rob who was calling."

"She only screens call for the guys. You may be the art director, but you're a girl. I'll ask her to ring you in here."

"Don't tell me we have a reverse-sexist receptionist."

Tara laughed. "In all this time you haven't noticed that she never acknowledges anyone but Rob, Jules, Fred and a few of the editors? No one can stand her. By the way, she mentioned that Danny called twice."

"Thanks, Tara. I'll call him back in a few minutes." Where was Rob when she really needed him? Becoming the big star of his agency, no doubt. But there was no time to think about him or, for that matter, Danny. She was on her own and there were still calls to make. As she picked up the phone, Fred poked his head in and said he might have a stage actress who would do the shoot. She thanked him, optimistic that a real actress might take attention off the dress.

The phone next to her rang. She picked it up hoping it was Rob, or second best, some, or any, good news about this freaking shoot.

"Hello, Maddie," Danny said, sounding unusually serious.

"Hi, Danny. Sorry I haven't gotten back to you. There's a small disaster here that I'm trying to fix."

"I hear you were at Twenty-One last night with MacLeod."

A stab of panic gripped her stomach in a vise. "Yes, Danny. He had a successful day at LRG and asked me to celebrate with him."

"That's not exactly what I heard, although the news about LRG keeping the Cosette account is all over the industry this morning. MacLeod made quite a splash, apparently with you as well. From what I was told, he was all over you and you were kissing him back. Maddie, have you been dating him?"

Dating him? She wasn't sure if she should laugh or cry.

"Look Danny. I worked with him for four months." She wondered if he thought that answer was as lame as it sounded.

"We need to talk Maddie. You know how I feel about you. Now I'm beginning to understand why you've been putting me off."

"I'm sorry. I didn't think I was."

He was abrupt. "Just so you know, we also got a new account yesterday. Dr. Pepper. Thanks to that I had to work late last night, but I did call you at home to tell you about it. Now I know why you weren't there."

She sighed. "Danny..."

He cut her off. "I'll call you."

She put the phone down slowly, her mind suddenly blank. It rang again, startling her back to reality. Picking it up, she wondered just what that reality would now hold for her.

Chapter 6

Every man has a breaking point. Rob's had been reached by around eight that Saturday night. Allison had been sniping all day about how bad he was, not to mention a failure as a father, that he cared about no one but himself and that he slept with whores. Despite his triumph at the agency she was intent on making him feel not only irrelevant but that his accomplishments were insignificant. He had tried to hold it in and not respond, but it was becoming harder as the day went on.

Returning home each night had become more difficult than the previous one. Before Allison had surprised him with the photographs, he had tried whenever possible to arrive home in time for dinner or at least to see the kids before their bedtime. Since she had found out about Maddie, she wasn't even leaving crumbs out for him. Each time he asked if they could talk, she shut him out. If she was trying to shame him into some sort of guilt, it wasn't working.

Instead he had gotten into the routine of meeting Maddie a couple of times a week for quick dinners. They'd discuss their work, friends, movies—anything to avoid talking about what was happening at home. Then he'd look at his watch and they'd rush to her apartment to make love before he caught a late train.

=

It was the last Saturday in February and Allison had become obsessive. After yelling at him all morning, she began making denigrating comments in front of the kids. He asked her quietly to stop; her anger was only making the kids cranky and argumentative. When she didn't, in an effort not to retaliate, he left the house and drove to Ernie's for a hamburger and a couple of beers. Frustrated, he went to a pay phone and called his lawyer at home, telling him he wasn't sure he could take any more, that Allison's overt anger and the tension at home was impacting his work not to mention the rest of his existence. The lawyer advised him hang in and do his best to ignore her; a meeting was coming up shortly and hopefully he could move out soon.

When he returned home, the kids, aware of the tension between them and Allison's unconcealed rage, were restless and irritable. Later, after kissing them goodnight, he hugged them tighter than usual.

Making sure Allison was downstairs, he went quietly from Tommy's room to the attic and brought down a couple of suitcases. He threw some clothes into them and grabbed a few suits on hangers. After taking everything downstairs, he went to get his skis. *Why?* He didn't know. Skiing made him happy and maybe he needed to feel that.

He was loading everything in his old station wagon when Allison came storming out. "What the hell do you think you're doing?" she screamed. He told her to shut up; the neighbors would think she was being murdered. *An attractive thought.*

Looking back at her, he felt a strange calmness overtake him; he was suddenly beyond arguing. "I'm leaving, Allison. I can't do this anymore."

She ran to him and slapped his face. "No. You're not! You can't leave me."

His calm evaporated into a flash of rage. He stepped back from her; otherwise he might have hit her back. He had never raised a hand to her although there were times he had been sorely tempted. He wasn't about to make a bad situation even worse.

"I'll call you," he said, barely able to control his fury. She was still standing, fists clenched, in the driveway as he drove away. He was sure her next move was to call Daddy, but he didn't give a shit anymore. He stopped at Ernie's for a beer. He suddenly felt empty, wrung out. In the act of getting away from Allison's venomous accusations he hadn't thought even one minute ahead; his anger having overtaken any coherent plan. He thought about Ken, or Pete, a neighbor, knowing he could camp out with either of them for a few days or at least until the surfeit of emotion had quieted down.

After a few beers, followed by a couple of scotches his emotions shifted from anger to despair to a growing feeling of exhilaration and freedom. A few drinks could do that.

Without thinking much more about it, he got in the car and drove to New York.

=

Maddie was about to get into bed when the doorbell rang. "You're kidding," she muttered to herself, convinced it was her horny neighbor who invited girls he met at singles bars to come home and try out his waterbed. All too often he came creeping over to her apartment at midnight to ask if she had any extra scotch. Did anyone ever have extra scotch?

Throwing on a robe, she opened the door about to tell him to go screw himself. Before she could say a word, she stopped in wide-eyed shock. Instead of her sleazy neighbor, it was Rob. In one hand he was holding skis and in the other a martini.

"Say something Maddie. Anything will do. 'Hi Rob,' is a good start."

"What happened? Why are you here? Why didn't you call me? And what's with the martini?"

He rested his skis against the wall. "Let's take it one question at a time. Did you know there's a small bar, almost hidden, across the street? It's run by three lesbians. I figured if I was going to show up at my girlfriend's apartment at midnight, I needed a little something to fortify myself with. They suggested a martini."

She had noticed the bar; it was a few steps below street level and was simply called "Three." So now she knew about the martini. *Great, but unimportant.*

"Okay, Rob. Come in and tell me what's going on."

He finished what was left of the martini and put it down on the small table where she threw her keys. "Only if you kiss me first."

She put her arms around him and kissed him deeply, the unspoken implication of his presence beginning to sink in. He nodded as if satisfied and looked down at her, his face serious. "The reason I didn't call was because I wasn't sure what to say. But now I know. I've just left Allison."

Chapter 7

Rob woke to the sound of splashing water. He felt displaced, unsure of his surroundings. Becoming more awake, he realized he was in Maddie's bedroom and wondered briefly how he had gotten there. Maddie came out of the bathroom wrapped in a towel.

"Shit. Did I really leave Allison last night?"

"It appears you did. I believe those are your suitcases are in the living room, not to mention your skis."

He shook his head trying to clear the unaccustomed cobwebs. He hadn't had that much to drink, so what was it? *Anger, emotion?*

"Rob, are you all right?"

"Yes, sure. Maybe. I have to let this sink in."

"We should talk."

He touched her hand as if for reassurance, not knowing if it was for her or himself. "We will, Maddie. Later." He lay back on the pillows. There had been a few times in his life when he had been unsure about what to do, but this had to be the granddaddy of them all. What had seemed clear the night before had turned to uncertainty in the all-too-harsh light of day. He considered calling Allison, but he had no desire to listen to her bitch at him. He decided he'd cool it for a few days, although he worried about the kids and what she would say or not say to them.

He glanced at Maddie who was watching him with questions in her eyes. He wasn't even sure he could speak much less answer anything she might ask.

Maddie broke the strained silence. "It's after eleven. Why don't we go out for breakfast?"

He nodded. "I could use a Bloody Mary or two for that matter."

She smiled. "Me too."

=

Hoping the cold air would help clear his head, Maddie suggested they walk to Yellowfingers, a popular spot for Sunday brunch
across from Bloomingdale's.

As they followed the hostess to their table, Rob saw some people
he knew from his days at *Cavalier* and stopped to say hello. After
introducing Maddie, he chatted with them for a couple of minutes,
mostly answering questions about the agency. Maddie could see he
was savoring the attention and she was relieved that it seemed to be
lifting the pall from the morning.

After a couple of Bloody Marys, he finally spoke. "So here we
are Maddie. What does one do on Sunday in New York?"

She gave him a coy smile. "I usually pick up a New York Times,
maybe a couple of bagels from the deli and go back to the apartment.
Sometimes in the afternoon I go for a walk or to a museum."

He glanced around, clearly preoccupied with his own thoughts.
She waited, not wanting to push him. "You decide Rob. Anything
you want, just tell me."

Stroking her fingers, he nodded absently. "I don't feel like going
anywhere. The *Times* sounds good. Can we read it in bed?"

She leaned over to kiss him. "Where else?"

For the first time since the night before she saw a small grin. "Maybe that's why I love you, Maddie," he said softly. "We think alike."

On the way home they bought the newspaper and spent the rest
of the day alternating between making love and reading, laughing as
they traded sections. Although she had tried asking a couple of sub-
tle questions, he refused to discuss Allison and what had prompted
his decision. What worried her was that he had made a snap decision and guilt-ridden, he would decide to return home.

At *Today's Bride* she had worked with Anne, an editorial assistant who had been dating a married man. After a couple of years
and repeated promises that he would leave his wife, she had given
him a final ultimatum: her or the wife. When he chose to stay home,
she refused to answer his increasingly frantic calls. One day, un-
announced, he had shown up at her door with a several pieces of
luggage, declaring defiantly that he had left his wife. Anne had been
ecstatic until the evening she returned home to find him throwing

his belongings back into the same luggage and sniveling that he "just couldn't do this." Six months later, after his wife had thrown him out, he returned to find that Anne, in reaction, had quickly married someone else. (And would just as quickly get divorced.) He ultimately reconciled with his wife who from that point on tracked his every move.

Maddie shivered, suddenly thinking about Danny. He still hadn't called her back after their terse discussion last week. When he did, she wondered if she'd have to explain a bit more than just kissing Rob at Twenty-One.

=

By Monday morning Rob was a bit more relaxed. He left first and with a quick kiss, said, "See you later." She smiled, thinking that sounded pretty good.

Her good thoughts lasted until she arrived at the office. Eleanor wasn't at the reception desk and when Maddie entered the bullpen she saw three assistants packing up their belongings.

Tara came over. "Jules just fired them, Eleanor and one of the ad salesmen. He asked them to leave today. Now, in fact."

"It's Monday. Who gets fired on a Monday? Do you know what happened?"

"No. All Fred told me was that I'd have to sit at the reception desk and manage the switchboard. He said he'd have one of the other girls back me up. Besides you and Cynthia, there aren't many girls left."

"I'm not sitting at the reception desk. That's crazy."

"Not so crazy if the magazine is losing money."

Maddie nodded. Tara was right; there were fewer ad pages every month.

She went to call Rob but was told he was in a meeting. She left a message for him to call back. As she hung up, Fred came over and asked to see her in his office. Holding her breath, she followed him.

"I guess you know by now what's happening here."

"No, Fred. I really don't."

"There was a meeting over the weekend. It was far from pleasant. It was decided by the powers that be that it has become necessary to let several employees go."

"In other words, they were fired."

"Maddie, you don't have to worry. We need you here, but..."

She took a breath, waiting.

"...there's a problem with your shoot. We've been ordered to cut costs and Jules refuses to pay the location fee for Tavern on the Green. He says it's too expensive and can be done in the photographer's studio. As I understand it, there's no charge for that."

"No, Fred. Photographers don't charge for studio shoots. That's not a problem. The problem is that dress doesn't make any sort of a statement. At the very least we need to have some props." She stopped to think. "Would you want to ask our actress if we can, perhaps, shoot her on a stage?"

Fred nodded. "Not a bad idea. I'll give her agent a call."

"The shoot is scheduled for Thursday. We're already over deadline. This can't be put off."

"I understand Maddie. I'll get on it."

As she left his office she glanced back, satisfied to see him pick up the phone. It had felt good giving him an order and even better knowing he'd followed it.

=

Rob called back a couple of hours later and hearing the anxiety in Maddie's voice said he'd be there by six.

It was closer to six-thirty by the time he arrived. Rather than coming to her first, he waved as he went directly to Fred's office and closed the door. *What was that? He goes to Fred's office for what, a man-to-man talk?*

"Screw this," she muttered to herself. "If I were Matt instead of Maddie, I'd fucking well be in that meeting."

She tapped on Fred's door and then opened it. "I assume you're discussing *my* photo shoot. Shouldn't I be part of this?"

Obviously surprised, Fred looked at Rob. Rob grinned. "Come in, Maddie."

She took a breath and sat, at the same time noticing the two glasses half filled with amber liquid. She wondered if Fred would offer her some. He didn't.

Fred said, "It looks like there's an off-Broadway stage you can use Thursday morning. They won't charge a fee since our actress,

Lily Prism—now there's a name—is a member of their theater group. She'll be in later today for a fitting. This better go well; a lot of ad pages are riding on it."

Not too much pressure. She nodded, still having no idea what, besides a girl in a boring dress, she was going to shoot. Even Neil, the photographer, was worried.

She had hoped Rob would have time to talk, that maybe they could go to Allen's for a few drinks. But after leaving Fred's office, Rob said he had to get back to the agency; they were finishing up a client pitch for the next day. Life wasn't slowing down just because he'd suddenly moved in with her.

=

As she unlocked her door, the phone began to ring. She was afraid it might be Danny and wished she'd had more time to rehearse what she would say to him. But the voice she heard was shrill: "Let me speak to Rob."

"He's not here, Allison. I asked you not to call me again."

"Of course he's there. Where else would he go? I called his office, they said he wasn't there."

Maddie felt her stomach lurch. *Not there?*

"Get him. I have to talk to him. Now. He has to come home. His kids need him."

"Allison. He's not here. I thought he was at the office."

"See?" her tone was sharp. "You think you know where he is and he's not there. He'll do the same to you as he's done to me. Count on it." She hung up.

Feeling ice coursing through her veins, Maddie dialed his office. Whoever it was that answered—the switchboard was long closed—asked cautiously who was calling. After a pause, Rob picked up.

"What is it Maddie?"

"Rob. Thank God. Allison just called. She said she tried you at the agency but you weren't there."

"That's because she hasn't stopped bugging me. I'll call her when I'm ready. Don't listen to her. I'll be home soon."

Don't listen to her? As if he had known what she said.

=

When she, Neil and his assistant arrived at the theater, Lily was already there. Maddie was relieved to see she had done her own hair and makeup since Fred had also nixed not only the stylist, but a hair and makeup person as well. She was pretty in a bold, actressy way, and most importantly, very enthusiastic about the shoot. Finding the stage bare, Maddie went in search of props. Amongst assorted couches, desks and tables she found a large gold painted chair upholstered in red velvet; almost a throne. That sparked an idea; as unlikely as it seemed, maybe she could make Lily into a princess, albeit in a dumb red dress. Unfortunately, there was no ermine-edged cape or even a tiara to be found.

After pinning Lily into the dress, they directed her to sit, to perch on the arms, and to lean against "her throne." They told her to smile, laugh, look serious and appear coy. No matter what they tried, it still came down to a somewhat pretty girl in a nondescript, weird colored dress interacting with a large chair. Neil looked as alarmed as Maddie felt; this wasn't exactly what either of them had in mind for the cover of a magazine.

As they were wrapping up, Lily's overly eager agent strode in asking about the article that would accompany the photos. With forced enthusiasm Maddie promised it would be at least a two-page spread. What she didn't say was she doubted Lily would garner much recognition from it; she wasn't convinced anyone was still reading the magazine.

=

When the transparencies came in a few days later, she made sure to have Fred help select the one to be used for the cover. She wasn't about to take sole responsibility for the final choice. The shot they chose was of Lily sitting on the arm of the chair and smiling directly into the camera. They had put a small fan below her and her short brown hair was ruffled in the slight breeze.

She looked fine; it was the dress that was still ridiculous. In the article it would be described as "Royal Carmine, The Must-Have Color for Summer '67." Added to that was the line on the cover which erroneously stated, *Lily Prism, New York's Newest Princess of the Broadway Stage*. Maddie hoped Lily, having had only small parts in a couple of off-Broadway shows, would one day live up to the hype.

Frustrated by the entire debacle, Maddie went into Rob's old office and called him. He answered, sounding rushed. "Don't freak out, Maddie. I know there are problems with the magazine, but you also know I love you and I'll be there for you. We'll talk later."

She hung up and looked across the sadly depleted bull pen. There was little doubt that the magazine was in a downward spiral and she wondered if the wealth/snob/society angle was beginning to wear thin. The world was changing rapidly and The Village Voice and San Francisco Oracle were becoming the new voices of a younger generation whose mantra was, "Don't trust anyone over thirty."

After releasing the cover to the printer, she picked up the phone and called Mr. Collins at the employment agency.

Part 3

Buy the ticket, take the ride.

Hunter Thompson

Chapter 1

November 1967

It was the day before Thanksgiving, a year since Rob invited Maddie for that fateful drink and eight months after he had rung her doorbell, complete with skis and martini. Their only challenge, other than his ongoing divorce, had been in July when Maddie had been unceremoniously fired from *Status*. Although it wasn't a surprise, Rob had been more upset than she. Between he and Ken they'd gotten her several interviews, the first at a new magazine called *Weight Watchers*. But since she couldn't comprehend why women would want to read a magazine about dieting, the interview hadn't gone well. After a month and several more interviews, she accepted a job as an art director in the illustrated book division of American Heritage. The book she was to design was on nineteenth century American antiques, something she knew almost nothing about. Nevertheless, on her first day the head creative director, Irwin Gluck, challenged her, saying he wanted a design that was bold and unusual — not the all-too-expected small rectangular pictures centered on the page. She obliged by creating a unique format that combined large and small images, silhouetting and bleeding photos off the page, as well as enlarging details of carvings or paintings as headers for each chapter. When she nervously presented her first layouts, Irwin and her editor, Miles, were not only thrilled with the originality of the pages, but highly complimentary as well. It was a gratifying moment; as the first female art director in the company, she was well aware that Irwin had taken a chance on her.

Although she hadn't been sure she'd like designing five hundred page books, she was finding it far more satisfying than continually juggling magazine layouts while at the same time cajoling bickering editors into meeting deadlines.

=

Due to the Thanksgiving holiday, everyone had left early. As Maddie was putting on her coat, Irwin called her into his office. Sounding a bit frazzled, he said, "Maddie, I may need you to work this weekend. I hope you're staying in the city."

She looked back in surprise. "I am. But why?"

"I was just informed that President Eisenhower has been taken to the hospital. If he dies, I need you to put together a special magazine about his life and his presidency. It's all in a morgue file that we keep on important people so when something like this comes up we can publish quickly, within a few days. This may be one of those times."

"And you want me to do it?"

"Yes. You're creative and you work fast. The editor in charge of it asked for you. After the Six-Day War in June, we published a special edition within a week, one day longer than the war itself! We even beat *Time-Life*," he said with a self-satisfied look on his face. "I know it may be an imposition, but we need you."

=

Although flattered that Irwin had chosen her, she hoped President Eisenhower would at least survive the holiday weekend. On her way home she made a quick stop at the supermarket to pick up steaks and potatoes—Rob's favorite. She also bought a small cake to celebrate their first year together and Rob's latest success, this time on a campaign for pantyhose. She mused that he seemed to do his best work on accounts dealing with women. Once, when she had asked why the agency didn't hire women copywriters for such feminine products, he'd shrugged. "Other than Mary Wells or Jane Maas at Ogilvy, what agency has women copywriters? Anyway, who needs them when they have Doug and me?"

"Aren't you being a bit conceited?"

"Not at all, Maddie. It's what I do."

"Maybe," she'd laughed. "But it's still self-congratulatory."

=

As she was putting everything away, the phone rang. She ran to the bedroom to answer it. It was Cynthia, sounding agitated. "Maddie, I just got fired. They let everyone go."

"Cynthia, slow down. Tell me what happened."

"*Status* is folding. Over, kaput." Her laugh was bitter.

"You knew this was coming."

"Yeah. We all did. But it's still a shock. Lucky you got out before it all hit the proverbial fan, although I still think it's unfair that they fired you because of that cover."

"Someone had to take the fall for it, Cyn. It was the owners' decision to use that dress. They weren't going to fire themselves or Fred for that matter."

"Well, it's over. How's your new job?"

"It's great. Deadlines in book publishing are a lot longer than magazines. I won't finish until next summer."

"How are you and Rob doing? Is he being a good boy?"

"Yes, Cyn. Everything is great. We've just moved into our new apartment."

"Who would have guessed? I remember telling you how difficult and arrogant he was. If anyone can handle him, you can."

Maddie shook off a whisper of unease. "What about Tara?

"You won't believe this—she got a job at Danny's agency. By the way, have you spoken to him?"

She sighed. "Not since the day I told him Rob and I were living together."

=

After hearing the gossip about Maddie that night with Rob at Twenty-One, Danny hadn't called again for three weeks. By that time Rob had already moved in. She knew she should have taken the lead and called him; after all the time they had spent together he deserved that. But she honestly didn't know what to say to him.

He had asked her to meet him after work at a bar near his office. When she arrived he kissed her and before she could say a word, he acknowledged that perhaps he had overreacted. He said he had forgiven her and hoped they could resume their relationship. Of course, he expected her to give up seeing or even communicating with Rob.

She had been astonished first by his forgiveness and then his demands. She explained as gently as she could that it was far too late for either, adding that she truly cared for him. When he asked gruffly if she had been seeing Rob at the same time she was sleeping with him, she admitted she had and that he was now staying with her. (*Staying* sounding a bit less dramatic than *living*).

He drained his drink and slammed his glass down on the table. "I can't fucking believe you were cheating on me."

Maddie blinked. "Danny, please try to understand; there was never anything exclusive between us."

He glared at her, his voice deep and sarcastic. "How exclusive could it be? You were sleeping with two men. What the hell were you thinking?"

She looked away. "It wasn't something that either of us planned. It just happened."

"Yeah, sure. It just happened when I thought I was falling in love with you. I didn't want to believe you were going out with a married man, not to mention that you're now living with him. I thought you were a lot smarter than that. Don't come crying to me when he breaks your heart. And from what I've heard about him, I promise you he will."

Speechless, she watched him walk out, her body and her tears frozen by his words.

=

"That's too bad, Maddie," Cynthia said. "He's a nice guy. I wish I could find one like him. I thought you two were great together."

"Maybe we were, Cyn. But I just didn't love him. How's Michael?"

"We're still on and off. He's another bad boy, although it sounds like you've tamed Rob. Maybe when I find a new job, I'll find a new boyfriend."

"I wish you luck. If you're around this weekend, come see the new apartment."

"Where is it?"

"Seventy-Seventh and Lexington. It's a small building, only ten floors. There's no doorman or for that matter even a dishwasher. But as Rob says, it's ours."

"Do you think you'll get married?"

"He's not divorced yet. But even when he is, why bother? Everything is perfect as it is."

=

After hanging up she returned to the kitchen. She had told her mother she'd make a pie for Thanksgiving dinner. Unlike her previous apartment, the kitchen was big enough to actually cook in. It even had a window.

Feeling the kitten rub up against her leg, she leaned down to pet her. Rob had brought her home, a tiny ball of soft grey fur, a couple of days after they moved. When she asked him why, he had simply answered, "Because I love you." Unable to agree on a name, they called her "Cat."

It was almost five. Surprised she hadn't heard from Rob, she called his office. He picked up sounding rushed. "Where are you?" he asked.

"I'm home. What time will you be finished?"

"I'll probably be another hour or so. We've been brainstorming on this new account all day. It's not going very well. I'll call when I'm leaving."

"It's a holiday, Rob."

"I know Maddie, but Doug and I want to get something down before the weekend."

"All right. Try not to be too late. I'm going to attempt to make a blueberry pie. We'll take it to my mother's tomorrow."

"Good luck with that, Maddie." She could hear the smile in his voice; he knew she wasn't much into baking. But she also heard a bit more and wondered if he'd been drinking. While she knew some drinking went on at the office, there seemed to be more nights lately that he was coming home with liquor on his breath. After she hung up she wondered if she should have reminded him that tonight was special. *No matter, we have the whole weekend to celebrate.*

=

Things indeed were not going well. Rob was beginning to worry that, after his first few agency wins, his magic was gone. He picked up a glass and drank some of the clear liquid. It may have looked like water, but water didn't sting his throat or calm his nerves. He had never felt this depth of tension at magazines—they were a piece of cake compared to the never-ending challenge of conjuring up new and unique ideas for everyday products that weren't very interesting. How exactly was he going to make a bar of soap so compelling that women just couldn't live without it?

He glanced at Doug, his copywriter, suggesting they call it a day. The pitch for the bath products account was repeatedly hitting a wall. They had piles of comps with different copy lines, but it just wasn't coming together. Maybe after the long weekend they could start over again.

They were preparing to leave when Larry came in trailed by Kimmy. He said a few people were stopping at Rattazi's for a drink and asked if they wanted to come. Doug nodded, saying he would. Rob started to say no, but reconsidered. One drink might not be such a bad idea; definitely better than the vodka he had been nursing all afternoon.

He was surprised that after what seemed like only a drink or two, his watch showed it was almost nine. By then a few more copywriters and assistant art directors had drifted in and everyone was having a fine time drinking, gossiping and telling stories. He was about to leave when Larry said he had snagged a table for dinner and insisted that everyone stay, especially Rob and Doug, their new creative stars.

He went to the back to call Maddie. Holding the phone close so she wouldn't hear the racket in the background, he told her he was running late and not to worry about dinner; he and Doug were still working and would bring something up to the office. He promised he'd be home soon. He wasn't sure why he'd lied to her; maybe he just needed some space.

=

Maddie was troubled by the call, particularly the part about not worrying about dinner. Hadn't he told her earlier he'd only be another hour or so? The old thread of uncertainty, silent for so many months, suddenly began to scratch.

And yet, she rationalized, there had been plenty of late nights that had ended with her meeting him along with other art directors or copywriters either at PJ's or Max's. Those nights, filled with booze and advertising gossip had often gone on till closing at four in the morning. Despite the inevitable hangover the next day, she loved the industry talk and the fact that as an art director, albeit in publishing, she was included in their conversation while the other girlfriends and even an occasional wife sat mute and basically ignored.

Then there were the nights he came home close to midnight, exhausted and not far from drunk. Those were generally in the heat of completing a presentation or preceding a big client meeting. So far, despite Allison's warning—and Danny's as well—she'd had no reason not to trust him. But the night before a holiday? It didn't sound right.

Thinking she was over reacting, she decided to call him back. She would use a seductive voice, remind him this was a special night and that she had a very special dinner planned. When no one answered after a dozen rings, she hung up, her mind churning.

Returning to the kitchen, she fed the kitten, opened a can of blueberries and turned her attention to making the crust for the pie. *Maybe everyone is still there, just in a room where there are no phones.* She took the dough from the mixer and began rolling it out. When it stuck, she kneaded it into a ball and put it in the fridge to chill for a few minutes. When she looked at the clock it was close to ten thirty. Dusting flour off her hands, she went to the phone and called again. No answer. With tension flooding her entire body, she went back to the kitchen and picked up the roller. *Maybe he's on his way home by now.* She rolled the dough out but it stuck, curling around the roller. She peeled it off and tried again. After four more tries she scraped it off and in a fit of frustration, threw it against the wall where it stuck. She glared at it, her heart pounding.

Everything is perfect. Wasn't that what she had just told Cynthia?

After another couple of hours with no word, she worried that perhaps something terrible had happened to him. But how would she know unless he called and the phone wasn't ringing. She couldn't even call Suzanne—it was one in the morning. All she could do was wait and she wasn't good at waiting. After her parents had divorced, there had been weekends when she had waited for her father to come for her. Too many of those Sundays he hadn't bothered to show up, nor had he called, giving her mother and grandmother even more ammunition for criticism. She had been wired for anxiety from childhood and not only did she resent it when someone said they'd call and didn't, but waiting for someone who never showed up was pure torture for her.

=

Rob knew he should leave. After calling Maddie, he returned to the table noticing the only vacant chair, the one with the half-finished drink in front of it, was in between Kimmy and a copy assistant named Patty. After ordering another round, Larry, already a far distance from sobriety, began telling stories of raucous office parties from years past, no doubt in anticipation of Christmas revelries coming up. Doug, also having had at least one too many, jumped in and began gossiping about the senior partners and their peculiar tastes in hiring secretaries. When he finished skewering them, he went on to describe the curious and occasionally depraved excesses of some of their clients, adding how he and others at the agency had been appointed to "take care" of them. There had been meetings in so-called "hot sheet" hotels and even inferences of whips and leather with various apertures and appurtenances. Between the drinking and raunchy stories, Rob felt Patty, who was laughing and somewhat beyond half-blitzed, repeatedly grab his arm as though trying to get his attention.

By the time they split up the check it was almost midnight. When Rob went out to find a taxi, he wasn't completely surprised to find a slightly unsteady Patty waiting. Looking up at him, she asked if he'd like to have a drink at her place.

=

The sound of the lock turning spooked the cat and awakened Maddie from a restless doze. Glancing at the clock, she saw it was just after six. She lay back feeling her heart racing, no doubt in anticipation or more realistically, fear.

Rob walked into the bedroom, tie loosened, looking haggard and holding his coat. She wanted to tell him to put it back on and leave. Instead she stared at him, not uttering a word.

He picked up the cat and put her carefully on the bed. "I'm sorry, Maddie. I don't know what to say. The night got out of hand. It was so late Doug and I ended up sleeping at the office."

She shook her head in disbelief. "Do you really expect me to believe you worked all night?"

He sat down next to her, but she moved away. "We did work late, but when we were leaving a couple of the guys wanted to go for one quick drink. Then someone started telling stories and suddenly the bar was closing and we were both drunk. We barely made it back to the office."

"That's the best you can come up with? There were no phones anywhere? Or in your drunken haze did you forget our number? I don't believe a word of it Rob. No way." She paused, her anger giving her strength. "Maybe you should just go back to whoever you really spent last night with."

He shook his head. "I swear to you, Maddie, I wasn't with anyone but Doug."

"Then explain why you would go back there when you could have gotten a cab and come home?"

He sighed deeply. "I was so bombed I couldn't function. The office was across the street and I guess I just wasn't thinking. I'm sorry."

She shook her head. "I'm not buying it."

"Please, Maddie," he pleaded. "You know how much you mean to me. Look, I'm here, we're living together." He paused and stood up. "But if you want me to leave, I will."

She felt a stab of panic. While in her mind she pictured herself pointing to the door, the truth was she couldn't imagine living without him. Her life revolved around this man and, no matter what his trespasses, she still wanted him. She shook her head with a barely audible, "No." He took her hands and pulled her close. "You're the only woman I will ever want."

She wanted to believe him with every cell in her body. "I guess you didn't remember that it was a year since our first night together," she said, as tears began to run down her face.

"Oh my God. I wish you had said something. I would never have gone out with the guys."

He wished I had said something? Would that really have prevented this long miserable night? She sat down on the bed, unable to stop weeping.

He kissed her tears and then her lips. "Maddie. I'm sorry. Let's try and sleep for a couple of hours. We don't have to be at your parents' house until later this afternoon."

=

When they had gotten up later that morning, Maddie was still a knot of raw nerves and uncomfortably aware that Rob was watching her as though expecting an explosion at any moment. Her instincts were screaming *lies* and yet she was afraid of the truth. But why would he cheat? She knew he loved her.

She had to let it go, if only for the moment. They had planned that Rob would have Thanksgiving dinner with her family and then take the train to Darien to see his parents and spend time with his kids the next day. They would have to wait until the weekend to talk.

=

Her mother still didn't trust Rob. She had deep suspicions that he wasn't, as Maddie had told her, living temporarily with one of his photographer friends. From the moment they arrived, she watched the two of them like a hawk.

After settling himself on the sofa, drink in hand, Rob became the charming focus of her mother's guests which this year included a few of her country club friends. The neighbors with the kids were also in attendance—the kids taller and more pimply. Kitty, in a repeat performance from last year apparently felt it was important to remind Maddie that her hair was still too short. On the other hand, she fussed over Rob, even going so far as to feed him the occasional appetizer.

The conversation, particularly amongst the men, revolved around the Vietnam war—an endless discussion on a seemingly endless war. When Norman, Kitty's husband, commented that President Johnson had only days before confirmed that the "enemy is losing," Harry shook his head. "I don't believe Johnson or any of them anymore. This thing isn't going away. Every day is a different story."

After a moment of awkward silence, Rob reached for a shrimp and asked, "Has anyone seen *Cool Hand Luke*? Maddie and I saw it a few weeks ago."

Kitty practically swooned, declaring that she was in madly in love with Paul Newman. After that the war was put aside and everyone went on about violence in the movies, particularly *Bonnie and Clyde*, which everyone had seen last summer.

After a few minutes, Maddie chose to disappear into the kitchen, ostensibly to help her mother. After last night she wasn't in the mood for light conversation.

"I thought you were bringing a blueberry pie," her mother said.

"I was, but I'm not very good at crusts and it finally got the best of me. I gave up."

She frowned. "That's not like you. You never give up." Maddie glanced at her, wondering if that was some sort of compliment. "How are things with Rob? You seem very quiet today."

"I'm tired Mom. It's been a busy week."

"What's going to happen with him? Is he ever going to get divorced?"

"As a matter of fact, his lawyer told him it should be finalized by March or April. He's had a hard time of it. Allison has made it as difficult as she could."

"Well," she said archly, "he left her for you. I'd be angry as well."

"No, Mom, he didn't. I've told you before, there were problems between them before."

"Believe what you want, Maddie. But you better be honest with yourself and think about where you're going with him. Does he want to marry you?"

Maddie put down the serving dish she was holding and looked at her incredulously. "What kind of question is that? No, we've never discussed it. We're happy the way things are." She stopped suddenly, not quite sure that statement was entirely valid at that moment.

Her grandmother walked in, her antennae up. "You better not live together; then he'll never marry you. You know the old saying, 'Why buy the cow if you can milk it through the fence.'"

=

After an endless dinner, Maddie drove Rob to the train. Both of their parents' homes were, fortunately, on the same New Haven rail line. At the station he came around and opened her door, asking her to get out of the car. He took her face in his hands and kissed her deeply, as though he was leaving for weeks. "This will hold you until Saturday. I love you Maddie. You must believe me."

She nodded and whispered she loved him as well. She didn't want him to go, afraid she might never see him again.

=

Maddie was unpacking boxes when Rob arrived back at the apartment. He hadn't bothered to call—just showed up. Without a word he scooped her up in his arms. Before she could react, he deposited her on the bed, and in almost one motion threw off his coat and began pulling her clothes off.

"Rob, stop…"

"Shhh. No talking, Maddie. I'm going to make love to you." He began by kissing his way up and down her body, caressing her until he felt her respond to him. Without warning, he grabbed her wrists and held them above her head on the pillow, all the while looking down at her. He wasn't smiling as his knees moved her legs apart. "Tell me you want this."

She looked up at him and nodded. "No, Maddie," he demanded. "Say it."

His heat was palpable. He gripped her wrists tighter and she tried to twist away. "Rob, you're hurting me. Let me go." It came out as a gasp; she was barely able to breathe.

"No," he growled, his desire obvious and intense. "Tell me you love me and you want me to fuck you."

Trembling with unaccustomed pain that was somehow mixing with an uncontrollable craving, she whispered, "Yes, Rob. I love you and I want you to fuck me."

"That's more like it," he muttered, running his tongue over her nipples. "Say please."

"Please," she moaned. As he moved into her slowly and deliberately she felt an electric current surge between them. He didn't rush; he was, as always, in control. Finally, when he could sustain the sensation no longer, he kissed her and releasing her hands, whispered, "Come with me."

"Yes," she sighed, wrapping her arms and legs around him, pulling him deeper into her.

They lay back, sweating and spent. After some time, he turned and silently traced her face with his finger, stopping at her lips which he leaned over to kiss.

"I love you today," he said.

"What does that mean?"

"I don't think it requires an explanation."

"But why just today?"

"Maddie, you don't have to analyze everything."

She closed her eyes, understanding his message all too well; there was nothing more to be said about *that* night. Within it was also the underlying implication that he could control her, her response to his touch, to his love, to his sex. He knew she couldn't resist him, sexually or emotionally. He had become her addiction — one she had no desire to break.

Chapter 2

Maddie was relieved the long weekend had ended in relative peace. When she arrived at her office, she found a note on her drawing board. It was from Jay, saying he wanted to meet her in the conference room at eleven.

Since she began working at American Heritage the only negative had been Jay Connell, a senior art director who was designing a book on American history, a companion volume to hers. From the very first day he had been decidedly cool to her. He arrived every morning with a curt hello and left at night with an equally brief, "See you." At thirty-one, he was tall with slate blue eyes and light brown hair worn fairly long. He dressed elegantly in dark suits, no doubt for evenings out with the many girls who called during the day.

He left a note? Why? They shared an office, their work areas only separated by a floor-to-ceiling partition. She glanced around it. "You want to meet with me?"

He barely looked at her. "Bring your latest layouts. We have some things to go over."

She wanted to ask why they couldn't walk to the conference room together and, by the way, what was his problem with her? He was friendly with everyone else in the office, but she seemed to have some strange negative effect on him. *So be it. Maybe better to keep my distance.*

Although she brought her most recent layouts to the meeting, Jay showed up with only a few sheets of paper. He sat down opposite her and without even a greeting, proceeded straight to the business at hand.

"Since this is your first book, I want you to be clear on timing. Although our deadlines are months away, you'll now have to start adhering to a weekly schedule of submitting pages for approval." He pushed a typed sheet across the table and waited while she scanned it. "Will that be a problem?" he asked as if it were a challenge.

She looked back at him, refusing to be intimidated. "As long as Miles gives me the photos and text on time, I'm sure it won't be."

"Well, we both have to stay on track."

"Miles reviews layouts with me almost every day. I'm sure you know he's been very pleased."

He nodded and asked to see some of those layouts. She pushed them over to him.

He looked through them with an expression of vague surprise. "I haven't seen these before. They look pretty good."

That's it? That's the best you can do?

"By the way, I heard you were up for the morgue file this weekend." She was surprised to see him actually smile. "I'll bet you didn't know that it's an honor as well as a curse. I'll also bet that Irwin didn't mention that you would have had to work sixteen hours a day to get the magazine out on the newsstand before anyone else."

With the chaos of the weekend she had forgotten all about it. "I didn't know," she said, suddenly grateful that President Eisenhower had survived.

=

When he arrived home that night, Rob announced he had great news: he was going to Connecticut the next day to finalize his separation agreement. It was the first week in December and the negotiations, an ongoing study in frustration, had dragged on since he had moved in with Maddie in February.

At one point he hadn't been sure it would ever end: It had been the last Friday in July, just after he had picked up his new motorcycle, a Honda 350. Maddie hadn't been exactly overjoyed by it, but it was something he wanted and he'd had the means to buy it. He figured he'd better buy it before the divorce was final, because by then he might not have quite the same means.

That day he'd had to leave the agency in the middle of a presentation. There had been no choice; the lawyers and his soon-to-be ex were waiting in Stamford. Despite that he was running late, he stopped at Ernie's for a couple of quick beers. Otherwise he'd never get through it.

By the time he arrived at the lawyer's office, everyone was waiting impatiently. Allison stopped pacing long enough to glare at him. His lawyer made a few statements and next thing he knew they were harping away. Trying not to become impatient, he pictured himself saying *Chuck it Farley*, getting on the bike and riding off somewhere, anywhere away from all this bullshit. He looked up seeing Allison staring at him —*smug bitch.* It was all about money and the kids; she dangled visitation rights out there like bait. She already had the house and everything in it except for his clothes and skis. One weekend he'd had to sneak his artwork and portfolio out of the den and into his father's car. As for the small wood carving he was making for Maddie, he had found it on the basement floor, broken to pieces.

He was trying to keep his cool, but when Allison whispered something to her WASP lawyer, the best Daddy could buy, he couldn't take another minute of it. Standing up, he shouted, "Fuck you," practically in her face and walked out, slamming the door behind him. He heard her yelling at the lawyers to stop him; this had to get done today; her father had insisted. *It had to be today? There are no other days? Ever?* He stopped, turned around and opened the door to the conference room where everyone's mouth was hanging open in shock. *Good,* he thought, as he pointed to her and said in a calm voice, "And fuck your father as well. He's not going to control me any more than you are. No one is."

"What about your slut in New York?" she screeched. "I'll bet she's controlling you."

He faced her, "Don't you dare call her that. Unlike you, she has never laid any trips on me about anything, including getting divorced."

He loosened his tie and looked at his dumbass lawyer. "Make sure I can see the kids every week if I want to. Then make your best deal and call me."

"Where?" he asked in a squeaky voice.

"At the office, asshole." He shook his head and walked out. All he heard was silence.

=

Now it was December. Six months had passed and this time he returned with great news; his separation agreement was signed and his divorce would be final by January. Maddie shrieked in happiness and ran into his arms. "January? So soon?" she asked, looking surprised.

"It's Allison's father, Maddie. He's friendly with some judges in the town and hates me so much that he's getting it done quickly." He laughed and went to the fridge for a beer. "Just think, in a few weeks I'll be a free man. And by the way, while I was there I asked Allison if I could bring the kids in a couple of days before Christmas."

Maddie looked up. "Really?"

He nodded. The summer before, he had borrowed his father's car one Saturday morning and brought them to the city. Maddie had joined them at The Museum of Natural History where Rob had introduced her as a friend. The kids had been shy at first, but after the excitement of seeing the exhibits, especially the dinosaurs, they had warmed up to her. On the way back to the apartment, Maddie picked up sandwiches so they could have lunch and a short nap before heading back to Connecticut. They had loved the apartment, having never been in one before. When Val asked whose it was, Maddie glanced at Rob and said it was hers. Val said she wanted to see Daddy's apartment. Rob smiled, saying, "next time."

Rob had been concerned that they'd report the part about the apartment to Allison but strangely she never said anything about it.

=

That afternoon, after signing the final papers, Allison had been un-usually placid, almost friendly. He decided to take a shot and asked if he could take the kids to the city before Christmas. When she had answered calmly, "Yes, Rob. They shouldn't miss Christmas with their father," he had been completely blown away. While he was adjusting to this new reality, she went on, "Rob, I know you're living with Maddie; so tell me, are you planning on marrying her?"

That stopped him, big time. He'd had no idea that was coming or what to say. But if the right response would allow him to bring his kids to the city for Christmas, he already knew the answer. "I think so Allison. We're not quite there, but things are very good between us." He hoped it would be enough for her.

"Since you seem to be in a stable relationship, then yes, you can take them for the day. They seem to like her." By now he was sure she must have popped a few Valiums; she had never been that mellow.

=

After weeks of wild Christmas parties and booze filled nights, Rob took the train to Darien to borrow his father's car and drive the kids back to the city.

They had lugged home a good-sized Christmas tree the week before and Maddie had gone to Woolworth's to buy a few boxes of brightly colored ornaments and tinsel. They wrapped presents but only partially decorated the tree, leaving some of it for the kids to do.

He arrived with them around noon and they had lunch at the coffee shop across the street where Val and Tommy eagerly ordered hamburgers and French fries. Afterwards they took a taxi to Rockefeller Center so they could see the tree and skating rink. Val held Maddie's hand as they crossed Fifth Avenue to look at the animated windows at Saks and Bonwit's. Rob put Tommy on his shoulders as people milled around, glancing at the two of them with the excited kids and smiling their approval.

They returned to the apartment where Maddie made hot chocolate and Rob handed out ornaments so Val and Tommy could finish trimming the tree. By four, the floor was littered with tinsel, discarded wrapping paper, assorted toys and even a few game pieces underfoot. After being wired all afternoon, the kids were becoming tired and whiny. Anxious to preserve Allison's magnanimous mood, Rob said they could nap in the car. Maddie got them into their coats and scarves and fished out lost gloves amongst the torn-up wrappings. She looked up seeing Rob staring at her. "What?" she asked.

"Come with us," he said quietly. "I think you should meet my folks."

Casting a doubtful glance back at him, she said she wasn't sure it was a good idea. She knew his mother was a deeply religious Catholic who doted on her only son. But, as that son had told her more than once, she also doted on her grandchildren and was very displeased about his divorce.

"Please Maddie. I have a few gifts for them. We'll just drop them off and say hello. My father will drive us to the train."

She shook her head. "It's too soon. You're not divorced yet."

He put his arm around her and kissed her lightly. The kids giggled. "Don't make a big deal about it. I want you to come with us." While she was aware he was using seduction to get her to agree, she also knew when he was this adamant it was easier to give in, although she did so with great apprehension.

The kids slept the entire way home, hardly waking even when Rob parked in front of a big white house. Maddie realized with a twinge that this was where Rob lived, before…well, before her. As he extracted the groggy kids from the car, the front door opened. She wanted to slide down in her seat and hide; she hadn't anticipated seeing Allison.

Val, wriggling out of Rob's arms, insisted on hugging her. Reluctantly, she opened the door and got out. Val gave her a quick kiss on the cheek and excitedly ran up the snowy path to her mother. Rob carried Tommy, still half-asleep, and handed him off. He spoke briefly with Allison, her eyes never leaving Maddie.

Back in the car, he said, "That went better than I thought. Allison seemed very laid back." He laughed, "Maybe laid is the right word. Val mentioned she had a date last night." Maddie shot him a look and shook her head.

They arrived at Rob's parents' house only a few minutes later. It was a long white clapboard house surrounded by large trees and dense shrubbery. As she got out of the car she picked up a bad vibe, a feeling that Darien might not be a good place for her.

Rob opened the trunk and took out several wrapped gifts. Maddie followed him to the front door. His father, a tall man with white hair, a white moustache and familiar green eyes was waiting with a welcoming smile. Dressed in a flannel shirt and pressed khakis, he looked like he had just stepped out of an L.L. Bean catalog. Maddie shook his hand and tried to relax.

The living room was furnished with subdued blue, grey and ivory sofas and high backed chairs. A large console television in the far corner was dwarfed by a lavishly ornamented Christmas tree. To the left, through a darkened dining room, Maddie could see a bit of the brightly lit kitchen and the shadow of someone, no doubt his mother, moving about.

Rob placed the gifts under the Christmas tree as his father sat down on a sofa and motioned for Maddie to join him. "Rob tells me you're also an art director. Is that how you two met?"

Trying not to look surprised, she answered, "Yes. We met at *Status*," omitting the part about being his assistant since it was obvious Rob hadn't bothered to mention it. "I'm now an art director at American Heritage."

He nodded slowly, murmuring, "Very nice," and proceeded to tell her about his long and evidently satisfying career as a production engineer at CBS. She listened attentively, at the same time wondering why Rob's mother hadn't yet emerged from her kitchen. While his father was still talking, she glanced at Rob, who, becoming aware of her discomfort, finally got up asking what everyone wanted to drink. His father looked at his watch, mentioned something about the sun being over the yardarm and said he'd have a scotch and water. Maddie said a Coke would be fine. Rob went into the kitchen where she heard some less than quiet words being spoken.

She turned to his father. "Maybe it would be best if we leave."

Mr. MacLeod shook his head and patted her hand. With a deep sigh, he stood up and walked toward the kitchen, pausing to turn on the dining room lights. At that moment Rob walked out carrying their drinks. His mother followed, her face blank and wiping her hands on her apron. Maddie stood up ready to shake her hand, but she kept her distance, murmuring a curt hello. At that moment the front door was flung open and Melanie, Rob's sister stormed in. She glanced at Maddie with an obvious sneer, threw out a sarcastic hello to Rob and her father, took her mother's arm and hustled her back to the kitchen.

Maddie was aghast, her face burning with humiliation. Rob, looking chagrinned, put his arm tightly around her as if to protect her from such abuse. "I'm sorry. You were right. We shouldn't have come. I had hoped they'd be over it by now."

Mr. MacLeod looked toward the kitchen and shook his head. "Please try to understand, Maddie, my wife doesn't believe in divorce. To her Allison is still Rob's wife, the mother of his children. My daughter appears to feel the same way."

Maddie whispered, "I think we should go now."

"Give it a minute and I'll drive you to the station. There's no train for another half hour anyway."

At that point she would have happily walked to the station or even New York. To add to the tension, Melanie reappeared about five minutes later, glanced at her with derision and stamped out. Rob went after her and Maddie heard them arguing on the steps. His mother never left the kitchen.

After an endless twenty minutes Mr. MacLeod drove them to the train station, apologizing again and giving Maddie an affectionate peck on the cheek. Rob admitted that it was a big screw-up on his part. At least his father had been nice; but then he appreciated pretty women.

=

When they arrived back in New York, Maddie insisted on going straight to Allen's where she downed two Old Grand Dad sours in about five minutes. She had hardly spoken on the train despite Rob holding her close and apologizing for his mother's and sister's behavior. It was only as she was working on the third drink that she spoke to him. "Why, Rob, would you think your mother would be even somewhat accepting of me, much less polite? She sees me as the interloper here, the evil siren who lured her innocent son away from his wife and kids."

What could he say? The day with the kids had been close to perfect. Even Allison was still chilled out when he had brought them home. Seeing Maddie in the car, she did make one crack, asking sarcastically if they were house hunting. He had laughed it off, not wanting to ruin the mood.

On the way back to the apartment Rob stopped abruptly in the middle of Third Avenue. "Let's throw a party," he said.

"What? Why?" Maddie asked, pulling him out of oncoming traffic.

"Because 1968 is going to be a great year. We're going to have a New Year's Eve divorce party."

Chapter 3

Everyone loved the idea of a divorce party on New Year's Eve. Friends who had already made plans said they'd be sure to stop by and a few acquaintances even called to ask if they could come. Maddie invited Jay who thanked her but said he had a date and had committed to several parties. He added that they should go out for lunch one day soon; they never had much time to talk. Maddie, surprised at his sudden friendliness, said she'd like that and got back on the phone.

The excitement of planning the party made her pretty much forget the dreadful evening at Rob's parents. The truth was that neither of their families approved of their relationship and were very obvious about it. While she felt it drew them even closer, she wondered if Rob thought about it at all.

=

Their friends began arriving at nine. Suzanne and Andrew miraculously managed to find a babysitter and arrived with three bottles of a California Cabernet as well as a bouquet of flowers to celebrate Rob's impending freedom. The stems were tied with red ribbon and after Maddie put the flowers in a vase she hung the ribbons on a doorknob in the kitchen.

Evan and Danielle brought two bottles of Cristal, and Ken called saying he and his wife would be there later with a couple of bottles of Rob's favorite Johnnie Walker. Six of Rob's coworkers, all art directors and copywriters from LRG, showed up with their wives or girlfriends and a case of Almaden red. Larry and Doug brought their girlfriends and two bottles of Dom. Maddie wasn't sure if all the booze was prompted by New Year's or if they were really into celebrating Rob's divorce.

The party went on raucously until after two, often with twenty or thirty people coming and going through their living room, a space that would, perhaps, hold fifteen comfortably. By that time, everyone was pouring their own drinks and most of the food was gone. The Stones were blasting that they got no satisfaction and everyone was laughing and shouting until a neighbor tentatively knocked on the door and asked politely if they could turn it down. Rob was pretty buzzed by then and Maddie was afraid he might be rude. But he apologized and lowered the sound.

Some people left but most of the agency crew—drinkers to the end—remained. Doug went to his coat and brought out a few joints. Not wanting their nice neighbor to call the police, Maddie opened a window to let out the haze of smoke. About twelve of them sat around, drinking and smoking and telling jokes until Doug suddenly shouted, "Does anyone know the definition of balls?" Humoring him, several people yelled back, "No."

He stood up unsteadily. "Okay guys, get ready. Balls is coming home late after a night out with the guys with lipstick on your collar and stinking of perfume and beer, then slapping your wife on the ass and having the balls to say, 'You're next.'"

Everybody laughed and one of the other writers chimed in with another joke: "Question, How many elephants will fit into a Volkswagen? Answer, Four: Two in the front, two in the back. Question, How many giraffes will fit into a Volkswagen? Answer—none. It's full of elephants." That started a run of stupid elephant jokes.

Larry moved next to Maddie asking woozily what she thought about the hippies and what had been called the "Summer of Love" in San Francisco. It was an odd question, out of sync with the rest of the conversation but by then everyone was stoned, and context, along with smoke, had basically drifted out the window. Unsure what he was getting at, she responded that the idea of a counter culture was a good thing and if it took the hippies to shake up a rigid American society with their anti-war rallies and views on free love, so be it.

"I think it's time this country emerged from the miasma of the fifties—the stifling conformity and the hypocrisy that sex is acceptable only if you're married. My parents think having sex without marriage is anathema." She blinked, having no doubt the pot had prompted that profound pronouncement.

"Well then," he laughed. "Your parents must be thrilled about you and Rob."

"My mother won't even come to this apartment. If she did, she'd have to admit that we're living together. She refuses to accept that it's a new world, our new world. We can do anything we want. We're free to make our own rules. No longer do we have to follow anyone else's. I have friends who have already gotten married and have kids. Some of them have moved back to Scarsdale where we went to high school. They've bought into the same conformist BS as their parents. That's not going to be my life."

"So how do you see your life?"

Knitting her brows, she thought for a minute. "I want to be the art director of a big, important magazine." She stopped and shook her head. It was something she had never articulated before. *Way too much grass tonight.* "Did I really say that?"

"Sure, why not? It's cool and I'll bet you'll get there. Rob's a lucky guy," he said topping off both their glasses from the dregs of a bottle of Dom.

A bit dizzy from the grass, the wine or perhaps her spontaneous declarations, Maddie got up: she had almost forgotten the cake. Thanks to Betty Crocker, she had managed to bake what she de-scribed as a divorce cake: dark chocolate icing on one side and white on the other. When Rob saw it, he said it didn't make quite the de-sired statement. After cutting a piece of paper into a small square, he scrawled "Marriage License" on it, placed it on top of the cake and stuck a knife through it. Maddie had to admit it did make the point.

She was plugging in the percolator when Larry trailed her into the kitchen. He was still going on about their discussion, particu-larly the free love part. Laughing, she noticed Rob standing in the doorway with a sullen expression on his face. He asked if she need-ed help. Still giggling, she said. "No, Rob. I've got it under control." He glanced at Larry and then at her, looking less than pleased. Lar-ry shrugged and carried a stack of dessert plates back to the living room.

Everyone applauded when she brought out the cake and af-ter toasting Rob with what remained of the wine and champagne, wished him a great year now that he was days, or even hours, away from being single. He thanked them and drained the last of the Cristal. By the time everyone finally got up to leave it was close to three. Larry, who was totally trashed and hanging on his girlfriend, gave Maddie an unexpected and rather wet goodnight kiss.

After locking the door, she returned to the living room to straighten up. The place was a shambles: empty bottles, half-filled glasses, overflowing ashtrays and crusty plates on every surface. Rob came up behind her, put his arms around her waist and whispered, "We're not cleaning up now. We have other things to do." She wriggled out of his grasp. "Come on, Rob. Let me just take some of this stuff into the kitchen."

Without a word, he picked her up and carried her into the bedroom, dropping her less than gently on the bed. She looked up at him in surprise. "What's wrong with you? We just had a great party."

"Nothing Maddie. I suddenly have this great desire to make love to you. Now." She had heard that tone before. Despite the fact the apartment was a mess and she was tired and half-drunk, she knew better than to say no to him. He'd had far too much to drink, not to mention smoke, and she was all too aware that he could become volatile in an instant. Before she could say a word, he practically ripped her dress off.

Frightened at his sudden ferocity, she moved away from him.

His face hard, he snapped, "Don't move," and left the room, seconds later returning with the ribbons from the flowers Suzanne had brought.

"Rob, what..."

"I'll show you what," he smirked. Ignoring her protests, he grabbed her wrists and bound them tightly with the ribbons. With narrowed red-rimmed eyes, he got out of his clothes quickly and straddled her, his hands and fingers becoming rough and demanding. Her obvious discomfort further aroused him and in a brusque voice he asked if she liked Larry. She shook her head, whispering, "We were just talking. That's all."

"He kissed you, didn't he? I'll bet you liked it," he scowled, squeezing her nipples. She pulled away. "Stop it, Rob. It was nothing. He was drunk."

"So am I, Maddie. And now I'm going to fuck you. Hard." That was all he said before he took her with force, pushing her legs back and sucking hard on her neck. Once again he was branding her with what would become red bruises despite knowing she hated hickies. He held her arms back until they ached, anger escalating his lust until she couldn't help responding to his domination. At once harsh and seductive, he whispered coarsely that he wouldn't stop until he had made her come, more than once. It was only when he was finally sated, and convinced by her muffled screams that she was as well, that he pulled her close, telling her how much he loved her and that no other man would ever touch her. He demanded she tell him she loved him and it was only when she whispered breathlessly that she did that he removed the ribbons, putting them away carefully in the chest next to his side of the bed.

Turning back, he held her tight against his body, kissing her neck and hair. She felt him becoming aroused again, but he relaxed and lapsed into heavy but regular breathing. She moved away from him, anxious and sore and asking herself how it was possible that his mood had gone from euphoria to jealousy to rage after seeing her just talk with another man. And while the sex had been deeply erotic, it had been more out of anger than love.

It was noon when they finally got out of bed. Rob hugged her, saying he'd make breakfast and help her clean up. She looked at him with disbelief; was he simply ignoring his fury from the night before? Or, thanks to the booze, had he just forgotten it?

Chapter 4

Several weeks later on a frigid February morning, Maddie awoke to a kiss. Forcing her eyes open, she saw Rob staring at her. They had been out the night before attending the annual Advertising Awards gala at the St. Regis. Other than John Langer and the other senior partners, only Rob, Doug and two copywriters from the agency had been invited to the formal affair. Maddie had gone out and bought a new black cocktail dress.

Several of LRG's ad campaigns were represented and two had won awards. As expected, Doyle, Dane, Bernbach's, "You don't have to be Jewish to love Levy's," won the highest accolades. Nevertheless, Rob was ecstatic; his Cosette campaign had been awarded an honorable mention.

As always, many eyes had glanced their way as they entered the baroque ballroom. Maddie never fooled herself about whom they were focused on. In his tuxedo, Rob was impressive, confident and well aware of his recognition by the top tier of agency aristocracy. John went out of his way to introduce him to Bill Bernbach, David Ogilvy and George Lois who spent some time chatting with him. He had looked forward to meeting the already legendary Mary Wells, but she had been continually surrounded by a wall of people. Maddie was happy for him and even happier that he had kept her close by his side. He had smiled each time someone asked to meet his wife.

By the time the ceremonies concluded it was almost midnight. The entire LRG contingent moved first to PJ Clarke's to continue celebrating, and finally, at four a.m. ended up having a somewhat drunk and boisterous breakfast at the Brasserie.

=

Rob kissed her again, as though trying to wake her further. "It's too early, Rob," she murmured. "It's only seven, we just got home."

"I think we should get married."

She burrowed into his chest, convinced she hadn't really heard what she thought she had heard; it had to have been a half-awake dream. She looked up at him. "What?"

"I said we should get married."

"Why?" Now coming awake.

"You're kidding. I'm asking you to marry me and you're asking why?"

She didn't move. "You didn't ask me. You just said 'I think we should get married.'"

"Do you want me to get down on one knee? I can do that." he started to get out of bed. She reached over and grabbed his arm. "Why?" she asked again.

"Why, what?"

She sighed. They had never discussed marriage, not once, and all she could think of was why now? *Or why at all?* "Was it because people thought we were married last night?"

"Don't be silly, Maddie. I love you and want to spend the rest of my life with you."

She sat up and rubbed her eyes. "I love you too. But you just got divorced. Besides, lots of people are now living together. We don't have to get married. I'm happy—aren't you?"

"Maddie, I can't believe we're having this conversation. If I have to explain why I want to marry you, forget it," he said, sounding piqued. He paused a moment and added, "Not to mention that your mother is having apoplexy that we're living together." After almost a year, her mother had figured it out. She had called one night after New Year's exclaiming hysterically, "What will the women in my bridge club say?"

Wondering if her mother had already imbibed a cocktail or two, Maddie asked how they would even know, unless they stopped by the apartment building and saw two names on the mailbox.

"She won't be any happier that we're getting married."

"Yes, she will. Eventually. She'll see how happy you are. We have everything going for us. We love each other, we work together without having to explain anything and we want the same things in life. We're soul mates, Maddie, and this will just make us more special. That's a promise." He gathered her in his arms.

She pulled back. "But everyone who's married says it changes things. I'm happy the way we are. I don't want anything to change."

"Maddie, I promise nothing will change. It's not complicated. Trust me."

She took a breath. Could she really trust him? Up until that debacle at Thanksgiving she had. But since then, except for a few flashes of jealousy on his part, they'd been happy. And if he wanted to get married, didn't that imply that he'd be faithful? She hoped this wasn't one of his sudden impulses. "Can I get up first? Maybe we should make coffee and talk about this."

"No."

"Why not?"

"There's nothing to talk about. I asked you to marry me. Yes or no."

"You really think it's a good idea? We're doing just fine this way."

"Let me show you a few of the reasons I think we should."

She wanted to talk more, but stopped. His desire, as always, was irresistible and it sparked hers. All she could think about was that he had just told her how much he loved her and that he wanted to marry her. As it began to sink in, she felt a joyous warmth pervade her entire body, a warmth born of pure happiness. It was a moment to savor and never to be forgotten. Somehow they had met and fallen in love. And how better to experience the wonder of that love than to surrender herself body and soul to the man she adored.

Afterwards, their fingers entwined, he asked, "So are you going to marry me?"

"I guess I am," she whispered.

When he went to shower, she lay back in bed, her mind and body suffused with the wonder of an unforeseen moment. Basking in the afterglow of lovemaking, she lightly traced a line from her breasts to the fur between her legs. She closed her eyes, still tingling; *maybe he loves me so much he wants me to be part of him. But then on the other hand, isn't that possession?* Inadvertently her thoughts reverted back to Thanksgiving, the old thread of unease doing a brief tap dance on her memory. She pushed it aside, letting the overwhelming pleasure of being so desired wash away all her doubts.

Rob came in, stretched, put his hands on his hips and shouted "Hello, world. Maddie Samuels is going to marry me." She laughed with tears of happiness in her eyes.

While he got dressed, she showered. Drawn by the scent of breakfast, she quickly finished and, wrapping a towel around herself, went into the kitchen. Rob was working away on the stove, bacon in one pan and French toast in another. She laughed as he fed her a piece of crisp bacon and went to get dressed.

After breakfast she washed the dishes—it never mattered who cooked, she always ended up with the dishes. Rob said he needed to do some errands; a stop at the hardware store to get a pair of pliers to fix something or other in the apartment, Woolworths for something else. She was in a happy daze and hardly listened.

After he left, she saw a note on the sideboard in the hallway. It was the place they dropped their keys and occasionally left one another messages. All it said was, "I love you and can't wait to marry you." Smiling, she picked it up and went to the bedroom to call Suzanne.

=

Suzanne's first comment was not "Great" or "Congratulations," as one would expect from a best friend. It was, "Why?"

Maddie laughed. "That was my first question as well. All I know is that he keeps insisting that he wants to marry me. Who am I to deny him? He makes me happy."

"Yes, Maddie. But he's also made you miserable. You know what happens when he drinks. He becomes impulsive, or I should say more impulsive than he already is. You know you can't control him."

"I have no desire to control him. And since this is his idea, I'm hoping that's all behind him. I think this will be good for both of us."

Maddie heard her take a breath. "Well, congratulations, I guess. I hope you're not being naïve. Have you told your mother yet?"

"No. Maybe later," she answered in a small voice. She hadn't called because she didn't want to destroy her happy mood.

Suzanne laughed. "Ask Rob to call. She won't yell at him."

=

Despite Suzanne's suggestion that she ask Rob to call her mother, she avoided mentioning it all day Saturday. By Sunday morning Rob finally said if she wouldn't call, he would.

She nodded solemnly. "I didn't want to ask you. Maybe say you wanted to be the one to give her the good news."

"Don't worry. I know what to say."

All things considered, it had gone well. Her mother hadn't gotten hysterical, not at first. She seemed to appreciate it was Rob who called to tell her they were making it all nice and legal.

After a few minutes he handed the phone to Maddie who looked like a scared rabbit. But her mother remained calm and asked if they had set a date.

"We're thinking in a couple of weeks."

"What? Why so fast? Maddie, you're not pregnant are you?"

"No, Mom."

"Then why the rush? You don't have to have a big wedding, but it would be nice to have a few months to plan. We can take one of the smaller rooms at the Plaza or even The Pierre. Not to mention that you'll have to look for a wedding dress."

Maddie took a breath. This was the part she was dreading. "Rob's already had the big wedding. Honestly, we both prefer to have just family and a few friends. I don't want the fuss of having to invite all your club friends and Harry's business associates and other people I don't know." Closing her eyes, she hesitated. "And I don't want a wedding dress."

Her mother's voice began to rise. "Is this all part of your never wanting to get married nonsense? Every girl should have a wedding dress."

"I'm not wearing a wedding dress to City Hall."

Hearing nothing but silence, Maddie looked at Rob and shook her head. That's when the hysteria kicked in. "City Hall? You cannot possibly think of getting married in City Hall. What are you thinking? Don't be ridiculous."

Maddie held the phone away from her ear. "Mom. Calm down."

"Are you really sure this is what you want and not what Rob told you to want?"

Through gritted teeth, she said, "No. I'm a big girl now and this is what I want. Rob says he'll do whatever pleases me. Maybe we can find a judge."

Her mother sighed, no doubt thinking of the people she wouldn't be able to invite as payback for all the weddings and Bar Mitzvah's they'd attended. Sounding resigned, she said they would ask about a judge; one of their friends would surely know one. She asked if they wanted to at least go to lunch or dinner afterwards.

"I think lunch would be perfect. I'll let you know who of our friends will be there. I'm sorry you're disappointed, but this truly is what both of us prefer."

"All right Maddie. I only hope you won't regret missing a very special day.

"It will be special. At least for Rob and me."

"What about his family?"

Maddie answered evasively that she wasn't sure if they would be there.

Hanging up, she breathed a sigh of relief. "Now she'll be able to tell her friends her daughter is married and no longer living in sin."

Chapter 5

They met at Ratazzi's instead of the Cattleman. Rob hadn't been there since the night before Thanksgiving and he quickly squelched the flashback of Patty sitting by his side.

Looking doubtful, Ken lifted his glass. "Here's to you, Rob. I hope to hell you know what you're doing."

"I think I do."

"The question is why? Why get married again so soon? Or for that matter why get married at all? You signed your divorce papers a month ago. Is Maddie pressuring you?"

"No. Not at all. I surprised her. We had gone to the Advertising Awards dinner the night before and everyone wanted to meet my pretty wife."

"By the way, congratulations on your honorable mention."

"Thanks, Ken."

"Have you considered that you're being impulsive? You don't want to regret this later."

"Not a chance. I love her and I love to come home to her every night. I've never felt that way about a woman."

"You never felt that about Allison? Give me a break."

Rob sat back, lit a cigarette and sipped his drink. "Last Saturday Maddie and I decided to go to a few galleries in Soho. Afterwards, instead of taking the subway, we began walking uptown. We got so deeply involved in a discussion about art, our jobs and whatever, we weren't even aware that we had walked all the way to the apartment on Seventy-Seventh Street. That would never have happened with Allison. The only thing we had in common was the kids."

"I get that you're completely into her. But what are the advantages of making it legal? More important, what about other women? You're going to give up your so-called extracurricular activities?"

He shook his head. "I've had a few moments, you could say, since we started living together. You know the scene: a few drinks, the girl was cute and available. Most of it she never knew about but I did screw up once. However, due to my inimitable charm and seductive ways, we got past it." He lifted his glass. "Come on Ken, we're guys. There are some things we just have to do."

Ken grinned and they touched glasses. "Good luck pal. Be careful, I'm not sure this one will go for your so-called 'moments' a second time. If she ever stops to think about it she'll realize what she's got going for herself. She's pretty and talented and underneath that low-key exterior, she's ambitious. Eventually she's going to get where she wants to go. You may find yourself having to deal with her success without fucking up."

"Hell, Ken. That's one of the things I love about her. It's like a partnership. I help her with presentations and we go back and forth on the ads I'm working on. It's great."

"Well, I wish you luck. She's good for you. Don't blow it."

Rob signaled the waiter for another drink. "I expect to see you in the judge's office next Friday."

"I wouldn't miss it. Evan's excited as well."

Rob glanced around. "By the way, where is he?"

"He had an appointment, but he'll show up. He always does."

As they were ordering Evan rushed in. "Sorry I'm late. I thought the meeting would never end. I ran the whole way here." He sat down looking flustered and waved at a waiter. "I need a drink."

After catching his breath, he turned to Rob. "Well, congratulations, I guess. Are we really losing you to matrimony?"

Rob nodded.

"Why so soon? Didn't you just decide this a week ago?"

"Why wait? It's not exactly a blow-out at the Plaza. It's just a few of our friends and her parents who are giving us a lunch at Twenty-One. A private room, no less."

"I'm devastated. What about all your other girls? I live vicariously through you."

Before Rob could say anything, Ken cut in, "We'll just have to play that one by ear."

Chapter 6

The first thing Maddie did the Monday after Rob proposed—still a word that sounded strange to her—was go to Irwin's office. Not only was he her boss, he was also an iconic figure in the world of New York publishing and she considered herself fortunate to be working for him. His door was open, but she knocked lightly. He motioned for her to come in.

"What's going on Maddie? Is everything all right? Have a seat."

"Yes Irwin. Everything is great. I just want to ask for a few days off."

"May I ask why?"

She blushed. "I'm getting married."

He sat back, a smile playing on his lips. "So old MacLeod finally popped the question. How long have you two been living together?"

"About a year." He was about the same age as her mother and Harry, yet, not surprisingly, his views were far more contemporary.

"Congratulations. He's a great guy, although a bit of a wild man. Guess he's decided to give it all up. I keep hearing good things about him even though he's abandoned publishing for advertising. I think if any woman can handle him, you can."

She stared at him, remembering Cynthia saying almost the identical words. Taking a breath, she stood up. "Thank you, Irwin. Well, I better get back to work."

"Maddie. Aren't you forgetting something?"

"What?"

"You asked about taking some days off."

"Oh," she said, a bit embarrassed. "Is it okay if I take next Friday and the following Monday and Tuesday off?"

He leaned forward, a look of alarm replacing his smile. "Why so quick? Are you pregnant?"

"No. No, I'm not." she said, her face scarlet. "Since we're both so busy and didn't have time to plan a trip, we decided we'd take a long weekend to go skiing."

He nodded, looking relieved. "You have a great career ahead of you, Maddie. It would be a shame to end it now."

"We haven't even discussed children. With child support and alimony, Rob has enough to deal with. I need to live my own life before I can even begin to think about having a baby."

He nodded. "You're not only a good designer, you're smart. I wish you luck."

She returned to her office hoping she was indeed as smart as he thought.

When she told Jay, he wished her well. She knew he wasn't fond of Rob; he had heard too much gossip about him. He asked her to lunch again but she told him she had to go look for a dress; there were only two weeks before the wedding. He looked at her as though he wanted to ask why, but held his tongue.

=

They were due at the judge's office at eleven. Harry had arranged it.

Rob could see Maddie was nervous. When she put on her dress, he kissed her, telling her she looked beautiful. It had taken days of searching every department store in the city until she found the right one at Bonwit's. It was a calf-length ivory silk, bias cut with tiny covered buttons down the back, just like a wedding dress. At a hundred and twenty dollars, it was far more than she could afford. Nevertheless, she bought it along with shoes to match. *After all, how often does one get married?*

She glanced at the clock. "We should go, Rob. It's almost ten thirty. We have to find a taxi."

He shook his head. "Trust me, ten forty-five is enough time."

She had looked back at him curiously, but by then it was almost time to leave. As she went to the elevator, he said he had forgotten his keys and returned briefly to the apartment.

Downstairs he took her arm, guiding her to a black limousine idling at the curb. She stopped. "Rob, you shouldn't have. This must be costing a fortune."

"It's our wedding day, Maddie. I want it to be special for you." The driver opened the door and on the back seat she saw a small bouquet of lilies and freesia wrapped with yellow and white ribbons. There was also a box with a white carnation for Rob's lapel. With all the excitement she had forgotten about flowers. But he hadn't. Without a word to her, he had not only ordered them, he'd also arranged with the limo company to have the driver pick them up earlier. She hugged him with tears in her eyes.

=

Harry and her mother were already chatting with the judge when they arrived. Suzanne and Andrew had arrived early as well, as had Cynthia, who, despite her complaints, was still with Michael. Ken, Evan and their wives joined them minutes later, along with Larry and Doug. Maddie was sure Larry had no clue about Rob's jealous rant on New Year's Eve.

Strangely enough, all the women were wearing white, except for Maddie and her mother. Her mother wore a deep purple dress, which as Suzanne later quipped, was as close to black as she could get. Maddie was relieved her grandmother had migrated to Florida for the winter.

The ceremony was brief. After handing the judge the marriage license, he said a few words and asked Rob to take out the rings. They were solid gold with a thick finish of what looked roughly like waves and had been hand made by Rob's friend in the village. After he placed the ring on her finger, she did the same. But his ring wasn't made for the third finger on his left hand; it had been sized to fit his pinkie. As she slid it on, she prayed that it had the same significance.

Afterwards, they trooped over to the The Twenty-One Club where her parents had arranged lunch in a private room. After everyone toasted them with champagne her mother pulled her aside. "Why aren't Rob's parents here? And his kids?" she whispered.

Knowing this was coming, Maddie sighed. "He asked them and his sisters. His younger sister is away at graduate school, but his mother and middle sister refused."

Her mother looked shocked. "Why?"

Maddie glanced around, hoping someone would come to her rescue. "Because, Mom, they don't consider this marriage to be valid. Rob never got an annulment and I'm not exactly Catholic. Since his parents weren't coming, there was no way the kids could come."

Her mother frowned. "Is it because you're Jewish?"

"I don't know. To be honest, we've seldom discussed religion. It's not an issue for either of us. But even if I were Catholic, I think it would be a problem."

"Have you even met his parents?"

"Yes. His father was very nice, but his mother didn't even acknowledge me."

Her mother shook her head. "How sad."

"Yes, it is. But Rob seems to be all right with it. Can we go back to the party now?"

"One more thing."

Now what?

"Why is Rob wearing his wedding ring on his pinkie? Who does that?"

"He says it's more comfortable."

Her mother gave her a doubtful look. "And you believe that?"

Do I have a choice? "Mom. It's my wedding day. Let's just enjoy it."

Her mother rolled her eyes and headed for the bar.

=

When they returned home, Rob went to the living room to put down the gifts their friends had brought. Taking off her coat, Maddie noticed a note on the sideboard: "Welcome home, Mrs. MacLeod." She recalled Rob rushing back to the apartment that morning. When she looked up he was watching her. "Are you happy?" he asked.

She went to kiss him. "I've never been so happy. And it's all because of you."

=

"I'm really looking forward to teaching you to ski," Rob said, strapping his skis to the rack of the rental car. "You'll have to start in a beginner's class, but I'm sure you'll love it."

"I hope so," she murmured, not quite so optimistic. All she could think about was the freezing temperatures and trying to navigate with two boards strapped to her feet.

He had reserved a room at a small, charming bed and breakfast at Sugarbush, his favorite ski destination. After what seemed like an endless drive, they arrived at midnight and found the proprietor, an older man with a long grey beard, drowsing in the parlor in front of a dwindling fire. He stood up stiffly and welcomed them, directing them to their room on the second floor.

Tiptoeing cautiously around an enormous, loudly snoring Saint Bernard, they made their way upstairs. Their room was small but cozy with a queen-size bed covered in colorful quilts and soft pillows. Looking out the window, Maddie noticed dots of lights moving high up on the darkened mountain. Rob came up behind her explaining they were snow cats grooming the slopes for the next day. Then he picked her up and carried her to bed.

The next morning, dressed in enough layers to make her look like the Michelin Man, she followed Rob to the ski shop. On the way she glanced anxiously at a thermometer. It read a frigid seven degrees.

After being fitted with leather ski boots, poles and terribly long skis, almost a foot longer than she was, she trailed Rob to the bunny slope where the beginner's class was about to begin. She was ruefully aware that she was by far the tallest; the rest of her classmates were, at most, seven or eight years old.

She was grateful that Rob accompanied her since the first thing she did was fall down. She looked up at the instructor who ignored her. She quickly discovered that contrary to popular belief, not all ski instructors were handsome young guys. This one was in his forties and looked as though he'd had a long, hard night. His name was Carl, not even spelled with a Nordic K.

Rob grinned, helped her get up and re-balanced, which meant leaning on her poles in order to stay vertical. He kissed her, wished her luck and went off to buy a lift ticket. She wanted to beg him to stay, but she was freezing, off balance and too scared to even speak.

After he left, she scraped along after Carl and the kids to what appeared to be a fairly flat area. On the other side was what Carl described as a gentle slope. To her it looked like the Matterhorn. He said the first thing they had to learn was how to stop. She was in full agreement; she wasn't anxious to even start. Knees together, skis kicked out behind, he demonstrated something he called the snowplow. The kids went first. It didn't look so hard. She took one step and fell over.

She looked at Carl. "Can you please help me get up?"

"No," he answered with a sneer. "You have to learn to get up by yourself."

"And how am I supposed to do that?"

"Push off the ground."

"These skis are seven feet long and there's nothing to push against. It's flat here. Help me up." Hearing the desperation in her voice and the giggles of the kids, he came over and hauled her up. That's when she noticed his stale breath and red eyes. She decided she hated him.

She tried a few snowplows, each time clamoring back up the small slope and cursing whomever had invented this insane sport. The kids were having a much easier time of it and she wondered if she could borrow a pair of their skis; shorter looked better. Back at the top of the hill for the fifth or sixth time, as Carl explained the next basic move, she fell again. Lying on her side, ski poles askew, she looked at up him. He shook his head. "Use your poles," he said. "You have to learn to get up by yourself."

If she had a knife she would have crawled to him and despite the skis, stuck it in his boot. At that very moment, Rob glided by as though on air. She yelled at him, "Help me get up."

Laughing, he came over and pulled her to her feet as Carl watched with a malignant snarl. "Just get through the class," Rob whispered with a grin. "I'll show you the rest." *The rest?* She wasn't sure she wanted to learn anything more.

By the end of the class she was frozen and pissed off. But she understood the basics, and most importantly, how to stop. She was relieved to see Rob skiing toward her. Suddenly he was intercepted by a blonde wearing a pink and white ski outfit and a matching ski cap topped with big pink pom-poms. Maddie had noticed her before; she had been standing around and appeared to be looking for someone. Maddie guessed that someone was Rob. She looked very chic—too chic. She tossed her pom-poms and giggled as she flirted with him for a couple of minutes. He smiled, shook his head and pointed to Maddie. Glancing her way, the girl laughed and skied off.

Great. I'm freezing, off balance and holding on to my poles for dear life and he's chatting up a blonde who just laughed at me. She hated her as well.

Rob skied effortlessly over, put his arm around her and pulled her close. After a deep kiss, which banished all her bad thoughts, he asked her to show him what she had learned. She slid a few feet downhill, did a wide turn and completed a very awkward and shaky snowplow. But she stopped! He applauded and she fell down again. Laughing, he once again got her vertical and announced it was time for lunch. After shucking their skis, Rob led her to the restaurant in the base lodge. He ordered a Bloody Mary and Maddie asked for a Coke; she wasn't taking any chances nor was she trusting fate. She said her feet were freezing and after he loosened the laces of her boots, she happily kicked them off. He sat across from her and she tucked her feet between his legs. "Don't move those feet," he said with the hint of a smile. "We are definitely going back out on the slopes." *Damn,* she thought, *not all plans work as we would like them to.*

=

After lunch, he helped her on with the skis and she skidded behind him to a chair lift.

"No," she said looking up what appeared to be a gigantic mountain. "I can't possibly go on that. It's way too high, I'll never make it down alive and I'll freeze to death."

"Maddie, you can. You don't want me going by myself, do you?"

She looked at him, imagining the dire implications of that statement. "No, Rob. I promise I'll do anything you want. Anything. Just not the chair lift."

"Too late," he said laughing. "I already know what you can do for me. Let's go"

He held on to her getting on the lift, which was scary enough, and also getting off, which was pure terror. Out of control, she plowed directly into a pile of snow. Trying not to laugh, Rob helped her out of it and gently brushed her off, promising it would get easier.

When they got to the trail, she knew she was doomed. There was no way she was going to make it down alive. She was convinced that standing on top of a mountain on two planks constituted pure suicide. But Rob had rare moments of extreme patience and this was one of them. He coaxed her into making enormously wide, slow turns until she finally ended, intact, at the bottom the hill. She looked at him with relief and he hugged her. "Let's go."

"Great," she said, leaning down to loosen the bindings.

"No. Back to the lift."

=

That night, she discovered that taking off ski boots was only second to having an orgasm. She lay back on the bed wearing only bikini panties and socks, massaging her still frozen feet while Rob took a shower.

When he emerged from the steamy bathroom, he said, "Maddie, today you learned to ski. I'm proud of you."

"I'm not sure what I did out there was skiing."

"Yes, it was. And you'll do better each day. Eventually you'll love it. It's like sex. The more you do it the better it gets."

"It won't get boring?" she asked, teasing.

He leaned down to kiss her, running a finger over a bare nipple. "With you sex will never be boring," he whispered. As she reached up to kiss him, he backed away. Taken aback, she watched as he walked around the bed and picked up her new furry après ski boots.

"Put these on," he said.

"After I get dressed."

"I didn't want you to get dressed. Take off your panties and put these on."

"What?"

"You heard me. It's time for après ski. Put the boots on."

=

Tuesday night they returned home finding a long rectangular box wrapped in brown paper in front of their door. Maddie took it into the kitchen while Rob brought in their bags. She ripped off the paper and opened it.

"Ohmigod," she screamed, backing away with her hands covering her face. Rob came running in. "What's wrong?"

"Look." She pointed to the box.

Inside was a bouquet of flowers or what had been flowers. They were now unidentifiable, shriveled brown stalks. Looking solemn,

Rob pulled out a small white card: "Congratulations from the MacLeods."

He shook his head. "My foolish mother. She couldn't be bothered to have them sent by telegraph through the flower shop in Darien. She mailed the damn things. I'm sure she thought they'd arrive by Friday. They probably did, but after we left."

He picked up the box and carried it to the trash room. Maddie watched him take it away. Dead flowers were bad enough, but what parent signed a card to their son and his wife in such a cold, terse manner? Although she said nothing to Rob, she couldn't help thinking desiccated flowers were a singularly bad portent for a new marriage.

Chapter 7

In early April Rob took the train to Darien to see the kids and returned with his motorcycle. It had been stored in his parents' garage for the winter and, despite the still cool days and nights, he was impatient to take it out. To him, it signified freedom.

When he arrived at the apartment he kissed Maddie and asked if she wanted to take a ride around the city. He was surprised when she stepped back. "What's wrong?" he asked.

"You smell of booze. I can't believe you were drinking before you drove here."

His placid mood, no doubt owing to that same booze, dissolved in a flash of anger. "What the fuck. Are you kidding me? You never said anything last summer about me driving the bike after a drink or two. I know how much I can drink and if I should drive or not. Is this what happens when you're married? When you were my girl-friend you didn't seem to care, but all of a sudden *my wife* doesn't want me to drink?"

Maddie stared at him wide eyed. "No Rob. I know you know your limits, but still…"

He cut her off. "Back off Maddie. Don't ever try to control me." He grabbed his coat and walked out, slamming the door behind him.

She stood frozen in place, having no idea of what had just happened. Or why.

=

On the sidewalk he glanced at the bike. He would have preferred to get back on it and ride…anywhere, but he had left the key upstairs.

Instead he headed to Allen's; he'd developed a rapport with Stu, the bartender. He hoped he'd be there.

Fortunately, he was and Rob sat at the bar and BS'ed with him, mostly about women and how unnecessarily difficult they tended to be. After a couple of hours and several more fuck-you-Maddie scotches, he returned to the apartment. The cat ran to him, rubbing against his leg and purring. The apartment was silent and it wasn't until he went into the bedroom that he saw Maddie on the bed placidly reading a book. It was "No Exit," a play by that nutcase Sartre. Rob couldn't fathom Maddie's fascination with philosophy in general and existentialism in particular. She often talked about choices and responsibility and assorted other crap. After a drink or two it all sounded the same to him. Unless he could use it in an ad, why the hell would he care anyway?

He didn't, but he had made up his mind to apologize anyway. He sat on the bed next to her. "I'm sorry Maddie. I reacted too quickly. But please cut me some slack. I know how to drink and I know when not to ride the bike. You should know that by now."

She put the book down and looked at him with tears in her eyes. "Don't do this Rob. I was just concerned for you. I'd never try to control you. You know that."

He held her and began to caress her. She may not have chosen to control him, but he knew how to control her.

Chapter 8

The first week in May, John Langer received a call from a small but aggressive company that had developed a line of hair-care products for men. Shampoo specifically for men was unheard of; most men used whatever soap was in their shower or their wife's Prell. This was an entirely new category and John wasn't convinced the world was quite ready for it. Nevertheless, he asked Rob—the marketing group had mentioned his Cosette ads—to sit in at the meeting.

Rob recognized Rachel the second she entered the room; she had been part of the Cosette marketing team the day he had saved the account. He recalled her handing him her card as she left. At the time he hadn't really paid much attention: too much was happening in his life. This time she was introduced as a senior product manager.

During the presentation Rob found it impossible to concentrate; he couldn't stop looking at her. She was tall and curvy with long dark hair and blue eyes and she looked smashing in a white mini dress with black stripes and heels to match. He couldn't really tell her age, but he was pretty sure she had a good ten years on him. Who cared? She was really put together.

When the meeting broke up around noon, Charlie, who always showed up for new account meetings, commented that he thought the product had potential, though how much, he didn't quite know considering it was an unknown and un-researched market. John said they'd discuss it and get back to them. In other words; don't call us, we'll call you. As Rachel left she again handed Rob her card.

Unable to get her out of his mind, he waited until around three and called. Her secretary put him through and she answered in a breathy voice. *Nice.* He congratulated her on her new job and she asked him what he thought of their men's product. Rob replied that it was too early to know what the agency might choose to do. He asked if she'd like to have lunch the next day. She paused, saying she was busy for lunch but perhaps a drink might work.

He sat back and lit a Marlboro. Since he had married Maddie no woman had crossed his path who he gave a damn about. And no doubt, sooner than later, he wouldn't give a damn about Rachel either. But at that moment she was a challenge—one he hadn't had in a while and hadn't missed. Until now.

He told her that was good for him.

=

They agreed to meet at Toot's Shor at six. It was dark, crowded and smoky, and if anyone saw him with Rachel, he was just having a drink with a client. As he expected, she was about ten minutes late. It was a well-known fact that fashionable New York women preferred to make an entrance, therefore never arriving first. She strode in wearing a black mini dress, looking even better than she had the day before. A couple of guys at the bar turned to glance at her.

He ordered drinks and they laughed about the coincidence of meeting twice in client meetings. Picking up her Chivas on the rocks, she sat back, her look and voice seductive. "I was surprised you never called after we met, all too briefly, at the Cosette presentation."

"Rachel, I did think about it. But my life was in chaos at the time."

She smiled. "I assume it's not so chaotic now?"

He shook his head. "Nope. Not chaotic at all."

"I hear you got married."

He sipped his drink. "Yes. I did."

Changing the subject, she asked. "So tell me your opinion of the meeting yesterday. Do you think LRG is interested?"

"To be honest, it's an odd product. I think John will want to find out if there's a market for men's hair products before we take it on. Either way, it's not my decision. I'm just a lowly art director."

"Not so lowly from what I hear."

He took out a Marlboro and offered her one. She took it, guiding his hand as he lit it. He asked if she'd like to join him for dinner.

She looked directly back at him with a confident smile. "I'm not sure, Rob. Are we on the same page?"

He stared at her. *That was fast. I didn't even have to make a move.* Covering her hand with his, he said, "I believe we are."

"Then maybe we should skip dinner." Her voice was husky, almost a purr.

He nodded and put his drink down. "I have to make a call."

On their way out, the same guys at the bar gave him approving nods.

They barely made it out of the cab before she was all over him. As she slammed her front door he moved her against the wall and began kissing her. She kicked off her panties and he took her right there, standing with one of her legs wrapped around him. It was intense and quick and somewhat awkward, as fucking against walls tends to be. They moved to the bedroom where they continued almost non-stop for another hour or so. When they finally lay back, she asked if he wanted a drink. Lighting two cigarettes, he handed her one, saying that would be great.

He checked his watch. It was only around ten; he could still get home without Maddie knowing. But then Rachel returned, her long hair falling wildly around her face and wearing only a tiny dressing gown that barely covered her butt. She was holding two stemmed glasses and a pitcher of martinis.

Chapter 9

When Rob had called Maddie he told her the meeting on their new account was running late and not to wait for dinner. He had sounded sincere and her usually sharp instincts had remained passive.

So why, after fewer than three months of marriage, was she pacing her apartment at two in the morning with tears in her eyes.

She was still wide awake at sunrise, propped up against pillows, an unread book on her lap and the cat warm against her leg. By then disbelief had morphed into anxiety and churning humiliation. She glanced at the clock having no doubt, judging by his last performance that he'd be showing up shortly.

As before, she wondered briefly if something terrible had happened to him. *Not something, more likely someone.* She went into the kitchen and poured a glass of orange juice, trying to recall if there was something she had done that had made him do this, whatever "this" was. There had been no real problems that they hadn't been able to work out and they seldom argued. They made love every night so what was he seeking that she couldn't give him?

Hearing the lock turn, she went back into the bedroom and sat on the bed.

"How could you?" she asked, unable to stop the tears running down her face.

He shook his head, his voice placating. "I didn't do anything, Maddie. I swear to you that all I did was get drunk and ended up sleeping it off at the office. I'm sorry."

He sat down next to her, putting his arm tentatively around her shoulder. She shrugged him off and moved away. "What's going on here Rob? How can you say you love me and then stay out all night without even calling? Or maybe it would be better to ask, why is it you stay out all night at all?"

"Maddie," he pleaded. "It just happened, I didn't plan it. I love you and I had no intention of hurting you. After the meeting I went out for a few drinks with some of the guys and that led to a few more. You know how it goes; suddenly it was three in the morning and we were all drunk. It was easier to go back to the office and camp out there. I must have passed out."

She got off the bed and faced him. "No. I don't know how it goes. You never pass out when you're with me, so why does it only happen when you're out with the guys? Come to think of it, has there ever been one night that you were too drunk to make love? So maybe it's more than just the guys or perhaps you should stop drinking so much—it seems to be getting in the way of this relationship." Although she had begun talking quietly, she was practically shouting by the end of it. She saw his eyes flicker and knew she had struck a nerve. But why should she suffer because he had one, a few, or even many too many drinks.

"I think you'd better come up with something more original than 'sleeping at the office.' You used that one last time."

He sighed and shook his head. He looked beaten down. "What do you want me to say?"

Listening to his lies made her feel even more hollow than she had felt all night waiting for him. She wanted to scream, *How about the truth?* But stopped, unsure she was ready to hear it.

"Maddie, I need you in my life. I promise it won't happen again."

Of course it won't. Not until the next time. There was a choice in that thought: accept his ludicrous explanations or tell him to get out. She already knew her decision but wished she was strong enough to tell him to take his clothes and leave.

She went to the living room window and opened it, breathing in fresh air.

Seconds later he followed, putting his arms around her. "This isn't getting us anywhere. It's almost six, we can sleep for an hour. I love you and I promise everything will be all right." He took her hand, leading her back to bed. He went into the bathroom and took a shower. By the time he came out she was dozing. He lay down and pulled her close to his naked body. She didn't move and in seconds she heard his deep, regular breathing.

=

Usually he drove her to work on the bike, but that morning she told him she preferred to walk. He looked chagrinned and continued to apologize. She slammed the door as she left.

When she arrived at the office, she sat down and stared unseeing at her drawing board until Jay came over.

"What's wrong?" he asked. "And why are you wearing dark glasses?"

"I don't know," she answered, taking them off.

He pulled a chair next to her. "Have you been crying? Is this about Rob? Do you want to talk about it?"

She shook her head. "It's not worth talking about."

"Come on. Let's get some coffee. Then we can go over the forms that have to be released to the printer."

She nodded, "Give me a minute." She was grateful that Jay had become friendlier, but she was far from ready to confide in him. This was no time to feel sorry for herself. Both books were nearing the deadline for completion and they had to prepare at least half the approved layouts to send the printer for page proofs. In September they were scheduled to go to Virginia for several days to oversee their books being printed. Having never been on press before, she was looking forward to it. If it could have been the next day, she would have welcomed it.

=

When she arrived home that night she was surprised to find Rob already there. He handed her a bunch of white roses and hugged her, apologizing again. He already had a beer in his hand and asked if she wanted a drink. She shook her head and backing away, thanked him for the roses. Seeing his smile, she realized he was already thinking about something else or, more likely, he had put last night behind him and no doubt expected her to as well. *Probably both.*

"Maddie," he said sounding excited, "I have a surprise for you. I know how much you like the beach so I've taken a half share in a house on Fire Island. Our first weekend is Memorial Day."

She looked at him aghast. "Rob. How are we going to afford that? You're behind on your alimony." It was something he would never have told her; the only reason she had found out was because whenever he was even a few days late Allison invariably called. It didn't matter who answered the phone, she'd threaten and scream at either of them.

A look of irritation replaced his smile, like a small child whose candy has been taken away. "Let me deal with that," he said sounding petulant. "It's every other weekend. The house is in Fair Harbor and it's only four bedrooms. I took the last one. Come on, it'll be a blast. You'll love it."

"How did you find out about it?"

"The guy who runs the house is a friend of Larry's."

"Larry. Is he in the house?"

His eyes narrowed in annoyance. "No, Maddie. He's going to Ocean Beach. A lot of people at the agency have houses in Fire Island."

Ocean Beach, Fair Harbor. How nice. Fire Island was obviously the cool place to be. The only problem was he had just committed to a share in a house that must have cost a couple of thousand dollars. She wondered where all that money had suddenly come from.

Rather than asking questions, which would only create another confrontation, she smiled and said, "Thank you."

Chapter 10

The Friday evening of Memorial Day weekend they took the train to Bay Shore. Despite arranging for the superintendent to feed Cat, Rob knew she'd still turn her tail to them when they got home. They lugged their duffle bag on the ferry and went up to the top deck where they watched a glowing orange sunset that promised a spectacular weekend.

By then Maddie's anger had cooled and she had finally shown some excitement getting everything together for the long weekend on the beach. Since his night with Rachel he'd made sure to leave the office by seven, waiting until he got home for that first drink. He hadn't called Rachel. He had gotten the immediate satisfaction he desired but wasn't about to endanger his relationship with Maddie any more than he already had. And yet he wasn't surprised when Rachel phoned a few days later asking if everything was all right and wondering why he hadn't called. He told her it had been great but he had to cool it for a while. In that breathy voice, she said she understood and suggested they meet for lunch at her place. He considered it for about five seconds and said he'd be there at twelve thirty. He'd get his rocks off, grab a sandwich and return to work; and no fighting with Maddie. Sounded pretty cool.

After returning to the office, far more satisfied and relaxed than when he left, he thought about Maddie. Why couldn't women comprehend that guys just had to get out there and do their thing once in a while? He required a lot of sex and when he saw a woman who turned him on he simply had to have her. More often than not it was a moment, quickly forgotten. Monogamy didn't work, certainly not for him or for most of his friends. They'd all had flings at one time or another.

In truth, at the beginning, Maddie's attraction for him had been as strongly sexual as his attraction for her: a raw desire seeking nothing more than immediate satisfaction. And yet if he tried to explain, she would ask the obvious: "Then why get married?" His answer would have been simple: "Because I love you and I want us to be part of one another's lives, hopefully forever." When he told her he saw no ending to their relationship, he meant every word of it.

Yet he greatly doubted she'd understand or accept that message. He'd just have to keep winging it and try not to fuck up. Sometimes that proved to be impossible.

=

Arriving at the town of Fair Harbor, if indeed a general store, a ramshackle café and a liquor store could be called a town, they threw their duffle bag into one of the red wagons that appeared to be Fire Island's sole conveyance.

They found Arnie and his girlfriend Susie sitting on the porch having a couple of cold ones. After helping Rob bring the duffle in, Arnie said, "Everyone else is on the next ferry. Come back outside; it's time for a drink."

Maddie shook Arnie's hand, aware that practically the first words out of his mouth had to do with drinking. It was going to be a wet summer, the ocean no doubt taking a back seat to booze. Rob took a beer from the fridge and Maddie said she'd make the bed and put their stuff away.

Their room was stark white and sparse; just a bed, a scuffed wooden chest with a mirror over it and two night tables with small tin lamps. Above the bed were two high, horizontal windows and on the left wall a vertical one overlooking a slice of beach.

After making the beds Maddie returned to the porch and sat on the steps. Susie had gone inside, but Arnie and Rob were lounging in old Adirondack chairs and talking quietly. The night was pleasantly warm for the end of May and the ocean shimmered in the light of a full moon. Arnie told them he had not only run the house for the past four summers but was the chief cook as well. Maddie was to discover that he was also the instigator of pranks.

An hour later, four more people arrived all pulling the ubiquitous red wagons piled with suitcases. Ted and Carla were lawyers and in their early thirties. The other two were young women about Maddie's age who were sharing a room. Maddie overheard Arnie whisper to Rob that they had small tits. She rolled her eyes. *Tits, ass, legs. Is that all we are?*

=

One weekend in late June there were warnings a hurricane might brush the New York coastline. The radio reports were sketchy; none of the weather people seemed quite sure which way it would go. Since no one had any desire to return to the city, they all decided to stick it out. Saturday was hot and sunny, but by nightfall heavy clouds began rolling in. In anticipation they lit candles and began telling their own special hurricane stories, and of course, drinking like there was no tomorrow.

The next morning despite waking to bright sunshine, Rob declared there was no rush to get out of bed and reached for Maddie for, as he liked to say, a quickie. She would just as soon have preferred to get a quick coffee but knew he'd be in a spiteful mood all day if she refused. Denying Rob was seldom a peaceful option.

A short while later, just as they were getting up, someone yelled "hurricane" and a cascade of water poured through the windows above the bed. They both leaped away in shock. Neither had gotten very wet. The bed, however, was soaked. Maddie started laughing, but Rob, furious, grabbed his cut-offs and stormed out of the room. Outside she heard shouts, water splashing and then raucous laughter. By the time she went outside, arms full of soggy sheets and pillows, Arnie, Ted and Rob were sitting on the porch nursing Bloody Marys.

=

The weekends they didn't go to Fire Island, Rob went to Darien, spending Saturday with Val and Tommy and returning that night. Occasionally Maddie went with him. Other times, when he had matters to discuss with Allison or wanted to take the kids to their grandparents, he went by himself. She never questioned him, always saying she understood and to hug them for her. One weekend in July he casually mentioned that he wanted to have dinner with his parents and stay overnight. Although she was curious as to why he couldn't have dinner and then return home, she chose not to make an issue of it.

Two weeks later he asked her to come with him to Connecticut, saying he wanted to take the kids to the beach in Westport. She had been thrilled, her previous doubts vanishing in an instant.

They drove first to his parents' house to borrow his father's car. His father came outside, gave Maddie a hug, and handed Rob the keys. She was relieved; she had no intention of ever going into that house again.

When they arrived at Allison's, the kids practically flew out the front door and, armed with pails and shovels, piled excitedly into the car.

At the beach they grabbed Rob's hands and ran shrieking into the chilly water leaving Maddie stranded with toys, towels and assorted bags to find an open spot to perch. Twenty minutes later, after emerging slightly blue and shivering, she toweled them off and had them change into dry bathing suits. Rob yawned, declared that he needed a nap and lay back on his towel.

After digging holes and filling up buckets with sand, the kids announced they were hungry. Once again Maddie toweled them off and unpacked sandwiches they had picked up on the way. After nudging Rob to wake up and get some sodas, she took a breath, unused to the constant demands of small children. *If this is what it's like being a mother, working is definitely preferable. Not to mention a lot easier.*

Val took a bite of her sandwich and looked up at Maddie, her face unusually serious. "I'm happy you came with us today Maddie. We haven't seen Daddy in a long time."

"Val, he was here with you two weeks ago. Don't you remember?"

Val shook her head. "No, he wasn't. He called and said he had to do something."

Maddie felt a sudden chill. Val was six; wasn't it possible she had forgotten? Or was that overnight at his parents' something else entirely? She felt the thread coiling again, but brushed it away; there was no point in ruining the day with her doubts, no matter how strong they were.

Despite being tumbled in small waves and tears of frustration at collapsing sand castles, both Val and Tommy deemed the day, "super-duper fun." After returning them, tired and sandy, to their mother, Maddie mentioned what Val had said to her. With no change of expression, Rob merely shrugged. "Why are you even mentioning this? Val is six. She has no sense of time. Of course I was here two weeks ago."

Maddie took a breath, thinking a six-year-old suddenly seemed far more credible than her husband. Or was it just her imagination?

Chapter 11

Rob had been assigned what he considered another dubious product—a shaving cream targeted specifically to women. Although its potential was still being researched, he and Doug were under pressure to prepare for the pitch. He was becoming frustrated; it was time to get on something other than women's products.

He appealed to John who, with a smile proclaimed that although women and their various products seemed to be his special gift, said he would consider him for a French Brandy client they were having preliminary discussions with.

As he was about to leave, John asked, "Will you be ready with the shaving cream presentation tomorrow?"

"Yes. But I'm leaving early tonight. It's Maddie's birthday and I surprised her with tickets to *Hair*."

John shook his head. "Lucky you. My wife's been bugging me about taking her, but I'm afraid she might be shocked at seeing nudity on stage. I keep telling her it's sold out."

=

Maddie called in the afternoon telling him she was running late and would meet him at the theater.

"No, Maddie," he said, sounding concerned. "It's rough in Times Square. Better to meet me on the corner of Forty-Sixth and Sixth. We'll walk over together."

He was waiting and took her hand. They had just reached the corner of Forty-Seventh Street and Broadway when a young woman sidled up to Rob. "Wanna party?" she asked in a breathy voice.

Maddie grabbed Rob's arm, not believing a hooker would approach a man walking with a woman and proposition him so brazenly.

"I have a friend if you want a threesome," she announced, glancing at a redhead in hot pants lurking nearby.

Without missing a beat, Rob pointed across the street and shouted, "Get over there. This is my side of the street."

The girl shrunk back, staring at him in wide-eyed shock. With a smile he took Maddie's hand and continued walking.

"Rob. What the hell was that?"

"Maddie, it happens all the time. That's why I wanted you to meet me. Times Square has become a zoo populated with junkies, pimps and prostitutes. I was walking up Sixth Avenue one day after work when one cruised by in a Cadillac. She lowered the window and asked me to jump in. I think her pimp was at the wheel."

"Are you kidding? You never told me that."

"It wasn't important. It's happened to every guy in the office."

=

After the show they had dinner at Sardi's. Sitting under caricatures of Ava Gardner and Mickey Rooney, Maddie remarked that she couldn't get over the nudity in the last act. "I'm surprised it got through the censors."

Rob laughed. "That was cool but there was nothing sexual about it. I heard it was up to the actors whether they wanted to take their clothes off or not."

"Well, I loved it. It was a great birthday present," she said giving him a kiss.

=

When they arrived home, Rob took her in his arms and began to undress her. She reached for his shirt buttons but he gently removed her hands. "Let me do this. This is still your special night and I have another surprise for you."

She looked at him with suspicion. "What is it?"

"Be patient, Maddie," he said with a grin.

In bed he told her to lie back and close her eyes. Taking the ribbons from under his pillow he tied her wrists as he had before, over her head.

She opened her eyes. "What are you doing?" she whispered.

"Shhh. Maddie. No talking. Close your eyes."

When she did, he caressed and teased with his tongue and fingers until he felt her relax and sigh with pleasure. Making sure her eyes were still shut, he took out a white plastic vibrator from the nightstand. Gently parting her legs, he turned it on, touching her most sensitive place. She jumped in surprise, her eyes wide. "Rob. What …?"

Holding it in place he leaned in to kiss her. "Just lie back. Feel what I'm doing to you."

"Oh God," she whispered. "What is it?"

He moved it and she gasped. "It doesn't matter. Just tell me what you want me to do."

She was breathing heavily and he knew she was ready for him, but she had to say it; she had to beg.

Arching her back, she whispered, "I want you."

"I know you do, Maddie," he murmured, sucking her nipples. "Now tell me exactly what you want me to do."

"Make love to me, Rob."

"No. I want to hear more."

Breathless: "Fuck me. You know what I want."

Touching his lips to hers, he whispered, "Not yet. You have to wait." He intended to keep her on the edge for as long as he could. He waited, playing with her until her hunger became his and he was barely able to control himself.

As he entered her she went wild, clinging to him in a fit of intense craving. He pulled her up to sit on his lap, knowing she would feel him even more. They came together in a long and violent orgasm.

Trying to catch her breath, she stretched out close to him. "What did you do to me?" He kissed her deeply. "You just had the best sex you ever had. And I promise it will only get better."

Chapter 12

It was Monday night, a week after her birthday and the day before she was to leave for Virginia. After ten months of work, both her book and Jay's were about to be printed. When Rob called at six saying he had a meeting and not to plan on dinner, something in his voice sparked her instincts. She seldom questioned him, but this time she pointedly asked him why.

Without hesitation, he responded, "We're meeting with a potential men's product client. The entire team is required to be there."

"Okay, Rob. Please don't be too late. I'm leaving tomorrow."

"I'm aware of that Maddie. Don't sweat it."

After packing, she made a sandwich and turned on the TV, finding *Citizen Kane* on channel nine. After she finished, she lay down, only to awaken several hours later to the cat asleep against her leg and a public service announcement on the screen. Alarmed, she sat up; not only was Rob not home, he hadn't called. As the all-too-familiar tension begin to surface, all she could think was they had spent half the weekend making love and suddenly he wasn't coming home. Again.

A couple of hours later she heard the door open. The cat flew off the bed as Rob walked in.

This time she wasn't passive; she shouted, "Where the hell have you been?"

His stare was blank, unconcerned. "Calm down Maddie. It's not five in the morning. We had our meeting and went out for dinner and a few drinks. I'm here, aren't I?"

"It's after two. You expect me to believe, again, that you were just out with the guys?"

"First of all, stop shouting at me. And you can choose to believe it or not."

His tone was unusually aggressive, not apologetic as before. They faced each other, Maddie becoming aware that she was seeing something new; his usual defensive posture had suddenly turned offensive as if he was trying to make her feel she had no right to question him about coming home at only two as opposed to five in the morning. Rather than have a screaming argument she went to the living room to calm down. He didn't follow her.

Frustrated, she returned to the bedroom. He was sitting on the bed sipping a beer. She lay down with her back to him.

He finished his beer and put the bottle on the night table. "Look Maddie, I should have called, but you know when I drink time gets away from me. I'm sorry. Come on, don't be angry. You know I love you."

"Rob, please. I just want to sleep. I have a long day ahead of me."

"Oh yeah, you're leaving tomorrow. Come on, just one kiss."

She turned over, reluctantly giving in to him. As he kissed her, she picked up a light scent; one she happened to know well. It was Joy, one of her mother's favorite fragrances. Furious, she got out of bed. "Did your meeting include getting close to someone wearing perfume?" she asked through gritted teeth.

"What are you talking about?"

"You stink of Joy. Maybe you should take a shower after you screw someone."

She picked up her pillow and stamped into the living room.

He followed a second later, his tone softer, the aggression gone. "Come on Maddie. There was a girl at the bar who was having a birthday. She was smashed and kissing everyone. It was nothing."

"She unbuttoned your shirt and rubbed against your chest? Are you kidding me?"

He shrugged. "She was wearing a lot of perfume I guess."

"You'll have to do better than that."

"I can't Maddie. That's what happened." He went into the bathroom where she heard water running. He came out drying his face and neck.

"Come back to bed. You can't sleep out here."

She glared at him. "Then you sleep here."

"You already know I don't sleep on couches. Please, Maddie."

She sighed, knowing she didn't have much choice. Beginning with her flight to Washington, tomorrow was going to be a long day. The cat realigned herself between the two of them and ignoring Rob's entreaties for kisses, she fell into a fitful sleep.

=

Jay had said he'd meet her in the Eastern Airlines lounge at La Guardia at ten. At nine thirty, after making sure the cat had water and food, she dragged her suitcase to the door. On the sideboard Rob had left a note: "I love you today." She crumpled it up and threw it into the trash.

In Washington, an air-conditioned car was waiting. Maddie was grateful; in the minute it had taken to descend the stairs from the plane to the tarmac, the heat and humidity had enveloped her like a soggy blanket. New York had been hot and sticky when they left, but it was cool and dry compared to this. After a blissful air-conditioned hour, the driver dropped them at their hotel in rural Virginia, advising them to get settled. He said the presses ran twenty-four hours so he or another driver would be back for them, no matter what time of the day or night.

After they checked in Maddie glanced around the featureless lobby seeing a restaurant and a bar, now closed and dark. But through a large window a turquoise pool surrounded by a flowering garden beckoned. She told Jay she'd unpack and go for a swim.

After an all-too-short half hour he came to get her saying they had to go. As she got out of the pool she suddenly felt self-conscious, aware that he was watching her.

They were greeted by Mr. Ross, the production director who informed them that the first form of Maddie's book was just beginning to run. In the reception area she could already hear the heavy thrum of the presses. When he opened the door to the pressroom a wave of sound hit her with an almost physical force—a deep chugging beyond anything she had ever experienced. Standing too nearby to a rapidly speeding train would be a close description, and the press wasn't even up to full speed yet.

What surprised her most was the sheer size and majesty of a Heidelberg web press. It was almost a New York block long with an enormous roll of paper at the far end. Several pressmen, dwarfed by the sheer size, were climbing on it, adjusting dials as it chugged along slowly. Jay glanced at her and smiled. She returned his smile, her eyes wide in awe of the scene before her. It wasn't just the machine, it was the comprehension that it was her design, her book with her name in it that was at that very moment about to become real and all those people were there to make it happen.

The first pages began to come up: the text grey, the color flat and uneven. The press began to rev up, the volume increasing as the pages began to move faster. After about fifteen minutes, the pressman sliced off a form and took it to a light table. The colors had become more vivid, but still off in certain places. After more adjustments and another forty-five minutes, they finally had it right. The pressman pushed some buttons and the machine came up to full speed. No longer aware of the sound Maddie stared, mesmerized at white glossy paper becoming pages with color and text as they sped through the rollers.

Outside, the silence hit her with the same intensity as the clamor they had just left, the roar receding to a gentler drone of nearby traffic mingling with the twittering of birds. Mr. Ross said they wouldn't be called again until sometime that evening. Since there was nothing else to do, they decided to spend what was left of the afternoon sitting at the pool.

After taking adjoining chaises and talking briefly about the printing plant, Jay lay back and closed his eyes. Trying to break what seemed like an awkward silence, Maddie asked where he had grown up.

"Huntington. On Long Island."

"Is your family still there?"

This time he glanced at her. "Yes. My parents, brother and three sisters all live within a couple of miles of each other."

"I didn't realize you came from a large family," she said, trying to keep the conversation going.

He seemed to lighten up. "I'm the youngest of five. Not unusual for an Irish family, although I've always believed I was an unplanned accident. By the time I came along, my brother was in his late teens and my mother and sisters treated me like a little prince." He laughed. "Not a bad way to grow up. The best part was as I got older they loved having me draw pictures of them. My mother and sisters recognized my talent, if you will, and encouraged me."

"How about your father?" she asked, thinking of Rob's parents and how he had told her of their arguments with him about wanting to go to art school.

"When I was sixteen, my father, who runs a large corporate accounting firm, took me into his den, poured a couple of Irish whiskeys and sat me down for a "man-to-man" talk. Not about sex, you understand; it was a little late for that. He told me that since my brother was well ensconced in his accounting firm it was all right with him if I wanted, in his words, 'to waste a couple of years at art school.' His only warning was about those 'queer boys' that I should watch out for. I assured him it wasn't a problem. They might be my friends but not my boyfriends. Still, he was firmly convinced I'd come to my senses and ask to join the family business."

Maddie looked at him with a grimace. "You? An accountant?"

He shook his head. "But it turned out great. The day I graduated he was the first to congratulate me, especially since I already had gotten a job. He was proud of me."

"You're kidding. A job? Where?"

"You won't believe this. At Harper's Bazaar," he said with a wide grin. "The creative director, Alexey Brodovitch hired me. The man himself. I was the only male assistant in a sea of women."

Maddie smiled, imagining this great looking guy at a fashion magazine. She was surprised they ever let him leave.

"How lucky for you. He's considered the father of modern magazine design. He must have been amazing to work for."

"He was, although it was his last year."

"Do you see your family much?" she asked.

"Yeah. Almost every Sunday. We all go to my parents' house for dinner. My sisters and brother are all married and have kids. It's pretty hectic."

Maddie smiled, thinking how different his life was from hers and Rob's with their fractious parents.

"Now, Maddie. Tell me about you."

Maddie gave him the short form: California to New York to art school in Providence where she had majored in illustration, hoping to come to New York to freelance for magazines that, by the time she graduated, were moving, thanks in part to the very same Brodovitch, from illustration to photography. "It was only in retrospect that I realized I should have taken graphic design." She shrugged. "I learned as I went along."

He smiled. "It couldn't have been too difficult for you."

She shook her head. "No. Not at all. I loved working at *Today's Bride*. That's what made it easy. I did get to illustrate a few book covers, but I knew it would never be enough to support myself."

He nodded and lay back. "I know what you mean. By the way, how's Rob?"

The question was unexpected. Still unsettled from the night before, she said he was fine. She had no desire to discuss him with Jay. Since he had brought up Rob, she in turn, asked him about his girlfriend. He looked at her in surprise. "What girlfriend?"

"Sorry," she said, her face reddening. "I thought you were seeing someone."

"Well, I guess you could say I was. But it seems every time I meet a girl I like, after a few dates she wants to discuss the relationship. What relationship? A few dates do not make a relationship. Why can't women just take it slow? What's the rush? It's a turnoff." He paused and turned to her. "Sorry, I didn't mean to get into a rant."

"Maybe you just haven't met the right girl yet."

He shook his head and stood up. "Not sure there is one. All the good ones are married." He dove into the pool.

She watched him, thinking briefly about his comment and that he looked lean and strong in his swim trunks. She was sure he must have had relationships with scores of women. He reminded her of Danny; two overly cautious men who kept their emotions in check. Her thoughts turned to Rob, wondering why whenever things were really good between them, he somehow created a situation where they'd end up in a confrontation. She decided she'd try to talk with him about it when she got home.

=

At nine thirty she and Jay were finishing dinner when the bellman ran in saying the plant had called and the driver would pick them up in ten minutes. By the time they returned to the hotel it was after one in the morning and they were both exhausted.

The next two days were a repetition of the first, except for Wednesday night when they were called at three a.m.

They spent most of Thursday at the plant watching her book finish printing and Jay's just beginning. By the time they returned to the hotel they were starving and went straight to dinner. Maddie was scheduled to leave the next day, while Jay would remain until Saturday to finish up his book. As they left the restaurant, he asked if she would join him for a drink. It wasn't late and since they were still on call she agreed. They found a booth in a corner of the dimly lit bar and Jay ordered B&B's. Touching his glass to hers, he said he had a confession to make.

Maddie frowned. "A confession?"

"You probably weren't aware of this, but when you first began working at American Heritage I didn't like you. I actually told Irwin I thought he made a mistake by hiring you."

"Are you kidding? It was so obvious. You never said a word to me unless you had to. I didn't understand why."

"To be honest, I resented you being there. We'd never had a female art director and even though Irwin interviewed a couple of other girls, they didn't look like you. To me you didn't look like a book designer."

"And what exactly does a book designer look like? Does one have to wear pants?"

"No, Maddie. Not at all. I know it sounds stupid, but in your miniskirt you looked like a model or an actress, not an artist."

"Everyone wears miniskirts," she said with a grin.

"True. But they don't all have legs like yours."

"Thank you Jay. Are you telling me my legs are why you basically ignored me?"

"Actually, I didn't. I was very aware of you and your work. I was surprised that you didn't follow the grid. More important, you weren't afraid to take chances."

"I only did what was asked of me."

"Yes, but I bet you didn't know there were two art directors who tried to design that book before you. They were both let go. They couldn't cut it."

She looked at him with surprise. "I didn't know that. Why didn't you do it?"

"I was already involved in a couple of other projects and Irwin said he wanted a fresh take on it. You gave him something new, something no one had done before." She gave him a cautious smile. "So, am I to assume you like the book?"

"Yes, Maddie," he said covering her hand with his. "I like your book and I like you. Probably more than I should."

She stopped breathing and stared back at him. This was unexpected. They were basically co-workers, barely even friends. And yet she didn't move her hand.

Taking her face in his hands, he kissed her gently.

She took a breath. "Jay."

He kissed her again and put a finger to her lips. "Don't say a word."

The bellman suddenly appeared; the car was waiting.

=

The entire way to the plant and back, neither said a word. When Jay took her hand, she didn't pull away. She looked out the window, the darkness unable to provide answers to questions she was sure should not be asked.

By the time they returned to the hotel it was after midnight. The night pressman had told them they didn't have to be back until nine the next morning.

As they entered the lobby, Jay turned to her. "Do you want to have a drink?"

"I don't know. Do you?"

"No," he said taking her hand. In the elevator she held her breath, asking herself what the hell was she doing. She decided that whatever it was, she wanted to do it. In his room he took his jacket off, throwing on a chair. She stood frozen, unsure whether to stay or go. He put his hands on her shoulders, giving her a light kiss. She pulled back, whispering, "I don't know, Jay."

"Maddie, there's nothing to know." Drawing her into his arms, his kisses became more assertive. He unzipped her dress and un-hurried, he caressed her as though she were made of glass. Moving her to the bed, his kisses became insistent, his hands stronger and probing. She lay back letting sensation build and reached for him. He whispered, "No," and moving back, parted her legs. Entering her, he kissed her deeply. She gasped and wrapped her legs around him, pulling him closer. He came quickly but waited, holding her tight even as her nails raked his back. Finally moaning and calling his name, she lay back with a sigh.

Still entwined, Jay whispered, "You are amazing."

"I thought you didn't like me."

"Think again, Maddie. But now we have a problem."

"A problem?"

"I want more of you."

"I don't know, Jay. In New York this will be impossible."

He hugged her. "Maybe it doesn't have to be. We'll work something out. This can't be our only time together." As he leaned over to kiss her, the phone rang, startling them both.

"That can't be the plant," Maddie said. "They told us we had until tomorrow morning."

As Jay turned to pick it up, it suddenly dawned on her who might be calling. "Oh, please. No," she whispered.

Jay put his finger to his lips and said a tentative, "Hello."

He glanced at her quickly, too quickly. "Rob," he said, steadying his voice. "No. Of course she's not here. We just came back from the printer. I thought she went back to her room." He stopped and shook his head. "Yes. I know it's late, but there's a garden here. Maybe she went out for some air."

Maddie sat up and covered herself as though Rob had just walked into the room. Still looking at her, Jay said, "I'll go down and look for her. Do you want me to have her call you? Okay then." He hung up.

They stared at one another until she broke the strained silence. "It's like he knows. What am I going to do?"

"Maddie, go back to your room and wait till he calls or call him. Tell him you went out for a walk. It will be fine."

"You don't know him. It won't be fine."

"Do you want me to come with you?"

"No. I have to deal with this myself," she said, hunting around the rumpled covers for her clothes. At the door, Jay put his arms around her. "I'm sorry," he said.

"You know what? I'm not." She kissed him. "I'm really not."

"Not about making love. I'm sorry you have to leave me."

=

She wasn't in her room five minutes when the phone rang. Picking it up, she could already hear Rob yelling, calling her every derogatory name he could think of. And, as she was well aware, he had quite an extensive vocabulary in that regard.

"You fucking cunt. I called you at the hotel hours ago. They said you had gone to the printer, so I left a message. Then," he snarled sarcastically, "I called the printing plant and was told you had just left. When I called the hotel again and you didn't answer the phone in your room, I figured you were with Jay, probably in bed with him. Am I getting it right so far, bitch?"

Trembling, she held the phone away from her ear. What was most astonishing was his strange clairvoyance, no doubt the result of his own years of philandering. In a weak, shaky voice, she said, "Stop it Rob. You have to stop calling me names. I haven't done anything wrong." *Not anything you haven't already done.* "And, by the way, why are you calling at two in the morning? Perhaps you'd like to tell me what you've been up to tonight?"

That made him even angrier as she knew it would and he started calling her names again. This time she wasn't about to be intimidated and while he was still shouting, she said she'd see him tomorrow and hung up. Strangely there was no guilt. Time and place had always played a significant role in her life and she had always followed her instincts, promising herself there would be no regrets. Although she didn't regret one second of this night, she thought, sardonically, that the timing could certainly have been better.

Now she'd have to deny it to Rob, actually lie to him. She cringed at the thought. But if she wanted to keep her marriage together there was no choice. Rob's jealous anger at seeing her just talking with another man would no doubt pale compared to what he considered a betrayal. Not that she had any intention of ever confessing that she had slept with Jay; confession would only create more pain. She asked herself if a "walk in a garden" correlated to his well-used excuse of "sleeping in the office." Not that it really mattered. What did matter was that the next days and weeks were going to be spent trying to pacify an enraged Rob.

=

After the final press run the next morning, Jay insisted on accompanying her to the airport, holding her hand the entire way. At the departure gate he gave her a lingering kiss, which despite her anxiety, she felt all the way to her toes. "Are you going to be all right, Maddie? I can come with you if you want."

She touched his face. "There's nothing you can do, Jay."

"Then I guess I'll have to wait to see you Monday," he said, finally letting her go.

She walked nervously out to the tarmac, but before ascending the stairs to the plane, she looked back. Jay was still there. He waved and she waved back, his small gesture renewing her confidence.

=

She unlocked the door cautiously and breathed a sigh of relief that Rob wasn't home. Cat greeted her with her customary leg rub and as she dropped her keys on the sideboard she noticed an ashtray with a note under it. Curious, she picked it up and looked closer. It contained what appeared to be short pieces of hair. Having no idea what she was looking at, she put it down and read the note: "You've had the best, now here's the rest." *What?* She looked in the ashtray again and with a shock realized the clippings weren't just hair, they were pubic hair. She stared at it, trying to imagine Rob in a rage grabbing a scissor and snipping what he called his "short hairs." She didn't know whether to laugh or cry.

She was nervous but composed when, just after seven, she heard the front door open. Having positioned herself strategically in a corner of the couch, she took a deep breath of anticipation heavily tinged with fear. Rob stared at her, his face a mask of anger. Maintaining the outwardly placid demeanor she had worked on all afternoon, she looked back at him and silently sipped a glass of wine. Cat jumped off the couch and ran to him. He leaned down to pet her and went to put his keys on the sideboard. He returned holding the ashtray. "Did you like my message?" he asked, his voice dripping with sarcasm.

=

She didn't answer. The unfaithful bitch wasn't moving. "Talk to me, Maddie. Tell me about Jay. Is he a good lover? Can't possibly be as good as me."

She sipped her wine or whatever it was and shook her head.

"You are such a fucking whore. How could you have slept with him?"

"I didn't sleep with him, Rob. It was hot out and I took a walk in the garden. Why are you doing this?"

Her calm fueled his anger. He couldn't fathom her even looking at another man, much less kissing and fucking him. No way. And

Jay? There was nothing special about him; he was just a guy she happened to work with. All he wanted was to know if she had gone to bed with him. He was like one of those preachers who demanded confession; he needed her to acknowledge her sins. And yet she sat gazing at him as though nothing had happened. He wanted to grab her, to shake it out of her.

He approached her. "Tell me," he shouted. She shrank back which at least gave him a second of satisfaction.

"I didn't do anything Rob. I love you. You're the only man in my life and the only one I want. Why can't you accept that?"

He reached for her arm and she dropped the glass. As it shattered on the floor, the cat howled and ran for the kitchen. Rob scooped her up and carried her protesting to the bedroom where he dropped her on the bed. She started to get up and he pushed her back. He was going to do what he had to do. When he began pulling off her jeans she stopped fighting and stared at him through narrowed eyes. Maybe it was that look that made him snap out of his frenzy but he suddenly backed off. With tears in his eyes, he sat down next to her, his head in his hands. "Oh God, Maddie, I can't take this. Please tell me you didn't have sex with him. I can't imagine another man touching, much less making love to you. I have to trust you. You belong to me."

He got up abruptly and went to get a beer. He needed more than that, but it would suffice for the moment. He had almost blown his marriage but he had stopped in time. And yet he still felt rage; she had challenged his manhood. No matter what her explanation, he wasn't convinced she was telling the truth. It also occurred to him, if only briefly, that she might still be angry about his coming home at two in the morning the night before she left. No matter what her explanation, he wasn't ready to forgive her. What she had done was a transgression; one that wasn't going away anytime soon.

=

Maddie watched Rob leave the bedroom. Still frightened, she sat on the bed hugging a pillow to herself. She had never seen him act with such violence before. Though the moment appeared to have passed, she was sure it wasn't over. She was also well aware that if this had been his indiscretion, it would have been dropped in an instant, and that instant usually occurred after sex. She was afraid that with or without making love, hers wouldn't disappear so quickly.

=

Unfortunately, she was right. The rest of the night Rob was morose, sitting silently, scotch in hand, in front of the small television that he normally disdained, calling it a "boob tube." Grateful he hadn't slammed out of the apartment, Maddie took a book and curled up in a chair out of his line of sight. Finding it almost impossible to concentrate, she got up several times attempting to make conversation or ask a question that he either ignored or answered in a sarcastic tone: "No, I don't want dinner," and "Yes, since you offered, I'd like another scotch." It was only when they had gotten into bed that he looked directly at her with a challenge in his eyes. She wasn't in any mood for lovemaking but she knew better than to refuse him. One moment he was gentle, arousing her until she moaned, the next, holding her down while roughly thrusting into her and whispering in a harsh voice that she couldn't come until he told her she could.

After, without a kiss or even a word, he turned away. She lay back with tears in her eyes.

=

In the days that followed he was unusually distant. When she repeatedly asked what was wrong, he shut her out, saying things were difficult at the office. She found his frequent silences and petty nit-picking unnerving, yet she didn't want to create another scene by referencing his obvious infidelities. To her surprise he came home every night by eight in those weeks and she wondered if this was some sort of truce or simply the basic awareness that she could do the same as he.

Chapter 13

Rob needed to get away and soon. After Maddie returned from Virginia, he never went home without stopping for a few beers or a scotch or two. His favorite bar was only a few blocks from his office and there was usually an exotic black haired barmaid serving drinks. One night after a brief conversation, she introduced herself as Denise. At least he had someone to talk with before going home to Maddie's either chilly reception or fake attempt at being friendly. Even the nights out with their friends felt forced.

He purposely waited until the last Friday morning in September to face her. As she was getting ready for work he announced in a firm voice that he was going away for the weekend. Startled, she asked why.

"I have to get out of here. Away from you and away from all the tension between us."

For the first time in weeks, he saw her cool exterior crack. "What is it, Rob? What's going on? I thought things were better."

"No, Maddie. Things aren't better. I'm not even sure we should stay together."

She sat on the bed, eyes welling with tears. "How can you say that? We love each other. What do you want me to do?"

"It's not only you," he admitted. "It's also the office. Everything was going well and suddenly it's all turned to shit. We've actually lost a couple of accounts."

Unfortunately, that was true. He and Doug had been given the account of a popular sport shirt company. The client had been adamant, insisting he wanted something original, not just the expected photograph of a man in a shirt that other agencies had proposed. They had drawn on Rob's first concepts for Cosette, showing young men riding bikes, playing tennis and interacting with pretty girls. The client had gone for it, saying he liked their ideas, but only a few days later asked for more. Then, before their second presentation, the account had suddenly and without explanation been pulled. Although it may have been irrational, Rob felt that John somehow blamed him.

Before Maddie could say anything, he said, "I don't want to discuss it with you. I need space. I'm leaving tonight after work."

He felt a surge of satisfaction seeing the surprise on her face. "Tonight? Where are you going?"

"I'm not sure. Maybe to the Cape." He went in to the bedroom and brought out a small satchel already packed with the few things he would need.

"What is it you want, Rob?"

"I don't know, Maddie. I only know I have to get away. Also, I prefer not to come back here. I'd like you to meet me Sunday afternoon at the boat pond in Central Park. Five o'clock. Will you do that?"

He watched as she caught her breath, obviously afraid to ask what that statement meant. But she nodded, saying she would. Seeing her so distraught he began to feel his dominance over her again. As a girlfriend she had been close to perfect, but he didn't need a wife who was quite so independent, not to mention free-thinking.

"Come on, Maddie. We have to go. I'll drop you at your office."

=

When they arrived at her office building on the corner of Forty-Fifth and Fifth, Rob cut the ignition.

She dismounted the bike and took off her helmet. "Well, Rob. Have a good trip or whatever it is you're doing," she said, her voice tinged with irony.

"Wait a minute. What the fuck does that mean?" he shouted. "I told you why I'm doing this."

She backed away. "This isn't the place to talk. You've given me a lot to think about as well."

A flash of anger flickered across his face. As she turned to enter the building, he got off the bike and followed her. "Don't be a bitch, Maddie. You're beginning to piss me off again. That's why I'm out of here."

Before she could respond, she saw Jay walking toward her. He glanced at her and then at Rob. With a wicked grin, he said, "Hi Rob. Nice to see you."

Rob's eyes narrowed, ignoring him.

Jay turned to Maddie, "Coming up? I think we have a meeting this morning."

She glanced at Rob. "I guess I'll see you at the boat pond."

Jay was silent as they walked to the elevator. Maddie was too stunned by that harangue to even speak.

It was he who broke the silence. "Are you going to be all right? Do you want to talk?"

"Not right now, Jay. I have a meeting with Miles on my new book. Thanks for coming to my rescue." *My marriage may be fucked up, but the book has to go on.*

"Let me know when you're finished. I'm taking you out for lunch."

=

Since returning from Virginia they had been having lunch together once or twice a week; in good weather going to the recently opened Paley Park, a peaceful sliver of green tucked in between two buildings on East Fifty-Third Street.

Jay went to the kiosk near the waterfall and brought back sandwiches. "Do you think Rob wants to end your marriage?"

"I don't think so, but he's still furious about that night in Virginia and no matter what I say, he argues with me. I also think something or maybe someone is going on at LRG. I don't know what to think or even do anymore."

"Maybe you should ask yourself what it is that you want, Maddie."

"Other than making love with you again?" she said lightly.

He laughed. "I only wish you would."

"To be honest, I wish Rob and I could go back to where we were before we were married."

He took her hand. "I preferred your other statement. Let's think about that. You'll be alone this weekend. Have dinner with me?"

She was tempted, but despite Rob's transgressions, she knew there was no way, emotionally and without guilt, that she could manage an affair. She kissed his cheek. "Probably not the best idea."

=

After what seemed like an endless day, she decided to walk home. The evening was crisp with the scent of dry leaves that crunched underfoot. She longed to be walking those streets with Rob's arm firmly around her rather than alone and confused. Was her supposed infidelity so unthinkable compared to his? Was he somehow entitled and she wasn't? Did "free love," only apply to the male of the species and if so, what did that mean for the female—that she would forever be branded, by that same male, as a slut or worse? And yet, she mused, what happened between her and Jay couldn't be considered free love; it was a spontaneous moment—albeit one with unfortunate timing—and, although she wished otherwise, unlikely to happen again.

And what if Rob told her he wanted out of the marriage? It was hard to imagine having to endure everyone's false sympathy while they whispered they knew it would never last. Her mother, on the other hand, might just plan a parade.

At home, with the cat curled up against her, she fell into a restless sleep filled with ragged dreams:

She is walking into an old, grungy men's bar with low ceilings and sawdust on the floor. She knows she doesn't belong there. Several well-dressed young women are drinking and laughing at the bar—not prostitutes but career girls like her. A barmaid with dark hair is rinsing a shot glass. Suddenly they all look toward the door as if expecting someone. Not her. She's there searching for Rob, but she can't find him. She sees Jay walk through a doorway, his hand extended to her. She woke up with a start, feeling an eerie apprehension. The dream had been vivid, maybe too much so.

Jay called Saturday afternoon and begged her to meet him, if only for a drink. "I'll even break my date tonight Maddie. Come on. We deserve this."

She demurred: "You're tempting me, Jay. But I can't. I don't want to do what may be the right thing for the wrong reasons."

Chapter 14

Rob was experiencing an exhilarating sense of freedom, every mile distancing him from that fucked-up scene in front of Maddie's office and the senseless arguments that had taken over his life. He asked himself for the hundredth time why it was that women always became so resentful? *Why can't they just be happy we're with them and let us be ourselves, at least from time to time? Is that too much to ask? And why do they feel it's their job to change us?*

Although he doubted that Maddie believed him, he really was going to Cape Cod. The season was over but he knew a guy in Chatham who ran a boat dock. He made a pit stop at Ernie's, downed a couple of beers and kept going, arriving in Chatham about eleven. It was a mild night for late September and he figured boats would still be coming in even at that late hour. He was right. When he got to the boat shack, Tony slapped him on the back and asked what he was doing there. Jokingly, he said he was hiding out.

"From?" Tony asked with a grin.

"From my wife," Rob answered, taking a swig of the beer Tony had offered.

"That short girl you brought up here a couple of summers ago?"

"No, Tony. This is another one."

Tony guffawed. "Guess some guys just don't learn."

They laughed and touched bottles. Tony asked if he had a place to stay. When Rob said he hadn't thought about it, Tony offered a bunk on one of his boats. Rob said that was fine with him.

Tony brought out a bottle of Cutty Sark and they talked for an hour or so catching up on old times. Tony mentioned that he was recently divorced and "happy to have lost that bitch." Rob told him he loved his wife, but they weren't getting along at the moment. "That's why I came up here. I need to think about what I want to do."

Tony touched his glass to Rob's. "And so it goes, Robby. You can't live with them and you can't kill them. Just fuck'em is what I say."

They both drank to that.

Tony closed the shop for the night and showed Rob to a bunk on a giant motor cruiser he was boat-sitting until the owner took it south for the winter. Between the booze and the slow rocking, he fell asleep in minutes.

After a late breakfast in town Rob picked up a couple of sandwiches and a six-pack and rode over to the beach. It was a sunny day though with an early autumn bite in the air. He popped a beer and thought about Maddie. Despite that she had repeatedly denied being with Jay, he still didn't believe her. Or maybe he didn't want to believe her. Why? Because she never believed him? But, shit, that was different; women weren't the same. What he did with other women was of no consequence. He loved her and that meant she had to be his and his alone. He didn't want to destroy what they had together, but that was now tainted. And yet he kept asking himself how he could deal with her, with their marriage. Not having an answer for those rare emotional questions, he took a long walk along the deserted beach.

By the time he returned the sun was low on the horizon and some of the locals had come out loaded down with blankets and coolers. After they built a fire on the beach a couple of girls came over and asked him to join them and their friends. He thanked them saying he didn't want to intrude, but they wouldn't take no for an answer.

Soon there were four married couples and a couple of single girls warming themselves around a roaring fire. They had brought quite a feast of clams, lobsters and corn. They told Rob they were celebrating the end of summer, both sad and happy that the tourists had finally departed.

By nine it was getting cold and they began to pack up and head back to their cars. Everyone shook hands and he thanked them for inviting him. One of the single girls, Lorna, tagged along with him and asked if he would give her a ride home; she had never been on a motorcycle before. Rob thought she was about twenty-four or five and attractive, although a bit on the chunky side for his taste.

He handed her his helmet and she gave him directions. Once she mentioned that she lived alone with a couple of cats, he knew this was a no-brainer.

When they pulled up in front of a white painted cottage, she asked if he'd like to come in for a beer. He followed her to the door.

The small living room could only be described as Cape Cod cute: chintz fabrics, colorful pillows and painted tin lamps all set off from sky-blue painted walls. After Lorna brought a couple of Narragansetts from her tiny kitchen she began showing him her crafts: trays and dishes trimmed with shells, small quilts sewn from antique fabrics—the usual tourist-friendly stuff found in gift shops all along the Cape.

He was sitting on a light blue couch with big pink flowers. As she sat down next to him he put his arm around the back of it. When she leaned in for a kiss, he obliged. As they moved apart he realized he felt nothing. No challenge, because there was none—not even desire. He took a breath and put his beer down on the driftwood coffee table. She was looking at him expectantly with a small smile.

"Lorna," he said, taking her hand. "I can't do this. You're a lovely girl, but I'm married." He stopped cold. He had just told a woman who wanted to go to bed with him that he was married. That had never happened before and he wasn't sure where it had come from.

"That's all right, Rob. I know this isn't going anywhere. I just thought we liked each other."

He shook his head, still amazed at himself. "I do like you. But I should go."

The look on her face was so pathetic that he put his arms around her and gave her a light kiss. She pressed close, trying to make him change his mind. Usually he would have had her in the bedroom in a flash, but all he wanted was to get out of there.

He pulled back, picked up his helmet and let himself out.

=

There was no one in the shack so he went directly to the boat, finding Tony in the salon, sitting on a large sofa with his arm around a hefty girl with stringy brown hair. Holding a bottle of beer, he beckoned Rob in.

"Join us. This is Sally." Sally waved and giggled. "Want a beer?"

"Thanks, Sally. But I need to get some sleep. I have a lot to think about."

He lay down on the bunk. He'd only had a few beers and his head was clear. Glancing out the porthole, he saw the bobbing shapes of nearby boats. Suddenly he wanted to be home. *Home.* The word began to take on new meaning. The apartment was home, with Maddie close and Cat curled up against them. With unusual clarity he realized he had to get past his anger and that if he continued having affairs his life with Maddie would deteriorate further. He didn't want to destroy this marriage; he'd been there before with Allison.

Maybe the real question was could he be faithful to her? New York was a smorgasbord of women, all of them constantly flirting and teasing. It was that occasional, special one who, for whatever reason, just got to him—the one who looked like she had to be fucked. And only by him. He promised himself he'd try to be faithful, or if that proved to be impossible, at least more careful.

The next morning, he thanked Tony and said he'd try to make it back to the Cape next summer.

Tony laughed. "Are you going to bring your wife?"

"Yes. I think I will."

"Good. Have a safe trip home."

It was around nine when he got on the bike. If he could make it to Darien by two it would give him time to see the kids and still get back in time to meet Maddie in Central Park.

=

Sunday was a day that normally flew by, but each time Maddie glanced at the clock, the minute hand barely moved.

After doing laundry, she vacuumed and even dusted the books, anything to keep from thinking. She left at four, killing time by walking down Madison Avenue window-shopping for things she didn't need and couldn't afford.

At four-thirty she entered the park at Sixty-Forth Street, bypassing the overcrowded zoo. The day was warm and she passed a few couples tanning themselves in the late September sun. Seeing many of the men shirtless she recalled a sweltering July afternoon the year before when she and Rob had gone to the park. After spreading out a couple of towels he had taken his shirt off. A few minutes later a cop came by informing them there was a law requiring men to wear shirts in the park. He had remained, impatiently tapping his nightstick against his leg until Rob put it back on.

This summer, things had changed dramatically. "Be-ins," "sit-ins," and anti-war rallies had begun in July when thousands of kids, barely clad and mostly barefoot, had swarmed and eventually occupied the park, destroying the lawn in the Sheep Meadow. The cops had enough to deal with and finally backed off some of their petty regulations, shirts becoming the least of their concerns.

When she arrived at the boat pond it was still surrounded by children sailing small boats and shrieking whenever one rolled over. Several agitated fathers were leaning precariously over the concrete edge with long poles trying to fish them out before they sank. She continued to the north end, not far from the Alice in Wonderland statue and found an unoccupied bench. It was almost five and the air was beginning to cool. She wasn't sure how this day would end and yet, in happiness or pain, it invariably would. Her present had become entwined with her future, both floating like clouds shifting in the air.

=

It was almost five-fifteen when she saw Rob circling the pond; she couldn't miss his long confident stride. He was wearing jeans, a dark T-shirt and his leather jacket. Watching him approach, her heart began to race and her hands were suddenly cold and damp. Taking off his dark glasses, he stopped and stood over her, casting a cold shadow. She looked up at him, tears stinging her eyes. They stared at one another until he reached out and took her hands, bringing her to her feet. Putting his arms around her, he kissed her lightly on the lips. "I love you, Maddie. I want us to be together. For now, forever."

She clung to him, silently weeping. "Come on," he said. "Let's go home."

Chapter 15

A week after a blessedly non-eventful Thanksgiving weekend, Rob came home one night half-drunk. It was the first time since their reconciliation two months before. Worried, Maddie asked him if something was wrong. He avoided answering her, saying that he had stopped to have a few drinks with a guy from an employment agency.

Surprised, she asked tentatively if he was thinking of leaving LRG, but it was obvious he didn't want to discuss it. Later in the evening, he took his portfolio out of a closet and started putting his work from the agency into it. Doug had recently left for a new start-up and the gossip all over Madison Avenue was that LRG hadn't won any new accounts in several months.

When she persisted, he ranted that he had a great reputation and didn't want to be with an agency that wasn't allowing him to do his creative best and, by the way, had clients that were too cheap to appreciate what he presented. "Every time I come up with an original idea, someone shoots it down. I did some great visuals—a couple skiing, another on a boat—for a new suntan lotion and then the client says he just wants another pretty girl on a beach. But we didn't let it go. We showed him more concepts and talked about shooting a commercial. That, he liked."

"So what's the problem?"

"Carl, a new copywriter and I came up with a few story boards. They're dynamite, Maddie. I'll bring them home to show you. Anyway, the asshole flipped over them. Even after we gave him the costs for the shoot, he said to go for it." He stopped and went to get a beer from the fridge.

After taking a long pull from the bottle, he said, "We met with him this afternoon. He was solid until the account guys submitted

the media plan and budget. That's when he went ape shit. He started yelling that there was no way he could afford the commercial
plus the media. These guys think it's cool to shoot a commercial, but
what's the point unless you've got the bread to run it? We ended up
going full circle and now we're back to square one—a print ad of the
broad on the beach." He shook his head. "Fuck it. If you must know,
I have a job interview tomorrow."

She went to him, taking his hand and kissing him. "Come on
Rob. We're in this together. Who is it with?"

"Maddie, it's just an interview. It's not a company you've ever
heard of." He picked up the portfolio and put it next to the front
door. "And besides you of all people know how superstitious I am
about these things."

=

A few days later, after leaving a production meeting on the scheduling of their new books, Jay dragged his chair into Maddie's side
of their office. In a low voice, he said, "I want to tell you I've had a
couple of interviews for a new job."

She looked at him with surprise. How was it possible that he
and Rob were both interviewing for new jobs? "Jay. How come you
never mentioned it? You can't leave me behind."

"I wasn't looking. A head hunter called me." He took her hands
in his. "I'll never leave you behind."

She bit her lip. "Thank you. That was a sweet thing to say."

"I mean it. You know I want more of you."

She shook her head. "I wish we could but I don't think I'd be
able to handle it."

"I understand, Maddie. And yet I just keep hoping. Anyway,
this job is in Europe. It's not a done deal; they want me to come back
next week. Please don't say anything."

"I won't. But Europe? I'll miss you and then I'll have to deal
with a new art director. It won't be the same."

He laughed. "I would hope not." He got up and looked around
outside their office. When he came back, he leaned over to kiss her.
"Don't worry about it now. But think about this; if I leave Irwin will
make you the senior art director."

A couple of weeks later Maddie had practically forgotten their conversation. Since Jay hadn't mentioned it again she assumed it hadn't worked out.

She was in her office, preparing to meet Rob at a Christmas party when the phone rang. Picking it up, she was surprised to hear his voice.

Before he could say anything, she said, "I'm running a little late, Rob. I'll meet you at the party."

"That's not why I'm calling, Maddie. There's something I have to tell you." He sounded solemn and she began to worry that he had lost his job.

"What is it?"

"Actually, there's something I want to ask you."

"Okay. Ask me."

"Are you ready?"

"Yes, Rob," she said, trying to keep exasperation out of her voice.

"How do you feel about London?"

"London? I love London. Why?"

"I know you've always dreamed of living there. You've told me several times that you wanted me to see it."

"Are we taking a trip?" Worry had turned to anticipation.

"Better than that, Maddie."

"Stop teasing. Tell me."

"I've just been offered the position as creative director for a big real estate company. It's based in London."

"Be serious. Is everything all right?"

Laughing, he said, "Everything is great. Better than great. And yes, I'm perfectly serious."

"Say it again."

"We are going to live in London. We leave in February. Look, I have to go. We'll talk about it later. Now we really have something to celebrate."

Maddie sat down and looked at the phone. Was it really possible?

She got up as if in a daze and went to tell Jay. He was on the phone and raised one finger, mouthing, "Just a minute."

He hung up, took a breath and looked up at her.

"What is it?" she asked.

"You know that interview I mentioned a few weeks ago?"

She nodded, suddenly experiencing a weird sense of déjà vu.

"They just called, Maddie. I've just been offered a job as creative director for a huge off-shore company."

"What does that mean?"

"It's in Europe."

"What?" she looked at him in shock.

"What's wrong? I told you there was a job in Europe."

"Yes. But just tell me...where?" she managed to croak.

He looked at her curiously. "It's in Switzerland. There are two companies doing overseas investments. They're growing like crazy and the competition is apparently fierce. One is Amrelco, which I think is in London and the other is IOS in Geneva. That's where I'm going. Strangely enough they were both in New York looking for creative directors."

Through tears of laughter, she said, "Yes, I know. But I can't fucking believe it!"

Part 4

The world is seldom what it seems;
to man, who dimly sees, realities appear as dreams,
and dreams realities.

Samuel Johnson

Chapter 1

February 1969

London

A limo was waiting at the curb, the liveried driver holding a sign: MacLeod/Amrelco. Touching his cap, he muttered something unintelligible which likely had something to do with "good morning" and stowed their bags in the boot.

"Did you know they were sending a car for us?" Maddie whispered.

Rob shook his head, trying not to appear surprised. "Peter never mentioned it."

The limo deposited them at a pristine white townhouse on Curzon Street in the heart of Mayfair. The front door opened and Peter Hutchison stepped out attired — dressed would have been too simple a word — in a sky-blue jacquard silk robe complete with a navy ascot. As one of Amrelco's directors and Rob's direct superior, Peter was the overseer for all promotional materials and advertising. He was middle aged, paunchy and Maddie was sure he dyed his jet-black hair. It wasn't that she didn't like him; he was the sort of man who, after he had shaken her hand, made her feel that she needed a shower.

She had met him only once before in New York, the night Rob had signed the two-year contract as creative director for Amrelco. Peter had opened a bottle of champagne and made a toast to Rob, promising that in London he would make him a star. Maddie had almost choked on her champagne but saved the moment by saying that Rob was always her star.

At the curb, he shook Rob's hand and kissed Maddie's cheek. "Welcome to London and a glorious future." Maddie thought he was a bit overly ebullient for seven a.m. on a Saturday morning.

"First, breakfast," he announced as they followed him into a large wood-paneled dining room lit by an enormous crystal chandelier. A sideboard was set with an elaborate English breakfast: porridge, scrambled eggs, bacon, kippers, sausages and fried mushrooms on toast, most of which was beyond Maddie's ability to look at much less consume so early in the morning, especially after a seven-hour flight. When Peter offered Bloody Marys both she and Rob took him up on it.

Rob filled his plate, as did Peter. Maddie took a spoonful of scrambled eggs and one piece of toast. She was grateful the coffee was American; from her earlier trips she remembered it being weak and slightly red hued.

Peter flipped a switch and suddenly there was loud music; *The Year 2525* came on followed by *Sugar Sugar*. Maddie asked if he would mind turning it down.

"What? You don't like my music?" He looked a bit miffed.

"It's not that, Peter. It's seven in the morning. We've just gotten off a long flight."

He went to a wall switch and lowered it. "Only for you, Maddie," he said in a seductive voice.

Maddie glanced at Rob who was draining the last of his Bloody Mary. He looked back at her with only the slightest movement of his head. His message was clear, *Don't rock the boat.*

=

After breakfast Peter took them upstairs to a bedroom on the fourth floor. He suggested they get settled and go out for a walk; they would adjust more quickly to the time change. He said he'd see them downstairs.

Maddie surveyed the room; it wasn't large but it was lavishly decorated with a canopied bed and dark wood furniture dating from at least a century past. Heavy, mustard colored silk drapes covered the windows. When she drew them, the view was over the surrounding rooftops, each sprouting chimney pots of all shapes and sizes.

Rob sat down on the bed. "We did it Maddie. We're in London."

She nodded. "Until yesterday it still seemed like a dream."

"I'm glad I was able to make your dream a reality," he said, getting up and kissing her.

"Rob. It's more than a dream. It's like everything is new again. I think we'll be happy here. Don't you?"

"As long as I have you I'll be happy. Come on. Let's go for a walk. You can show me why you love London."

"I'd think I'd like to take a shower first. If there is such a thing."

He looked at her with a leer. "Anything you want, my dear. Just be prepared for the consequences."

She laughed as he followed her into the white tiled bathroom. As she expected, there was an ancient high-sided bathtub with only a hand held shower. Rob started peeling off her clothes.

"Rob, this may not be a good idea. This bathtub is narrow and it's sure to be slippery. I think we should do this one at a time."

"Not going to happen Maddie. This was your idea. You know the rule about making love in every room."

"Yes, Rob. But look at this tub. We'll kill ourselves."

"Don't worry. We'll improvise."

She pointed to the bed.

"Nope. We're doing this."

She stepped gingerly in the tub as he turned on the shower. "Rob," she screeched as cold water hit her. He laughed, regulating the weak pressure to at least some semblance of warmth. Handing her the soap, he made a couple of suggestions where he thought she should begin.

"I think it's fairly obvious," she giggled.

Seconds later he grabbed the soap, turned her around, quickly soaping her back. "Hold on to the edge. Tight," he said suddenly, his voice hoarse with desire. By the time they were finished they were both laughing and the entire bathroom was soaked.

They got out and dried each other with thick towels. "That was cool," he said. "Actually quite British from what I understand."

"What are you talking about?"

"I hear they like to do it doggy style."

"How do you know that?"

His grin was sly. "I have my sources."

She hoped they weren't first hand.

=

When they went back downstairs, Peter smirked, "Everything all right up there?" Maddie cringed as Rob nodded. "Thanks, Peter. It's a lovely room."

Handing Rob a map of Mayfair and the West End, he warned, "Pay attention. The streets tend to wind around and names change when you least expect it. I suggest you go first to Shepard's Market. There are some nice old pubs if you want a pint. And watch that you look right; we don't want to lose you on your first day." Rob assured him they'd be fine.

"We're having dinner tonight with Kevin and Rafa. Since they're Amrelco's founders they're quite anxious to meet my New York award-winning creative director."

Stifling a yawn, Rob said they'd return well before that.

"Why is it I don't trust him?" Maddie asked as they strolled the narrow lanes of Shepard's Market.

"I know what you mean. There's something off about him. But we can't complain. It's because of him that we're in London and we're lucky he invited us to stay at his house. Hopefully we'll find a flat quickly and get out of there."

"I'll start looking Monday. Look at that." Maddie said, pointing at pansies already in bloom. It was only February and New York was still in a deep freeze. After covering a good portion of West One from Park Lane to New Bond Street, they returned to the townhouse by three. Crawling gratefully into the canopied bed, Maddie said. "I have to sleep. That walk did me in."

"Maddie, this is our first day in London. I think a proper British shagging is in order, don't you?"

"The shower wasn't proper enough?"

"Consider it a start."

=

For dinner she put on a slim-fitting black and white mini dress with black medium heels. With her fur coat, Rob told her she looked very chic. As she climbed into the limo Peter took her hand, complimenting her as well.

The driver let them off in Soho at what Peter had informed them was the hottest of London's "new style" Italian restaurants,

La Trattoria Terrazza. The stark white modern façade stood out in sharp juxtaposition to the ancient, crumbling buildings surrounding it. Inside, the angular space was brightly lit, probably Maddie thought, so everyone could watch everyone else. Rob nudged her arm; Michael Caine was sitting at a corner table with two men and a stunning young woman. Peter whispered her name was Shakira and she was a beauty queen from Guyana.

They had just ordered drinks when a tall leggy girl walked in and with an exaggerated hip-slung pose glanced around the room. Peter waved to her and she glided to their table. With a melodramatic sigh, she removed her oversized dark glasses revealing aqua shadowed eyes rimmed with black and lashes longer than Rob's. Her arrival prompted approving looks from every male in the place while their dates blinked in disdain and tossed their hair. Maddie had already come to the conclusion that she was the only wife in the room.

"Sorry I'm late," the girl said, striking another pose and brushing long golden ringlets over a fur-clad shoulder.

Maddie glanced at Peter and then the girl. She was at least twenty-five years younger. Not only that, but beneath her fluffy fox jacket, she wore a mini that was a good four inches shorter than Maddie's—a length currently considered very fashionable in New York. She wasn't the only one; all the girls had the same heavily shadowed eyes, false eyelashes and dresses the same length, if indeed, length was what it could be called. A few were wearing hot pants with high boots, furs flung casually over bare arms. And every one of them was having dinner with a man easily twice her age.

Peter introduced her simply as Ava. She sat down next to Rob, her eyes doing a quick appraisal. Smiling, she said, "Nice ta meet cha."

Maddie watched her, thinking there'd better be a seamstress near the townhouse; every dress and skirt she owned was going to require severe shortening. While she was stressing over apparel, Kevin Barron, one of Amrelco's founders and C.E.O. came in with Raphael Santiago—known as Rafa—a co-founder and president of European operations. Kevin, originally from Florida, was short but imposing in a bespoke Savile Row suit and handmade alligator loafers. Rafa, a slight, wiry Spaniard from Seville had a dark, compelling stare and seldom smiled—clearly not a man to be tangled with.

With them were two stunning girls whom they introduced as associates. As everyone settled in, Maddie glanced at Rob who didn't seem to be able to stop grinning while doing his best to charm Ava.

Picking up his drink, Kevin said he was finally glad to meet Rob about whom he'd heard such great things. Rafa nodded silently, his arm around the blonde "associate" he had introduced as Caroline, his fingers tracing circles on her shoulder.

Other than welcoming Maddie and Rob to London and Amrelco, not much business was discussed; everyone was too busy gossiping and celebrity gazing. Maddie prayed the secretaries at Amrelco didn't look like these three girls.

=

The next morning, they went down to breakfast finding Peter once again in a dressing gown and reading the Sunday Times, a mimosa on the table in front of him. He was about to pour himself a cup of coffee when Ava marched in looking angry.

"What's wrong?" he asked.

Without a glance at Maddie or Rob, she hissed. "My back is burned. That's what."

With a bored look, he said, "I have some salve. We'll rub it on after breakfast."

"After breakfast?"

"Yes. Can't you see I'm reading the paper? Have a mimosa."

Grabbing her fur off the chair where she had so elegantly dropped it last night, she told him to piss off and slammed out of the house.

Rob looked at him. "What was that?"

He shrugged. "Nothing really. I was just a bit over-zealous in the sauna last night. If you'd like, you and Maddie can join me later." Maddie shot a warning glance at Rob.

"Thanks Peter. But we plan to use the day to look around, maybe find neighborhoods where we'd like to live."

"I have a list of estate agents for you. I assume you'll want to live in the West End, although the office is a trek from anywhere. Why Kevin chose Millbank I'll never know. Nothing's there but the Tate Gallery."

"Do you know if there's a seamstress nearby?" Maddie asked. The Tate Gallery could wait.

Looking at her over his glasses, "Why yes, Maddie. You looked stunning last night, but your dress was a tad conservative. We like micro minis on our birds here."

Maddie held her tongue. Forgetting that he was one of Rob's bosses, he was fifty if a day. And he was advising her about the length of her dresses?

Chapter 2

The limo came to a stop in front of a modern glass building facing the Thames. The drive from Curzon Street had taken about a half hour through Monday morning traffic, giving Peter enough time to explain to Rob the reasons for his presence in London. "Our previous creative director, a London chap, was decent enough but the company was growing so rapidly he couldn't keep up. Kevin and I came to the conclusion that Brits just don't move fast enough. We decided an American was the way to go, someone from advertising who was used to getting work done on short deadlines. Nevertheless, you'll find the pace a good deal slower here. Too slow for me and I hope it doesn't become frustrating for you. Be it type, photos, whatever, nothing comes in at the speed you're accustomed to in New York."

"It might be nice moving a bit slower," Rob said.

"Won't happen. There's too much work that has to be produced every month. There's a forty-eight-page monthly magazine that goes to the salesman and current investors, a never-ending variety of promotional mailers, as well as trade and consumer ads to maintain our image.

"Interestingly enough, the UK isn't even our primary market. We're selling real estate to Europeans who think it's glamorous to own a piece of America. Especially the Germans, although we have over a hundred salesmen covering every country in Western Europe, including a few in the Middle East. They use the glitzy sales brochures you'll be producing to help them sell all those Florida condos, which through their rentals guarantee the buyers a generous return on their investment. It's astonishing how huge this market is and up until now no one has thought to tap into it. Kevin, of course, is the genius behind it. IOS in Geneva is doing the same thing, but with mutual funds. The problem is we're going after the same investor so although we shouldn't be in competition, it turns out we are. There are only so many Francs, Lira and particularly Marks to go around. It's pretty fierce out there and that's why we put out all this glorified promotional crap to help the salesman. Some of them, the ones we call 'elite,' are cleaning up. With their commissions, they're making a couple hundred thousand a year."

Rob could practically see dollar signs emanating from Peter's greedy little eyes.

"I assume you've heard of IOS and Bernie Cornfeld? They're making money hand over fist as the saying goes. But they're crazy. There are rumors of girls running around the office half naked and that coke, grass and other drugs are readily available to everyone who works there. Of course we're not exactly pussies here either," he said with a grin.

Rob didn't bother to mention that Maddie's friend Jay was now in Geneva, no doubt producing the same sort of "crap" as he would be.

Peter turned to him and in a confiding voice, said "Speaking of pussies, Rob, why don't you and your pretty wife join me and Ava or one of my other birds for an evening at home. I have all sorts of fun toys and we can do a foursome. It would be a blast."

Rob stopped himself from responding with a sarcastic retort; this pervert was one of his bosses.

"Peter, that sounds interesting. But I really don't like to share."

Peter sighed, "Too bad. Well, thought I'd take a shot. You can, of course, join me on your own. I'll invite two or even three girls over."

Rob laughed, hoping he sounded sincere. "Great idea, Peter. Just let me get settled first."

"Good man. I knew I was reading you right. You're a player. We'll get along just fine. Wait until you see your secretary, not to mention the other girls at the office. They're competent but none of them were chosen for their brains if you understand my meaning."

Rob nodded; he couldn't get out of the car soon enough.

=

They rode the elevator to the eighteenth floor, entering an expansive reception area with large contemporary paintings on the walls. Rob recognized two Francis Bacons and a De Kooning.

A spectacularly made-up-and-coiffed "bird," as Peter called her—which Rob thought was a bit over the top since Peter was from New York—sat at the reception desk and smiled as they walked in. He noticed Peter wink at her.

On the way to Rob's office—with a city rather than river view—Peter made introductions to various administrators and editors Rob would be working with. At his bidding, Rob's four assistants came in and gathered around a circular table in the corner. His secretary, Abigail, a tall willowy blonde, brought tea, coffee and cookies which he quickly discovered were an essential component of the morning ritual and called "biscuits."

Gilbert, the senior assistant, was a small man with a narrow, pale face and a ready smile. Although Rob listened carefully as each assistant described his job, he was having some difficulty understanding their different accents.

=

While Rob was meeting with his staff, Maddie gathered up all her dresses and skirts to take to a seamstress in Shepard's Market. Later she met a broker to look at flats. By the end of the week she had seen several and rejected every one as either too small, too dark or too grungy. Although Rob was making a big salary, fortunately in U.S. dollars, alimony and child support still took out a significant chunk.

The estate agents—as agents will—repeatedly told her she'd have to spend more to get what she wanted. And yet despite the screams and moans emanating from a nearby bedroom on several nights, she wasn't about to be intimidated.

The next Monday she spoke with another agent who told her he had a nicely furnished one bedroom on Upper Berkeley Street, just north of Oxford Street and conveniently close to Selfridges and Marks and Spencer. It was on the ground floor in one of a row of narrow white townhouses. Although it wasn't as bright as she would have liked, it did look out on a small park.

After taking Rob to see it, he signed the lease the next day. The following Saturday they were loading their bags into a taxi when Peter came out, still blitzed from another dinner at Terrazza the night before, and moved to kiss Maddie on the lips. She saw it coming and at the last second turned her head. As Rob shoved their suitcases into the cab, she saw him grimace.

Chapter 3

The following Monday was Rob's first attempt at taking the tube to work and with an underground map firmly in hand, he left early. After straightening up the flat, Maddie wrote short letters with her address and telephone number to her parents, Jay, Suzanne and Cynthia. Her parents had been alternately happy and anxious about her moving to London, her mother cautioning her to "keep an eye on Rob."

As for Suzanne, she had come over the day before they left. Seeing the apartment bare and Maddie packing, she began to weep. "You can't leave me Maddie. Who will I call when I want to complain about Andrew?"

Maddie tried to calm her down. "We'll write, and I'm sure we'll have a phone so we can call each other once in a while."

"Once in a while isn't enough."

Maddie hugged her. "Don't fret. I'll send you my phone number as soon as we find a flat."

=

After putting the letters aside to mail, she made coffee and relocated a few things around the flat until there was nothing more she could think to do. Admitting she had procrastinated long enough, she took a breath and looked at the phone; it was time to look for a job. She didn't know why she was so nervous, but London, unlike New York, was as yet unknown and therefore a bit frightening. She went to the bedroom to retrieve an envelope Irwin had given her.

She was still sad about leaving American Heritage and Irwin. His shock at Jay's resignation had turned to dismay when she had come in with the same news only a few days later. Their resignations had everyone in the office speculating that they were either running away together or starting their own publishing company, a patently absurd example of gossip reeling out of control. Both she and Jay had assured their co-workers that it was all a coincidence and they were doing neither.

The day she had given notice Irwin had expressed disappointment that she wouldn't be there to finish her second book. "I don't know how I'll find anyone to replace you." She had blushed and thanked him, saying she hated to leave.

"I'll miss you Maddie, and yet I hope you understand that you're being given a unique opportunity. Not only live in London but to work there as well. You're a lucky girl."

She smiled. "It's hard to believe it's actually happening. I just hope it won't be too difficult finding a job."

"You shouldn't have a problem. I'll give you a list of contacts and a letter of recommendation. I have no doubt you'll do well."

She had hugged him, praying he was right.

=

Before Jay left in mid-January they had gone to lunch at Larre, a small French café on West Fifty-Sixth Street. They each had a couple of glasses of wine, whether to celebrate or commiserate, Maddie wasn't quite sure. On the walk back to the office, Jay said, "I'll give you the office address in Geneva so you can write me when you get settled in London."

With tears in her eyes, she reached for his hand. "I will Jay."

"What's wrong?"

"I guess I'm just sad. Who knows when we'll see one another again."

"Oh, Maddie," he said, steering her into the doorway of an old townhouse. Taking her in his arms, he kissed her. They held each other for a few seconds. "I don't want to lose you," he whispered.

She took a tissue out of her bag and wiped her eyes. "Somehow this seems so final."

"It's not, Maddie. As long as we stay in touch, it'll be okay. Once I hear from you I promise I'll write."

She had nodded, wishing she didn't feel so empty inside.

=

Overcoming her nervousness, she resolved to make three calls beginning with Weidenfeld and Nicolson, a large publisher of illustrated books. After mentioning Irwin's name to the receptionist, she was surprised when the director, Mr. Browning picked up and in a booming voice asked, "And how is my friend Mr. Gluck?"

Startled at the loud and unexpected question, she stammered, "Oh, um, he's fine. He gave me your name and suggested I call. I worked for him as an art director and I've just moved to London."

"Then you must come see me. How's the day after tomorrow?"

She stared at the phone; no publisher in New York had ever been so quick to respond. After the same thing happened with the next calls, she couldn't believe she had two more appointments within the next week. Excited that she had accomplished far more than she had anticipated, she decided the only thing left to do was to go shopping.

She walked to Marble Arch and took the bus to Knightsbridge, getting off just steps from Harrods. Unlike the department stores in New York, the ground floor was one shop after the other of high priced bags, jewelry, scarves and other outrageously expensive accessories. Even the food court was pricey. Upstairs she found most of the clothing somewhere between boring and dowdy. It wasn't till she got to the fifth floor that she saw contemporary fashion. And yet nothing appealed to her. Disappointed, she walked to Harvey Nichols where the prices were better but there was still nothing she particularly liked. The style in New York was sharper, more structured; here everything was too girly for her taste.

That night, still determined to buy something British, she asked Rob to come with her to Mary Quant on Saturday. "I promise you'll have a fine time gazing at the birds shopping on King's Road."

He reluctantly agreed. "Always glad to look at birds, as it were. I'll go with you if we can have a look at Carnaby Street. Although those skinny Beatles suits aren't exactly my style."

=

The following Monday, wearing a new black and white striped Mary Quant mini dress and with her portfolio and Antiques book firmly in hand, she took the tube to Tottenham Court Road, the stop for Bloomsbury, the home of such revered authors and poets as Virginia Woolf and T.S. Eliot.

Mr. Browning welcomed her warmly, chatting about his visits to New York which he considered a rather crass place, except for his good friend Mr. Gluck who always took him to Peter Luger for steak. He seemed to have the ability to combine positives and negatives within every sentence.

After looking through her portfolio, he removed his glasses and regarded her seriously. "I have to say that we've been looking for someone like you, although I wouldn't have expected this sort of work from a woman. Maybe it's because you're American and have what appears to be extensive experience in book design. Although you do seem a bit young. However, as much as I'd like to offer you a position here, I doubt it will be possible. I don't believe we can obtain working papers for you. However, I may be able to offer you a book to design off-premises, freelance, if you will."

Listening to him, Maddie wasn't sure if she should be disappointed or optimistic. Cautiously, she ventured, "Freelance sounds fine, Mr. Browning."

It indeed, sounded fine until he told her the book was on the history of eighteenth-century British war ships. After asking herself what the hell she knew about British war ships, or any other watercraft for that matter, she smiled enthusiastically and thanked him, grateful she had gotten a book to design.

"Good then. It's settled. Come back next Monday and we'll get you started. We don't pay as well as New York, but I'm sure we can work out something satisfactory for you."

Maddie left elated. What would be satisfactory as far as payment, especially on such a book as war ships, however, was a matter of conjecture.

As soon as she returned to the flat she called Rob, telling him about the meeting. He congratulated her. "Why don't you meet me at the pub here. Say around seven. You can meet the blokes I work with."

"Blokes?" she laughed. "Just tell me where it is."

=

Rob was finding it relatively easy settling into the routine at Amrelco. After the first few days, Peter, obviously satisfied with his choice of a creative director, came in only sporadically, barely glancing at the work and asking Rob how things were going. Unless he had a question, Rob assured him everything was fine. He and his assistants were already working on a series of ads and a variety of promotional materials.

He had been relieved that Peter hadn't brought up anything about girls again. If anything overt was going on at the office with girls or drugs, he hadn't picked up on it, at least not yet. True, not a day went by without one or two secretaries casually wandering into his office to flirt and flutter their fake eyelashes at him. One, a bit more forward, even suggested lunch or a drink. He hardly gave them a passing thought. What mattered was that he and Maddie were back to loving and trusting one another.

Each evening after work Gilbert and the other assistants had an established routine; before heading to their various trains and tubes, they stopped at the Marquis of Granby, a nearby pub. On Rob's second day at Amrelco, they invited him to join them. Gratified to be accepted so quickly, he thanked them. Soon he began stopping by every night, spending a lively hour with his blokes while consuming pints and BS'ing about the day.

When Maddie arrived and, before Rob could introduce her, Gilbert intervened. "Nice ta meetcha, Mrs. M. Now I know why Rob ignores all the birds that chat 'im up every day." He turned to the others, "Wot say? Am I right?" As if on cue, they all nodded their agreement.

Maddie blushed and thanked him, at the same time wondering about the birds chatting up Rob.

"So what are you drinking Mrs. M?" Gilbert asked. Rob, unable to get a word in, stood aside, observing with an indulgent grin.

"I'm not sure, Gilbert. I don't like beer and I'm not in the mood for whiskey. I haven't found anything I particularly like."

"I've just the thing for you luv," he said, patting a stool at the bar. She heard him order a Shandy.

"Try this," he said. She took it feeling strangely self-conscious; Gilbert and the other assistants had formed a semi-circle circle around her and were watching expectantly. She took a sip. "I had one of these the other day. It's still beer," she said wrinkling her nose.

"That's so, but it's partly lemonade," Gilbert said.

She shook her head. "Any other suggestions?"

"Yeh. I've got it," he said, snapping his fingers.

This time the barkeep handed her a glass with a strange looking blob of orange at the bottom and what was apparently brandy poured over it. She sipped it, a less than optimistic look on her face. Looking up, she nodded. "What is it?"

"Brandy over orange crush, sort of a concentrated syrup. We'll now name it "The Maddie Crush."

The guys stayed for another half hour teaching her how to play darts. They left asking her to join them again soon.

=

Maddie's second interview at a small publishing company was the direct opposite of the first. The office, on a murky side street in Soho was dark and musty, smelling of tobacco and moldy paper. Following a frumpy secretary, she passed several poorly-lit rooms occupied by middle-aged men hunched over desks. The place had more the aspect of an old accounting firm than a book publisher and was grimly reminiscent of a scene out of Dickens. Since the publisher who was acquainted with Irwin was out of town she met with the associate publisher who turned out to be curt and dismissive. She couldn't wait to get out of there. One day of success didn't necessarily mean there would be more to follow.

A couple of days later she once again she took the tube to Tottenham Court Road and walked to Bedford Square. Entering Two Rivers Publishing, she asked for Claudia Newkirk, the creative director and daughter of the late founder.

As they shook hands, Claudia mentioned that Irwin had rung a couple of days before to let her know Maddie would be calling. When Maddie looked surprised, Claudia said, "He's obviously very impressed with you."

After looking through her portfolio, Claudia thumbed through the Antiques book. "I now understand why Irwin rang me. Your design is quite unique." Putting it aside she glanced at her watch. "It's almost tea-time. Will you join me? We can talk some more."

"That would be lovely." Maddie thought it sounded quaint; tea-time never happened in New York. After chatting briefly, Claudia said, "How would you would like to work here?"

Maddie almost dropped her teacup. She'd gotten the freelance book only days before and now a job offer. Was it her portfolio, that she was American or had the stars suddenly aligned just right? Whatever it was, she prayed it would continue.

"Yes. I'd love to work here."

"Good. I already have the perfect book for you. It's an overview of Pop Art and you'll be working with John Russell, the famous journalist. I can start you off at thirty pounds a week although my accountant will no doubt tell me that's too high. The only snag may be obtaining a working visa. But leave that to me."

Maddie wanted to hug her. Instead she shook her hand.

She could barely contain her excitement. Rather than taking the tube, she walked home along Oxford Street thinking about how fantastic her life had become. Rob was happy at Amrelco and his anger seemed to have magically disappeared. He called every afternoon, on most days asking her to meet him at the pub. After a drink or two with his "blokes," they'd take the tube to random spots in the West End, Chelsea, and Soho, trying different restaurants.

Rob had found a local pub he liked, The Carpenter's Arms, around the corner from their flat. It was old, actually Victorian, and served steak and kidney pies, bangers and mash and other British "cuisine" that Maddie could barely look at much less desire to eat. One night after working his way through a Shepherd's pie and a couple pints of ale, Rob watched, amused as Maddie picked at a basket of fish and chips.

"I really miss Allen's and PJ's. I wish there were someplace in London where they made a real American hamburger."

Rob nodded. "Wimpy's just doesn't cut it. But you wouldn't trade this for New York, would you?"

"Not a chance."

"I never said anything, but when I took his job I wasn't sure how things would play out here. But it's turning out great isn't it?"

"Especially now that I have a job."

He leaned over to kiss her. "I love you, Maddie. This is the best thing that could have happened to us."

"Speaking of love, all everyone is talking about is John and Yoko getting married. In Spain I think."

Rob shrugged. "From what I see in the tabloids the other Beatles don't appear to like her. I wonder if that'll change anything."

Maddie sat back and lit a Rothman. "Whether it does or doesn't, I still prefer the Stones."

Chapter 4

The activity in the office was frenzied. And yet things definitely moved slower in London, far too slow, Rob thought, as he attempted to cajole type setters, photo houses and printers into moving faster on the materials for the sales meeting, the company's most important event of the year.

Although Peter had warned him about the leisurely attitude of his suppliers, Rob was actually finding it much more frustrating than he'd imagined. Not one of them seemed to arrive at their offices before ten, or if they did they didn't bother to answer the phone. Soon after, as he already knew, the teacart would come around and they'd settle in for twenty minutes of gossip while throwing down coffee or tea along with their ubiquitous biscuits. Then, at four it all went round again. He continually asked himself why it was that in London no one could manage to answer a phone while consuming a cup of tea and yet the entire population of New York City had the ability to drink coffee while working, typing, talking on the phone, smoking or doing just about anything else? Exactly how complicated was it? After a few weeks, he learned to just go with it. Yelling at printers made them move even slower.

The night before the sales meeting, Rob met Peter at the Grosvenor House. Gilbert and the other assistants had already hauled in cartons of promotional materials and, according to Peter's instructions, set up posters with pretty pictures of moneymaking properties that had been designed to impress investors and motivate the salesmen. In truth, the salesmen's *only* motivation was purely money and how much of it they could squeeze out of those same investors.

Despite Peter's anxiety, the meeting turned out to be a success. Most of the secretaries from the office showed up in their micro minis to help out. For much of the day, Rob sat on the sidelines watching the men split their attention between the presentations and goggling at the girls' legs. He couldn't blame them; charts and spread sheets were pretty boring stuff.

At the end of the day, Peter found Rob helping Gilbert disman-tle the displays. "After the dinner and speeches, I'm having a little get together back at my house. Most of the birds from the office are coming plus shall we say, a few friends. Kevin and Rafa will be there and it's important that you spend a few minutes with them. Especial-ly Rafa. He's leaving for Spain tomorrow to spend some time with his family. It's been so busy he hardly gets home and he's never had a chance to get to know you."

"No problem, Peter. I'll be there."

He rang Maddie from the hotel to let her know he was going to Peter's and he'd be home as soon as he could. She told him not to worry; she was working on what she jokingly called the "boat book." He was pleased to hear her so relaxed; there were no unspo-ken questions in her eyes these days. The pure excitement of having a great job in such an exciting city and having Maddie to share it with was, for once, enough for him.

By the time he arrived at Peter's—only a ten-minute walk—the place was a madhouse or more realistically a cathouse. The regional directors, as well as the highest performing, so-called "elite" salesmen, many of them already drunk, were chatting up scantily dressed girls.

Peter snagged him at the entrance and brought him to Rafa and Kevin who were holding court in a small wood paneled library. In a whisper, Peter reminded him that it was they who had perceived the niche market and had chosen to go up against the competition, the much larger IOS. As if to prove his point, he had framed several magazine covers, both U.S. and European, and placed them stra-tegically around the room. On almost every one they were labeled as "giant killers." While it was true that Amrelco was still dwarfed by IOS, they had managed to take a significant chunk of European investment for themselves.

Since meeting Kevin and Rafa at Terrazza, he had hardly spoken to either of them except for quick greetings as they passed one another in the hallways. They were both anxious to hear his thoughts on the direction of Amrelco's promotions and advertising and Rob was glad to oblige. Rafa, who spent much of his time in Europe, told him there would be another meeting in Amsterdam in a couple of months and he'd like to have Rob join him there to discuss further projects.

Twenty minutes later they got up to leave, thanking him for his excellent work. As he shook their hands at the front door, he noticed three girls, including the blonde from the night at Terrazza waiting in the limo.

Peter came back rubbing his hands. "So, that went well. They like you Rob. By the way, I'm off to New York Tuesday so you're on your own for a couple of weeks."

"It's okay, Peter. I think I have everything under control."

"You do. You're doing great. Everyone here likes you." That he said it with a wink was disturbing. He looked around, catching the eye of a girl across the room. She glided over in a crotch length skirt and sequined top that hid little of her ample chest.

"Rob, this is Amanda. She works for one of our lawyers and was kind enough to join us tonight. I think you two should get acquainted." Rob picked up an edge to his voice, almost as if it was a command. His first reaction was to tell Peter to fuck off. And yet he had the distinct feeling this was some sort of initiation and it might not be smart to refuse. There always seemed to be a sense of threat about Peter.

"Sure," he said. As Peter walked away, he asked, "Which law firm do you work for?"

She shrugged. "I do a bit of work for several of them."

After a couple of drinks, she said she wanted to show him something upstairs. Why not, he thought, she's beautiful, sexy and more than willing. At the same time, he wondered if this was a scenario he didn't quite understand.

He had to admit, as his first—and so far only—British chick, she was lively in the sack. She wasn't wearing much to begin with and he didn't even have his clothes off before she was firmly planted between his legs. He took a breath and stopped asking himself questions.

A short while later he suggested they return to the party. She looked at him with big blue eyes. "There's no rush."

"Actually there is. I have to get home."

"Oh tosh," she murmured, reaching for him. But keeping it light, he caught her hand and whispered, "Next time. Now get dressed."

He watched her, feeling nothing but the desire for her to leave the room. The sex had been good, but then when wasn't it? After she left he locked the door and took a quick shower. He wasn't making any mistakes this time, nor was he overly pleased with himself. If he was going to play with a girl he wanted her to be his choice, on his time and his terms. The whole evening felt squalid to him. He prayed she didn't have a disease.

Downstairs he looked for Peter. Amanda was fortunately nowhere to be seen and although the party had thinned out there were still a few scantily clad couples making out on couches. He asked tentatively, "Does anyone know where Peter is?"

One of the girls, pulling her blouse closed, looked up. "Well luv, I think he's having a sauna. He and a couple of girls went down there a few minutes ago. If you're looking for a room upstairs, you better knock on doors first." She giggled and turned her attention back to her date, a fat, balding salesman.

Rob found his coat and left. He was just as glad not to have to face Peter. He decided to walk home; it wasn't very far and he needed to clear his head.

It was well after midnight and he expected Maddie to be asleep or reading. She had recently discovered Agatha Christie and a couple of other British mystery writers and had become obsessed with them. He was surprised to see her still at her drawing board — they had picked it up cheap on Portobello Road one Saturday — her head down on crossed arms, fast asleep. He dropped his coat on the couch, turned off the radio — playing the ubiquitous if somewhat tedious "Lady Madonna" — and kissed her neck. She blinked and looked up at him. "What time is it?"

"Late, Maddie. How come you're not in bed?"

Still groggy, she said, "I was working on the book. It was so boring I guess I fell asleep. It's due in a few weeks and it's very slow going."

He picked up a few photos. Most were overblown eighteenth and nineteenth century paintings of large sailing ships, many with cannons blasting orange fire. "You're right. They all look the same. If you want, I'll help you tomorrow night."

She looked at him wide eyed. "Really?"

"Sure, Maddie. Why not? I missed you tonight."

"Oh, yes. The sales meeting. How was it?"

"The day and the dinner were fine. Peter was..." he stopped, about to say "having an orgy," but corrected himself. "Peter's party was too long and too loud. I couldn't wait to get out of there."

She looked doubtful. "Really? Weren't there, as you say, sexy birds?"

He laughed easily. "Yes, of course there were. He paid a lot of expensive girls to take good care of his elite salesmen. Art directors aren't included. Anyway, it's not my scene, as you know." The lie, while convincing was tinged with guilt. He hadn't liked being part of Peter's debauchery.

"Why don't you go to bed," he said. "I have a couple of things to do."

"Other than me, what do you have to do?" her tone was sleepy but seductive.

"I want to make some notes. You go ahead. I'll be in soon."

She gave him a questioning look but went into the bedroom.

He couldn't make love to her that night and yet he wasn't quite sure why. He'd made love to two women the same night before, Maddie included, but the night at Peter's had left him feeling unsettled. Besides, everything between them was good again and he didn't want to take the chance of blowing it.

He poured a short scotch and sat down on the couch. Despite his frustration with the leisurely pace of his suppliers, the days had been moving faster than he'd anticipated. He suddenly realized it had been several weeks and he hadn't even written a note to his folks or, more importantly, his kids. He'd make sure to call them from the office tomorrow. He was surprised Maddie hadn't mentioned it, but he knew she'd been consumed with finding a job.

Before leaving New York, he and Allison, who thought the idea of moving to London was "absurd, not to mention ridiculous" plus a few more unpleasant adjectives, had tried to explain to the kids that daddy wouldn't see them for a while. He told them he would send them letters and cards with pictures and they promised to write back. Allison's parting message was clear and simple: London or not, he better not be late with alimony and child support payments.

Feeling guilty, he found some blank airmail letters Maddie had picked up at the post office. After writing quick notes to his kids and parents, he left a note for Maddie asking her to pick up an assortment of picture postcards; they could send a couple every week. By the time he went into the bedroom, she was sound asleep.

Chapter 5

Maddie's workspace at Two Rivers Publishing—it could hardly be called an office—was in one of several attached eighteenth-century Georgian houses. Claudia told her as the company had grown they had bought adjoining townhouses, breaking through exterior walls and connecting the buildings with perilously uneven hallways and floors that creaked ominously with every step. Maddie considered it all part of the charm. Not quite so charming, however, were the loos. They were small and cramped, most likely afterthoughts of a time long past, with rickety toilets and pull chains that didn't always work. In addition, they were unisex. Going to the bathroom required careful consideration and timing.

Her desk—there were no drawing boards—was one of three in a small third floor room she shared with an editor and a proofreader. She liked to imagine that perhaps a century or two ago it had been some young girl's bedroom. A girl who would have worn long, layered and heavily brocaded dresses, perhaps even a bustle. While the miniskirts of this decade were preferable they did leave one a bit chilly on London's damp, grey days.

She had just completed formatting the first chapters for the Pop Art book when Claudia came into the room. With a look of concern she asked Maddie to come back to her office, two buildings away.

Rather than sitting down, she paced. "Maddie, we have a problem. It's been over a month and we haven't been successful in obtaining your work visa. We've been turned down twice. This is my fault. I was overly confident.'

"What does that mean?"

She sat down looking defeated. "I'm afraid it means that it will preclude you from working here."

Trying to maintain her composure, Maddie stared at her. "But I've just started the Pop Art book."

"Yes, and we want you to continue with it, but not on these premises. I think it's best if you work at home and come in a couple of times a week so we can review the pages together." She shook her head. "I'm so sorry. Maybe we can try one more time."

It sounded doubtful, but Maddie nodded. "It's all right, Claudia. I'll do whatever is necessary."

Looking relieved, Claudia said. "The government makes it so bloody difficult. We couldn't justify why we needed an American book designer, even a really good one. It has to be for something special."

=

Trying not to panic, Maddie walked home with tears in her eyes. What if no publisher could get her working papers? What would she do then? Would the freelance even dry up?

She never imagined that she might not be allowed to work or, even worse, that she might end up having to ask Rob to support her. Although he paid the rent and other basic expenses, her salary kept her in spending and house money. It was unthinkable that she would have to be dependent solely on him. Not that she thought he would mind, but it was her own concept of independence that was now threatened.

By the time she called Rob she was sobbing with anxiety.

He tried to calm her down. "Maddie. You have names of other publishers. Everyone loves your work. I'm sure one of them will be able to do something."

"But what if they can't. What will I do?"

"First of all, don't future-trip. That's not like you."

"I don't know, Rob. This is awful. I should probably be making more calls but I can't even think."

"The calls can wait. I have an idea. Meet me at the pub later."

When she arrived Rob was waiting at the bar. Seeing tears in her eyes, he took her in his arms. "Don't worry Maddie, I have good news. I called Ken in New York and told him about the debacle with Two Rivers. He said you should call Cowen and Greenstreet. They're a large publishing group and have a relationship with *Time-Life* in New York.

He's already called them and was told they may be able to accomplish what the others haven't." He handed her a piece of paper. "Of course, it's not a given. You have to get the job first."

Tears turned to smiles and she hugged him. "You're amazing. Thank you."

He kissed her lightly. "You know I'll do anything for you."

"I love you Rob. What else can I say?"

"That you want to go to bed with me?"

Her smile was coy. "Here?"

He laughed. "Later. Come in the back room; the guys are having a fierce game of bar billiards and there are a couple of people I want you to meet."

Maddie shook hands with James and Claire McDowell, the owners of a graphics studio called LonDesign. "Pleased to meet you," Claire said in a distinct Scottish accent. "Rob never stops talking about you."

Maddie glanced at Rob. "Really?"

"Of course, Maddie," he said putting his arm around her. "Claire and James are taking on some of our work. Amrelco is growing so fast we don't have the time to produce everything being asked of us."

"Maddie," Claire said. "Rob tells us you're having problems with working papers. You're welcome to come freelance with us."

"But you haven't seen any of my work."

James shook his head. "Rob told us everything we need to know" He handed her his card. "Call us."

She looked at him with relief. "Thank you. It appears that my disastrous day has just improved."

James nodded and looked at his watch. "Time for dinner. We'll go to Terrazza."

Although there was a queue to get in, James knew the manager, who, for a generous gratuity, quickly found a table for them. Maddie sat next to Claire while James and Rob discussed business, interrupted occasionally by mini-skirted birds gliding by. Maddie was delighted to discover that Claire had a uniquely droll take on those same girls and their elderly dates. They ended up giggling throughout the entire meal.

On their way out, James introduced them to a couple he knew, Scott and Gwen Frost. James told Rob that Scott worked for Grey Advertising and was someone he should get to know.

By the time they parted that night, Claire had asked Maddie to have lunch later that week and Maddie was happy to have found a friend.

=

Although grateful for James's generous offer of freelance work, Maddie was still anxious to find a full time job. With the speed of a true New Yorker, she was in the offices of Cowen and Greenstreet by the next afternoon. With offices on Berkeley Square, it was an easy walk from the flat. She met with Mr. Cowen, the director, and Mr. Braithwaite, a senior editor.

After looking through her book and portfolio, Mr. Cowen nodded, "Mr. Henderson told me you would likely be a proper fit for us. From what I see of your work, I tend to agree with him. Although you will become our first female art editor, I believe you will fit in here. Also, since we specialize in illustrated books about the UK as well as other countries, I think we will be able obtain a work visa for you." He sat back, apparently in deep thought. Maddie watched him, holding her breath.

"We'll just say we're planning a volume on American history and you're our expert. Working at American Heritage should give you the credentials required." Glancing at Mr. Braithwaite, he grinned. "As long as no one tattles, who's to know?"

Maddie wanted to hug him.

"However," he continued, "The book I have in mind for you is on touring the UK. How does that sound?"

"Wonderful," she replied, barely able to contain her excitement. Anything sounded better than war ships.

"Well, Mrs. MacLeod, you might not find our salary so wonderful. It doesn't compare to New York. We can pay thirty-five pounds. I know it doesn't sound like much, but it's a fair salary and it will include any costs on your work visa."

Maddie quickly calculated; eighty-four dollars a week, more than Two Rivers but still only a fraction of her salary in New York. *I'm definitely coming up in the world*, she thought sardonically.

"Thank you, Mr. Cowen."

"You'll be working with Mr. Braithwaite as your editor. I hope you can start with us next Monday."

"Monday is fine. The only problem is I have to finish a book on Pop Art for Two Rivers. I'm sure I can go there at lunch time."

Mr. Cowen nodded. "I've heard about that book. Very impressive. It's quite an honor to be working with John Russell. Particularly after only a matter of weeks in London." He stood up and shook her hand. "I'm sure this will be a productive relationship for us both."

Maddie smiled with relief. "I hope it will."

=

When she arrived back at the flat, she checked the post. There was a note from Suzanne, a letter from her mother and a picture postcard of Geneva from Jay. She wasn't too worried about Rob seeing any correspondence from him; she usually went through the mail first. And if he did, so be it; Jay was still a friend.

His message was brief, basically that he liked working at IOS but as he had been told, it really was a pretty wild place. He said he'd elaborate in a letter to follow. He asked if she was working and, if so, where. He ended by saying that he missed her and signed it "Love, Jay."

Suzanne had written that the baby was good and at the moment everything was calm, but she still missed their conversations. She said she'd write again in a few days. As for her mother's letter, Maddie put it aside. She wasn't in the mood to read the gossip from the golf club.

Chapter 6

Peter was on the phone from New York telling Rob he needed him to go to Paris to pick up some documents.

"Why me, Peter? There are other people here who can go." He didn't like the idea of being asked to be a courier.

"C'mon Rob. You'll be doing me a favor. I'm giving you two plane tickets to Paris for next weekend. It's only May so you shouldn't have a problem finding a hotel. I'll be back in London the following Monday and I need those papers. Besides you've never been to Paris, have you?"

"No. Maddie has, but not me."

"Then consider it what the Brits like to call a 'dirty weekend,' with your wife. Or leave her at home and take Ava. I can see if she's available."

That suggestion made Rob even more uncomfortable. "That's okay Peter. I'd rather take Maddie."

"So we're all set. You'll have the tickets and the information about the pick up tomorrow."

Rob put the phone down wondering why he always felt slightly soiled after dealing with Peter. Still, a trip to Paris for the weekend sounded pretty good.

=

They flew to Paris Friday afternoon. When Maddie questioned Rob about having to pick up something for Peter, he put her off, saying he just had to meet a guy who would give him an envelope. It would only take half an hour, no big deal. After that it was dropped.

The next morning, they strolled through St. Germaine. Rob, captivated by the ancient streets of the Left Bank, stopped frequently to take photographs. After crossing the Seine to the Louvre, they braved the crowds gawking at the Mona Lisa. Extricating themselves from the tour groups, Rob proclaimed it was too mobbed and he wanted to leave. Maddie insisted he had to see the Marie de' Medici paintings by Rubens. Entering the vast room with twenty-four huge and flamboyant paintings, many of them depicting fleshy nudes, Rob nodded. "Now these I like."

Returning to the Left Bank in the afternoon, they browsed through small shops and galleries. Maddie stopped, pointing out a heavy silver chain link bracelet in the window of a tiny jewelry store on Rue du Bac. Without a word, Rob went inside and bought it for her, sliding it on her wrist next to the bracelet he had given her two years before. With their arms around each other, they returned to the hotel, Maddie thinking how truly perfect their lives had become.

The next morning Rob left the hotel, returning an hour later with a bulky, heavily sealed envelope that he immediately shoved into their suitcase. Still curious, Maddie questioned him about whom he had met and what could be so important that it had to be hand delivered. Rob replied it was just some guy, he didn't know his name and he had no idea what was in the envelope.

Chapter 7

By July Rob was complaining that the all too rare eighty-degree day didn't count as summer and both he and Maddie were far too pale from lack of sun. Since everyone was going off to Marbella, Capri or some other beach in the Mediterranean, they each asked for and were granted a two-week holiday. Rob rented a VW minibus with the singular intent of driving to the beaches in the south of France.

After taking the ferry from Dover to Calais, Rob drove and, armed with maps, Maddie navigated their route. The van gave them unlimited freedom; they required neither hotels nor campgrounds, which they had been told were dirty, smelly and overcrowded.

In Provence, they took back roads through miles of vineyards broken by patches of shimmering yellow sunflowers or fields carpeted with lavender. To their delight they discovered no one bothered them if they pulled off on a side road at the edge of a vineyard or a beach and spent the night, often making love under the stars. In the mornings, waking with the sun, they drove to the next small town where they stopped at cafes or patisseries for croissants and café au lait.

After a couple of days in Nice, they turned west, beach hopping along the French Riviera on the way to Spain.

One afternoon, while sunning themselves on a crescent beach outside the ancient town of Hyeres, Maddie leaned over to kiss Rob.

"What was that for?" he asked.

"I feel like this is our honeymoon."

"You're right, Maddie. It is our honeymoon. We're lucky to have found each other."

She grinned. "And that you were wise enough to hire me."

A few minutes later, he got up, saying he'd be right back. She watched him go up to the van. When he returned he asked her to hold out her left hand.

"Why?" she asked.

"No questions."

Taking her hand, he placed a narrow blue and gold lacquered ring on her finger above her wedding band. Looking in her eyes, he said, "Blue and gold are the colors of the Mediterranean. I want you to always remember this trip and how much I love you."

"Rob. It's beautiful. Where did you get it?"

"In an antique shop in Antibes. You were across the street buying sandals. I wanted to wait until the right moment to give it to you."

She threw her arms around him, telling him she loved him and wished the trip would never end.

=

After calculating how long it would take them to return to Calais, they drove only as far as a small town named Roses in northern Spain. It had a wide, sandy beach and was far less crowded than the coarsely pebbled beaches in France.

On their last afternoon Rob went to buy cigarettes leaving Maddie on the beach reading one of her British novels. Hearing a commotion, she looked up, seeing a few older men exclaiming loudly and gesturing at a newspaper. Having not seen one in two weeks, she walked toward them trying to get a glimpse of what could be so exciting. What she saw stopped her; she didn't need a translator to interpret the huge headline proclaiming that a man had walked on the moon. Noticing her, the men started speaking in a rapid Catalan dialect. When she tried to explain that she was "Americano," one of them opened the paper, eagerly pointing to a blurry photograph of an astronaut planting a flag on the surface of the moon. She ran back to tell Rob, who had just returned with a pack of unfiltered and terribly smelly Spanish cigarettes that they had labeled "El Ropos." He went over to the men, indicating he wanted to see the paper and offering them cigarettes. Trying not to laugh, she watched Rob who, not understanding a word, just nodded and smiled.

=

After returning to London, the summer passed in a flurry of un-remitting news from the States: The Vietnam war appeared to be escalating despite President Nixon's ongoing promises to end it, Senator Ted Kennedy received a suspended sentence for the death of a female campaign worker, and the gruesome Charles Manson killings had many Brits remarking how violent the States had become. Just over a week later the unlikely Mets won the National League pennant and the Brits were once again nattering on about what they considered the American madness at Woodstock. Rob's only comment was he was sorry he missed it.

One Thursday night in late August, while Woodstock was still provoking debate about how crazy the Americans were, Rob told Maddie he and Peter were going to Amsterdam the next day for a meeting but would return Saturday. When Maddie asked what the meeting was for he replied that it was with a group of salesmen. "It's only one night Maddie. Not a big deal."

"Yes Rob. But with Peter?"

He kissed her. "Not to worry."

The next afternoon he called from the airport. He said he loved her and would miss her, even for one day.

=

On the plane Peter explained that Kevin and Rafa were worried that the Netherlands were lagging behind in sales and they were going to Amsterdam to plan some local promotions and advertising. Suddenly he winked, which Rob always found irritating, and said, "This is Amsterdam. There's more to life than advertising."

When Rob asked him what he was talking about he grinned. "You'll see."

After checking into the hotel, Rob dropped his bag in his room and having time to kill, went for a walk along the canals, stopping at several pubs to sample the local beer. He wished he had been able to bring Maddie along.

After a short meeting and a long, raucous dinner at an Indonesian restaurant, Peter led them on a tour of Amsterdam's infamous red-light district. While the salesmen sniggered amongst themselves, Rob was intrigued by the scantily clad women framed in windows exhibiting their most intimate charms. After traversing several alleys, Peter stopped at an unassuming door and rang a bell. The woman who answered welcomed him by name. Despite heavy makeup Rob could see she was no longer young but still quite beautiful.

They followed her to a room painted a deep burgundy and lit with flickering lanterns. Perched seductively on deeply cushioned couches were several girls in various stages of undress. Rob stood aside as the salesmen grinned at one another and went to choose their "dates."

Peter touched Rob's arm. "How about it Robby. Don't I always take care of things? I told you it wasn't all work." He nodded at the woman who took Rob's hand, guiding him to a small shadowy anteroom where an exquisite blonde draped only in a long gauzy shawl reclined on an antique Recamier. When he looked back, the woman was gone. The girl stood up silently, her shawl dropping to the ground. Speechless, Rob stared at her slender body: firm breasts curving to a small waist, nipples rouged with pink. She was shaved clean, something he had never seen before. Her perfection immediately aroused him. He reminded himself that she was a whore, but he didn't care. Taking his hand, she led him to yet another room lit only by tall candles. She began silently undressing him, her hands moving about his body with a skill born of her profession. He let sensation overtake all thought as she kneeled before him and took him in her mouth. Suddenly all-powerful, his hands roughly gripped her shoulders, pulling her tighter to him. He came with a groan and she licked her way up his body before leading him to the bed where she washed him off with a soft-scented sponge and continued her ministrations. He spent the night fucking her in every way possible. She was accepting and responded energetically to his every desire. He was insatiable and she was his slave, there only to please him and he penetrated her in ways he would never have asked of another woman. As ravishing as she was, he was well aware that fucking her was far from making love.

In one quiet moment, he mused that she was his first prostitute, although he still had questions about Amanda, the girl at Peter's house the night of the sales meeting. And while there had always been girls willing to satisfy his every need, this had been an entirely new experience.

All too quickly he heard Peter knocking on the door and saying they had to leave. He wanted to tell him to go ahead, he'd see him later at the hotel, but glancing at his watch he was shocked to see it was already six in the morning.

As they left, Rob avoided meeting Peter's eyes; he had no desire to invite, much less answer any questions. It wasn't until they were at the airport that Peter, noticing a flower shop, suggested he bring Maddie flowers.

Rob nodded. "Thanks, Peter. That's a good idea."

On the plane Rob was relieved that Peter kept the conversation to business, only discussing a new promotion. As they were about to land, Peter turned to face him. "You know Rob, I'm pleased that you came along yesterday. I'd really like it if you'd consider joining me for dinner one night. Preferably by yourself. I know many, many people in London, people I think you'd, ah, like and who would like you. How about it?"

Rob took a breath. Peter had been far more circumspect about the night before than he would have imagined; in fact, other than discussing work, he hadn't even mentioned it. *What the hell*, he thought. "Thanks, Peter. Sure. Why not?"

By four o'clock they were back in London. Maddie was thrilled with the yellow tulips Rob brought her.

Chapter 8

In September Maddie received a funny yet worrisome letter from Jay. He wrote that things — although he wasn't specific about what things — were becoming difficult and there were rumors of government probes, whatever that meant. He quipped that despite the setbacks, the party atmosphere the company was famous, or infamous for, depending on one's point of view, was still continuing. Apparently the government wasn't quite as interested in probing sex in the office as it was about fiscal inconsistencies. The drug supply, however, had pretty much dried up. He ended by saying he missed their conversations and he would be in touch soon.

As perfect as their lives had been since arriving in London, Maddie was becoming aware that there were more days when Rob called telling her not to meet him after work and more nights when he came home well after the pubs had closed. At first she didn't think much about it, not until it dawned on her that the frequency was increasing and he was including her less. Whenever she asked him about it, he became impatient, saying only, "Maddie, it's work."

He called one afternoon telling her he had to make another quick trip to Amsterdam. A couple of weeks later, there was another overnight trip, this time to meet Rafa. He always returned with flowers.

=

One night in late September she returned from work surprised to find Rob already home.

She had barely opened the door when he approached her, shouting. "Where the fuck have you been? I called your office. They said you were out all day."

Incredulous, she faced him. They hadn't argued since they'd arrived in London. "What's wrong with you? I told you a few days ago that I was going with a photographer to spend the day on a houseboat on the Thames. Mr. Braithewaite wants some new photographs for the book and asked that I go along. No big deal."

He didn't back off. "Who's the photographer. Do I know *him*?"

Annoyed, she shook her head. "She was a woman. Okay?"

"Book publishers don't often send art directors out on shoots," he said, still sounding suspicious. "I guess I should be glad you're doing so well at Cowen."

She stared at him; his comment was not only sarcastic but patronizing and she didn't understand why he was so belligerent. She was tempted to remark that she could say the same about him, but seeing a half empty bottle of scotch on the kitchen counter, the last thing she wanted was to provoke him further.

As she took off her coat, he caught her arm and after pulling her into a rough kiss, he reached under her skirt. That day she had chosen to wear a new maxi skirt; they were suddenly all the rage. Instead of panty hose, she had put on stockings and a garter belt. When she backed away, he grabbed her hands. "I want to make love to you," he said in a soft but firm voice.

"Now? I just got home."

"Yes, Maddie. Now." His voice was curt. After guiding her into the bedroom, he sat on the bed. "Strip for me."

She pulled away, the aggression in his voice all too reminiscent of what they had left behind in New York. "What? Are you kidding?"

He sat on the bed and took a long drink from his glass. "You're looking very hot tonight. Leave your stockings and heels on."

She didn't like his commanding tone, but rather than make him angry, she played along. As she stepped out of her skirt, he said, "Good. Turn around, unbutton your blouse. Slowly. I want to see you touching yourself." Feeling awkward and self-conscious, but trying to please him, she turned her back and in a seductive voice asked him to unhook her bra. He shook his head. "No. I just want to watch. I'll be touching you soon enough." She glanced back at him, thinking it sounded like a threat. As she slid off her lace panties, he grabbed her and fully aroused, pulled her down on his cock. She gasped in surprise and pain.

"Put your arms around me and leave your heels on," he demanded. After moving back on the bed, he kept her on top, kissing and
fondling her until he could see that she was ready to come. Stopping
suddenly, he turned her on her back.

"Rob, no…"

"Quiet, Maddie," he said harshly, looming over her. "Spread
your legs." Going down on her, he teased her with his tongue and
probed with his fingers until she screamed for him. After leaving
light but discernable teeth marks on her thighs, he pulled her to her
knees. Standing behind her, he fucked her until she begged him to
stop. Instead he pulled her tighter until hearing her gasp, he whispered coarsely, "I'll stop when I'm ready."

The next morning, he again moved toward her. She asked him
quietly to leave her be; she was still tender from last night's activities. Ignoring her, he had taken her roughly.

Although aroused by his dominant sexuality, she was beginning
to sense that something other than drinking was driving his sudden
compulsions. And yet afterwards he always held her close, giving
her soft kisses and reminding her how very much he loved her. Nevertheless, he wasn't the same affectionate Rob from their their first
months in London or the loving man who, one day on a beach, had
given her a very special ring.

Chapter 9

Rob had never felt so powerful, so in control. He was receiving almost daily accolades on his work, Amrelco's business was soaring and he had found the perfect lay, even if she was a whore and he had to fly to Amsterdam to have her. Just thinking about her aroused him and while he was well aware that Maddie was paying the price for his excessive sexuality, there was no way he could, or even desired to stop. Anyway, despite Maddie's protests, he knew she liked it. *And if there are times she doesn't, tough luck. She belongs to me.*

He had returned from Amsterdam with an implicit understanding, if not a bond, with Peter. Now when Peter asked him to accompany him at night, he went, not with disdain, but with expectation and looking forward to the action. He felt liberated, in command of his life, enjoying having people look at him with admiration when he walked into trendy restaurants and clubs with a tall, elegant girl on his arm, especially one who wasn't his wife. He was excited when new acquaintances laughed at his jokes and called him "witty." It fed his ego and enhanced his confidence

Occasionally when he suggested taking Maddie, Peter would shake his head, saying there was a time for wives and a time for playing, making it clear that, like himself, Rob was "a player." Although Rob experienced moments of guilt and occasionally acknowledged his deceit to himself, he tried to make it up by taking Maddie out, often with Claire and James or other friends, to the theater or expensive restaurants on the weekends. While it assuaged his immediate guilt, the next time Peter called, he went—the rush too strong and the girls too beautiful, even if they were bought and paid for. And if, after a few too many cocktails, he occasionally was forced to admit conceit, even egocentricity, it was always with a self-effacing laugh and half joking. Besides, he deserved it, didn't he?

=

On an afternoon in early October he and Peter were called to Kevin's office to review their upcoming advertising campaign in Europe. The two of them had ended the night before at a gentlemen's club and they glanced at one another with knowing smiles. A few minutes later the door opened and Rafa walked in. As Rob jumped up to shake his hand he glanced out the still open doorway seeing a striking young woman chatting with Jennifer, Kevin's secretary.

After the meeting broke up, he stopped at Jennifer's desk. "There was a blonde girl talking with you before. She looks familiar but I can't place her. Does she work here?"

Jennifer raised one eyebrow. "Rob dear, her name is Caroline and if I were you I wouldn't ask anything more."

He nodded, recalling meeting her with Rafa that first night at Terrazza. She hadn't had much to say but their eyes had met more than once. In a seductive voice he said, "Come on Jenn, give me at least a little bit more."

"There are plenty of willing birds here, Rob. She's not for you."

He blinked. "Pretty please? Just tell me who she is."

She shook her head and sighed. "If you must know, she's Rafa's girlfriend."

He backed away. "Thanks, Jenn. Now I understand."

She looked up at him. "I hope you do."

He did, but it hadn't mattered. When he returned to his office he called Abigail in and closed the door. "Tell me about Caroline. I hear she's Rafa's girlfriend."

Like Jennifer she shook her head. "Please, Rob, don't even think about her. She's not just his girlfriend, she's his mistress."

He nodded. "Go on."

She sighed. "Caroline was a secretary here a couple of years ago. It was before I started so I never really knew her. But the word was that Rafa took one look and immediately began an affair with her. That continued until the day he fired her, the next installing her in a townhouse in Belgravia. Since Mrs. Rafa doesn't come to London very often he takes her everywhere with him."

"Why was she here today?"

"I don't know. Rafa's in town for a few days so I imagine she just came along and then left to go shopping. His driver probably took her to Harrods." She looked at him with a frown. "You know Rafa. Stay away."

"Thanks, Abigail."

With a worried glance back at him, she left.

=

A couple of weeks later, Amrelco's Public Relations agency organized a cocktail party, ostensibly to introduce a new director. The reality was that the tabloids had been running negative stories about Amrelco's sales strategies and Kevin was trying to mollify the press. Writers from the local and financial newspapers as well as the European bureaus were invited. Rob asked Maddie, thinking she might like to meet some of the writers. He knew she was feeling left out and thought it was a good opportunity to include her as well as show off his new work.

About thirty journalists showed up and each one, after shaking Kevin's hand, headed straight for the bar. Peter effusively kissed Maddie's cheeks and commented on how gorgeous she looked. Seeing her fake smile Rob quickly put his arm around her and introduced her to a writer from the Evening Standard, one of the few who had written kind words about Amrelco. While they chatted Rob noticed Rafa come in followed closely by Caroline.

She wasn't the tall willowy type he was usually attracted to. On the contrary, she was petite, as perfect as an English doll with porcelain skin and large blue eyes.

A short while later, seeing Rafa in a discussion with Kevin and Maddie engrossed in an animated conversation with a couple of journalists, he approached her. He introduced himself, asking if she remembered meeting at Terrazza.

"Yes, I do. I believe you had just arrived in London."

He asked if he could get her a drink. "That would be lovely," she said in a soft voice. After bringing her a glass of champagne they spent a brief time talking in a quiet corner, Caroline's eyes never leaving his face. It only took a few minutes before Rafa, giving Rob a pointed look, swept her away and out the door.

Rob didn't think much more about her until a couple of weeks later when, about to make a phone call, he saw her in the hallway outside his office. Hanging up quickly, he went to say hello. With a shy smile she handed him a card, asking if he'd like to take tea with her the next afternoon at the Dorchester.

When he arrived at the hotel, she was waiting just inside the lobby still wrapped in her sable coat. It had only taken one look for him to ask the doorman for a taxi to take them to Belgravia.

Chapter 10

By the middle of November, Maddie began to realize that Rob had reverted, at least somewhat, to his more normal self. Suddenly there were no more trips to Amsterdam, he was spending less time with Peter and although he was still coming home late a couple of nights a week, he was more attentive and less aggressive. When they were out with friends, he seemed almost laid back. Maddie began to relax.

One night she asked if he thought they should invite their new British and American friends for Thanksgiving dinner. Giving her a kiss, he said he liked the idea.

She shopped every evening that week on the way home, ordering a turkey from a poulterer and scouring the green grocers for sweet potatoes and cranberries—which she finally found at Fortnum and Mason. Unable to find pumpkin, she settled for a cherry pie from a bakery on Edgware Road.

That Thursday she left work early and by the time everyone arrived the roasted turkey was resting in the kitchen. There were eight at the table, including James and Claire, Scott and Gwen Frost, with whom they had gone to the theater several times, and Claudia and her husband.

It turned out to be a pleasant and successful evening of food, conversation and far too much wine. Despite the fact everyone had work the next day, they stayed until well past midnight. As Claudia left, she reminded Maddie the party for the Pop Art book was coming up. Maddie had completed it a couple of months before and although she had received many compliments, she hadn't heard anything since.

As they left, James kissed her on both cheeks and Claire made her promise they would all do it again the following year.

Part 5

I went into the luminous night,
to those pleasures that were half real,
and half reeling in my brain.
And I drank of potent wines, as only the
valiant of voluptuousness drink.

Cavafy

Chapter 1

London
March 1970

Rob tried to figure out how so many things could have gone wrong at once. When he left the office the night before everything had been groovy. The next morning, he walked into chaos.

As he stepped off the elevator the receptionist glanced at him and quickly looked away. He wanted to ask what was wrong, but two official-looking men both wearing dark raincoats, were talking with her. A few minutes later they showed up in his office. The bigger one flashed a badge and announced they were investigators from Inland Revenue. He said they wanted a word with him.

Taken aback, Rob said, "Sure. What's it about?"

The smaller one took out a notebook. "We'd like to ask you about Peter Hutcheson."

"Peter? What do you want to know?"

"Tell us about those envelopes you carried back for him." They sat down opposite him.

He felt a stab of alarm. "They were just envelopes. If there's a problem, you should ask him. He's in New York."

The bigger one nodded. "We know. He won't be returning anytime soon."

"Why not?"

They glanced briefly at one another. "He's being questioned about possible fraud, forgery, and money laundering. That's why we want to know more about you and those envelopes."

Rob tried to hold back his astonishment. "I'm not sure I understand what this has to do with me. I simply met different guys and brought back the envelopes they handed me. They were taped closed. I had no idea what was in them." He shrugged. "That's it."

"You didn't think there was anything a bit queer about carting back packages that could very well have been put in the post?"

"Not at all. Peter was always in a hurry and he knew I wanted to visit those cities. As far as I knew, I was doing him a favor."

"You're telling us you didn't know you were transporting forged documents and in some cases thousands of Francs and Deutsch Marks?"

"How would I know? I've already told you they were sealed. Peter gave me tickets to Paris, Amsterdam, Munich and Dublin and I brought back envelopes. My wife was with me on some of those trips."

The bigger guy smirked: "Maybe we should talk to her. I'll wager she wasn't with you on any of those trips to Amsterdam. Do you fancy Dutch whores over our homegrown British tarts?"

Rob stared back at them suddenly aware that this might be far more serious than he had first thought. Most important, he had to keep them away from Maddie. Envelopes were one thing; Amsterdam was something else entirely. "No. You can't get my wife involved in this. She knows nothing. I told you, Peter gave me plane tickets and I did him a favor. That's all there was to it."

"What about the parties at Peter's townhouse?"

"Look, he liked to drink and play. He'd bring in girls for the salesmen."

"What about the girls? He knew all the upscale slappers in town from what we hear."

"I don't know about that. I tried not to get involved."

"C'mon MacLeod. We know you were at those orgies."

"I was there as an employee. I don't like someone choosing women for me." That wasn't quite accurate, but he was sure they'd never find out that he and Ava had gotten it on once or twice. And if they did, so what?

"And the other nights you were out with him? Did you meet any of his friends outside of Amrelco?"

Rob sat forward, elbows on the desk, trying his best to look sincere. "I went with him a few times to restaurants and after hour bars. When he wanted to gamble we went to the Playboy Club. But there were too many nights out and my wife was getting annoyed, so I backed off. Since October the only interaction I've had with Peter was at work."

"Why October?"

"I told you I was too busy and I'd had enough of his crazy nights." He didn't mention that he'd met someone else he preferred spending his time with.

"What did he pay you?"

"Nothing. Other than tickets he never gave me any money. The hotel and everything else was up to me."

The smaller looked up from making notes. "You should've asked for more. How about the trips to Amsterdam?"

He felt his face color. "I paid for those on my own."

The note taker smirked again and shook his head. "You'd think you could get enough twat here. No accounting for taste I s'pose."

Rob stared at the guy, keeping his impatience at bay. He needed a drink, and soon.

They finally stood up, advising him they might be back. The bigger one stopped in the doorway. "What about the salesmen? Was there anyone he was close to?"

Rob shook his head. "Not that I know of. He liked to party with what we call the elite guys. You might want to talk to them."

He nodded. "We'll be doing that. See what the blokes say about you as well."

After his office door closed he got up and trying to keep his hands steady, poured himself a whiskey. This was no longer as simple as an angry, scorned wife. If Maddie ever found out the truth about Amsterdam he was sure it would be the end and he didn't want that. He shook his head. London had been so much easier to navigate than New York; Caroline was close by and there had been fewer late nights. Maddie had never even become suspicious. *Why is it that just when you think you have the world by the balls, reality comes along to bite you in the ass?*

=

It was almost five. Ignoring the unfinished work on his desk, he called Maddie telling her not to meet him at the pub, he might be running late. When she asked why he said he was in a rush and would tell her when he got home. As he hung up, Gilbert knocked and came in.

"What's happening, Rob?"

"Apparently, Peter had some sort of scam going on. I don't know much about it, but not to worry, it has nothing to do with you or the guys." He put on his jacket. "I have to get out of here. I'm not going to the pub tonight."

"Nor am I. With those inspectors around today the blokes are nervous. They'll want to get home to their missus'."

=

Twenty minutes later he rang the bell at a narrow townhouse in Belgravia. Caroline opened the door and pulled him inside, her mouth on his before he could speak. He stepped back and walked in silence to a small octagonal library. Every room, decorated with antique furniture upholstered in silks and damask, was pristine; no dust mote would dare to stir the air of this opulent maisonette.

She followed him, her smile fading. "What's wrong Rob? Has something happened?"

"Can you get me a drink, Caroline?"

He watched her as she went to a silver tray set with crystal decanters and glasses. She poured two drinks and handed him one.

"Rob. What is it?"

He drained his drink and handed her back the glass. "Another one."

She sighed and got up. "Rob, please."

"Caroline, Peter is being held by the police in New York. Two government guys came to the office today to talk to me and Kevin sent word that he wants me in his office at eight tomorrow morning. This is serious."

She sat back, her hand brushing his thigh. "What do you think will happen?"

He shook his head. "I have no idea. I've done nothing illegal, at least that I'm aware of. But I'm worried they'll find out about you."

"How can they?"

"Are you kidding, Caroline? Wake up. You're Rafa's mistress."

She shrugged. "So what?"

He wondered how she could be so fucking dense; she just wasn't getting it. But then, thinking wasn't exactly her strong suit. "Caroline, Rafa's keeping you in this place. If it comes out that you and I have been seeing one another whenever he leaves town, I'm out of here for sure. I also doubt he'll be pleased about sharing you."

She shrunk back, hands going to her face, her voice tinged with fear. "Oh no. That can't happen. You can't let it happen."

"Somehow they know more than I'd imagine. And I don't want to go into it."

"No, you have to tell me. I have to know what to say."

He finished his drink and lit a cigarette. She was right, it was better to give her some sort of script. Who knew what she'd come up with on her own. "If anyone from Inland Revenue comes here just tell them you know nothing. If they ask about me say I've been over for tea, that you wanted my opinion on some paintings you were thinking of buying. But I don't think that will happen." He took her hand and kissed it. "I hate to say this but I'm afraid we'll have to cool it for a while, at least until I see how this shakes out."

She stared back, sky-blue eyes welling with tears. "No. Rafa is in Germany and then he's going to Spain to see his wife." She practically spit the word out. "He won't be back for a week."

"I'll bet he'll be back a lot sooner than that." He put the glass on the table and leaned over to kiss her. "I should go. I have to get home."

She moved closer. "No Rob. You can't leave. I'm too upset. I'm sure your wife can wait."

He needed to get the hell out of there but he couldn't leave her, not like this. Taking her face in his hands, he kissed her tears. He pushed her gently back on the sofa, his hand already probing beneath her skirt. She sighed and reached for his belt. So another meeting had run late. Maddie would just have to wait. It wasn't as though he'd be staying all night.

=

At the front door, Caroline wept and clung to him, saying he simply had to come see her the next day. He glanced at his watch; it was already too close to the next day and he had to get out of there. He kissed her and said he'd ring her tomorrow.

He found a taxi quickly; they were never in short supply in Belgravia. He wanted, actually needed another drink, at least one. But there was no time and the pubs had already closed. He wasn't in any rush to go back to Caroline, not now anyway. He wasn't in love with her but she was hard to resist.

There were more important things on his mind now, first among them his wife.

=

Maddie was becoming worried; it was almost midnight and Rob wasn't home yet. Although it had been months since he'd gone out with Peter—he had told her that Peter was spending more time in New York—he still came home late once or twice a week. And yet she couldn't really complain. They now spent more nights out with friends as well as photographers and suppliers who continually invited them to dinner or events, if only to gain his favor.

There were still moments when the old thread stirred, her instincts on alert that something else was going on, but she was finding it hard to believe that he was having an affair; he was usually home by eleven when the pubs closed and desiring to make love to her.

She heard the front door of the building slam shut followed by his key in the lock. Without a word he went to the fridge and pulled out a beer. Sensing trouble, she asked if something was wrong.

"Maddie. I think you should sit down."

Shaking her head, she remained standing

Lighting a cigarette, he inhaled deeply. "Peter's been arrested."

She looked at him wide eyed. "Why?"

"Apparently for forgery and money laundering. A couple of inspectors from Inland Revenue came by the office today."

"Does this have anything to do with those envelopes you picked up for him?"

"They asked about those. But since I know nothing, I think they've backed off."

"Is that why you're so late?"

"Late? Oh yeah. I had to spend some time with Gilbert and some of the other guys in the office."

"You look tired."

"To tell you the truth, I'm exhausted. I have an early meeting with Kevin tomorrow. I guess I'll find out more then." He took her in his arms. "Not to worry. We'll get through this. Right now I just want to sleep."

=

It was still dark when he had woken her with soft kisses. Moving close to him, she was barely awake when he silently and gently made love to her. It had been uniquely sweet, as if in a dream, and they had fallen asleep in each other's arms. It was a night Maddie would always remember; it was the last peaceful moment they would have together in London.

=

The next morning Rob left early for his appointment with Kevin. At the door, Maddie asked if she should meet him at the pub after work.

"Let me see what happens today. I'll ring you at the office. You know I love you today."

Startled, she looked at him; she hadn't heard that phrase since they had left New York.

Chapter 2

Maddie was impatient to get to her office. This was the day she'd find out more about her new book. As she walked through Grosvenor Square, she realized it was late March and the morning light was returning. She had hated walking to work on dark winter mornings when the sky only brightened well after nine. Those months had been raw and damp, although never as frigid as New York. The office was poorly heated and one January morning, finally fed up with the constant chill, she had gone to Mr. Cowan to ask if he would mind if she and the other girls in the office wore pants to work. As the newest fashion statement they were becoming accepted in offices in New York and the trend was beginning to pick up in London as well.

He had stared back at her as if in shock. "No, Maddie. We wouldn't consider such a thing. Fashion or not, we can't have women wearing trousers. We like having our girls in miniskirts."

She was speechless. Women couldn't wear pants because the guys in the office wanted to gawk at their legs? Finally, she stammered, "It's really cold in our room."

"No one has ever complained before. Perhaps it's because you're American. Actually we rather like the chill. However, my dear, you will have an electric heater in an hour. That should help, don't you think?"

What she was thinking was that the Brits were perhaps even more chauvinistic than the Americans. She moved away before he could pat her bottom.

Later that day, as promised, she received a small electric heater along with a note that read, "Compliments of Mr. Cowan." After that, always attired in a heavy woolen sweater, she carried the heater with her to every meeting all winter long.

=

Rob arrived at Amrelco at eight fifteen and went straight to Kevin's office. Since he didn't see Kevin's secretary, he knocked lightly on the door.

Kevin opened it and looked around. "Looks like we're alone Rob. Come in. Jennifer will be along soon. She'll bring coffee."

Rob nodded, thinking Kevin looked fatigued but calm — maybe too calm.

Kevin sat down and lit a cigar, the odor drifting unpleasantly across his desk.

"So, Rob, we might as well get right to it."

Rob nodded, waiting.

"This thing with Peter is bad. Until a few days ago we had no idea he was receiving kickbacks, not to mention forging documents and signatures. I've also been informed that he set you up to be a courier although I understand that you knew nothing about it."

"That's true, Kevin. I had no idea. As far as I knew I was doing Peter a favor."

"You couldn't have known this, but even before Peter's arrest, Amrelco was being targeted not only by Inland Revenue but the U.S. Feds as well. After that fucking Bernie Cornfeld at IOS got himself in trouble, they set their sights on us. The discovery of Peter's fraudulent activities will now create even more problems for us."

He took a deep puff on his cigar. "It appears these investigations, as you experienced yesterday, will subject us to a great deal of unwanted scrutiny which, to be honest, is something we can ill afford. Especially with the tabloids snooping around. In light of these unfortunate developments we had an emergency board meeting last night and decided it would be best for all involved to close this office and move our entire operation to Miami."

Rob shifted in his chair, unsure he'd heard Kevin correctly. "What?" he asked in a stunned staccato.

"I said we are moving to Miami."

It was abrupt, too abrupt. *This can't be happening*, was a silent scream that seared his mind as a flash of rage surged through his body. With a clenched jaw, he asked, "What exactly does that mean?"

"I'm afraid it means you will have to inform your assistants of their termination as early as today." He pushed a folder across the desk. "Everything you need to know is in there. We've offered each of them severance as long as they finish out this week. There's no point to continue or complete all your projects. I'll let you know which ones we will still require."

Rob sat back attempting to slow his rapidly beating heart while containing his anger. How was it possible that a company that appeared solid the day before could, only hours later, be going down the tubes? There had to be more that Kevin wasn't telling him. Before he could ask, there was a knock on the door and Jenn came in holding a silver tray with coffee and two cups. "Just leave it on my desk, Jenn. Close the door on your way out." She glanced at him, obviously irritated at his curt manner. She left in a huff.

He poured coffee and handed Rob a cup. "I can see you're upset Rob, but take it easy. Let me tell how you fit into this. I'm offering you a choice. You can resign or you can go to Miami and help us sort out the problems. I'm afraid there will be a good deal of negative press and we'll require as much positive presence in the media as we can place or buy. You have a contract and I'm willing to honor it for as long as I can, although how long that will be I cannot tell you. But if you choose to leave the company, I suggest you consider returning to the States as soon as possible."

Aware that his hand was shaking, Rob put his cup down. The first surge of anger was subsiding, leaving in its wake the dregs of disbelief. "Why? What's the rush?"

Kevin stood up and walked to the window. He turned to look at Rob with narrowed eyes. "Because you're fucking Rafa's mistress."

Rob felt like he'd been hit with a baseball bat.

"Don't look so shocked. Rafa's a genius at business but he also happens to be extremely possessive of his women. I don't think you want him to find out that you've been stupid enough to trespass on what he considers his very private property."

"How do you know about Caroline?"

"Rafa has security, although to be honest, it's pretty lax. You've been observed ringing the bell. More than once. I would guess she wasn't serving you tea for three hours. The reports have come back to me and I'm willing to tear them up. Rafa will never see them. If

I were you, I'd have chosen Amsterdam over Caroline. Your little whore is far less of a threat than she is."

Rob stared at him, this time shock mixing with apprehension.

"Come on Rob, I know all about her. I've had her as well, so has Rafa and the other directors. She was a one-time gift to you from Peter, sort of as one of the guys. We never expected you'd go back for more. Although," he said almost wistfully, "I can understand it. She truly is a great fuck."

Feeling a knot grinding in his gut, Rob wanted to jump up, shout "Fuck you and the horse you rode in on," and escape from this insanity, but he wasn't sure he could stand, much less speak.

Kevin sat back down and poured more coffee. His look was hard. "It's your call, Rob. I want your decision in twenty-four hours. And by the way, if I were you I'd consider staying far away from Caroline."

=

He was sitting in his office staring unseeing at the wall. He couldn't even recall how he had gotten there. Finally, he stood up, closed the door and poured a couple of shots. Downing them neat, he closed his eyes as the alcohol worked its way through his body, calming him.

He had never been paranoid but he was beginning to question if he was living in some sort of Orwellian hell. Were unseen observers tracking everyone's moves? And yet it no longer mattered. It was over, all of it, and there was no choice but to accept the fact that he was royally screwed. All that was left to him were his decisions about what to do, although in truth, hadn't they had already been made?

Knowing he had to get his act together he looked through the folders Kevin had given him. At least they had been generous with his guys. He poured another drink, dreading the arrival of Gilbert and the other assistants.

=

It had been a hellish day. He wasn't the only one dismissing his team; the entire office had been reduced to a state of hysteria. Everyone was asking questions that no one could answer. Secretaries ran by his office sobbing and after packing up their belongings, several of the lesser executives came in to ask what he was going to do. His answer was simple: he didn't know.

As he left that night he passed darkened offices, empty except for overturned waste bins and papers strewn about. At the end of the hallway he heard a commotion. He stopped at what had been Peter's office, seeing several guys from accounting frantically destroying documents. One of them looked up and waved him away, shouting, "I think you'd best get out of here."

He backed off and went straight to the pub. He'd asked his assistants to join him, but they all begged off, too depressed about being sacked. Even the pub seemed oddly quiet, as if all the life had been drained from it. Or maybe it was just him, the reality beginning to sink in that he'd have to face Maddie and explain why, without warning, they had to return to the States. Since she loved living in London, probably even more than he did, he knew she'd not only be angry but she'd have a million questions, too many that he wasn't about to answer. After a few more whiskies, he had no choice but to return to the flat. He couldn't even call Caroline. Not that it mattered; she was a toy and sometimes toys had to be put aside.

=

Maddie was home and about to cook dinner. Rob noticed sacks from the green grocer and butcher on the kitchen counter. He kissed her and said they needed to talk. She looked happy and said she had something to tell him as well, but he should go first.

He took a beer out of the fridge and led her to the living room. Looking at him, she realized something was off. "What, Rob? Is something wrong?"

He nodded, sat down next to her on the couch and began telling her about his conversation with Kevin, omitting Caroline and Amsterdam.

She looked at him in wide-eyed horror. "No," she shouted. "No way. I'm not leaving."

"Maddie, calm down," he said, trying to put his arms around her.

She pushed him away. "Absolutely not, Rob. We've been happy here. London has changed our lives for the better. I figured we'd go back to New York one day, but not now. Not yet. If Amrelco is having problems, I think you should talk to James. He has contacts at some of the ad agencies. We've also met other people you can call. You already have a work visa; it won't be difficult finding another job."

"No, Maddie. I have to go to Miami."

"There must be other options. You don't even know if this job will last. It could all fall apart tomorrow."

"I don't believe that. This is the right thing to do. We'll probably have to leave within two weeks."

"No Rob. I can't do that. Why the big rush?"

The big rush is getting out of town before Rafa finds out about Caroline. "Look, maybe I can go first and then you follow me."

She sat down on the couch, wiping tears from her eyes. "I refuse to believe this."

"Maddie. You said you had something to tell me?"

She took a breath. "Cowan wants me to go to France for a couple of weeks to work with another publisher. My next book will be published in both countries. I don't get an opportunity like this every day."

He shook his head. "I'm sorry it's come to this. We can talk about it all night, Maddie, but it won't change anything. If you want to stay to finish up your book for a few weeks, then go ahead. I won't like it, but I understand."

She shook her head. "No, Rob. I don't think you do."

Chapter 3

Rob had been correct; all the talking led nowhere. The truth was she couldn't afford the flat on her own. She even went so far as buying a newspaper and searching through the "Flats to Let" section. It only confirmed that she'd have to leave Upper Berkeley Street and move somewhere far less expensive, most likely Bayswater where some of their friends lived, or even Hampstead, a long commute to Berkeley Square. It also implied a separation, which despite her anger and severe disappointment was not something she wanted.

When she told Mr. Braithwaite, he almost leaped out of his chair. "Maddie. Is this definite? Is there no way you can stay? Even a few months just to get the new book started?"

She shook her head. "I don't see how, Mr. Braithwaite." Trying to lighten the moment, she added, "Not without divorcing my husband."

He looked at her as if about to suggest just that, but stopped. "What about the book you're working on now?"

"Rob is leaving in a couple of weeks, but we've agreed that I'll stay for another month to finish it. I'm sure you can find someone to design the new one."

He shook his head. "It's not that simple, Maddie. I never told you this, but the French publishers approached us. They saw the marketing brochures you designed and, at their request, we also sent them some of your layouts. We've never had a book designer who got involved with research and worked with photographers. No. This is your book and they insist on you."

At once gratified and sad, she took a breath. "I don't know what to say."

=

Arriving home, she wrote Jay with the less than happy news. He responded within days, saying things weren't going well in Geneva either and asked her to send him a number or address in the States where he could reach her. After thinking about it, she realized the only possibility was her parents' house in New York.

=

Two weeks before she was to leave for Florida the phone rang just as she arrived home from work. She expected it to be Rob; he had been calling every few days. So far everything seemed to be running smoothly; the office was busy, Florida was hot and he couldn't wait for her to get there.

When she answered, it was Claire asking if she'd have dinner with her and James the next night.

"That would be nice Claire. But you must know I'm not in the best mood these days."

"Then we'll just have to cheer you up. Meet us at the Chinese Dragon in Soho at seven."

As she put the phone down, it rang again. She answered, thinking Claire was calling back. "Claire?"

"Is this Rob MacLeod's flat?"

"Sorry. I thought someone was calling back. Can I help you?"

"My name is Caroline. Is this Maddie? We met at Amrelco. At a party last summer."

"Yes, I remember. You were with Rafa."

"Yes. Well. I'd really like to speak with Rob."

"He's not here. He left for the States two weeks ago."

Unexpectedly she heard sobbing. "That can't be. He never called."

Maddie felt her blood ran cold. "What are you talking about?"

"I haven't heard from him. I've tried calling Amrelco, but they kept telling me he was out of the office. Finally, someone gave me your number. I'm sorry, but I had to call."

"Why do you want to speak to him? Is there something I can do?" All she heard was silence. "Caroline. What is it?'

"I, I think I'm pregnant." Her voice broke. "Oh God, I must speak with him. How could he have left without calling?"

Maddie stopped breathing. Through clenched teeth she asked, "How long have you been involved with him, Caroline?"

Maddie heard her hesitate. "Ah, several months, I would say."

You would say? Maddie forced herself to remain calm. "I will certainly let him know you called. I assume he has your number?"

"Yes, of course. But where is he?"

"Miami."

"Oh no. How could he do this to me?"

"To you?" Maddie could feel her heart pounding. It was becoming more and more difficult to maintain her composure.

"Yes. To me." Her pleading had turned to anger. "Listen Maddie, I wasn't going to say anything, but you do know about Peter's little orgies, don't you?"

This just keeps getting better and better. "What are you talking about?"

"You don't know? Whenever the elite salesman came to London, Peter would throw a party at the townhouse. A few girls from the office would always come. They got paid overtime, if you know what I mean. Mostly though there were high-class prostitutes."

Maddie paused. *Wasn't there a phrase, something like "Ignorance is bliss?"*

"I assume you know about this because you were there?"

She hesitated. "Yes. Well, actually Rafa took me once or twice. It was before..." she hesitated, "... before we were really together. I don't like doing threesomes."

She doesn't like doing threesomes? How fucking sweet!

"And Rob was there?"

"Yes, Maddie. He was sort of Peter's sidekick. Sorry, but I thought you should know."

Of course, you little bitch. You're angry with him so you're laying it on me.

"So Caroline, now that I know, is there any more information you'd like to impart?" She didn't intend to sound quite so sarcastic, it just came out that way.

"I'm sorry. I know this must be upsetting for you. Are you going to meet him in Florida?"

She took a breath, taking a few seconds to mull over that salient question. "Look Caroline, I have a better idea. Why don't I give you the number at his office? Then you can call him and discuss your problem."

"Oh, Maddie. I can't believe you're so understanding. Do you think he'll be back in London soon?"

Understanding? Was this girl a total twit or just out there in the twilight zone? Rob obviously wasn't screwing her because of her brains. "Maybe you should ask him. And Caroline, make sure you tell him exactly how understanding I am."

"Oh yes. I will. You're a dear. Thank you so much."

"Good luck Caroline." *And good luck to you Rob, you fucking bastard.*

She put the phone down carefully. Otherwise she might have thrown it against the wall. For a while, everything had been so good — and when it hadn't, she had ignored her instincts and put on blinders, refusing to believe that Rob hadn't really changed.

She picked up a framed photograph of Rob with his arm around her. He was holding up a glass of beer and laughing as she looked up at him with a happy, adoring smile. Gilbert had snapped at the pub one night around Christmas — no doubt when Rob was already screwing Caroline. She let go of it and it dropped to the floor, the glass shattering at her feet. She looked down with grim satisfaction; she'd sweep up the glass but leave the fractured picture next to the phone. The next time Rob called she intended to be staring at it.

Chapter 4

Her last day in London was spent saying goodbye to her friends and co-workers. As Mr. Braithwaite and Mr. Cowen shook her hand, each lamented that they were losing, as Mr. Cowan put it, "Our star designer." He promised to send her book to New York when it was printed. She left with tears in her eyes.

Later, after a last dinner with James and Claire, Claire hugged her, saying she still wished she didn't have to leave. "It's just that too many things went wrong at once. None of us really believed that Amrelco was being investigated for fraud and tax evasion. And yet I still don't understand why Rob couldn't have stayed in London. He'd surely have found a job with one of the agencies here."

Maddie shook her head. "I guess it wasn't meant to be."

"Well," Claire said, perking up, "maybe you'll like Miami. At least it will be warm there. We'll come visit."

=

The phone was ringing as she unlocked the door. She hadn't answered since the night Caroline had called. Glancing at the scratched photo in the broken frame, she went to pick it up.

"Maddie? Thank God you finally answered." Rob sounded even more desperate than she had expected. It didn't offer her much in the way of satisfaction.

"What do you want Rob?"

"Why haven't you answered the phone?"

"What was I going to say? Ask about the weather and by the way, is Caroline really pregnant?"

"It's not what it seems."

"No? I think she made it pretty clear."

He paused. "She's not pregnant."

"You know, Rob, I didn't think she was. She was so desperate she had to come up with an excuse. Just telling me about the affair and the prostitutes at Peter's might not have been quite enough?" She brushed away unexpected tears; this was no time for weakness.

"Maddie, it wasn't like that. You're the one I love. You're my wife and the only woman I want."

"Apparently that's not quite the truth."

"Look, we'll talk when you get here. I promise I'll change. You have to understand that place was crazy. I never intended to get caught up in it. You're my soul mate, the woman I love. We'll work it out. I'll pick you up at the airport Sunday."

She took a breath. "Rob, I'm not coming to Florida. You've screwed me around for the last time. I'm going to New York."

"You can't."

"Try and stop me."

"I can't believe this. Why? You belong here, with me."

"Are you seriously asking why? If you can't figure it out on your own, I suggest you call Caroline or maybe Ava or one of the others. I've had enough of your bullshit lies. If you want, you can reach me at my parents' house. That is, until I get a job and find an apartment."

"How can you do this?"

"Well, I get on the plane. My mother meets me…"

"Shit. Stop it. Maddie, you have to come to Florida."

"No I don't…bye, Rob."

He shouted, "Don't hang up."

"Why not? There's nothing more to say."

"Look. I have to think. Things aren't that great here. I'm afraid the whole thing might collapse. I'll come to New York. I need a few weeks."

"Take your time. Make sure you don't give any girls down there my number."

"That was unnecessary."

"Was it? I have to go."

She hung up feeling no satisfaction, only emptiness. Wiping away tears, she asked herself for the hundredth time how she could still be in love with him. He drank, he lied, he was unfaithful, not once but innumerable times. Why? Because the girls were there and available; she knew he had no feelings for them. Rob was a man determined to live by nobody's rules but his own, which in truth, were no rules at all. He did what he pleased when he pleased, not to mention with whomever he pleased.

She recalled the phrase, "Whatever doesn't kill you, makes you stronger." While she hated to leave London, she was beginning to get past it. There would be new jobs and new people. Maybe Jay would return soon. New York beckoned and anticipation was beginning to replace disappointment. An incredible year had ended in disaster and yet it was a year she would never forget.

Part 6

*This is how we bring about our own damnation you
know — by ignoring the voice that begs us to stop.
To stop while there's still time.*

Stephen King

Chapter 1

Maddie had barely put one foot in her mother's new Jaguar when she started in. "What's going on with you and Rob? Why are you here when he's in Florida? Are you separated?"

Maddie took a breath. "Mom, I just got off a seven-hour flight. Give me a minute."

Deciding what to tell her mother was something she should have considered on the plane, but all she had thought about was Rob and how their lives were now going to play out—together or apart.

"Everything is fine Mom. I told you on the phone; they decided to close the London office because the company was being investigated by Inland Revenue and the Feds. That's all I know." *Well, almost.*

"But that man who hired Rob, Peter. It was all over the papers that he was arrested for some sort of fraud. And then it disappeared. Whatever happened?"

"To be honest, we never found out anything more. I don't think anyone at Amrelco knew what he was doing. Not until it was too late. By then the company was already in trouble."

"So why didn't you go to Florida?"

"A couple of weeks ago Rob began to feel the company was about to dissolve, so there was no point. Of course we're not separated. He'll be here in a week or two." She hoped she sounded convincing.

"What will you do?"

"If it's all right, I'll stay with you and Harry until I can find a job and an apartment."

"Of course, Maddie. We'll be glad to have you. You should call American Heritage. Maybe you can get your old job back."

"I plan to do that, Mom. I'd love to go back there. That is if they'll have me."

"Why wouldn't they? Your book won an award."

=

Ten days had passed since she had returned to New York and despite that it had been six weeks since she had seen Rob, she was far less concerned with him than she was about getting back to work. When she called American Heritage she was told Irwin was no longer there, the company had been sold and the book division closed. It was a huge disappointment on many levels. But it wasn't until she called the first headhunter, her old friend Mr. Collins, that she discovered she'd returned to an economic recession, something she had never heard of, much less experienced or understood. Despite her impressive resume, every employment agency she spoke to had been unusually pessimistic about the availability of jobs.

It was almost another week before Mr. Collins called back with a slim possibility; a new financial magazine called *Modern Securities* was looking for an art director.

"There are a couple of problems with it Maddie. I don't think you're very familiar with the stock market and the office is all the way downtown in the Financial District. Also, there's stiff competition and since it's not exactly the area of your expertise, you might want to pass on this one."

"Not at all, Mr. Collins. Make the appointment. I'll go to the interview even if it's in Brooklyn."

=

Maddie took the #1 train to Cortlandt Street. The only problem was finding her way out of the subway. Several exits were blocked due to the construction of two enormous buildings that were being called the World Trade Center. "Do Not Enter" or "Sidewalk Closed" signs on almost every corner made walking precarious.

Bruce Wagner, the publisher of *Modern Securities*, turned out to be very handsome. Cobalt blue eyes and designer-cut blond hair were set off by a deep charcoal grey suit that fit as though it was made for him—which she had little doubt it was. Not a wrinkle or crease was out of place. His associate and financial partner, Phil Decker sat off to the side, more observer than participant. Tall, with dark hair and intense eyes, he was nothing to scoff at either. She reminded herself that she was still married. Or was she?

She observed all this as she entered the office, sizing up the two men with more confidence than she felt and smiling as she met their appraising stares. She had purposely worn a deep mahogany patent leather coat and a large floppy hat, both the latest rage in London. Underneath she was wearing one of her shortest minis and high boots. As she slid off her coat, she watched as both pairs of eyes widened in what she hoped was appreciation. She had dressed for impact and was aware she had at least achieved that goal. Now she had to sell herself and her portfolio.

She had expected Mr. Wagner to be older, certainly not in his early thirties and she wondered briefly where the money was coming from to fund this venture. She had done her homework, but when she mentioned there was another well-established magazine in the same category, he waved it away.

"Phil and I have been working on this project for two years and we now have the backing to launch it. The statement we make with this publication will be our own." He came across as energetic and self-assured.

Taken as she was with both men, they, in turn, appeared to be captivated by her. After discussing how she had liked living and working in London, Mr. Wagner asked to see her portfolio. Without much more discussion, Mr. Decker, who said to please call him Phil, surprised her by asking if she could start the following Monday. After negotiating her salary, Maddie citing a figure and they countering by referencing the current recession, they came to an almost satisfactory number, at least for her. If she was careful, she could now get out of her mother's house and find an apartment, one she could afford on her own.

On the street she took a much needed breath. The feminist credo about women being objectified be damned, at least for that moment. When it came to getting a job in a crunch, her presentation, not to mention her miniskirt, had worked like a charm. Of course she'd had the portfolio to support it. She looked out at the world and smiled, beginning to comprehend what confidence felt like.

That weekend she began hunting for an apartment. As she walked from building to building she thought of the apartment on East Seventy-Seventh Street and wished she and Rob could return to it. But that was ancient history. The Maddie of two years before had dreams that had no chance of coming true. And yet how could she have known? The conflicts she had endured with Rob in that apartment and later in London hadn't hardened her, they had taught her that she could depend on no one but herself. She had no idea where Rob's head was or what he planned to do, but unless things changed, she was now on her own.

Chapter 2

Rob should have been loving Miami. When he left London he had relished the thought of a few weeks of freedom before Maddie arrived. He'd found a garden apartment on a quiet street in Coconut Grove, one he thought she would like. And yet it wasn't working out quite as he had anticipated. He was unexpectedly lonely, particularly at night. Having never lived alone — he had gone from his parents directly to Allison and then to Maddie — he missed having someone to come home to.

He'd also rented a well-used 1968 Mustang, more because it was cheap than stylish. It served the purpose of driving to the Amrelco office, or more realistically what was left of it, in downtown Miami, not a particularly pleasant place. The mood in the office was grim and although he was still getting a paycheck he worried it wouldn't continue much longer. He figured he'd wait for Maddie and they could decide together what to do. He'd also had enough out of control sex for a while and promised himself he wouldn't screw around. He laughingly told himself he could manage to wait until Maddie arrived.

The first two weeks his calls to Maddie had gone well. Although she was still sad about having to leave London, she said she was coming to terms with it. Her only questions were about finding a job in Miami.

He had assured her there would be no problem. "There are quite a few magazines being produced here. Some in Spanish, others bilingual. I'll bet one of them would love to have an art director from New York and London."

She had laughed. "Maybe I'll have a chance to learn Spanish. But what happens if there's no more Amrelco?"

He had chosen not to mention how close that reality was becoming. "There are a few ad agencies here. I'll check them out. Who knows, maybe we'll like living in Florida. It's pretty laid back and the best is, it's always warm." As he was saying it, he considered it might actually be an option. With his experience he could very well become a big fish in this little swamp. So could Maddie. Yet down deep he knew Maddie was unlikely go for it; she was becoming too ambitious for this backwater. Still, it was important to at least sound optimistic.

Everything changed the afternoon the receptionist told him there was a call from London. Expecting it to be Maddie, he was surprised and not a little alarmed at hearing Caroline's breathy voice.

Grabbing a cigarette, he had cautiously asked how she was and apologized for not calling before he left.

Suddenly he wished he hadn't asked. As she began to describe her conversation with Maddie, he began to sweat. Thinking he'd heard enough, he tried to wedge a word into her insidious chatter by saying he had to go to a meeting. But she didn't stop, and it was only when she repeated exactly what she had said to Maddie that she had gotten his full attention. After holding himself back from shouting that she was a mindless twit who had fucked up his life, he finally got her off the phone by promising to ring her the next day.

Taking a much needed breath, he looked at his watch. It was almost eight in London. He had to call Maddie and try to explain. Explain what? He shook his head. He had thought it was all behind him, that he'd gotten away free.

In retrospect, his mistake was in deciding to wait. He convinced himself that she'd cool off and call him, if only to vent. After three days of silence, curiosity overcame his apprehension and after a couple of shots he picked up the phone. There was no answer at the flat and the next day when he called her office, her voice was ice. In a clipped tone she said she couldn't talk. When he called that night and every night following, she didn't answer.

After almost two weeks, he had become frantic. It had gotten so bad that when he finished work he began hitting the bars around the "Grove," as the locals called it. Despite his promise to himself, he picked up girls, mostly secretaries or shop girls, working out his anger and frustration by getting shitfaced and fucking all night. Whenever one of them — he didn't even know their names — asked what was wrong, he'd refuse to answer. He counted the days till Maddie's arrival.

When she finally answered the night before she was to leave, things hadn't gone quite as he had hoped. It was his own fault; after all those ignored phone calls he should have realized that she would be less than amenable to his explanations, much less his apologies. But when she told him she had changed her flight to New York he had been truly shaken. He would never have believed she'd have the balls to do that to him.

After she hung up, he had stared at the phone. *The bitch hung up on me?* He wanted to go out and get drunk, but he knew it was time to act, not react. He had to think, make a decision about what he was going to do. In truth, Miami sucked. It was time to blow the joint and go home.

Chapter 3

Maddie was in the basement when she heard the doorbell ring. She ignored it, knowing her mother would answer. She was grateful that her parents had let her store several cartons of housewares, her paintings and books as well as her bed and a few basic pieces of furniture. It wasn't much, but enough to start; the rest she could buy later. She was so absorbed she barely heard her mother yelling for her.

"Now what?" she muttered to herself, wiping dust off her hands. It seemed her mother continually required her attention if only to listen to her bridge scores or what she and her friends had shot that day at the golf club. In Maddie's opinion, golf was boring enough to play, much less talk about. She went upstairs curious as to why her mother sounded so excited. Entering the foyer, she stopped abruptly; that Rob was standing in the doorway was shocking enough, but seeing her mother happily embracing him was almost too much to bear.

"Maddie, what's wrong with you. Your husband is here," she said effusively. "Finally." The last said with a touch of pique.

Knowing there was no choice, she went to Rob. He enfolded her in his arms. "You can't know how much I missed you," he said, his voice deep and low. As he kissed her she hugged him, purely for show. Her mother still had no idea what was going on between them and it wasn't the moment to provoke questions. As she began to pull back he clasped her closer and whispered in her ear, "Kiss me, Maddie. At least look like you're glad I'm here."

Her mother chimed in, "Maddie. Say something. Aren't you thrilled that Rob's home?"

"Of course, Mom. I'm just surprised. I thought he wasn't coming for a few more days." *Or at all.*

Rob laughed easily. "I realized I couldn't live without my girl for another moment."

Maddie rolled her eyes as her mother nodded her approval. "You look wonderful, Rob. Miami must have agreed with you. Leave your suitcases here. I was just making lunch. You arrived just in time." Maddie wondered when she had become a fan.

Forcing a smile, he put his arm around Maddie, steering her toward her bedroom. "We'll be right there."

After closing the door, he drew her into another embrace. She pulled away. "Come on, Maddie. Talk to me. We have to get past this. Being away from you has been torture for me. I've had plenty of time to think. I know I made mistakes and I promise we can start again."

She sat down on the bed and looked up at him. "I thought in London we had it all. I loved and trusted you. We had great jobs and good friends. I kept thinking how lucky we were. Then I found out it was all a lie."

He kneeled before her, taking her face in his hands. "Maddie. That's behind us. It was crazy with Peter and all the sex in the office. I knew you had no idea and it wasn't something I was ever going to tell you." He took a breath. "I don't care what Caroline said. It wasn't true. You're the only woman in my life. I don't want to live without you."

She pulled back. *Sex in the office?* That was a new one. Or maybe not. Jay had written: "It's like a brothel here. You can screw any girl any time you want. They'll even leave their typewriters for however long it takes."

No wonder the company had imploded; it had gone from a revenue machine to a mindless indulgence of too much money, sex and booze. Did big financial deals drive the need for sexual gratification, not to mention forgery and fraud? And did everyone at Amrelco just go about their business while Kevin, Peter and the other executives took short sabbaticals with the secretaries? What about Gilbert and Rob's other assistants? No doubt they were considered serfs, standing aside and watching while the big boys played.

She shook her head, thinking that while Rob was having daily bacchanals, she was trying not to get too close to her very nice editor who didn't bathe very often.

"I no longer know what's true or not."

His change of subject was abrupt. "Look Maddie. I understand why you took a new apartment. I wish you had waited but it's all right."

"You wish I had waited? You were in Florida. I didn't know when or, for that matter, if you were coming back. I wasn't sure I wanted you to."

"But you never gave me a chance to explain. The only time we spoke was the night before you left and you hung up on me."

"Rob. No matter what your explanation, I wouldn't have believed you. After the call from Caroline, I realized I had to take control of my life, that I could depend on no one but myself. That's why I came back to New York. You have to understand that I did this for me, not for us. There was no us."

She saw a flash of irritation cross his face. "Maddie. I am your husband."

"I'm not sure what that means."

"What it means is we belong together, not apart. I'm perfectly aware that it's up to me to prove that you can trust me. And I promise I will."

Maddie understood she was being seduced. And maybe that's what she really desired. She wanted to him to work to get her back; she needed to be convinced. At the same time, she was aware that this was the same sort of melodrama they had acted out before. In the past the same promises had been made and all too quickly broken. And yet it was a raw fact that when he touched her he left spots of fire on her skin. Resisting him was like trying to reverse gravity.

"Are you coming?" Maddie's mother yelled from the kitchen.

Maddie glanced at Rob and they both laughed. With the tension at least fractured if not entirely broken, he took her hands and kissed her.

"Come on Maddie. Let's have lunch and then I'll help you get organized. When are the movers coming?"

"Next Friday."

He nodded. "Do you think I can borrow your mother's car tomorrow? I'd like to see the kids and my folks. I should also probably take the motorcycle out for a spin. It's been too long."

"I'm sure it's not a problem. Ask her."

"Why don't you come with me?"

"No. You should go on your own."

"I don't want to be a minute without you."

"Look, Rob. Let's take it one day at a time."

"By the way, I called John Langer from Florida. I have a meeting with him next week. I hear it's rough out there."

Maddie nodded. "You have no idea. I've never seen so few jobs available. I was lucky."

"Lucky?"

"To be perfectly honest, I think it may have been the outfit I was wearing as opposed to any great talent on my part."

He looked at her questioningly.

She shook her head. "I'll explain it later."

=

Later he gave her no time to explain. They had chatted about London with her parents during and after dinner. He'd been careful not to drink too much, keeping it to one scotch before and a couple of glasses of Cabernet at dinner. After her parents yawned and said their good nights, he asked Maddie if she'd like to go outside for a few minutes. He picked up on her reticence; something he expected. He had no intention of rushing her.

They walked out to the pool. She let him take her hand and they sat together on one of the chaises. The night was warm with a full moon. Trees swayed in a soft breeze, throwing shifting shadows over them.

"I love you Maddie and I want to make love to you."

He heard her sigh. "I don't know."

"Maddie, please. We'll make a fresh start. No more screw ups, I promise. You're the only woman I want. We'll make it work."

"After all this, how can I ever trust you?"

"Just give me the chance to prove how much you mean to me." He put his arms around her and kissed her lightly. When she looked up at him, he kissed her again, this time feeling tentative hands on his shoulders. He pulled her tighter. "Let's go inside," he whispered.

"Rob…"

"It's okay Maddie. Let's just get into bed. We'll take it from there. If you're not ready, then we'll wait."

She refused to let him undress her and put on one of her old T-shirts. He didn't remind her that they always slept together naked.

In bed he moved close and put his arm around her. Feeling her relax, he leaned over to kiss her while barely caressing her breasts with a fingertip. Whispering how much she meant to him, he moved his hand, parting her legs and touching her gently between her thighs. He knew her spots and waited until he heard her soft sighs.

"Put your arms around me," he whispered, his fingers becoming more insistent. As she did, he took her slowly, each watching the other through deepening desire.

"Rob," she whispered.

He hugged her to him, saying, "I love you," as she came with him. They fell asleep in each other's arms.

Chapter 4

The Cattleman looked and smelled as good as he remembered. He'd forgotten how much he missed a real American steak.

As he sat down, Ted, his old waiter, came over with a JW Red. "Glad to have you back, Mr. MacLeod."

"Thanks Teddy. It's nice to be back."

"So?" Ken asked.

Rob took a breath and lit a Rothman. He still had a few packs left and rather liked the image of smoking British cigarettes. He reminded himself to check the tobacco stands to see if he could get them in New York. "Well, guess I'm back sooner than I thought. Talk about a cluster fuck."

"Why don't you start at the beginning or maybe the end. I never heard from you after you left for Florida."

"It went downhill fast. Amrelco was essentially ripping off its own investors and Peter ended up paying the price." He shook his head. "It was bad shit, Ken. I should have just come back to New York."

"What about Maddie. Is everything all right with you two?"

Rob drained his drink. "What can I say? I screwed up."

"You just can't keep it in your pants can you?"

"Listen. It was cool and I was careful. You could get girls, drugs, anything you wanted. Even after I started with Caroline I never stayed out very late. There was no way that Maddie would have ever known. I never thought the twit would call her."

Ken shivered. "Ouch."

"Yeah. Now she's acting like some sort of feminist. I can't believe she rented an apartment without me."

"Where is it? East Side, I assume?"

"Of course. Seventy-ninth and First. Another two blocks and we'd be in the damn river.

He laughed. "Good for her."

"C'mon Ken. Whose side are you on?" He shook his head. "She called me yesterday to meet her at Stern's. They got in a shipment of Spanish furniture and she saw a headboard she wanted to buy. I reminded her that I wasn't working yet but she insisted. It's not bad. Dark stained walnut with several rows of carved spools. I told her I thought it was too feminine but she was practically jumping up and down. If I didn't buy it, I think she would have and I didn't want that. Where's this sudden independence coming from?"

"I hope she was, um, appreciative."

"Yeah, and about freaking time. I finally did something right."

"To be honest, Rob, I'm surprised she didn't divorce you."

Rob drained his scotch and signaled for another. "I'd usually say, 'Fuck you' to a comment like that but, though I hate to say it, you're probably right. I'll get her back where I want her though. I've just got to get this job nailed down."

"At LRG?"

"Yeah. I have a meeting with John later. I'm afraid if I call, shit, what's the guy's name? Oh yeah, Chuck, he's the head hunter, he'll just tell me to try for corporate promotion. Here we go again."

"It's not such a bad idea, Rob. You should keep your options open."

"What I really want is to get back to the agency."

"That may not be so easy right now. The economy has changed everything. By the way, have you seen your kids?"

"Last weekend. They've really grown. The only problem, as always, was Allison. She was furious that I hadn't called or written often enough from London." He neglected to mention that Allison hadn't only been angry about his not being in touch; it had more to do with late alimony payments. After she threatened to take him to court, he'd placated her by saying a job at the agency was waiting and promising he'd catch up quickly. That it wasn't quite true didn't matter; it had shut her up and that was enough.

"By the way, what's happening with Evan?"

Ken smirked. "Danielle threw him out. He was having an affair with some chick at the office and she found out. He moved in with John until he can find a place."

"Is he all right?"

"I don't really know. He's been under the radar for a few weeks. When he realizes you're home, I'm sure he'll call. He'll want advice from the master."

"Some master I turned out to be. Another drink?"

"No, Rob. And if you're seeing John I'd lay off it."

"Shit. You sound like Maddie. Nobody'll know."

=

When he arrived at LRG, Mamie enveloped him in a bear hug and John welcomed him with a warm handshake. They sat in this office, Rob becoming slowly aware that the usual frantic hum seemed oddly muted. John told him they'd had to let several people go and that Charlie had left the agency six months before.

"It created quite an upheaval since he was a founding partner and there was a conflict on the buy-back of stock." Laughing without mirth, he said, "I guess he just got fed up with the lack of imagination on the part of our clients. Unfortunately, they're playing it safe just like everyone else in order to survive this damned recession." He shook his head. "One day in the middle of a meeting, Charlie stood up, pounded his fist on the table and shouted that the creative heyday of advertising was on its deathbed and he was cashing out and moving to Montana to paint. And that, as they say, was that."

"Too bad, John. He's a talented guy."

"I was sorry to see him go. He was the creative soul of this agency and although we brought in Dave Crimmins, it's not the same. I wish you had come back a couple of months ago Rob, because nothing good is happening now. That doesn't mean we won't need someone like you in the future. There may be some freelance work until a position opens up. You'll have to keep in touch or I'll call you."

As he left he felt that John had been open and candid, although it wasn't the conversation he had anticipated. He had thought it would be a no brainer and they'd be glad to have him back. *Fuck this recession*, he thought lighting up another Rothman. It was the last one in the pack. Crumpling it up, he tossed it into a trash can.

Noticing a phone booth on the opposite corner, he called Mary Diehl, still rumored to be the best employment agency for artists and writers. The problem, he was told, wasn't him; it was, as everyone was calling it, "The damned recession." No matter who he spoke to, they regurgitated the same message: no one was hiring and all the agencies were laying off talented employees.

The next call was to Chuck, who said to call back in a few days; there was a design group that might be looking for an art director. A bit more optimistic, Rob hung up and called Fred who was happily ensconced as the managing editor at Esquire. After making a lunch date for the following week, Fred said that unfortunately there were no jobs open at Esquire which, despite the recession, was still holding its own against Playboy. With a laugh, he said, "Our girls aren't as naked, but our articles are still better."

He suggested Rob call their mutual friend Chad, a graphic designer they knew from their days at *Cavalier*. "He started his own company, Studio 5, a few years ago. They do work for some of the agencies as well as promotion and packaging for Seagram's and Helena Rubinstein. Call him, Rob. He always liked you."

Rob took the number and called on the spot. Chad was happy to hear from him; he actually sounded like the one bright spot in a sea of depression. "Since all the companies are downsizing, we're getting plenty of work. Unfortunately, I don't need anyone full time, but if you want to freelance, come in next week for two or three days."

"Thanks Chad. How's Monday?"

"Great. Looking forward to seeing you again. By the way are you still married to…what's her name?"

Rob laughed, "Allison?"

"Yeah. Sorry I couldn't remember."

And I wish I could forget. "No, Chad. There's a new one. I'm sure you'll get a chance to meet her. She's also an art director."

"Hey, good going. I'm impressed, although knowing you I shouldn't be surprised."

=

It wasn't what he wanted, but it was work. What bothered him was that he felt he was starting over, not where he should be at thirty-two. Despite that he had gained a good deal of positive recognition before he left for London, he was well aware that people, especially agency people, had short memories. Finding a job was obviously not going to be the slam dunk he'd envisioned. As for Maddie, he asked himself how it was that she seemed to get hired so quickly. She probably turned on her sexy act, which, he had to admit, was pretty irresistible. That she was just beginning to understand her appeal to men was something he gave himself credit for. When he'd met her she'd been insecure and unsure of herself; it was one of the things that attracted him. But that had been replaced by a new confidence, something he had inadvertently triggered by his sloppy actions. It was the old Maddie that he preferred. He'd get her back where he wanted her, he was sure of it.

When he looked up he was already in the East Sixties. Across the street he saw a bar called O'Leary's. Inside, a white haired bartender swiped the bar with a cloth and dropped a cardboard coaster in front of him asking laconically what he wanted. Rob told him JW Red on the rocks. While he waited, he looked around. The place had the usual wood paneling and red-velvet booths plus a few tables in the middle. The lighting was dim except for stripes of daylight filtering through partially drawn blinds shielding the dusty front windows. A couple of older men were seated in the shadows at the end of the bar, but he was the only one wearing a suit. Loosening his tie, he drained his drink and looked around for the bartender. A few minutes later a different bartender appeared, this one a female. She asked if he wanted a refill. He nodded absently and before he could tell her what he was drinking, she said, "Johnnie Walker Red. Right?"

Bewildered, he stared at her.

"You don't remember me, do you? I used to work at Scotty's Pub on the West Side. You came in sometimes after work. You were working at some ad agency. Then I never saw you again and I wondered what happened."

He squinted at her. "Yeah, I think I remember. I've been away, living in London."

"Well, lucky you. Welcome back. By the way, I'm Denise."

He reached across and shook her hand. "Hi Denise, nice to see you again. But coming back hasn't been exactly welcoming. It's difficult finding a job."

She nodded; her long black hair shining in the glow of small spotlights above the bar. "So I hear. I guess the worse the job market, the more the need for bartenders." Rob smiled and took a closer look, vaguely recalling talking with her on a couple of problematic nights when he was in no rush to go home. Denise was a big girl, close to six feet tall with an olive complexion, large brown eyes and a pleasant, if not pretty face.

He watched as she served another customer, this one in a suit as well. When she returned, she asked him questions about London until the bar began filling up with men on their way home from work.

Rob got up and paid the tab. Denise gave him a warm smile. "Don't get lost again. I'm here weekdays, four till twelve."

Chapter 5

After completing two issues of *Modern Securities*, Maddie was beginning to realize the job wasn't quite what she anticipated. As art director it was her job to read the articles and have them illustrated, design and lay out the pages and complete camera-ready mechanicals. What hadn't been mentioned was she was also expected to assist Ed, the production manager, to coordinate the pagination, which meant spacing the ads within the editorial, a job he was unable to get done on this own.

She was becoming tired and frustrated. She seldom made it home before eight, more often nine and all too frequently by the time she left, all the other offices in the building were dark.

At least Rob was freelancing at Chad's. He'd had several interviews that so far had gone nowhere. Lately she was coming home to find him drinking and cantankerous. One night he'd growled at her, "I want a wife, not a workaholic. Why do we have to have dinner at ten every night?"

"Come on, Rob. You know this business. There's too much work and it has to get done. I don't like staying so late, not to mention that it makes me nervous walking to the subway when the streets are dark and deserted."

"Well, don't expect me to be here every night waiting for you."

"What the hell does that mean?" She realized too late she'd said it as a challenge. When he was drinking he was always on edge.

He looked at her through narrowed eyes. "It means you better start coming home earlier."

"Stop it, Rob. You're being ridiculous."

"Yeah, Maddie, that's me. The out-of-work ridiculous art director who has to depend on his poor over-worked wife. Fuck that."

He picked up the bottle of scotch and poured the little that remained into his glass.

"But you are working. I thought you liked it at Chad's."

"I belong at an agency, not some crappy studio."

"You'll find a job soon. I'm sure of it." She went to kiss him but he stepped back. "Well look at that," he said, turning his glass upside down. He watched as one drop hit the floor. "No more scotch. I guess I'll have to go out and get some more."

"Please, Rob. I picked up dinner for us."

"How nice of you," he said derisively. "But I'd rather go out."

She watched silently as he walked to the door. At one time she might have tried to stop him, but lately everything seemed to make him angry. She was finding it more and more difficult to placate him.

=

Rob was glad to get out of there. He was fed up listening to Maddie and her excuses about having too much work. He considered it might be unreasonable, but he didn't particularly care. His thoughts turned to Denise. She'd probably be at the bar tonight, but that was down in the Sixties and he wasn't much in the mood for friendly conversation. Instead he began walking uptown on Second Avenue. Deciding to go to Martell's he turned into Eighty-Fifth Street and headed toward Third almost missing a dimly lit, ramshackle one-story building. Curious that there was no sign out front, he looked in the window seeing several couples sitting at a bar and some guys standing and talking. He thought it might be a private club but decided to go in anyway. As he entered everyone glanced at him briefly and then resumed their conversations. He sat down at the bar and after asking for a beer watched a couple of guys boisterously cheering on a pony-tailed blonde playing an electronic pinball machine. He asked the bartender what the place was called and why there was no sign.

The bartender introduced himself as Roy and held out his hand. "Welcome to Pedro's. The best kept secret in Yorkville."

=

It was a couple of weeks later that Maddie realized she was going to miss her deadline to release the next issue of the magazine to the printer. No matter what she and Ed tried to do, there were too many loose ends and not enough time to tie them up. Bruce had been out all afternoon in meetings with investors and one of the reasons for her lateness was that he'd rushed her to design some last minute promotional materials for him. By the time he returned that evening almost everyone had left.

Frustrated, she went to his office and sat down in the chair opposite his massive glass-topped desk.

He looked up from some papers he was signing. "What is it? I don't have much time."

"Bruce, we have to talk. You must realize that a monthly magazine of eighty pages is too much for one person. There's no way I'm going to be able to finish it every month without help. If you can't afford a full time assistant at least let me bring in a freelancer a couple of days a week."

"Maddie, I'm about to leave. I have to meet some people. We're going to Washington for a march against the war in Vietnam. Can't this wait till next week?"

"Bruce. Did you hear me? The magazine is due out tomorrow. I'm not going to make it."

He dropped his pen and sighed. "Okay, I get it. Can you complete it by Monday?"

"Probably. But that's not going to solve the problem."

He smirked. "Maybe a guy could do it faster."

She wanted to tell him to fuck off. Instead she said, "Really? Then maybe you should find one."

"I'm sorry, Maddie. You're great. I'm just in a rush. Shoot for Monday if you can and we'll talk then. One day won't kill us."

She nodded. "All right. It's your call."

"If you're ready to leave, my car is across the street. I'll drop you at your apartment. By the way, where is your apartment?"

"Seventy-Ninth and First. I thought you were in a hurry."

"It's slightly out of my way, but what the hell. Maybe we can have a drink one night."

She glanced down at her hand; had he missed her wedding ring?

=

The following Monday passed in a blur, but she managed to complete the final mechanicals and release the magazine to the printer. Tuesday was taken up with organizing the next issue and finding artists who would illustrate a few articles for less than the going rate. It wasn't until Wednesday evening that she had the time to get back to Bruce.

Standing in his doorway, she asked, "Can we talk about a freelancer now?"

He finished writing something, put it aside and grinned at her. "Maybe. But I have another idea."

She stared at him, waiting.

"Why don't you come over here and get under my desk?"

"What?" She wasn't sure she had heard him correctly.

"Come on Maddie. Everybody does it."

"Everybody does what?"

"Don't be naïve. Girls are giving their bosses blow jobs every day in every office in New York City."

"You're joking."

"Not at all. I thought the Brits were big on that."

"You must be out of your fucking mind."

He didn't flinch. "Fucking. Good thought. Blow job first."

She left his office and went back to her drawing board. After scribbling something on a notepad she picked up her bag. When she returned to Bruce's office he was still smiling. "So Maddie. What you you think?"

"Bruce. I think you should take your blow job, your cheap one-horse magazine and your sick ego and shove them up your ass." She dropped the paper on his desk. "You can send my final paycheck to my apartment. Here's my address in case you don't have it."

Suddenly he wasn't smiling. "Hey, Maddie. Slow down. You can't quit. I was just kidding."

"No Bruce, you weren't. You apparently think you're entitled to sexual favors from all the girls in this office. Don't think I haven't heard about your 'under the glass desk' routine. Your secretary may be willing, but I'm not."

"Shit. You're probably a frigid bitch anyway."

She lowered her voice to a breathy purr. "No, Bruce. I may be a bitch, but I've been told I'm quite the lay. I was taught sex by a very talented older man when I was twenty. Quite an extensive education, I'd say. Think about what you're missing by being the very definition of a sick, chauvinistic pig."

She turned and left, feeling his eyes boring into her back.

=

It wasn't till she got home that she panicked. She'd have to be on the phone to the head hunters again first thing in the morning.

Although it was almost eight, Rob was still out, God knew where. So far nothing was happening at LRG and interviews were few and far between. He'd been called back on a couple, but never mentioned them again. No matter what she did or said, he was drinking heavily. She went to the window and looked out at the city she loved. Despite the August heat, she shivered, afraid of what was to come.

Chapter 6

Rob couldn't believe Maddie had quit her job. He told her she should have just laughed it off and stayed, at least until she could find something else.

She looked at him with surprise. "Really? It doesn't bother you that he asked me to give him a blow job?"

"You've been around Maddie. You could have handled it without quitting."

Rather than get into a fight, she said softly, "You're still working at Chad's. We'll be all right."

He wasn't so sure. The fashion client he'd been working with had, without warning, gone bankrupt. Chad had reluctantly told him he'd have to lay him off for a few weeks. He wasn't prepared to tell Maddie, at least not yet. He had a couple of interviews scheduled for the following week and was optimistic about both of them.

It looked like it was going to be a depressing evening and he was surprised when Maddie suggested they go to Martell's for a few drinks and hamburgers.

"At least," she said jokingly, "I don't have to go all the way downtown tomorrow. That in itself is a relief."

She had been right, they'd had a chance to relax and talk. She told him she was sure she'd find something quickly. She was always optimistic; she just kept going until she made something happen. He hoped whatever it was would happen sooner rather than later.

As they left he took her hand and they walked to Pedro's. She, like most of the residents in the area, had never noticed it before. They sat at the bar and he introduced her to Roy.

"Pleased to meet you Maddie. Rob has great things to say about you."

"Thanks, Roy. I have some nice things to say about him as well."

He laughed and turned to Rob. "So, Rob. It looks like your dream job has come true. If you want, you can start working next week."

Rob felt Maddie go still. She looked at him wide eyed. "Working? Here?"

He nodded. "I didn't want to mention it until I was sure. I think I'm going to like bartending three nights a week."

=

The next morning after Rob left for the studio Maddie called Mr. Collins. She was worried he'd be annoyed that she had quit *Modern Securities*, but after telling him what happened he was shocked.

"Maddie. I'm sorry. I know some of these guys are aggressive, but that's stepping over the line. I guess you never know. Look, you called on a good day. I have two possibilities that just came in."

"Great Mr. Collins. What are they?"

"Well," he paused. "The first one may be a stretch. But you're moving up and after London I think this might work. That is, if you want to stay with magazines."

"Book, magazines. Either is fine."

"This is a biggie and I'm not quite sure you're ready for it. *Woman's Weekly* is reorganizing and they're looking for an art director. They've always had men but I think they'd be willing to talk to a woman. Particularly with all this women's lib stuff going on."

Not about to enter into what always turned out to be a provocative discussion on feminism, she said, "That would be wonderful."

"They're looking for a heavy hitter and although you really don't have that experience, I think it may be worth a shot. I'll try and set up an appointment for next week." He paused and she heard papers being shuffled. "I also have another one. It's a trade magazine for the menswear business. It only goes to retailers and manufacturers but it's considered a bible in the industry."

Maddie held her breath. Two magazines on the first phone call was too much to hope for. She could barely manage to sit still.

"They've only had male art directors but I think the editor in chief, Mr. Morton would be willing to interview a woman."

"Mr. Collins, if I were in your office I'd kiss you."

He laughed. "Timing Maddie. It's all timing. I'll call you back."

Maddie was encouraged. She wanted to call Rob but knowing he was superstitious about discussing potential jobs, she decided to wait.

Although she'd been taken aback about the bartending job she was beginning to think it wasn't such a terrible idea. Rob was naturally gregarious, but two obvious things worried her: he'd be able to drink as much as he wanted and she was sure once word got out, even as unknown as Pedro's was, girls would be flocking to meet him. And yet she couldn't tell him not to do it, not that he would have listened to her anyway. She hoped it would get him out of the doldrums he seemed to be mired in these days.

The phone rang and she ran to pick it up.

"Your appointments are set Maddie. Got a pencil?"

After she wrote down the days and times, she thanked him, saying she'd call him after each interview.

"One thing, Maddie. Mr. Morton is a great guy. He's married, but he's also known as quite the man about town. He likes pretty girls. Be careful."

She laughed. "You should have warned me when you sent me on the interview at *Status.*"

"But look what happened. It turned out great. You married the art director and got to live in London."

Turned out great? She wasn't so sure at the moment. Although she loved Rob and wished only for him to succeed, she still wondered why he was having such a difficult time finding a job. She also wished he'd cut down on his drinking but she was becoming too afraid to say anything. The one time she mentioned it he'd gotten angry and walked out. True, he returned and apologized, but she didn't want to live in fear of saying the wrong thing, especially when she didn't know what the wrong thing was.

=

The interview at *Woman's Weekly* had gone well, or so she thought. Mr. Collins had suggested she dress conservatively. When she entered the large reception area cluttered with slightly musty furniture that likely dated from the thirties, she knew he had given her good advice; this was a big magazine with a long history. Although somewhat intimidated, she reminded herself that Mr. Collins had also said it was worth a shot.

She met with the managing editor who appeared to be impressed with her resumé and her portfolio. After asking the usual questions, particularly about marriage and babies, he offered to show her around. The hallways were active with editors and secretaries bustling back and forth and she counted five assistants working at drawing boards in the art department. Walking her out, he shook her hand, saying he still had several people to see and he'd be in touch. She thanked him, doubting she was even in the running.

Two days later she went down to lower Fifth Avenue to Men's, Inc.

Mr. Morton was a tall, elegantly attired man at least twenty years her senior. His perfectly styled brown hair had precisely the right touch of grey at the temples. He complimented her work and was entranced that she had lived and worked in London, his favorite city. After chatting with him for almost an hour, she felt it was less an interview and more a first date. By the time she left she thought she might be half in love with him. That lasted until Mr. Collins called a few days later to tell her he'd hired another man. The explanation? It was a men's magazine; the only women who worked there were secretaries.

The next day Mr. Morton phoned to say he was sorry, he had wanted to hire her but had been overruled by the publisher. To make up for it he offered to take her to lunch. She actually blushed, thanked him and reminded him she was married. After all, the guy was old enough to be her father, almost.

It turned out she didn't get the *Woman's Weekly* job either. Mr. Collins told her she'd come close but, as he expected she probably needed another couple years of experience. He said not to worry, he might have something coming up in the next couple of days and would be in touch.

By Friday, Maddie was worried. She hated being idle and considered looking for freelance work. It wasn't only her days; three nights a week Rob was coming home only to change and run to Pedro's at eight. Sometimes he went straight from work. Occasionally, she would walk up there between ten and eleven. After the first few times the regulars began to recognize her and came over to talk. Her presence seemed to deter most of the single girls from flirting but it wasn't something she was about to do every night.

=

When the phone rang the following Monday she was sure it was Mr. Collins. But the deep voice was only vaguely familiar.

"Maddie, I'm glad I found you."

"Who's this?"

"Maddie, come on."

"Jay. Ohmigod. Where are you? How did you get my number?" She wondered why her heart was pounding.

"I called your mother's house. She said you were, in her words, 'between jobs.'"

She laughed, "Good description. I had one for three months but I quit. It's a long story. Now I'm waiting for interviews. When did you get back?"

"Have lunch with me. I'll tell you everything and then you can tell me. How's that?"

"When?"

"Tomorrow? There's a little café near our park, the one where we used to go on Fifty-Third Street. Meet me at one?"

"Are you working?"

"Yes. I just started at *Holiday*. They were looking for an art director to give them a new image. It took a bunch of interviews though."

"That's wonderful, Jay. Congratulations. I had an interview at *Woman's Weekly* but I really didn't expect to get it."

He laughed. "I interviewed there as well. It didn't seem very creative, just recipes and home stuff."

"I agree. But there aren't many jobs out there."

"If I know you, you'll find something soon. What happened with the last one?"

"I'll save that for when I see you."

"That bad, huh?"

"I'll let you decide."

After Jay said he'd see her tomorrow, Maddie put the phone down. Closing her eyes, she felt an unexpected flush of warmth. She had missed him, perhaps more than she had allowed herself to admit. It was also nice to speak to someone with a positive attitude. She wondered if Rob had known about the job at *Holiday*. When she mentioned that he might want to go for an interview at *Woman's*

Weekly he had put her off, acting as though she had demeaned him by the very mention. He had practically snarled, "Are you kidding? I'm not going back to magazines. I'm beyond that."

Taken aback, she had snapped. "What about me?" She stopped herself from adding, *I'm the one bringing in most of the money, so what's your problem?"*

He had ignored her and walked out of the room.

She jumped when the phone rang again. Reaching for it, she hoped it wasn't Jay cancelling.

This time it was Mr. Collins. He'd already set a meeting for her on Wednesday at a magazine called *Beauty&Fashion*. He told her to look "chic."

Chapter 7

There were plenty of seats; the subway car was half empty. And yet there was no way Maddie could sit down; her mini dress was too short, but now it was at least covered by a long patterned sweater. Maxi over mini was becoming the newest trend, and thanks or not to the hippie influence, longer skirts were quickly following.

Mr. Grenier, the publisher of *Beauty&Fashion* welcomed her with a smile and asked how she had liked living in London, one of his favorite cities. *Is London everybody's favorite city?* As he spoke he seemed to be having a difficult time tearing his eyes away from her legs, which she kept modestly crossed. She smiled and answered his strangely insipid questions. She was sure she had the job nailed until he called Carla, the art assistant, into his office.

Maddie didn't particularly like having women, especially a potential assistant, brought into an interview; they tended to nitpick. Had she known, she would have dressed a bit more conservatively. But with the economy and jobs more competitive than ever, only the best man, or woman, most likely wearing a miniskirt, would win. While she was sure that was feminist blasphemy, she didn't particularly care.

Surprisingly, Carla turned out to be outgoing and friendly as well as highly complimentary on her portfolio. Despite Mr. Grenier saying he had a couple of more candidates to see, Maddie left feeling optimistic.

When she followed up with a phone call a couple of days later, he asked her to come in the next day. This time he introduced her to the managing editor, Letitia Parsons, a grey-haired woman in her fifties. Maddie breathed a sigh of relief that she had chosen a somewhat more conservative dress this time. After reviewing her portfolio and asking the usual questions, she glanced at Mr. Grenier with a barely perceptible nod.

Trying to contain her excitement, Maddie left with only slightly less than the salary she had asked for. By the time she arrived home she could hardly wait to tell Rob the good news. Picking up the phone, she realized she didn't have the number for Chad's studio. In fact, she had never had it; Rob had never given it to her.

After calling information, she dialed the number.

When a woman answered, she asked for Rob MacLeod.

The woman hesitated. "I'm sorry miss. You must have the wrong number. There's no one here by that name."

"No. I'm sure he works there. He's a freelancer."

"Everyone here is freelance. But I've only been here a couple of weeks. Maybe he worked here before."

Barely able to breathe, Maddie whispered, "Thank you," and hung up.

=

When Rob walked in she was sitting in the same place; the phone at her side, her portfolio on the floor where she had dropped it in her excitement two hours before.

"Maddie. What's wrong? Why are you crying?"

She stood up, her body stiff from lack of movement, her tears already dry. Her voice was steady. "I'm not crying. Not anymore. Where have you been, Rob?"

"What do you mean? At the studio."

She shook her head and shivered. "No. I called."

He sighed and took of his jacket. "Look Maddie. I didn't want to worry you. You had just quit *Modern Securities*, which as you know I thought was a mistake. So the guy came on to you. You could have laughed it off until you found another job."

"Explain to me why quitting *Modern Securities* has anything to do with why you weren't at Chad's when you said you were."

She saw his eyes narrow. "The account I was working on went out of business. Chad said he was sorry, that he'd have more work in a couple of weeks. I thought it would be easier all around not to mention it."

"Not mention it? How about mentioning that you've been lying to me. I can't believe that you put on a suit every morning as though you were going to work and didn't return until nighttime. Where did you spend those days?"

"I don't need to be interrogated. But if you must know I met some of the guys for lunch. I also went to coffee shops to call employment agencies and friends, anyone who could help with a job. I wasn't just sitting around Maddie. I was looking for work."

"What about the rest of the day?"

"What are you, some kind of Nazi? It doesn't matter. Look, I have to change. I have to be at Pedro's in an hour."

She followed him into the bedroom. "It does matter and we do have to talk about it."

"The fuck we do."

"Rob, this isn't going away. You've lied to me for weeks. How do I ever trust you again?"

"Trust me or don't, Maddie. That's the way it is. I was going through a rough time and I didn't want to discuss it with you. But maybe this will help. I spoke to John today and I'll be starting back at the agency next week. Freelance, but full time. He says he'll get me back on staff in a couple of months. See? Now you can back off."

"Congratulations. But I'm not backing off."

"What's done is done. Discussion over. Things will be better now. By the way I'm working till three tonight, four if there are still drinkers." He had changed from a suit to a white shirt and jeans. "Don't wait up."

After he left she put her portfolio away in a closet. She had been dismayed at how aggressive he'd been, first turning the discussion back to her and then ending it without apology. She hadn't even told him about her new job. But then, he hadn't asked.

She had never felt so alone. She needed to share her good news with someone. Calling her mother was an option. She was always happy to hear about a new job, but she'd end up asking questions that Maddie wouldn't want to answer.

She thought of Jay. They'd had a wonderful time at lunch the week before. He had been anxious to tell her more about IOS, saying it had been a blast at the beginning, but as the company had descended into chaos, desperation had taken over as rumors circulated that the owner was about to be indicted for fraud.

"It was incredible, Maddie. Within one day everyone was ordered to destroy whatever documents they had. They were even burning them in wastebaskets. I was glad to get out of there. And yet I wouldn't have missed it for the world."

She nodded. "I know what you mean."

"So tell me about that job you got and then left so quickly."

"You won't believe it or maybe you will. Maybe I'm just naïve."

After telling him about *Modern Securities* and what Bruce had asked of her, Jay lit two Parliaments and handed her one. "I hate to say this Maddie, but I'm not exactly shocked and I'm surprised you were. You know as well as I that guys, especially those with some sort of power, come on to their secretaries and assistants all the time, often with the promise of a better job. It's a game; they're racking up notches. But that Bruce did it to his own art director is off the wall. I'll bet you shocked the hell out of him by quitting." He banged his fist on the table. "Damn. I'm proud of you."

Maddie jumped and several people glanced their way. "Thank you, Jay. But there was no choice. I couldn't face him or that office again. Rob was annoyed though. He didn't think I should have quit."

"Are you serious? I'd have gone down there and punched him out."

She laughed. "I'd like to have seen that. To be honest, things are strained. Rob's having a hard time since we left London."

He reached for her hand. "Maddie. You know I'm here for you if you need me."

She smiled, feeling the warmth of his touch. "Thank you," she whispered.

The waiter came over, hovering. Jay looked at her. "Another glass of wine?"

She nodded. "Sure, why not."

"It's too bad about *American Heritage*. I have to find out what Irwin is doing."

"It would have been so simple just to go back."

"Too simple. We've both moved on. But it was great while it lasted."

She touched her glass to his, wishing him luck in his new job. When they left, he kissed her lightly on the lips. It was a kiss she felt all the way home.

=

Now that it was her moment to celebrate there was no one to celebrate with. Getting her nerve up, she reached for the phone and called him. It was already after eight and she wasn't surprised he didn't answer. Maybe, she thought, it was better that he didn't.

=

Rob was relieved; he'd escaped just in time. In his view the best defense was an offense, and he considered he'd handled Maddie's probing questions pretty well.

Did she really think he was going to tell her about his afternoons? That first Monday he'd gone to O'Leary's and talked with Denise for a couple of hours. The next day she changed her shift and they spent the afternoon at her apartment, a walk-up, two floors above a rundown bar called The Blarney Stone on Third Avenue in the East Fifties. It was pretty primitive: a living room with soot-covered windows that faced the street, a bedroom that looked out on a brick wall and a kitchen with a tub in the middle. But then she was a bartender, not a fancy art director like his Upper East Side wife.

He asked himself why Maddie would have suddenly called Chad's studio. The realization suddenly hit him that she had called to tell him something; maybe she had gotten the job with that magazine. *Shit.* Well, he'd make it up to her when he got home. He'd been screwing Denise all afternoon but he was sure he would have no problem seducing Maddie at four a.m.

It was just after three-thirty when he arrived home; the last of the drinkers having departed before closing time. Maddie was asleep, naked as usual with the covers pushed down to her knees. He was aroused just looking at her. Denise was a big girl with none of lithe elegance of Maddie. She stirred and looked up at him.

He sat down next to her on the bed and smoothed her hair. "Maddie. I'm sorry I was short with you before. I didn't know what to say and I was embarrassed that I lied to you. It's been hell these last couple of weeks and the last thing I wanted was to disappoint you. All I can tell you is that I love you."

She blinked and rubbed her eyes. "Rob. I don't know what to say anymore."

He leaned down to kiss her. "Now that I'm going back to LRG everything will be all right. When I told you there was no end to this relationship I meant it. I still do."

He kissed her again and this time he felt her respond, if just barely. "I never asked why you called me. It must have been important."

"It was. I got the job at the magazine."

He hugged her. "Congratulations. You deserve it."

"But I don't understand what you did all those days. We still have to talk about it."

Holding back a sudden surge of anger, he said, "We will Maddie. But not now."

He undressed quickly and got into bed, moving close to her. She moved away until he started stroking her. In the middle of her saying no, he took her quickly. She gasped, but he continued playing with her and whispering until he felt her respond. It was just where he wanted her and he knew there would be no more resistance.

=

The next morning, he awakened her with caresses. "Don't move," he said pulling her close, his hand already between her thighs.

"Rob..."

"There's no hurry," he whispered. "We don't have to go anywhere until Monday. We can spend the whole weekend in bed just like we used to." They were lying face to face with her leg over his hip and he heard her sigh as he entered her.

Sex, as he knew well, was an incredibly effective distraction and particularly useful in keeping Maddie from asking questions he had no intention of answering.

What he had told her was essentially true; he'd spent most mornings at a midtown coffee shop where he'd used their phone booth to make calls, endlessly checking on jobs. The afternoons, however, were his secret.

One day Denise had scored some Hawaiian Red and stoned out of their gourds, they'd gone to a rerun of 2001 at an obscure movie theater in the Village; a total wigged-out trip. Not a bad way to live if you could afford it. Since he didn't have a trust fund, however, work was of necessity the way to go. And yet he was beginning to feel he no longer had the energy or the drive. He didn't really understand it, but the fuck up in London and Florida had taken a lot out of him. He had always woken up in the morning eager to get to the office, impatient to discover what the day would bring. But lately it didn't seem to matter so much. Occasionally he considered he might want to cut down on his drinking, but then he'd meet up with Denise and after downing a few—the girl could outdrink an Irishman—life would again become just too much fun.

Chapter 8

For Maddie life was becoming a constant riddle. She never knew which Rob would come home—the one or two drink mellowed-out Rob or the half-drunk angry Rob. Every night seemed to evolve into an unending cycle of arguing and making up, promises made and promises broken, love spoken and silent remorse. She finally faced the fact that he had a problem and that was booze. Wasn't it F. Scott Fitzgerald who had written, *"First you take a drink, then the drink takes a drink, then the drink takes you?"*

One afternoon not long after they began their new jobs, Maddie called Rob at the office. Hoping for a tranquil night, she told him she planned to make his favorite dinner, steak and baked potatoes. For once he was home by eight and although she smelled liquor on his breath, he appeared to be in a good mood. As they ate he asked her about her work.

"I like it, Rob. The magazine has fashion as well as articles on makeup and skin care, even an advice column. It's like our days at *Status*, twelve issues a year and yet every day is something different."

"How's your assistant?"

"Carla's great. I've been showing her how to produce photo shoots. You know, model agencies, stylists, locations, the whole thing. The last art director didn't let her do very much and she's happy to learn. It's like what Joan did for me at *Today's Bride*. I feel like a mentor." She put down her fork and looked at him. "Wow. Am I old enough to be a mentor?"

"Sure, Maddie," he said with a grin. "You're all of twenty-eight. I'd call that ancient."

They had opened a bottle of wine and he touched his glass to hers. "You've had a lot of experience. Now it's your turn to teach someone else."

With a coy grin: "Like you did for me?"

He laughed. "Not quite the same."

After they cleared the table he finished off the wine. "Since I don't have to work at Pedro's tonight, let's go out for drinks."

She stopped moving and took a breath. Looking in his eyes, she said, "Rob. I really don't feel like going out."

"Come on Maddie. Just a drink or two. We'll go to Allen's."

"I don't think I want to drink anymore."

He stared at her, his good mood vanishing in a flash. "What the fuck are you saying? You won't go out with me for a drink?"

"Not at all. I just can't deal with hangovers anymore. My days are too hectic and I hate waking up feeling like I'm going to throw up. I think we both drink too much. Maybe you should also consider drinking less." *There, I said it.*

He grabbed his coat. "Then you're no fucking fun anymore." He walked out, slamming the door.

She winced, asking herself when the booze had become so important that he was now choosing it over her.

=

She spent the remainder of the night watching the clock, certain that Rob would be home any minute. When the phone rang at six, it startled her out of a light sleep. After fumbling with the receiver, she said a muffled hello.

"Is this Mrs. MacLeod?"

Immediately awake, she answered, "Yes."

"Look, your husband is here at the bar. He's in pretty bad shape. You'd better come get him."

"What?" she wasn't sure she'd heard him correctly.

"Please, Mrs. MacLeod. I'm the bartender at The Blarney Stone on Fifty-Fifth and Third. He needs help."

Panicked, she asked if he needed an ambulance.

"No ma'am. He needs to go home."

"I'll be there in a few minutes. I have to get dressed."

The Blarney Stone was an old, grubby, booze soaked bar. She must have passed it a hundred times without noticing it. The bartender, a heavyset man with salt and pepper hair had, to her dismay, been accurate; Rob was slumped over the bar and barely coherent.

"How did this happen? Has he been here all night?"

He shrugged. "I don't know. He was here when I arrived."

"How is that possible?"

"I don't know."

He sounded vague, too vague; something was off and she wanted to know more. How could the night bartender have left him there alone?

But there was no time for questions and the bartender helped her get Rob into a cab. His clothing smelled of something other than cigarette smoke, which meant he'd been doing more than just drinking. By the time she got him home and into bed she was physically and mentally drained.

She put on the percolator and dropped two Alka Seltzers into a glass of water. After helping him sit up, she managed to get him to swallow it.

"What happened, Rob? Can you tell me?"

"I don't know." His voice was barely a croak.

"Maybe I should call a doctor."

He put a hand on her arm. "No. Let me sleep. I'll be okay."

"Are you sure? I don't think I should leave."

"No. Go to work. There's nothing you can do."

"Will you call me when you wake up?"

He nodded.

By the time she got dressed he was sound asleep, or more realistically, passed out cold.

=

He called about noon, apologizing and saying he didn't know what happened; he'd gone out for a couple of drinks intending to blow off steam and return in an hour or two. A guy he knew had come by the bar and they had talked for a while. He told Rob he had a couple of joints and they went out to the street, which at one in the morning was deserted.

"It couldn't have been grass," he said. "It was too strong. It must have been hash. After he left I went back inside. I don't remember anything else."

"Rob. That's crazy. Why didn't you have the bartender call me then?"

"I guess I was too stoned. Please don't be mad at me. Maybe you're right about too much drinking. I'm just glad you were there for me."

"Why don't you take it easy for the rest of the day?"

"I can't. There's a meeting at four and I have Pedro's tonight."

"And you'll come home after?"

"Of course, Maddie. I'm sorry I yelled at you last night. Don't worry. Just know that I love you and I'll see you later."

She put down the phone not really believing his story. She couldn't fathom why he would go to such a downbeat bar as The Blarney Stone. It wasn't exactly his style. And why hadn't the bartender called her last night? Once again there too many questions or perhaps too many secrets.

Chapter 9

On an afternoon in late October, Mr. Grenier wandered nonchalant-
ly into the art department. That was unusual: normally he preferred
to call his employees into his office where he could command them
from behind his massive desk. There had, however, been occasions
when he'd pass by, ostensibly giving a potential advertiser a tour
of the office. He'd stop briefly and whisper, "Take a look at my art
director." The guy would leer until Maddie turned to glare at him.
Did he really think she hadn't heard him? He was right up there
with Bruce in the chauvinist pig category. Even worse was that he'd
wink before moving on.

Not knowing why he had suddenly appeared, Maddie asked
if he'd like to see a new idea for a cover. She had taken a photo,
a headshot of a beautiful model they had used in a previous issue
and Xeroxed it. What resulted was a grainy black and white image,
more illustration than photograph, which she then colored with eye
shadow, a touch of blush on the cheeks and red lipstick. The intense
color on the coarse black and white page was startling and dramatic.

Mr. Grenier's eyes lit up and grabbing it out of her hand, he ran
out to the hallway yelling for Letitia. Coming back, he asked "Can
you do a few more like this Maddie? Maybe try some different colors? I don't know where you got this idea but it's fabulous. No one
has ever done this before. We'll be the first."

Letitia came in looking concerned. "What is it? What are you so
excited about?"

"Tish, we're going with this for the cover of the next issue. I'll
bet when this hits the newsstand every magazine in the city will be
copying it.'"

She took the paper from his hand and glanced at Maddie. "How did you come up with this?'

"I was copying some papers and saw that photo. I was curious to see what it would look like if I Xeroxed it."

"Good job, Maddie. This is terrific."

Maddie breathed a sigh of relief and Carla applauded. They both had been unsure of their reactions.

On his way out, Mr. Grenier said, "I almost forgot. My wife isn't feeling well and I have to go to this damned industry dinner tonight. I hate to ask, Maddie, but will you go with me?"

Holding back a grin, Carla glanced at Maddie. Letitia rolled her eyes.

"Sure, Mr. Grenier. But I'm not exactly dressed for it."

"That's all right. I'll give you money for a taxi. If you leave here around four can you meet me at the Waldorf Ballroom at six?"

She nodded, thinking she didn't have anything remotely dressy enough. "Is a little black dress all right? I don't have a long gown."

"Perfect. On you anything would look good."

She tried not to grit her teeth. "Thank you, Mr Grenier."

After he left Carla looked like she had swallowed a cat. The laughter she'd held back erupted in a howl as tears of glee ran down her face.

Letitia, grinning said, "You should have seen your face, Maddie. You looked like a deer caught in the headlights. Watch out for him; he can get handy if you know what I mean."

Maddie handed Carla a tissue. "Just what I need, going to some stuffy charity ball as Mr. Grenier's date."

She picked up the phone to call Rob. Although it had been two months since she'd started at the magazine and Rob had returned to LRG, they seldom spoke during the day. Especially since the night she had told him she wouldn't drink with him anymore. Although she had gone back on that declaration several times, she still refused to sit half the night in a bar. Once, to pacify her, he promised to quit drinking for a week but it only lasted three days. Since then, what remained was an uneasy truce.

When the receptionist put her though to his office, a girl answered. "Can I please speak with Rob MacLeod?" she asked.

"Can I tell him who's calling?"

"His wife."

There was a pause. "His wife?" she asked in a squeaky voice. When Maddie didn't answer, she heard whispers and giggling. Rob must have grabbed the phone. "Sorry about that, Maddie."

"Sorry about what, Rob? That they don't know you're married?"

"Don't take it the wrong way. There are a couple of new secretaries here."

"Whatever you say. I have to go to a formal event with Mr. Grenier tonight but I should be home by eleven."

"Okay, Maddie. I'm bartending at Pedro's. I'll be home between three and four. And please, don't take these things so seriously."

=

The Waldorf Ball Room was a mob scene. Maddie stood on tiptoes scanning the room for Mr. Genier. He wasn't very tall, but one couldn't miss his toupee. Spying him on the far side of the ballroom, she began to make her way through the crush of formally dressed men, many with wives adhering to their sides. Since it was an annual award dinner for the publishing industry, everyone who was anyone was in attendance. Suddenly someone grabbed her arm and as she turned, Fred embraced her in a bear hug. "Maddie. How are you? I spoke to Rob last week and he told me you had a great job."

She laughed. "That's true. It's a small publication but I'm loving it."

"I knew you'd make it in this crazy business. Good for you. Next time it'll be a big one."

"Thanks Fred. But I'm happy right now."

"You know you have to keep moving. It's how you've gotten where you are."

"After five jobs in six years, I think I'd like to stay at this one for a while. By the way, have you seen or heard anything about Cynthia? I've called her several times since I've been back but nobody answers."

"The last time I spoke to her, maybe six months ago, she had dumped Michael. Good riddance to that one. Anyway, she was all excited. She had met some agent from L.A. and said she was heading out there to write scripts for *Laugh-In*. She's a bit off the wall so I'm sure she'll be great at it."

"I guess I'll just have to wait until she resurfaces in New York." She glanced around. "I'm supposed to meet my publisher here. I better go find him."

He hugged her again. "I told Rob we should go out one night. Have him call me and we'll arrange it. My book will be published soon. I'll invite you to the signing."

Great. A book on mixing cocktails. She gave him a peck on the cheek. "I look forward to it."

After squeezing through more men dressed like penguins, she finally saw Mr. Grenier at a table. He was standing and peering around. No doubt for her.

"Ah. There you are. Come with me and I'll introduce you to some of my friends."

She followed him as he cut into several groups, shaking hands with publishers who, she hoped, would remember her at some future moment. As she glanced past an editor from *Life* magazine, she saw Jay. He was talking with a slender blonde who, like she, was wearing a simple short black dress. Maddie was sure she was in the business. The wives had a different look; long colorful gowns, teased hair and ostentatious jewelry. Jay caught her eye and waved.

After dinner and the inevitable, endless speeches, a band began playing. Feeling a hand on her shoulder, she saw Jay smiling down at her.

"Dance with me?"

She glanced at Mr. Grenier who was in a discussion with the man sitting on his other side.

Taking Jay's hand, they walked to the overcrowded dance floor.

"I never expected to see you here," he said.

"Mr. Grenier's wife was sick. I'm filling in."

He laughed. "Are you sure he doesn't have other designs on you?"

"Oh, yes. He's a paunchy, fifty-year old man who wears a rug. Definitely my type."

He pulled her close. "Am I your type? I thought I was. Now I'm not so sure."

She blushed. "You already know the answer to that."

"We haven't been this close since Virginia. Do you ever think about that night?"

"Yes, Jay. Too often."

"What are you going to do about Rob? I know you're having problems with him. How long are you going to take it?"

"What are you talking about?"

He stopped dancing and moved her to the side. "Look Maddie, maybe I shouldn't say anything, but what the hell, I think you should know. Sometimes when we have too much work at the magazine we farm it out to Studio 5. Chad told me that when Rob was working there he was really good. But after a few weeks he began screwing up, coming back from lunch with liquor on his breath and wasting time chatting up the secretaries."

She stepped back. "Why are you telling me this?"

"I care for you and I don't want to see you hurt."

"I wish I could say I'm surprised. But I don't think this is the place to talk about it."

"I'm sorry."

"No, Jay. It's all right. I didn't mean to be short with you."

He glanced back. "It looks like your boss is about to leave."

"If you want I can meet you downstairs. Maybe we can have a drink."

She saw him hesitate. "Maddie. I have plans to meet someone later."

"Jay. Are you seeing someone?"

He shrugged. "Yes. I guess I am."

"I'm happy for you." *Really? Then why do I feel a knot in the pit of my stomach?*

He kissed her lightly. "We'll have lunch next week. I'll call you tomorrow. I'm sorry if I upset you."

She shook her head. "It's okay."

Mr. Grenier was waiting at the table. "Ah, there you are Maddie. Thank you for coming with me tonight. You've gotten quite a few compliments. My publisher friends are jealous that you're my art director."

She smiled. "Thank you, Mr. Grenier."

"Can I drop you at your apartment?"

"No, it's okay. I'd like to walk a little."

He handed her ten dollars. "Don't walk too far. Take a cab."

"This is too much. It's a two-dollar cab ride."

He shook his head. "I'll see you tomorrow."

=

Her mind was spinning. Since that all-too-brief night with Jay she'd managed to keep her emotions in check, sometimes only barely. He was the one who always spoke of wanting more. Although she did as well, she always demurred, fearing her emotional response. Just the thought of Rob's phone call that night in Virginia was enough to make her snap back to reality. She sighed, all too aware that when she was dancing with Jay she had again felt desire for him. And now he was seeing someone. Did she really think he would be there forever; that he was going to wait for her? Wait for what? She told herself to stop it; she should be thinking about Rob, not Jay. She flagged a taxi, telling the driver to take her Eighty-Fifth and Third.

Pedro's was the expected pandemonium. Every seat at the bar was occupied and a couple of guys had wedged themselves in between, shouting drink orders. At the pinball machine several others were waving bottles of beer while raucously urging on a young woman in hot pants. Maddie was surprised to see Rick Wellington, who alternated with Rob, tending the bar. Rick was an actor in a soap opera, but like Rob, moonlighted at the bar two or three nights a week. He liked to joke that he prayed to the TV gods every night that the writers wouldn't kill him off anytime soon.

He kissed her cheek. "Maddie, you look gorgeous. Where have you been all my life?"

"I don't know about all your life, Rick, but I just came from a charity dinner with my boss. Where's Rob?"

He suddenly looked uncomfortable. "He called earlier saying he wasn't feeling great and would I mind switching nights with him. I told him I would. Did he know you were stopping by?"

"No. I wanted to surprise him. I guess I'll see him at home."

"Sure, Maddie. Tell him I hope he feels better."

"I will," she said, thinking Rick might want to consider taking a few more acting lessons.

She walked home. Although it was almost midnight, Second Avenue was still swarming with couples and groups of singles entering and leaving bars. It wouldn't slow down for at least another hour or two.

Joe, the doorman greeted her. With him was Ralph, a short, solidly built man she'd met a few times before. He lived in the building and moonlighted as a security guard several nights a week. The building was heavily populated by singles who, returning less than sober from the bars late at night, occasionally got out of hand. His job was to back up the late night doorman.

"Joe, has Mr. MacLeod come in?"

He frowned and glanced at Ralph. "No, Mrs. M. I started at eleven. Maybe he came in before."

Ralph shook his head. "I've been here since nine. I haven't seen him."

She nodded. "Yes, well, goodnight."

As she expected the apartment was empty. She missed Cat who had always been there to greet her at the door. After she and Rob returned from London, Suzanne had balked at giving her back, saying she had bonded with her Siamese. She was right; whenever Maddie went to Suzanne's apartment, the two cats were curled up contentedly grooming one another.

Rob had told her he'd be home by three or four. She was sure he would; after all, he hadn't expected her to surprise him at the bar. She wondered how often he called in sick.

She looked out the window. There wasn't much of a view, but the lights of the city were visible between two buildings opposite. She felt a strange sense of aloneness, and yet it wasn't loneliness. It was more that she and Rob seemed to be living in two separate worlds, worlds that had very different values and no longer communicated very well.

She walked to the bedroom, looking at the bed and the beautiful carved headboard they had bought together. *What if he didn't come home? What if he wasn't living here anymore?*

She shivered, trying to imagine the emptiness of her life without him. *But he'll come home drunk and most likely having just left the bed of another woman, won't he? Do I really want to go on living like this? Isn't he, despite his promises, throwing his infidelities in my face?* The reality of those thoughts were too new, too raw, and she had no answer. She'd have to try and talk with herself about it, assess her feelings and address her future. Maybe the emptiness would one day give way to clarity. And clarity would begin to free her from his hold on her.

=

Rob congratulated himself. He'd gotten home before three. He could have left earlier, but he and Denise, along with a few of her friends had gotten so stoned they'd had to hit a twenty-four hour diner on the West Side to satisfy their munchies. It had been an evening filled with booze, pot, silly jokes and giggling, about what he couldn't even remember. At one point Denise had practically dragged him into the bedroom. When they came out the others were still going at it and they had laughed. He wished he could remember why everything had seemed so funny.

He was glad that Maddie was asleep. He wasn't in any shape to answer questions. Since the bedroom was dark, he tiptoed into the bathroom to get undressed. As he dropped his shirt into the hamper he noticed stains on it. He had no recollection of how they had gotten there.

=

The next morning Maddie was up early. The first thing she asked was about his night at the bar.

He yawned, "The usual. One night is a lot like the next. I may have to work Friday this week. I hope you don't mind."

"No Rob. Do whatever you have to."

"Come over here Maddie and give me a kiss."

She hesitated, but kissed him lightly. "Aren't you getting up?"

"I think I'll go back to sleep for twenty minutes."

"Are you all right? Did something happen last night?"

"Maddie. I'm fine. The bar was busy and I'm still tired."

"That's not like you."

"It's okay. Maybe we should go out tonight. I'll call Evan. He has a new friend. We can check her out."

"Whatever you want."

"What's with you this morning? You seem so, I don't know, laid back?"

"Nothing, Rob. I'll see you later."

"By the way how was the charity thing last night? What time did you get home?"

"Around midnight."

"I love you today."

As she walked out, she said, "Really?"

=

Rob watched her leave, thinking something seemed different about her. He shrugged; he had more important matters on his mind. But first he needed to get through the queasiness in his gut; no doubt the consequence of the long, wet, not to mention smoky night. He rationalized that it couldn't be the booze—maybe the bacon cheeseburger at the diner; it had tasted weird. He got out of bed slowly, trying to clear the smog in his head. After downing a couple of Alka Seltzers he turned on the shower. There was a meeting with a potential new account that afternoon and although he wasn't presenting he would, as the art director, be sitting in on it. Also, Rachel had been calling. LRG had ultimately turned down the men's shampoo account—research having shown that men had not a shred of interest in having their own line of hair-care products. As soon as she heard that he had returned to the agency, she had asked him to meet her. They'd gone to her apartment for a quickie once or twice, but he didn't really need her; he had Denise to play with. She was less demanding and always available.

After the shower he still felt sluggish. He reminded himself that he might want to cut down on the booze for a week or two; thirty-four wasn't quite as resilient as twenty-four. And yet, one beer couldn't hurt. It would help settle his stomach and get him going. Taking one out of the fridge, he went to get dressed.

=

Maddie was usually able to put her personal life on hold during the day but she was finding it increasingly difficult to keep her mind off Rob. She was approaching the point where she had to make a decision; one she would never have imagined only a year ago.

When she arrived home that night she called Suzanne. "How are things with Andrew?"

"Tolerable at best. He's grumpy all the time and almost never touches the baby. I'd ask how you are, but I have a feeling I already know the answer."

"You don't know the half of it. After the dinner last night with Mr. Grenier I thought I'd surprise Rob at Pedro's. He wasn't there. The bartender said he called in sick."

"Do you know where he was?"

"No. When he got home around three I pretended to be asleep. He has no reason to suspect that I know. Not unless Rick tells him." She stopped and took a breath. "Damn. And I'm sure he will."

"You'd better be prepared."

"You're right. I only wish I could get him to sit down and talk. Whenever I try or mention his drinking, he flies into a rage and walks out. I love him but I don't think I can go on like this. I'm surprised he even wants to."

"Until you face him with it, he'll keep on doing the same thing. Since you returned from London it's all been downhill."

"Yes. But he promised..."

"Come on, Maddie. Be real. His promises are meaningless."

"And yet I can't imagine living without him."

"Just stop and think about it. You won't have anyone coming home drunk and lying to you. You're becoming successful and if he continues on this path, which I'm sure he will, his career will go down the proverbial drain. You have to get away from him; otherwise I'm afraid he'll ruin your life along with his."

"It's almost the holidays. I'll deal with this in January."

"Listen to me. The holidays will only make it worse."

Hearing the lock turn, Maddie whispered, "Rob's home. Wouldn't you know it, for once he's on time. I'll call you tomorrow."

She hung up just as he walked into the bedroom. He looked sullen. "Talking to Suzanne? Telling her what a bastard I am?"

"No, Rob. Suzanne has her own problems."

"Yeah. I'll bet she does. You girls talk too much." He went into the kitchen, returning with a beer. "I told Evan we'd meet him at Dorrian's. Do you want to go?"

"Sure, why wouldn't I?"

"Maybe you'd rather call another one of your girlfriends and bitch some more."

"Why are you being so nasty, Rob?"

"I don't know Maddie. You bring it out in me."

=

He was trying to keep his rage under control. Rick had called earlier, supposedly to confirm that he'd be taking over his shift the next night. "Didn't Maddie look great last night?"

Rob frowned. "Last night?"

"Yeah. Didn't she tell you she stopped at the bar on her way home? She wanted to surprise you."

"Oh yeah. Sorry Rick. I was asleep when she got home and she left early this morning. Don't sweat it, I'll be there tomorrow night."

He hung up. No wonder she had been cold this morning. *The bitch knew.* Before, he'd have brought it up, made up a story and initiated make-up sex. Screw that. This time he'd wait for her.

=

They met Evan and Sally, Evan's new girlfriend, at Dorrian's. Evan didn't appear to be too broken up about his divorce from Danielle. Understandable, she was an uptight snob. Now he went out every night of the week, getting laid on most. On weekends he'd see his kid. Rob smirked; he'd had his chance, but he'd been in a hurry to marry Maddie. He tried to remember why.

They had drinks, dinner and a few laughs. After cheek kissing goodnight they had gone their separate ways.

When they returned to the apartment, he pulled Maddie into his arms. She pushed him away.

"Hey, what are you doing?"

"Leave me alone, Rob."

"Maddie," he cajoled, "I'm sorry I was short with you before, but you know I love you. Come here."

"No Rob. We have to talk. I can't live like this.

"You don't think I know why you're pissed? It's because I wasn't at the bar last night when you came by."

"Maybe you should go back to wherever you were."

"I was out with the guys. They wanted me to meet someone from another agency. It was important, otherwise I wouldn't have asked Rick to cover for me." He stood up abruptly and grabbed his shirt. "But if you really don't want me here, I'll get the hell out."

"Rob, please. Stop it. I don't want you to leave. Why can't we talk about this without shouting? I love you, but all I seem to do is make you angry."

"Maddie," he said, calming down. "I love you too. I get angry because you always think the worst."

He lay down on the bed and pulled her close. After a few minutes of silence, she thought he had fallen asleep. She was surprised when he spoke, his voice quiet and his eyes unusually clear. "You know Maddie, maybe the problem is that you expect too much from me. I sometimes think you see me as some sort of ideal, the man who swept you off your feet and told you he would love you forever. And perhaps you, and I as well, were right at the time. We thought things would never change. And yet life changed us. I think what I'm trying to say is I wish I could give you everything you imagined but it seems I can't. I'm simply not that man and now I don't know if I ever was."

She lay still, tears streaming down her face. "What do we do, Rob?"

She heard him sigh. "I don't know. I love you. But I just don't know."

Chapter 10

Suzanne had unfortunately been right about the holidays. Having missed the previous Christmas with the kids, Rob once again brought them into the city for an afternoon. As two years before, they took them to see the Rockefeller Center Christmas tree and the animated windows of the Fifth Avenue department stores. Although the kids were thrilled, Maddie thought Rob had acted horribly, constantly criticizing Tommy for no apparent reason and back in the apartment, asking Val to bring him things he could very well have gotten up to get himself. When Maddie glared at him, he repeatedly held up his bandaged right hand.

That little mishap had been his fault. The week before Christmas they'd had an argument. He'd gotten so angry—Maddie couldn't even recall why—that he'd hit the refrigerator with his fist. When she refused to fuss over him, he stormed out, shouting that he was going to the emergency room at Lenox Hill.

She didn't know if he had gone or not since he didn't come home till six in the morning. When she asked him why, he snapped, "Because the emergency room was wall-to-wall people. It took three hours before I even got an x-ray. If you cared you'd have come with me."

"But then you would have had to return home with me," she said sarcastically.

"Back off, Maddie. Damn it, after the x-ray I still had to wait for hours." He held out his swollen hand wrapped in an Ace bandage.

"So you didn't break anything."

"No." His tone was almost regretful. "But's it's badly bruised."

=

He was still in a nasty mood. While Maddie tried to make opening the presents and the tree trimming fun for the kids, he'd gone into the bedroom and closed the door. She'd heard him talking on the phone for almost an hour.

When he came out she asked who he was talking to. He said it was none of her business. She shook her head and went downstairs to get sandwiches at the deli. When she returned he appeared to have lightened up and was sitting on the floor playing Chutes and Ladders with the kids.

At the end of the day as she got them ready to return to Darien, Val hugged her, saying she missed seeing Daddy and making her promise to come to Connecticut soon. Maddie was sure Rob had told her he was visiting them far more than he truly was.

=

After they left she went to the kitchen and poured a glass of wine. She needed to think, to come to terms with what it was that she, and she alone, wanted. She had hoped they could have spoken more after Rob's unusually calm and lucid night, but with the usual round of holiday parties it had never happened.

He had been surprisingly perceptive in saying that she had naively expected him to be something that he wasn't, that he could never be. Maybe D. H Lawrence had been right; they had, indeed, outlived that all too "brief hour," and in pain and disillusionment it was now coming apart. *And yet in the first rush of love and intimacy, don't we all perceive our lover as our ideal? The one we truly and lastingly desire? And while we may thank that first evening star for the man of our dreams, we forget to wish for fate to continue to be kind to us.*

Despite that she was beginning to face an all too harsh inevitability, she still felt a powerful need for him, a profound love implacably entwined with intense sexual desire. In truth, sex was no longer a mainstay of the relationship—it had now become the entire relationship, the glue that was holding them together. While there were few nights that passed without sniping at one another, they'd still end up in each another's arms. Once, in the middle of an argument, Rob snapped, "Do you want to fight or fuck?"

The strangest part was when they went out with friends he always held her hand or put his arm tightly around her. She liked that he did; it made her feel more secure, hopeful that he really did still love her. Sex on those nights was always wild, as it had been in the early days. On the following morning he'd leave for work saying, "I love you today."

One morning she responded. "Rob. Tell me what that means?"

"It means I love you today."

"I'm not so sure it does. To me it means you love me for the moment. It has nothing to do with loving me yesterday or even tomorrow."

He opened the door and snapped. "Think whatever you want, Maddie."

Chapter 11

One gloomy afternoon in early February, Maddie heard Mr. Grenier running down the hall. She looked out to see what was going on.

He stopped, out of breath.

"Are you all right Mr. G?" she asked.

He put up one hand. "Just a minute," he wheezed.

Carla came up behind her. "What's is it? Is something wrong?"

He shook his head. "No. Quite the opposite. I just got a call. Your cover, the one you Xeroxed and colored, won an art director's award. We have another dinner to attend." He grabbed Maddie's shoulders and gave her a big kiss on the cheek. Carla started jumping up and down. "You did it," she shouted, twirling around.

Not believing what she had just heard, Maddie stared at him. "You're not putting me on, right?"

"Of course not, Maddie. This is incredible. We've never been recognized for anything like this before." He practically skipped down the hall. "I have to call…everybody."

Carla, still dancing around the art department stopped and hugged Maddie. "Congratulations."

"To you as well, Carla. You were part of this."

Letitia came in. "I just heard. Congratulations, Maddie."

They hugged each other. "This is amazing. Aren't you going to call your husband?"

"Yes. Of course. A little later."

=

When her phone rang late that afternoon, Maddie picked it up hoping it was Rob; that somehow he'd heard about the award and was calling to congratulate her.

When the receptionist announced it was someone from the Art Director's Club, she hesitated, feeling an unexpected rush of anticipation. She barely said hello before the voice on the other end boomed, "Mrs. MacLeod, we can't wait for you pick up your prize."

She laughed, recognizing Jay's voice. Playing along, she asked, "And what would that be?"

She heard him chuckle. "Anything you want, my dear."

"I'll have to think about that," she said laughing. "Really, Jay. The Art Director's Club?"

"Sure, Maddie. Why not? I'm here for lunch and heard about your cover. It'll soon be hanging on a wall for everyone to admire. I'm proud of you. Congratulations."

"Thanks, Jay," she said feeling a pleasant warmth. "We haven't talked in a while. How are you?"

Now it was he who hesitated. "Good, Maddie. I should have called sooner. Everything is going well."

"Maybe we should have lunch. Catch up with each other."

"For sure. Look, I'm going away for a week. I'll call when I get back." He suddenly seemed anxious to get off the phone.

"Where are you going? Vacation?"

"Ah, yes. St. Thomas. One of the advantages of working for a travel magazine."

She realized why he was uncomfortable. "Taking your girlfriend, I guess."

"Yes. But it's only a week."

No need to apologize, she thought. "Have a wonderful time, Jay. We'll talk when you get back."

"Thanks, Maddie. And again, congrats."

=

The magazine was picking up newsstand sales as well as subscriptions. Maddie's covers were attracting attention and one day Mr. Grenier called a meeting to announce that due to increased advertising he was adding eight more editorial pages every month. Afterwards he informed a pleased Maddie that he was granting her a generous raise. Although the extra pages meant more work and longer days, she didn't mind, she was seldom in a rush to go home.

One morning when Carla called in sick with the flu, she'd had to drop everything in order to art direct a shoot at a studio in Chelsea. By the time she got home it was almost nine and she was tired. Rob had called earlier, sounding upbeat and asking if she wanted to go out to dinner. Since he wasn't sure when he'd get out of the office, he said he'd meet her at home. That was fine with her, it would give her time to chill out.

After pouring a glass of Chardonnay, she took a few sips and lay down on the bed. Closing her eyes, she tried to unwind. She was lost in a peaceful trance when she heard the door open. Glancing at the clock, she was surprised it was almost eleven.

As she started to get up, Rob stamped into the room. She had never seen him in such a rage.

"Rob, what...?

"Shut the fuck up, you whore," he shouted.

"What are you talking about?"

"You went out with Neil and didn't tell me?

"Neil? He was about to do a shoot with me and we met at a Chinese restaurant to discuss it. His assistant and his girlfriend came along. You were working at Pedro's that night. What's the big deal?"

"The big deal, you slut, is that his girlfriend works at the agency. She told me how cozy the two of you were."

"That's not true. I didn't think she even knew I was married to you. If she did, why would she jokingly mention you as 'the art director who's always chasing the girls in the office.'"

"Fuck you," he shouted, taking a step toward her. She moved back on the bed, afraid he was going to strike her. Instead he lunged for the headboard, furiously wrenching it off the wall. She heard it crack as the wood splintered and spindles went flying.

She jumped off the end of the bed and bolted for the door. Ignoring the elevator, she ran down seven flights of stairs and straight to the front door. Joe looked at her with alarm.

"Mrs. M. Are you all right? Why don't you have shoes on?"

She leaned over, hands on her knees trying to catch her breath. "Joe. Call Ralph for me. Tell him to come down now. Please."

Looking confused, he nodded and picked up the house phone.

Five minutes later Ralph emerged from the elevator buttoning his shirt. She must have gotten him out of bed. If it had been Rob in that elevator she wasn't sure what she would have done. She was shaking from fear and shock.

"What is it Maddie? Are you okay?'

"No," she whispered, hugging herself. "Rob just tore the headboard off the wall. I was sure I'd be next."

His face clouded. "You were smart of get out of there. Come with me. I'll get him to leave."

"Can't you go by yourself? I'm afraid of him."

"No, Maddie. It's your apartment. I can only do this with you."

He knocked on the door and rang the bell several times. When no one answered he asked if Rob could have left.

"Only through a window. No. He's in there."

Ralph pounded on the door and Rob opened it a crack. He had put the chain on.

"You have to let your wife in Mr. MacLeod. Then I suggest you leave the apartment. Find somewhere else to stay tonight.'

"Fuck her and fuck you. I'm staying here. Let her go to one of her loser friends." He started to shut the door.

Ralph pushed it open. "Listen to me. If you don't leave I'm going to call the police. Do you hear me?"

"Call the police? What the fuck for?"

"Let's start with threatening your wife. You also destroyed something in the apartment."

He answered with a sullen, "It's my apartment. Why do I have to leave?"

"You're out of control and your wife fears for her safety. Get your things and come out of there before I call the cops."

She heard the chain being taken off. He opened the door looking gaunt and furious. "Fuck you," he shouted. Maddie cringed against the far wall. A few of her neighbors peeked out behind partially opened doors.

Giving her the finger, he grabbed his coat strode out. At the elevator he looked back. "This isn't over, Maddie."

"It better be," Ralph said. "Get your ass out of here." He turned to her with a look of concern. "Will you be all right?"

Trying to control her sobs, she nodded, unable to speak.

"Put the chain on the door tonight. Joe will call me if your husband comes back. I'll send the handyman tomorrow to help you clean up. I suggest you change the locks."

"Thank you," she said.

She took a couple of tentative steps into the living room. Other than an empty bottle of beer on the floor, everything appeared in order. It was the bedroom that terrified her. She stepped in with caution. There were broken spools and fractured pieces of dark wood everywhere. When she looked at what remained of the headboard tears came to her eyes. Perhaps this was an analogy for she and Rob—something (*or someone*) seen and desired, brought home with love and eventually destroyed by rage.

She cleared the bed of debris and picked up pieces of the shattered wine glass. Whatever hope she'd had was gone. The road before her had now become clear.

=

The next morning when she arrived at her office, she reluctantly pulled a piece of paper out of a drawer.

Over the last months she had become close to Letitia. One day when they had gone to lunch she had drawn Maddie out. Other than Suzanne, Maddie had never discussed Rob with anyone.

Instead of probing, she let Maddie talk, only interrupting to make observations, never pronouncements. Although Maddie expected her to be horrified by some of her stories, to her surprise Tish just shook her head. "Maddie, we're all too often attracted to handsome and charming men who aren't good for us. They're fun for a while but they eventually break our hearts. Most of us don't marry them."

"And woe to us who do?"

She nodded. "You're young and have your whole life ahead of you. It's time to let this go. As your career builds his will falter and he could very well drag you down with him. You can't let that happen. He's not the only man who will be in your life. There's someone else out there for you. Probably several someones and one of them will surely love you and make you happy."

Maddie shook her head. "I don't want to leave him. I still love him."

"You may love him until the day you die, but at some point you'll realize you can no longer live with him."

She had handed Maddie a slip of paper with the name of a lawyer on it. "He's a friend of mine and when the time comes, call him."

She had been tempted to toss it away. Instead she had put it in a drawer.

Chapter 12

After he stormed out of the apartment Rob went straight to O'Leary's where he downed four scotches in a row. He had no recollection of what happened next and when he woke up at noon he wasn't sure where he was.

Denise came in with a bottle of beer. "You're finally awake. You really tied one on," she said, shaking her head. "What the fuck happened last night? You were totally out of your mind. You were calling your wife every name in the book. At the beginning she was a bitch, by the time I dragged you out of there she was a motherfucking cunt. I had to practically carry you up to the apartment."

"I don't remember." It came out as a croak.

"Look, Rob," she said, sitting down next to him on the bed. "If she's driving you so crazy maybe it's time to get out of there. You can move in here if you want."

He sat up slowly, his head spinning. Denise had no real knowledge of his relationship with Maddie. Although she frequently probed him about it, he had avoided discussing it with her and he had no intention of starting now. To him she was a temporary refuge, someone to drink with, have the occasional laugh and fuck. He wasn't about to confide in her and he had no desire, despite his antagonism toward Maddie, to move in with her.

He shook his head as if clearing the cobwebs. "I have to call my office. I missed a meeting this morning."

She stood up. "Here. Take the beer. It'll help clear your head," she said, sounding miffed.

"No. Can you get me some coffee? I feel like shit. Maybe I should lay off the beer and booze for a few days. I think that's my problem. In fact, I'm beginning to think it may be the root of all my problems."

She laughed. "That's gonna be a trip. You without booze? But what the hell, go for it. You won't be much fun though." She turned her back and went to the kitchen. Hadn't he said the same thing to Maddie not so long ago?

He got up slowly and called the office. When he told the receptionist he was sick, she was sympathetic. "Go back to bed, Rob. You sound awful."

Denise came back carrying her coat and a mug of coffee that she handed to him. "I have to go out. Want anything?" She still sounded annoyed.

"Not right now. Thanks."

"There's more coffee in the percolator and some bread on the counter."

After she left he took a couple of aspirin and then went to shower, the combination reviving him a little.

His only clothes were from the night before and they weren't exactly fresh. Although he couldn't remember, he must have thrown up at some point. He had always been pristine about his hygiene and hated putting on clothes with the stink of cigarettes and booze, much less vomit. He pulled cash out of his pants pocket. He had over a hundred dollars, enough to get him through the weekend as well as a trip to Phil's. He needed underwear and a couple of shirts, maybe a pair of khaki's. He was glad he'd remembered to take his coat last night.

Before leaving, he called Ken and asked if he could come by later. He took a taxi to Phil's and after changing into clean clothes, he stopped for bacon and eggs at a coffee shop. Feeling somewhat renewed, he arrived at Ken's office around three. Seeing him, Ken closed the door and asked if he wanted a glass of water. Rob shook his head, sat down and told him the story of the night before. He had always been selective about sharing his experiences, but this time he desperately needed to talk, and who better than his good friend and mentor.

Ken got up and paced. "I can't believe you've let everything get so far out of control. How about the agency?"

He shook his head. "Not as good as it should be. I've been so fucked up between Maddie, Denise and Johnny Walker that I've let work slip."

"You can't afford to do that. Do you think you should talk to someone? A shrink?"

He shook his head. "No, Ken. I'm not an alcoholic. I just need to get it together. No drinking, a least for a while."

"Rob, if you're really serious you can stay at my apartment. Take as long as you need. But if you take one drink, I'll ask you to leave."

"I understand Ken. Thank you."

"What about Maddie?"

"I don't think I should go near her for a few days. Let me get my head straight and then I'll go and talk to her."

Chapter 13

Rob unlocked the door and stepped into the apartment. He had waited until nine to be sure Maddie would be home.

"Who's there," she yelled. He picked up the alarm in her voice.

Coming out of the bedroom she stopped abruptly, her eyes wide with fear. "What are you doing here?"

"Maddie, don't be scared. I want to talk to you."

"There's nothing to talk about, Rob. Take your clothes and get out."

He took a step toward her.

"Don't come any closer. I'll call Ralph."

He shook his head. "I guess I deserved that."

She nodded silently.

"Maddie. I haven't had a drink in four days. Not since I left that night."

Her look softened. "Are you serious?"

"Yes. I've been staying at Ken's. We've spent every night drinking Tab and talking. He keeps telling me what an asshole I am. I'm afraid I have to agree with him." He saw the hint of a smile. "Can I come in? Please?"

"All right. Rob. But I don't think there's much to say."

He went to the kitchen and took two bottles of Coke out of the fridge, holding them up for her to see. She nodded and went to sit on the couch.

He sat down in a chair opposite her and handed her one of the bottles. She took it carefully, as though afraid to touch him. "What is it you want from me?"

"I want one more chance."

"And what makes this different than all the other 'one more chances?'"

"I'm not going to drink Maddie. You were right, I think that's my problem. I have a couple and nothing matters. Not even you."

"I've asked you for months to slow it down." She sighed. "I just don't know."

"You know I love you and I think you still love me. Am I right?"

She bit her lip. "I won't say I don't, but that doesn't mean I can go on living with you. I'm afraid of your moods, your anger, not to mention your lies. I don't understand how you can say you love me and treat me as you have."

"No more, Maddie. I promise. I can't imagine living this life without you. You've been my inspiration, my muse, my love."

She stood up and walked to the bedroom. "Come here a minute."

He followed her. The headboard was gone, only the holes where he had bolted it into the wall remained.

"I am so sorry."

"That was wood, Rob. I'm not wood and I was afraid you were coming after me next. If you had touched me I would have had you arrested. That's not a threat."

"Maddie, I'd never hit you. I'd never hit any woman."

She went back to the living room. Watching her, he realized there was something different about her; she was more controlled, as though holding back all emotion. Booze or not, he'd have to be very careful.

"All right, Rob. I don't know why, but I prefer to live with you than without you. My friends will say I'm crazy and I should end it now, but I love you and if we there's a chance we can make it work, I'd like that."

"Maddie. I was stupid and thoughtless. I'm sorry." He went to her and put his arms around her. She closed her eyes as he kissed her gently.

"Do you want to go out?" he asked. "I'm starving. Do you know that food tastes better when you don't drink so much?"

"I don't know. Does that include wine?"

"No drinking at all. And by the way, our anniversary is next week. Would you like to go to go to Surabaya? I'll ask Ken and Evan to join us."

She nodded. "But no champagne."

"And that's okay," he said with conviction.

=

Maddie wasn't sure she was doing the right thing by letting Rob stay with her that night. Every time she looked at the naked wall she still wanted to cry.

The next morning they had gotten up as usual, but before she went to shower he took her hand and led her back to bed. She lay down next to him, responding to his caresses and allowing desire to flood her body. After the tears, the anger and the pain, the pure sensual pleasure was almost too much to bear and they held one another as if afraid to let go.

Later when he whispered, "It only gets better," she nodded and kissed him. She wondered if there was really no one like him, at least for her. Perhaps it was one of the unfathomable mysteries of love and hate that seem to eternally exist in an ever precarious balance between male and female.

Chapter 14

It was the end of March, the air still cold, yet with the tease of warmer days to come. By the time she met Rob at the restaurant there was a distinct scent of snow in the air.

They were meeting Larry and Doug, along with their dates, for dinner at La Goulue, a trendy restaurant in the East Sixties near Madison. Despite the candlelight and the large fin-de-siècle paintings on the walls, the place reminded her of La Terrazza. It was filled with grey-haired men and much younger women who swiveled their gaze to anyone who chanced to walk in. The only difference was the lengths of the skirts, the midi having become the latest craze.

Rob was already at a table talking animatedly with both couples. Seeing Maddie he jumped up and kissed her. Larry and Doug gave her cheek kisses and introduced their latest girlfriends. As she sat down she noticed a half-empty glass with ice and an amber liquid in front of Rob.

When he asked what she wanted to drink, she gave him a pointed look and asked what he was having. He laughed as though it was a funny question. "Scotch, what else?" he said, his tone taking on an edge. A few minutes later, he leaned over and whispered, "Just one Maddie. No big deal. Don't worry."

After the waiter brought her a glass of Chardonnay, Larry offered a toast to the gods of advertising—and publishing—who had been wise enough to grant them their awesome creativity. Everyone laughed and touched glasses. Maddie watched Rob sip his drink. She could see the alcohol beginning to work its effect on him; after one drink he was becoming looser, funnier and louder than he otherwise might have been.

She was relieved when they ordered. As Rob promised, he'd only had one. Larry ordered a bottle of Bordeaux and the waiter brought six glasses. Larry nodded at Rob. "You taste it, Rob. You're a wine person, aren't you?"

Rob shook his head. "I'm more of a scotch connoisseur," he said with a grin.

Despite his turning it back to Larry, Maddie was becoming uneasy. By the time they were halfway through dinner Rob had polished off two glasses of wine. Larry nodded to the waiter to bring another bottle.

Meanwhile the conversation swirled around her and when Doug asked about her magazine she hardly heard him. *Relax*, she told herself. *He'll be fine.*

By the time they left, they were all in some stage of inebriation and after cheek kissing goodnight, promised to catch up again soon.

As they walked toward Park Avenue she sensed Rob's mood darkening. "What the fuck is wrong with you Maddie? You were watching me like you were my jailer. Why didn't you just get up on the table and announce to the world that I had stopped drinking for a couple of months? All I had was one scotch and a couple of glasses of wine. No big fucking deal. See? I'm fine."

"You surprised me. I didn't know you were going to have a drink tonight."

He stopped walking. "Goddamn it. Do I have to call you every time I take a leak?"

She wasn't backing down. "I don't think you'd be yelling at me if you hadn't had those drinks. That was your decision, your promise."

"Back off Maddie. I don't need this shit."

She barely registered the long black limo slowing at the curb. They were standing on the corner of Sixty-Sixth and Park, no place for an argument in late March. The night had turned bitterly cold, slush freezing into black ice making the sidewalks treacherous. The wind lashed their faces but did little to restrain Rob's anger.

Out of the corner of her eye she saw the back door open. A young woman, maybe thirty-one or thirty-two, a couple of years older than she, stepped carefully out. Jet-black hair was piled on top of her head and her dark eyes were outlined in black. Despite the cold, she was wearing a short, form-fitting black dress, black stilettos and black gloves that came to her elbows. Long jeweled earrings swayed as she walked in what appeared to be slow motion toward them, all the while staring at Rob. He caught Maddie's look and turned, his harangue ending abruptly in mid-sentence.

She stopped a few feet away, her eyes never leaving his face. "Why are you standing there arguing with her," she said in a strong yet seductive voice. "Come with me."

Maddie stared in amused disbelief; the girl was a caricature of Holly Golightly, that is if Holly Golightly had been a hooker. As outrage replaced amusement, she took a step toward her.

"Get out of here and leave us alone."

Ignoring her, the woman repeated her offer. Without a word Rob walked to the car and slid in. The woman followed. Neither looked back.

Maddie watched the car for several blocks, sure it would stop and Rob would get out. But it continued on, slowly becoming a distant shadow. She stood on the corner frozen in shock. Light snow was beginning to fall and though an icy gust of wind billowed the scarf around her neck, she didn't feel a thing. *My husband just drove off with a hooker* was a chant repeating over and over in her mind. She tried to replay what had just happened. Had Rob even looked at her? She thought he had, his sullen expression turning to an eerie satisfaction as he glanced back at her and then walked toward the waiting car.

Taking a breath, she knew she had to snap out of it. She was shivering and her hair and coat were covered in snow. Relieved to see a cab coming, she ran into the street, hailing it.

Her mind was in turmoil; too many memories and emotions all coalescing into one irrevocable moment. As shock morphed to anger, she managed to ask herself how something like this could happen. How could Rob—her soul mate, her mentor, the man who told her their love would never end—walk away from her. And just not walk away, but go with a prostitute, leaving her stranded on a frozen sidewalk in the middle of the night.

Chapter 15

It was five days before she heard not from, but about Rob. She was torn between telling herself she never wanted to see him again and a visceral need to know if he was all right. Each day had been more difficult than the one before and every time she reached for the phone she stopped herself. *Maybe better not to know.*

It was Evan who called. "Maddie, are you okay?"

"Not really. I alternate between anger and worry, all day, every day. Not to mention that I cry myself to sleep every night. I just keep reminding myself the choices are over. This has become my new reality and I have to learn to live with it."

"He asked me to call you."

"Is he all right?"

"No. He's totally fucked up. All he talks about is wanting to see you."

"I don't think I can do that. I assume he's staying with you?"

"Yes. He called me from the street a few days ago. It was six in the morning. He was practically incoherent, not sure where he was or how he had gotten there. I finally got him to look at a street sign. When I picked him up in Chinatown he looked like he had been in a fight. His money was gone, probably stolen. That's all I can tell you. He refuses to say any more about it."

Maddie cringed, relieved to know he was safe but wishing Evan hadn't gone into such detail. No doubt he was trying to weaken her resistance by appealing to her feelings for Rob. It was too late; this time he'd finally gone too far.

"Evan, I'm sorry. Why don't you make yourself useful? Come over here and pick up his clothes."

"Please, Maddie. Just talk with him."

"I don't think I can."

"Not at your apartment. What if we meet at a restaurant?"

"Why are you so relentless?"

"When you see him you'll understand. He's miserable and I'm afraid he'll lose his job. He keeps calling in sick. I understand your anger, but aren't you concerned about him?"."

Tears were running down her face and it was difficult keeping her voice steady. "Of course I am. This has been torture."

"Maddie…"

She sighed. "All right, Evan. All right. But I expect you to be there. When and where?"

"When" turned out to be the next evening after work and "where" was not quite a restaurant, but an old Irish Bar in the East Forties. Evan met her at the door. "He's a wreck, Maddie. Please be calm."

He's a wreck? What about me?

She followed him to a booth across from the bar. Rob was seated with a glass of what appeared to be ginger ale in front of him. Seeing her, he mashed out a cigarette in an overflowing ashtray.

Evan was right, he looked like hell: a fading bruise on his cheek, dark shadows under his eyes, gaunt and thin. She asked herself how it had come to this.

"What is it you want, Rob?"

"To tell you I'm sorry, Maddie. Please listen to me. I don't want to live without you."

She sat down opposite him. "You should have thought about that before you got in that car."

"Look," he said holding up the glass. "I stopped drinking."

"Sorry. That's not going to work this time."

"What can I do to make you believe me? I'm not an alcoholic, Maddie. If you want, I'll go to a shrink. Anything. Just tell me what you want me to do."

"It's too late. I think we've become destructive to one another. Maybe that's why you're angry all the time. You drink and stay out all night, then I complain and question you. You say you're sorry, that you love me and then go out and do it all over again. It's become an endless circle and it's time to break it. If you want to destroy yourself, that's your choice." She was trying to hold her emotions in check as tears ran down her face.

"You can't do this to me. I love you."

"Then why did you cheat on me? Not once, but over and over?"

"Those girls never mattered. You were the one I loved."

"That's not an answer."

"That's the only answer. I always came back to you."

"That's it?" she whispered. *No way. There has to be more. Doesn't there?*

"It was the booze. I'd have a couple of drinks and suddenly nothing mattered but the next one. I always hated myself for hurting you. I promise that's over."

She raised her voice. "Are you kidding me? You never hated yourself."

Before he could react, Evan interrupted. "Maddie, do you want a drink?"

She stared at him, trying to collect her thoughts. "No, thank you, Evan. But maybe you can answer this. Why is it that you guys get married and then go out with other women?"

Suddenly uncomfortable, he shrugged. "I don't know. It's just the way it is. Maybe it's in our genes?"

She looked up at him. "Really? Are you asking me or telling me?"

"I'll be at the bar," he said, moving away.

"Maddie...please. Give me one last chance to make it up to you."

She took his hands in hers. She hadn't meant to, but she couldn't help herself. Holding back tears, she said, "I love you, Rob. Maybe I always will, but there's no way I can go on living with you. We thought we would last forever, but we didn't. It's time to let go of each other."

"This isn't all my fault, Maddie. You can't lay this trip entirely on me."

So much for pleading; he had returned to form. She pulled her hands back. "You're right Rob. It takes two. I was no angel, but I tried. I really did. After all those nights you didn't come home I listened to your lies and looked the other way. I cried but I didn't leave. If it was I who caused you to be angry and to drink, forgive me. I guess I wasn't the perfect wife you expected."

He sat back and lit a cigarette. "What about Jay?"

"Jay? What about him?"

"I know you've seen him. Are you still fucking him?" His voice had become harsh.

She shook her head. "I'm not discussing Jay."

Seductive again, he put his hand over hers. "Tell me you don't miss me."

How could she tell him that the man she missed was the one she had met five years before—the charming, talented, sensual man she'd fallen in love with. And yet, wasn't he the same man who was sitting across from her now? All the signs had been there—obvious to everyone but her. She moved her hand. "To tell you the truth I don't. I no longer look at the clock every five minutes wondering if you'll be coming home drunk or staying out all night."

Shaking his head, he said, "No more. I promise you."

"Sorry, Rob. When you stepped into that limo, you lost me." She took a breath. "I've spoken to a lawyer. He told me to change the locks. I haven't done that. You can come get your things whenever you want."

"You'll never have sex like we had."

"I'll take my chances."

"You are a bitch. Do you know that?"

It was enough. She stood up. "Thank you, Rob. You've confirmed my decision."

Evan, who had been watching from the bar, came over. "Maddie, please. Just give him one more chance."

She put her hand on his sleeve: "Evan. I told you before. There are no more one more chances."

She turned to Rob. "I wish you well. And whomever you're living with."

"I'm not living with anybody," he snapped.

"Of course you are. You can go out and be a bad boy all you want, but you still need someone to come home to. Someone who loves you unequivocally and who forgives you, not once, but over and over. Your mother did that, as did Allison and then I. Good luck with the next one."

As she walked out, she heard Rob shout at Evan to get him a drink. If she had had any misgivings left, that alone would have ended them.

=

Outside she took a breath and dried her eyes, well aware there would be many more tears to come. It was strange, but last week the apartment hadn't seemed empty, just quiet, as though what happened there was as yet left unfinished. Now she knew it would feel vacant, abandoned, as if half of her had gone.

From nowhere she recalled a line from George Bernard Shaw:

> *When your heart is broken, your boats are burned: nothing matters any more. It is the end of happiness and the beginning of peace.*

Epilogue

Yesterday is but today's memory,
and tomorrow is today's dream.

Khalil Gibran

New York City
September 1971

Carla stuck her head in the office. "Rob's on the phone. Do you want to take the call?"

Maddie looked up. "Sure. Why not?"

Carla frowned. "Because last time you had, um, a screaming fight."

Five months had passed and Maddie now had her own office, but even a closed door hadn't been sufficient to muffle the discord of divorce.

She picked up the phone. "What is it, Rob?"

"Hi, Maddie," his voice was seductive. "I just wanted to see how you are."

"I'm fine."

"How's everything at work?"

"The usual. Except that Mr. Grenier now has me doing promotional materials for the magazine. He decided he likes mine better than the studio he tried. Anyway, I don't have time right now for pleasantries."

"Then have lunch with me Saturday. I miss you and I think we should talk."

"About what? Every phone call has been another disagreement."

"Come on, Maddie. Time has passed. We have to put this behind us. I want to see you."

"I don't want to fight with you anymore."

"No fights. Everything is cool. Let's just catch up with each other."

Thinking she'd just spend the day working at home anyway, she said, "All right. Where?"

"I have to be at Pedro's at three. Meet me at Martell's at one?"

"I guess that's okay."

"By the way, I heard you went out with Rick."

She hesitated. "Yes. A couple of times when he wasn't rehearsing or bartending. He's a nice guy. That's about it."

"Good. Better to stay away from actors."

How about art directors?

=

He was sitting at a front table when she walked in. He stood up and smiled. "You look great. I like the bell bottoms."

She looked down. "Do you? I'm not sure."

Sitting back down, he said, "Do you want a drink? I'm having a Virgin Mary."

"Really? Then I'll have the same."

"Maddie, I'm drinking less. Only a beer now and then."

She paused. "Are you seeing a therapist or going to AA?"

He shook his head. "I've got it under control."

"I'm glad for you, Rob. How's the agency?"

"That was one of the things I wanted to tell you. I left LRG a couple of months ago. There was too much pressure and I was stressed out all the time. Besides, the new accounts we were picking up were pretty dismal. I'm not into package goods."

That wasn't quite what she had heard; rather that it had been more of an agency decision. "I'm surprised. I thought you liked the action."

He took her hand, entwining his fingers with hers. "I'm trying to slow it down — get my life back on track. Sort of where it was before. I'm working for a graphics studio now and I like it."

"That's great," she said, gently extracting her hand. Lunch was one thing but this seemed to be taking a somewhat different turn. "Where are you living?"

"An apartment on Third, near Fifty-Fifth Street. It's small but it works."

She considered asking if he was living alone but thought better of it.

"By the way, I heard you moved," he asked.

"Yes. About a month ago. To Eighty-Sixth and East End."

"Sounds swanky. I'm impressed."

"It's just a one bedroom. But it does have a working fireplace and a river view."

He stroked her hand. "I'd like to see it sometime."

Changing the subject, she asked him about the studio.

"We're doing a lot of work with fashion, something I always liked when we were at *Status*. Remember Neil and all the fashion shoots? Are you still working with him? Maybe I should give him a call. Those were crazy days, weren't they?"

She wondered at his chatty attitude, so different from the first months after they separated. She had neither asked for nor wanted any support from him. Nevertheless, they had argued for months. Even something as inconsequential as who got the wine glasses had triggered a heated discussion. Although emotions appeared to have calmed down, she wasn't up to a trip down memory lane. "Yes. I guess they were. And yes, Neil still shoots for me."

"I wanted to tell you we also represent some photographers and illustrators if you ever want to see them."

"Is this a sales lunch?"

"No, Maddie. Not at all. I'd like us to get back to at least being friends. When you love someone you don't want to lose them." His voice was low, intimate.

She was sure he saw her blush. "Rob…"

He took her hand again. "I've missed you Maddie. I'd like it if we could see one another. Haven't you missed me? Even a little?"

She hadn't expected him to be so seductive. Flustered, she shook her head. "I don't know." She seldom allowed herself to admit that she missed him. It had taken her months to stop replaying that final scene in the bar with Evan acting as referee. Whenever she thought of the good times, she'd force herself to recall the less-than-good-times, the many reasons they were no longer together.

He leaned over and kissed her lightly. "I think we need to talk some more."

She knew she should get up and leave, but for some reason she couldn't move.

He paid the check and stood up, his green eyes looking down at her. He was wearing tight jeans, Frye boots and a blue and white striped shirt, the sleeves rolled to his forearms; his dark hair was longer and tousled. She took a breath and asked herself how it was possible after all they'd been through that he could be as hard to resist as ever. She allowed him to take her hand as they walked uptown. When they reached Eighty-Fifth Street, where he should have turned to go to the bar, he didn't stop.

"Rob, it's almost three. Don't you have to be at Pedro's?"

He put a finger under her chin and kissed her lightly. "I put it off till four."

She stepped back. "I don't know if this is a good idea."

"I promise you Maddie, it's the best idea either you or I have had in months. Besides I want to see your apartment."

=

She had barely unlocked the door when he had her clothes off. In bed he was slow and deliberate, as though awakening her from a long sleep. Denial dissolved into submission as she allowed his hands and fingers to rekindle what seemed to be an unending desire for him. And when he arched over her she sighed and wrapped her arms and legs around him.

"Maddie," he murmured, kissing her breasts, "making love to you is always like the first time."

As they moved apart, she whispered. "I don't know what to say."

"Say you'll have dinner with me next week."

"I'm not sure we should be doing this."

"Why not? I care for you Maddie and I think you feel the same. Trust me, this is good for us." She saw him glance at his watch. "It's almost four. I have to go."

Something about the abrupt way he said it startled her. In bed all her doubts had been overtaken by desire. Now every instinct was suddenly on alert, making her question if making love with him had been a mistake.

As he dressed, she got up and put on a robe. At the door he moved it off her shoulder. "I like your apartment," he said with a smile. "Maybe next time I'll have a chance look at the view." He kissed her neck and then her lips. "I'll call you tomorrow."

=

At the elevator he turned and threw her a kiss. It had been more than just a pleasant afternoon; he really had missed her. Denise was good, but sex with her was an unrelenting battle for supremacy, a wrestling match of jockeying for position amidst grunts and shouts. It was erotic and satisfying, particularly after a few drinks, and yet he actually preferred the way Maddie abandoned herself to him. Even the times she had initiated sex, though he'd seldom given her the opportunity, she'd eventually surrendered to his lead. He missed her soft moans and the way she curled around him. The mere thought aroused him again.

And yet he hadn't been quite straight with her. True, he was trying to drink less, but he knew she'd be far more receptive if she thought he'd cut down—or off altogether. He'd been careful, using just the right amount of seduction and she had gone for it. After all the arguments of the last months, he'd wanted to crack her cool Ms. Successful Art Director exterior. It wasn't that she had become overconfident or lorded her success over him—she hadn't. But he was determined to get her to where he'd always been able to control her and, fancy new apartment or not, that was in bed. Just seeing the look on her face was enough to know he'd succeeded, that she wanted more. He smiled to himself, convinced he could have her whenever he wanted. He already knew he wouldn't call the next day. He'd let her hang out there a few days, create a little anxiety. He'd wait and see if she'd call him.

=

It was Thursday before Maddie heard from Rob and she was beginning to feel the all-too-familiar twinges of anxiety. She had considered calling him but reminded herself to be patient; Rob was a hunter, he'd call eventually.

"Meet me for lunch Saturday? Same time same place?"

"I don't know, Rob. I'm still not convinced this is a good idea."

"C'mon Maddie. It was great, wasn't it?"

"Well, yes. But..."

He cut her off. "What do you mean, 'but?' Either it was or it wasn't. I was trying to make you happy."

"But why Saturday afternoon again? Why not later or tomorrow night? We'd have more time together. I think we should talk about this."

He hesitated before answering. "Maddie. This week got screwed up and I have to work the next three nights. I was waiting to find out before I called."

She wondered about that hesitation but agreed to meet him. Still, there was something nagging in her mind. She brushed it away. He had called, hadn't he?

=

When she arrived at Martell's, she was dismayed to see a beer in front of him. He stood up and kissed her. "It's okay Maddie. I told you I have one from time to time."

"Rob. What are we doing here?"

"I told you. I miss you and I think we should try spending some time together."

"You mean like last week?"

"That and more. You know what we had, how good we were together. That's what I miss."

"And how do we do this? I mean spend time together. We're about to be divorced."

He shrugged. "So what? We can still do what we want when we want. Who's to judge us?" He took her hand and kissed her fingertips. "You know I could make love to you right here, right now. But then they probably wouldn't let us in here for lunch again."

"You didn't answer my question."

"Let's finish and go back to your apartment. Then I'll answer any questions you want."

=

Three weeks later, after a morning spent shopping at Saks, Maddie and Suzanne walked up Third Avenue on their way to their old coffee shop, the Third Avenue El. Hefting two shopping bags and trying to snap Maddie out of her doldrums, Suzanne quipped, "It's across the street from Bloomingdale's in case we missed anything."

As they stopped for a light, Maddie glanced across the street seeing Rob laughing with a heavyset man with salt and pepper hair. Something about him looked familiar but she couldn't place him. She also noticed Rob's motorcycle parked at the curb; the night-chain still on it. She paused, experiencing an uncanny sense of déjà vu. Before she could steer Suzanne in the other direction, Rob saw her and waved. Suzanne looked at her. "What are you going to do?"

"Nothing. Just keep walking."

=

Rob said goodbye to the man and walked toward them already sensing Maddie's tension. The last time they'd been together he'd arrived at Pedro's at four only to find a furious Denise waiting for him. She'd arrived at three intending to surprise him. Instead, she demanded to know where he'd been for the last hour. After he hustled her out to the sidewalk and endured the inevitable, screaming argument, he decided he'd better cool it with Maddie, at least for a while.

=

"Hello Suzanne, haven't seen you in a while," he said briskly. Taking Maddie's arm, he pulled her aside. "Look. I'm sorry I didn't call. Things got crazy and I really wasn't sure you wanted me to."

"You mean after I slept with you? Not once but twice? What weren't you sure of?" She shook her head. "I should have known better."

"Maddie. Listen to me. When I think about you I want us back where we were. It scares me." He glanced at Suzanne who was blatantly glaring at him. "We can't talk here. Can you meet me later?"

Before she could answer a tall woman with long black hair walked out of the building behind him. Her dark eyes swept over Maddie and Suzanne as if they weren't there.

"Rob, your father's on the phone. He wants to know when we're coming to Connecticut."

Maddie froze, surveying the scene before her. She looked at the woman and then at Rob. "You fucking bastard. You're telling me you want to get back together with me when you're living with her?"

"Maddie. Let me explain."

"Explain what?"

The woman squinted at her and turned to Rob. "Rob, what the hell is going on here?"

Without looking at her, he snapped, "Not now Denise." He turned to Maddie. "It's not what you think."

"You know what I think Rob? I think that in some weird and inexplicable way our lives have come full circle. Nothing ever changes with you. You're living with her and somehow, inconceivably, I've become the other woman. Again. Have you lost your mind?"

Suzanne grabbed her arm, pulling her away. "Come on, Maddie. Let's go."

Incredulous, Maddie looked back. The woman was in his face gesticulating furiously and screaming at him. But it wasn't so much the woman that caught her eye; it was the door she had come out of. It was next to The Blarney Stone, the same grubby bar where she had picked up an almost comatose Rob one freezing winter morning over a year before.

Three months later

It was twilight when Maddie left the building on Madison Avenue. A few brittle Ginko leaves twirled in a late autumn breeze that ruffled her hair as she joined the stream of pedestrians rushing by. The pulse of the city always beat a little faster in the fall.

Buttoning her coat against the chill, she pulled the fur collar up around her neck. This hadn't been a meeting for a miniskirt. In fact, she was sure the miniskirt had seen it's day and would soon go the way of the corset, no doubt to reappear in some future fashion cycle. Instead she wore a soft, calf-length suede skirt over high heeled suede boots. A long turtleneck sweater, wrapped with a wide belt around her hips completed the look. Her hair, now longer and straight, still had bangs that brushed her eyebrows. Her image wasn't what anyone would call corporate. She didn't intend it to be; she had always made her own statement and would continue to do so.

This evening had been her third appointment with the publisher of a new, high profile magazine. Although she'd already met with his editors and production people, this time she was to be vetted by his investors, an uptight, dour group in Paul Stuart suits. They had sat around around a mahogany conference table taking turns asking her questions and scrutinizing her portfolio. And yet since it was they who had sought her out, she hadn't been uptight and had answered their questions with an easy confidence.

It was now a moment to celebrate but there was no one she really wanted to call. Actually there was; Rob would be the one who would be happiest for her.

After the debacle in front of The Blarney Stone, he had called every day for two weeks. She had refused to take his calls until the afternoon Carla brought a bouquet of yellow roses into her office, saying someone had walked in and dropped them on the receptionist's desk. A card attached to a stem simply said, "Sorry." When Rob called an hour later, she took it, listening quietly as he apologized, saying it was all a misunderstanding and he wanted to explain.

"Rob, I'm not going through this again. There's nothing more to say."

"Yes, Maddie, there is. I want to see you and I don't want to talk on the phone."

"Please, Rob. You have to stop calling me. You're living with someone. It's time to get on with your life and let me go on with mine."

"Come on."

She was surprised at his determination; he wasn't giving up. What had attracted her before had now become a turn-off. "No, Rob."

His voice was deeper now. "All right Maddie. I hear you. I'll give you some time. I'll call in a few weeks."

=

Waiting for the light to change, she realized that it had been more like a few months. Not that she was surprised; Rob was all about immediate gratification and she was sure by now, Denise or not, he had found other girls to pursue. Yet here she was, thinking he was the first one she wanted to call.

Better to call her mother; she was always pleased to hear good news. Maddie had expected to hear shouts of glee the day she had called to tell her that she and Rob were getting divorced. Somehow she had subdued her elation, managing to hold back the predictable, "I told you so." And yet even over the phone, Maddie could feel her smug smile.

Suzanne was out of town with Andrew. In a rare spontaneous moment, he had taken her to the Bahamas. She had told Maddie she was leaving the baby with her mother and looking forward to a week of sun and sex, although she was sure he'd be more interested in playing golf. Maddie sighed; these days, sex was an all-too-rare occurrence in her life. Although she dated, most of the men weren't very interesting. *But then, after Rob, who could be?*

There was the older, bespoke suited lawyer who called every Wednesday—no doubt avoiding the Thursday deadline—to ask her out for Saturday night. Impressed that she was an art director for a popular woman's magazine, he took her to lavish dinner parties at his friends' posh Park Avenue apartments. But he was far too egocentric. No matter what she talked about, he would nod, offer a vacant smile and immediately turn the conversation back to himself, his famous clients, his golf game or whatever else he desired to hear himself say. Since she had limited him to a few goodnight kisses and a random feel or two, she was sure he'd be giving up soon.

She wished she could call Roger, a fashion photographer who had shot for her a few times at *Beauty&Fashion*. One day he had hit the big time and was currently in Spain on a photo shoot for *Vogue*. With perfectly tousled dark hair, just the right two-day growth on his craggy face and intense brown eyes, they had connected quickly. She imagined he connected equally as quickly with most of the girls he met. Since, however, she had learned her lesson—that the volatile concoction of attraction and lust was best taken in brief doses—their relationship, despite some wonderfully spontaneous and sensual sleepovers, had become more of a working friendship than an affair.

She had just stepped off the curb when a hand gripped her arm.

"If you don't pay attention, you'll get run over," a familiar voice warned.

"What?" she turned abruptly. "Ohmigod, Jay. Sorry. I just left a meeting. I'm in another zone I guess."

He kissed her cheek. "It's been too long, Maddie. I'm the one who should be sorry. I should have called."

She shook her head. "That's all right, Jay."

"Where are you coming from?"

She glanced up at the street sign, surprised she had walked almost ten blocks. "Actually I just left an interview."

"Are you looking for a job?"

"No. Not at all. They called me."

"Not *World* magazine?"

She looked at him with suspicion. "Yes. How did you know?"

"I got that call as well."

"Oh, Jay."

"It's okay Maddie. I'm not looking to change. From what I hear they're going with a female creative director. I'll bet that's you."

She nodded. "Actually it is. I can hardly believe I was offered the job. They won't be ready for a few weeks so I have plenty of time to warn Mr. Grenier. I've liked working at *Beauty&Fashion*, but I guess it's time for a change."

"That's a lot more than just a change. Congratulations and welcome to the big time. I'm proud of you. You're not even thirty and you got the job that every editorial art director in New York wanted. You'll be working with some of the most impressive intellectuals in the city. Of course they're all liberals, but what can you do?"

"Speak for yourself, Jay," she said laughing. "I'm sure I'll be excited once it really sinks in."

"That's one of the things I've always liked about you, you never take anything for granted. Tell me, how are you?"

She shrugged. "Good."

He looked closer. "One word answers aren't like you. What is it? Rob?"

She held up her left hand. It took a second. "Maddie?" he asked.

"There is no Rob," she said evenly.

"Are you divorced?"

"In a few weeks."

"Why didn't you call me?"

She had asked herself that same question all too often in the last months and rejected it every time. If she had called only to hear that he was happily living with someone or worse, married, she would have felt profound disappointment, possibly even rejection. With her emotions still raw after Rob, she didn't need more pain.

"Honestly, Jay, I didn't know what to say. The last time we spoke you told me you were seeing someone. Since I didn't hear from you I figured you might be married by now."

"No, Maddie. Far from it."

"How come? I thought you finally found that ideal girl."

"Actually, I thought I did. But as soon as I mentioned becoming engaged she went out the next day and returned with brochures from the Plaza and several other hotels for a big wedding. She even managed to find the time to try on a few wedding dresses. All in one day. Do you know how crazy that is?"

"I know a lot of girls who don't think it's crazy at all. Maybe it's only you and I who see things a bit differently."

He put his hands on her shoulders. "I've always known who my ideal girl is. Do you ever think of our night together?"

"You asked me that the last time I saw you. To be honest, even when I was trying to keep my marriage together you were there in the back of my mind. You unknowingly gave me confidence."

"I thought you were trying to make things work with Rob. I didn't want to interfere."

"I did try. For too long. And then one day there was nothing left to try for."

He hesitated. "Maddie, are you going somewhere now? Do you have a date?"

She took a breath, wondering if she shouldn't be so available. *But then, why not?* "No, not really."

He took her hands in his. "Good. Otherwise I'd have insisted you cancel it. This is our night to celebrate. Not only your new job, but do you realize this will be our first date? A little after the fact, perhaps, but what the hell."

She laughed, sensing his excitement. Maybe she had been wrong; maybe he had, indeed, been waiting for her.

"We'll go to the bar at Beekman Tower. It's got a great view of the city, it's dark and very romantic. I'm betting you can use some romance. What do you think?"

She hoped he didn't notice her blush. "As I recall, you're pretty good at romance."

He looked at her, eyebrows raised in a Groucho leer. "By the way, you've never seen my apartment, have you?"

"Jay. Slow down."

"No, Maddie. No more going slow." Taking her face in his hands, he kissed her deeply. She hesitated before putting her arms around him. He stepped back, suddenly serious. "I have to tell you something. Actually, I've waited a very long time to say it."

"Please. Not another confession."

"Not quite." He stood up straight and put his hand over his heart. "Maddie. I hereby promise that I will never, ever again answer the phone after I make love to you."

Laughing, she took his arm. "Jay, let's take it one day at a time."

Still round the corner there may wait,
A new road or a secret gate.

J.R.R. Tolkien

Acknowledgments

With very special thanks and appreciation to Lou Aronica, my extraordinary editor and publisher. Due to your encouragement, vision, and patience, *I Love You Today* became a far better book. Also special thanks to Laura Ross for her wise words and suggestions. And to my dear friends and readers: Maureen Baker who once again kept me going with her cookies, Joyce Fish, Suzanne Ruttenberg, Chas Dittell, Alan LeMond, and Ruth Reinhold who read, reread, and acted as both cheerleader and critic through many, many drafts. Also, special thanks to Bob Tulipan, Michael Fragnito, Sal Lumetta, and Dr. Samoon Ahmad who provided invaluable insights into the all-too-often inscrutable minds and actions of men. Thank you Sue Rasmussen, my favorite copy editor! Special appreciation goes to Eugenie Sills as reader, advisor, critic, and social media guru extraordinaire. And to Jeanne Buckley and Miranda Hines for conversations on history long past. And my love and appreciation to James, my ever-patient husband for putting up with me for (at least) these last four years.

About the Author

After graduating from Rhode Island School of Design in the 1960s, Marcia Gloster built a career in New York City as an award-winning book designer and art director. A decade later, she founded and ran a boutique ad agency specializing in fashion. Gloster is a member of the National Association of Women Artists and Studio Montclair and exhibits her paintings in the New York area. Her first book, *31 Days: A Memoir of Seduction*, was published in 2014.